I0755763

RENAISSANCE

Books by Vincent M. Wales

Wish You Were Here

One Nation Under God

The Many Deaths of Dynamistress

- *Book One: Reckoning*
- *Book Two: Redemption*
- *Book Three: Renaissance*

RENAISSANCE

The Many Deaths of Dynamistress

Book Three

Dinah Geof-Craigs
with
Vincent M. Wales

DGC Press • Sacramento

Model photo by Lisa Charrie Photography
Cover concept by Vincent M. Wales
Cover design by Brianna Flores

ISBN 978-0-9741337-7-5

First DGC Press printing, December, 2025
Printed on acid-free paper

Acknowledgments

Thank you to my wonderful test readers: Regis Harvell, Jacquie Jean Conway (RIP), Kat Kahoali'i, Lisa Kiner, and Miguel Tarrats. And to Keith Staten, for advice on fictional legal matters.

The character of Arsenal was co-created by Michael Krumm.
The character of Bloodmoon was co-created by the late Jacquie Jean Conway.
The character of Bronwyn Couch-Jones was co-created by the late Susan Wales.
The character of Fabian was co-created by Brent McKeehen.
The character of GlassMan was co-created by Kevin Benson.
The character of Half-Life was co-created by Amanda Brewer.
The character of Macy Zhang was co-created by Joe Martinez.
The character of Neon was co-created by Hayley Bennett.
The character of Nexus was co-created by Claudia Silva.
The character of Quanta was co-created by Lisa Kiner.
The character of Resonator was co-created by Kiet Nguyen.
The character of Sinta was co-created by M. Young.
The character of Vesper was co-created by Roland Martinez.
The character of Zero-Point was co-created by Miguel Tarrats.

My deepest gratitude to you all for allowing them to live in my world.

DEDICATION

This book is dedicated to the memory of my brother, Donald Wales, who introduced me to the works of Robert A. Heinlein, a major influence on my desire to become a writer. Thank you for being an exemplary model of a good human being.

And to the memory of my sister, Susan Wales, who practically raised me and shared my twisted sense of humor. Thank you for being my biggest supporter and my favorite person. The world is dimmer without your presence.

Also to the memories of Jacquie Jean Conway and Richard C. Barr, Jr., two great friends who left us far too soon.

"For he who lives more lives than one
More deaths than one must die."
~ Oscar Wilde

FOREWORD

Editorial
Supers
March 2010

Two years ago, in our January 2008 issue, our "Super of the Month" was a largely unknown meta named Dynamistress. Some on our staff thought this was a risky move, predicting a lukewarm response, at best. I, myself, said, "Who the hell is Dynamistress?" when she was proposed to be featured.

At first glance, she didn't exactly stand out from the crowd. But there were some things about her that were unusual even in the world of metas. For one thing, she was older than the average new hero by a good bit. Most metas debut in their late teens or early twenties, but Dyna hit the scene at thirty-two. For another thing, her meta abilities didn't manifest naturally, but were the result of her own actions, the only known example of self-induced meta mutation.

In the end, I went with my gut. This was a woman who was obsessed enough to become a geneticist specifically in order to manipulate her own DNA to bring about meta abilities. And my gut said this was someone who wouldn't be just a flash in the pan. She would really do something.

As evidence, we already knew she had been involved in Project Echo, colloquially known as "the Nevada Incident," and this was a large factor in causing that issue of *Supers* to sell out. At the time, though, none of us knew the extent of her involvement, as she downplayed her contributions to the event.

And I was right about her future accomplishments. She would be the one who not only determined the cause of the year-long disease outbreak that killed more than fifty people in the San Francisco Bay Area and sickened thousands more, but would also be the one who worked out how to stop it.

Just as Dyna herself was a virtual unknown when she graced our pages, her role in these events also isn't common knowledge, which is why she's not a household name. Maybe someday she will be. Many remarkable people were virtually unknown in their times: Dickinson, Poe, van Gogh, and so many more.

Sadly, there's a reason I compared Dynamistress to those who only became famous posthumously. As this issue of *Supers* was about to go to press, reports began to come in stating that Dinah Geof-Craigs – Dynamistress – had perished. Details have been limited, but the reports come from several eyewitnesses, including her own teammates.

As the saying goes, only the good die young. Dinah was only thirty-nine on that fateful day. Her career as Dynamistress spanned less than seven years. But the legacy she leaves behind will be long-lasting.

One thing we at *Supers* knew that had not been publicly revealed was that Dynamistress had signed a contract with a book publisher to bring her story to the world, including details of the Nevada Incident unknown outside of her team. Her co-author intends to move forward with the book, and the publisher has agreed to allow us the honor of printing excerpts in the pages of our magazine.

All of us here at *Supers* mourn her loss and will keep her memory alive, always. A memorial issue devoted to her career is forthcoming.

Malcolm Goodman
Publisher / Editor-in-Chief
Supers

One

"The timing of death, like the ending of a story, gives a changed meaning to what preceded it."

~ Mary Catherine Bateson

Golden Gate Park is where the kids hang out. I don't mean children, though some of them seem pretty damn young. I mean the ones celebrating their new status as registered metas in the city. They strut around, appropriately, in Peacock Meadow, where they pose in their costumes like jocks trying to impress cheerleaders. Recruiters for government teams swoop in on them like pimps on runaways at a bus station.

As it happens, I'm there as a pimp, myself, because I go there to look for potential recruits, too. But I'm much more selective than the government scouts. I look for those who aren't so puffed up with pride. I look for the humble, not the haughty. I watch for the ones who look lost or confused, or are there just to meet other metas, rather than boast and show off. In other words, the ones the government folks tend to ignore.

But I see them all, the timid and the bold, with mixed emotions. I look at them with fond nostalgia, for I remember being one of those neophytes, not so long ago. I look at them with hope, for that's what they are – the hope for the city's future. But mostly, I look at them with pity, for I know some of them will become part of another group – a group I call "The Disappeared."

We rarely talk about them. We never publicly admit that so many of us don't last. Nor do we wonder aloud whether those faces we haven't seen in weeks or months are gone because they moved, they quit, or they're dead. We pretend none of that ever happens in our bright, costume-clad worlds.

But it does. All too often.

In the past six months, I've counted at least ten faces in the park that I've never seen before. The names attached to those faces are logged into the computer in City Hall, and their deeds will be recorded as the days roll on. But, a year from now, how many of those names will still be active in the system? Six? Three?

City Hall might keep track, but we don't. It's too much like reading the obituaries every day. It's too morbid, reminding us of our own mortality.

But I can't stop thinking about The Disappeared.

Faces haunt my dreams, of friends not seen in too long, like Rachel and Esteban. And others never to be seen again, like Valora and Transcendant.

And of course, there is always the very real possibility that one day, when I'm off my game just a touch, when my attention is broken, my mind distracted...

I'll disappear, too.

Much to my surprise, I was in San Francisco. I was excited, and wanted nothing more than to explore this amazing city. But that would have to take a back seat. I had a mystery to solve. I had so many questions to ask, and could only hope that the combined answers would reveal what had really happened on February 12, 2010.

What was known was that Dynamistress had been out with several of her friends, celebrating her thirty-ninth birthday. There were few eyewitness reports in the news, and those few didn't all agree. Some said it was an explosion. Others said it was a fire. Her friends tried to avoid the press, which is why there was so much speculation in the media. Whatever it was – explosion, fire, or something else – it killed her and put her brother in the hospital, where he is still in a coma, weeks later.

Dynamistress had obviously not told her team about me. Except for Bloodmoon, they had no knowledge of me until just before we met. Though she explained the reason for my presence, none of them were comfortable with me. In fact, some refused at first to speak with me at all.

I really couldn't blame them.

Jasmine Cruz, a.k.a. Bloodmoon, is an imposing woman. In her early thirties, she stands about six feet tall. She is of mixed race, with Mediterranean features and a lovely *café-au-lait* skin. She is telepathic and empathic, and has a virtual arsenal of weapons. She told me that, these days, she focuses on the non-lethal sort. I didn't ask about the days before she had such a focus.

Bloodmoon was the first member of the Pariah Project that I met, so she has been my liaison to the team. She introduced me to everyone and tried to make things go as smoothly as possible for me. We laid down some "ground rules" for the interviews – which topics were off-limits, for example – and she would be present at each interview to make sure they were followed. She, herself, was naturally the first one I interviewed.

Bloodmoon served us tea in the conference area of the Project's building as we talked. It's not accurate to call it a conference *room*, since it had no doors. In most peoples' eyes, it would be the dining half of the living/dining area. I would have, too, if it had lacked the large monitor and lots of computer gear beyond my familiarity.

"I wasn't out with them when it happened, so I can't give a first-hand account. In the days following, as you can imagine," she said in a warmer voice than one might expect from such an intimidating woman, "the team fell into disarray. Even though our group doesn't have a 'leader' in the conventional sense, we all know the Project exists only because of one person. Dyna was the heart of the team. And we'd never had any formal discussions about what would happen in the event that she wasn't around, any longer." Bloodmoon sipped at her tea, seeming to collect her thoughts. "The two of us had spoken casually about it, though, so – as agreed – I stepped in to fill the role of facilitator," she continued, "since, after Dyna, I'm the most familiar with the inner workings of the group. And we wanted to continue, of course."

Bloodmoon explained that the Project was a young group, less than a year old. "We formed on August first, last year. That's not the date on our legal paperwork, but that's what we consider the anniversary of our founding."

It seemed obvious that the Pariah Project wasn't a typical team, I said to her. "What sets us apart," she explained, "is our goal of being more than just intercessors. We're not there just to stop the bad guys." She paused in her explanation and looked wistful. "Dyna had a deep sense of justice and was keenly aware that we have a system full of gaps into which victims often fall, where they fail to receive the attention they need."

Bloodmoon stopped, but I must have looked confused, because she went on. "For example, rather than just make sure the victim of a crime is physically unharmed, we assess their mental well-being. No, none of us are qualified to diagnose, but we've had enough training to be able to do a quick assessment. Being the victim of crime can be traumatic, after all, and everyone reacts differently. So if the person needs it, we'll escort them home, for example. If they need assistance, we have them come here, where we provide them with information on all the available resources out there that could help them, be it housing needs, drug counseling, financial assistance, or just about anything else." With a shrug, she said, "It's not that the police or other teams never do that sort of follow-up, but we make it a priority. All government teams are trained in crisis intervention, but the Project emphasizes it more than other groups I've been with. We're also trained in the basics of crisis *counseling*, which I've never encountered with other teams."

I understood, now. It was like a full-service team. Everything short of picking up the victim's dry cleaning. I wasn't sure if it was a cool idea or a bit pointless.

Vicky Valentine, a.k.a. Nexus, had been Dynamistress's girlfriend. Based on the photos and videos I saw, she was about thirty years old and quite pretty, with auburn hair and gray eyes that seemed to sparkle silver when she smiled. Her abilities are hard to describe, but she is able to open miniature portals into a number of planes of existence and use them offensively, defensively, and as teleportation-like transportation.

She was also not around. Nexus had taken a leave of absence from the team. "I'm not sure where she is," Bloodmoon told me. "I respect her need to heal in her own way, of course, but the truth is, we could really use her, right now."

I asked why, and Bloodmoon explained. "I recently received a call from Arsenal – my arms supplier – about a few strange weapons. From the description, they match those that Dyna and the others encountered before. Energy-draining weapons." She frowned before continuing. "The fact that these are here is quite disturbing. According to Arsenal, the weapons look new and unused. Apparently, the shipment came via Los Angeles, but that's about all we've got, so far. Vicky could be of great help in investigating this. I've left her a voicemail with details and suggesting that maybe doing some work would help her, psychologically. I'm still waiting to hear back from her."

Bridget Mason, a.k.a. Bricky, is Nexus's cousin and shares an apartment with her. Bricky is the youngest member of the team, at sixteen. But even that age was hard to believe, as she appears even younger. She's slim with long, blonde hair, and an adorably cute face. As her name hints, Bricky is able to transform the skin of her body into something resembling brick. She was young enough to still get an enormous kick out of her abilities and jumped at the chance to demonstrate them for me. She also didn't hesitate to tell me that she was probably the toughest member of the team, despite her size. That makes it sound like she's full of herself, but she's not.

The first thing she told me was how much she liked Dynamistress. "I was invited to join the team, even though we barely knew each other. I mean, yeah, I know it's because I'm Vicky's cousin and everything, but still... In the Gatekeepers, I was a reserve member, because I'm not eighteen, yet. That was fine, but here in the Pariah Project, I'm equal to everyone else. My opinion is as valued as anyone's. And that's so cool. I can't tell you how much it means."

Her enthusiasm disappeared, though, when I asked the inevitable question. "I wasn't there, thank God. And the others haven't been exactly gabby about it. Kinda thankful about that, too, honestly."

Jennifer Dusk, a.k.a. Vesper, is one of several members of the Project who is quite obviously a meta. It's the large, bat-like wings that give it away. She's one of the younger members, being just shy of twenty. She has deep red hair and a scar across one eye. Vesper can fly, produce deep shadows, and even has a form of echolocation, making darkness much less of a drawback for her than for most people. She was the first I spoke to who had witnessed the event.

"It was horrible," she said in a slight Texas drawl. "We'd all gone to lunch down to Fisherman's Wharf and then jus' kicked around for a while, goin' in some shops and whatnot." She paused, frowning slightly and glancing at Bloodmoon, who was, as always, present. "We'd just left the Ghirardelli store. Dunno why this sticks with me, but I remember Dyna was munchin' on a chocolate mint square. Next thing I know, she got this panicked look on her face and spit it out. She grabbed Jack's hand and they stared at each other. We all knew what that meant, of course. After a few seconds, she looked around at the rest of us, all wide-eyed and freaky, before blasting into the air and flying toward the water. We went after her..." Vesper looked away for a moment. "Got there just in time to see it."

Vesper got choked up and fell silent. I watched the emotions play across her face. She closed her eyes, shook her head, and stood up from the table. "Sorry," she mumbled. "I can't..." Then she hurried out the door to the street.

The Pariah Project headquarters is in a not-so-attractive neighborhood, to be honest. And this is what makes their HQ so amazing. It sits on a cul-de-sac accessible only to pedestrians, so the area is much nicer than the street beyond the gate. The front of the building is brick, with two doors and a pair of stained glass windows. The simple, white, wooden door off to the side reveals a staircase leading directly down to the basement level. The main door is much more ornate, with beautiful oak framing a grid of twenty rectangles of art glass. Just inside is a small reception area, separated from the main room by a glass wall and door. To the left inside the door is the reception area, and past that is a set of beautiful oak stairs to the second floor.

Beyond the glass wall, across the deep red tile floor, is the "living room," which is a sitting area in front of a gas fireplace, with a leather sofa and armchairs.

Past this is a small conference table. In the rear wall behind the table is a huge, flat panel monitor. The monitor is on at all times and has as its screen saver a revolving selection of art. I was told they were all favorites of Dynamistress, from van Gogh and Maxfield Parrish to Peter Max and Banksy, with lots in between. It made sense that she chose the art, because this building was more than just the Pariah Project's headquarters. It was also her home.

All the rooms on this floor are lined with oak paneling, and many of the wall panels are false fronts, as Bloodmoon showed me. When giving me the tour, she slid one open, revealing the building's security system controls. Another one hid a rack of guns. There was nothing unusual about most of the guns, she told me. It was the ammunition that was special. A regular-looking, shotgun, for example, fired rounds that delivered five hundred volts of shock to the victim, having a range of about a hundred feet. She showed me other munitions, too, including a variety of custom rounds from explosives to expanding foam to pepper spray. Before closing the panel, she told me she had "a few other surprises" in there.

Bloodmoon is a scary damn woman.

Through a door at the back of the room are two sets of stairs. A short flight leads up to the Project office. Bloodmoon showed me the room, briefly. "Here's where the magic happens," she said. Seeing my doubtful expression, she said, "Well, here's where a lot of important things happen, at any rate." I noted the stack of papers next to the computer keyboard. "Grants," she said simply. "The Project is funded primarily by them, and we continually have to apply and reapply for them." With her permission, I looked through them. There were grants for general non-profits, for the purchase of life-saving equipment, disaster relief operations, social support, and more.

In one corner stands a rack holding dozens of different brochures, many of them on victim resources, victim rights, and so on. Most are official brochures from different sources, but some are put together by the Project.

There are soda and snack machines. "No money needed," I was told. To test this, I pushed a button for a Dr Pepper, and the machine dutifully offered it up to me.

We turned to leave, and that's when the bulletin board caught my eye. The length of the wall is filled with a row of low windows that look out on the stairwell to the basement. Above the windows, a cork board stretches from wall to wall, filled with photographs. "This was Sinta's idea," Bloodmoon said. "Some of the people helped by Project members." There were quite a few. Most everyone was smiling. I noted that many of the photos appeared to have been taken there at the headquarters.

Bloodmoon followed me out of the room, and we headed down a full flight of stairs to the basement level. At the bottom is a landing. Turning right, there is a door leading to a few steps up into a guest room and bath. This is where her brother had been staying, and would again, when he returned.

To the left of the landing are a few steps down to the basement, which is actually a kitchen and dining area running the length of the building. It has a black and white tile floor and white, ceramic tile fixtures. As in many peoples' homes, the kitchen is where the group often congregates, so they made it a comfortable place. In addition to a couple round dining tables, there's also a small corner bar. The walls around it are lined with shelves holding a huge array of bottles, including probably two dozen different flavored syrups. Dynamistress used to work as a bartender, I learned, and enjoyed creating drinks for her team, including non-alcoholic ones for the younger members and non-drinkers. At the far end of the kitchen are the stairs up to the street level.

The second floor of the Project's building is the main bedroom. It's a beautiful room, with a herringbone parquet floor and two long skylights. There are no closets, but there are a few large, standing wardrobes. One of these holds nothing but shoes. The deep doors have shelves inside and there are even more shelves in the wardrobe itself. I estimated more than a hundred pairs. I dubbed it "the cavern of footwear."

There is a small vanity table with a mirror, a leather love seat, and a bed that spins upside-down and recesses into the floor at the flip of a switch. I couldn't help but think this was clever, but wondered how often such a thing would be needed. "So far, never," was Bloodmoon's reply.

On the vanity is a jewelry box, which I absently went through. Aside from the standard assortment of baubles, I found some items that deserved a closer look. One was a pair of silver earrings in the shape of DNA strands. Another was a gold necklace with a pendant that I recognized as the "drum" icon of the Pariah Project. The final one was a real curiosity, though. It appeared to be a spent bullet, flattened from impact and silver-plated, on a silver chain. What was the story behind this? I was sure I'd learn soon enough.

Near the stairs is a stone-tiled half-bath with a walk-in rain shower, separated from the sink and toilet by a glass wall. Talk about decadent.

At the back end of the room are stairs to a tiny nook with a skylight. The nook leads out to the rooftop deck, which itself is maybe ten by twenty feet, surrounded by a short wall. It overlooks the roof of the rest of the building. Bloodmoon said they had planned to convert the roof into a bigger deck, but had never gotten around to it.

But there is also another door at the back of the bedroom. "When Dyna bought the building," Bloodmoon explained, "this was a huge, walk-in closet and dressing room. Dyna converted the space into her lab," she said. I tried to open the door, only to find it locked. Bloodmoon shrugged. "I suspect she had the key on her when... you know."

It was strange for me to be living in her home, sleeping in her bed, and speaking with her closest friends. And it was all still just a mess of confusion. The brief talks with her team members helped provide some context, but for the most part, I was no closer to understanding than before.

Dynamistress, it seemed, was a prolific diarist. A small shelf held her journals, all hand-written in bound books with date ranges on the covers. I picked up the most recent volume and skimmed through a few pages until one caught my full attention. It was dated May 9, 2009.

"Well, I did it. I called K.T. today and told her that I was okay with the idea of a book about me, even though I still didn't think anyone would be interested. And besides that, I told her I hadn't the first idea of how to write a book, nor did I really have time to do it. She mentioned having a ghost writer, which is evidently the way we're going to go with it. I told her I'd start putting some things together for her. I have doubts, though, that this will ever happen, or that anyone will buy it."

I wondered why she would have doubts. The little I knew about her was fascinating. I couldn't imagine I was the only one who'd think so.

"It's still a bit uncomfortable, talking to her. I'm not sure whether I'm relieved or disappointed that she's not in the city any longer. I miss her terribly. It's difficult, sometimes, not to let memories of our time together just overwhelm me. I have to consciously remind myself that 'our time together' was just as friends, that she wasn't able to return my affection. And of course, I can't forget how I made an utter fool of myself. That bit in particular is usually enough to pull me out of the spiral of self-pity."

I closed the book and returned it to the shelf. I had known that reading her journals would feel uncomfortable, at times. I was going to be diving into someone's most private thoughts. But since it was unavoidable, there was no sense in feeling self-conscious about it. At least, that's what I told myself.

I located the earliest book. As curious as I was about her recent life, I knew if I was going to truly understand this woman, I had to start at the beginning.

Bloodmoon and I were to meet with other members of the Project, and I sat in the office, waiting. I spent the time looking over the photographs on the room-length bulletin board. In many of the photos, people were posed with members of the Project. But I saw none with Dynamistress. I suspected she was probably the photographer, in most cases.

One photo caught my attention. It showed a girl with black hair, perhaps about sixteen, wearing a blue t-shirt featuring a DNA helix and the words "Team Dyna" vertically along one side.

"That's Macy," Bloodmoon said from behind me, causing me to start. "You'll meet her eventually, I'm sure." I was about to ask about the shirt, but she beat me to it. "Macy founded a Dynamistress fan club. All the members got a shirt. They had other things, too, like mugs and whatnot."

I remembered reading somewhere that some supergroups had their own lines of merchandise. Bloodmoon escorted me downstairs to the kitchen. "Yes, some do, and they sell them to raise money for charity. We have some team items, too," she said, digging in her pocket. She pulled out a keychain featuring the Pariah Project "drum" symbol. "We don't try to sell them, though, since we're not exactly one of the popular groups."

We entered the huge kitchen, where I took a seat at a corner table. Bloodmoon poured her ever-present tea into black, Pariah Project drum logo mugs, and sat with me as we waited for the first of several "interviewees" to arrive.

Cara Desmarais, a.k.a. Caracara, was one of those most resistant to speaking with me until Bloodmoon convinced her. All during our talk, she was fidgety, clearly wanting it to be over. She looked to Bloodmoon frequently throughout our talk.

Caracara is a dark-skinned, brown-haired beauty in her early twenties. She's originally from French Guiana and has a lovely accent. She has enormous, feathery wings of brown and white, which fold neatly behind her when she's not in flight. The woman herself is about five foot nothing, but her wings, when folded, rise a couple more. They span probably twelve feet, fully extended. She was not a founding member of the Pariah Project, but voted into the group soon after its creation.

"*Oui*, I was *très supris*," she told me, and I was suddenly glad I'd taken French in high school. "We first met when I was rescued from that other world."

She was talking about what the media calls "the Nevada Incident," where several metahumans from our world were replaced by doubles from another Earth. It's a story many people have trouble believing and some flatly claim is a hoax.

"I was one of those exchanged," she told me, "and even I sometimes cannot believe it." She smiled awkwardly as she said this, but it quickly disappeared. "I next saw her at the memorial service for her *coéquipier*, Transcendant. A few weeks after that, she asked me to coffee, where she told me about her new team. I was asked to meet with them all. An interview. And then I was invited to join." She smiled sadly. "It has been difficult, the past month."

Caracara has a gift for understatement.

Nena Geissler, a.k.a. Neon had joined the group in January, and was the most recent addition to the Project. She was about the same age as Caracara. She's pretty, but doesn't think she is. And as her name implies, she's a colorful girl. Tall and thin, with a pixie-like smile, she dresses in bright colors and always has hair to match. The day we spoke, it was purple. The color isn't dyed, but is tied to her meta abilities. Neon, like Dynamistress, generates a form of bio-plasma. Dynamistress's energy manifested mainly in intense blasts of force, but Neon's plasma is of the more common sort: fire.

We sat at a corner table in the kitchen, a plate of cupcakes between us. Neon devoured one, then wiped frosting from her lips. "Lily brought me in," she told me, peeling the paper from another cupcake. "And I never met Dyna until the same day I met most of the others, which was maybe a week before... you know. I wasn't there when it happened. I'm sorry I can't be any more help."

Lily McKay, a.k.a. Half-Life, is almost twenty. Looking at her is, in some ways, like looking at the opposite of her friend, Neon. Her skin is extremely pale, with an almost gray tinge. She contrasts this with a variety of bright lipsticks and eye makeup. Her hair is silvery. "It's from the excess potassium I produce," she said. She explained that the decay of the radioactive isotope of potassium is responsible for the focused explosions she can produce. And when her hair got wet, she explained, lilac flames resulted, due to the potassium reacting with water.

"Dyna saved my life," she told me, with an intense gaze. "I was dying, being poisoned by my own abilities, which hadn't yet fully matured. She figured out what was happening and how to prevent it from killing me. And then she helped me get control of it all. Her brother helped, too... I wasn't in a good place, mentally. And of course, so did Kit," she said, leaning into her boyfriend.

Kit, a.k.a. Resonator, is the only member of the Pariah Project who maintains any sort of privacy about his identity. "Just Kit is fine," he said. Also in his early twenties, this quiet young man is, ironically, a master of sound. His armored battle suit converts noise into a variety of weapons that can deafen, cause dizziness or nausea, and even become a physical force.

"Dyna was special," Resonator told me. "What other meta would have taken the time to analyze Lily's condition and figure it out?"

"We weren't with them when it happened," Half-Life said. "It was hours later that we heard. They were all in a state of shock."

"Dyna and Sinta used to live next door to us," Resonator continued. "They share a birthday, you know. So it happened on Sinta's birthday. Nothing like having an in-your-face reminder every year, huh?"

"Sinta" is the only name people know her by, including her friends. She's the "catgirl" in the team, though I was told she hated being called that. Still, I wasn't sure why she denied it, given that she had fur covering her entire body, had eyes and ears like a cat, and claws. I was surprised she had no tail.

"Oh, she was born with one," Bloodmoon told me. "But she lost it when she was about two." Seeing my confused expression, she explained. "Her parents... um... chopped it off." I gasped and Bloodmoon sighed. "Yeah, that's the reaction I had, too."

She shared the details. Young Sinta was found at the door of a hospital, close to death from blood loss. As it so happened, this had been the same hospital in which she'd been born, and one of the nurses remembered her. They pulled her birth records, found the parents' names, and called the police on them. But when the officers arrived, the parents resisted. The official word is that they were both intoxicated and enraged. In the altercation that followed, the parents were killed. And thus began Sinta's terrible journey through the foster care system before being taken in by Scoutmaster when she was twelve.

She'd turned nineteen on the day Dynamistress turned thirty-nine. "Sinta has no family," Bloodmoon told me, "just her friends. Because of her traumatic childhood, with the numerous foster families and the abuse, she rarely became close to people. Oh, she's friendly with everyone and is far more trusting than most people would be, given her past. But despite the friendliness and the warmth, she still keeps her distance, emotionally." Bloodmoon smiled sadly. "Dyna was one of the few exceptions. Both of them."

Seeing my confusion, Bloodmoon told me that, through a strange series of events, Sinta had become close with the Dynamistress from that other world from the Nevada Incident. And the previous year, that woman had sacrificed her life to save the Dynamistress of this world. Sinta had been crushed by the loss. And now she'd lost a second Dynamistress, who'd been almost like a mother to her.

"To say she hasn't handled this well would be an understatement," Bloodmoon continued. "She withdrew, holed up in her apartment, and basically stopped communicating with the world. We urged her to get professional help, but she refused."

Referring to Bloodmoon's empathic abilities, I asked if there was anything she could do for the girl. "Not really," she said. "I'm not much good when it comes to trauma recovery. Anyway, as for meeting her... Well, I'll leave her a message, but I wouldn't expect an answer."

Jack Fullerton, a.k.a. Zero-Point, had chosen to bury himself in work as a way to handle the loss of his friend. Bloodmoon took me to visit him at his workplace, Wonderland Robotics. Zero-Point is in his early thirties with an athletic build and what some referred to as "movie star good looks." As for abilities, I had a hard time understanding them. He explained that he was able to tap into energy at the atomic level and manipulate it, to an extent. For the record, that explanation didn't help at all.

"Well," he told me as we sat in his office, "as an example, I can siphon energy from people. Or I can stimulate them, like an adrenaline boost. This sometimes results in minor wound healing, too."

While that was equally fascinating and incomprehensible, I couldn't stop looking at his mechanical arm. It looked so real. He'd lost his original in the same event that took the other Dynamistress's life. Late in the year, he had a series of surgeries to reinforce his upper body, allowing him to have superhuman strength by utilizing a variety of "battle arms." He was still in physical therapy to get his body used to the new additions.

I told him I wanted to know what happened in those final moments. The bits and pieces the others had given me were frustrating in what was missing.

Zero-Point glanced briefly at Bloodmoon, almost as if asking permission to share information. Then he said, "Dyna's abilities were the result of her own genetic manipulation. Periodically, she tweaked her DNA to fine-tune them. Her most recent adjustment was meant to help her get the most energy possible out of the food she ate, so that she wouldn't have to consume a frankly ludicrous number of calories every day." He chuckled suddenly. "My God, that woman could put away the food. It was amazing."

Then he stared vacantly into nothing for a moment. "Metabolism," he said, snapping back to the present, "the process of converting food to energy, is a chemical reaction. And in chemical reactions, there is something known as 'runaway.' Basically, it's an uncontrolled acceleration of the reaction. And that's what happened with Dyna."

Zero-Point went silent for a long moment. Then he cleared his throat and continued. "She knew what was happening," he said. "She figured it out a few months before. And she tried a number of things to reverse it, including further tweaks of her DNA, but she knew that would likely take too long. We spent a lot of time together in the last month or so, with me draining excess energy from her in an effort to give her more time. In the evenings, I'd drain her to the point of passing out. Toward the end, we were together almost 24/7." He smiled sadly. "But it wasn't enough."

Kim Choi, a.k.a. Kimera, is another obvious meta. Her body, while human in shape, is covered in fur like a lion's, including claws and a tail. Her head is another matter. The fur tapers off around the shoulders and lower neck, gradually turning to fine scales like a snake's. Her eyes look serpentine, as well. And she has fangs. She has no hair on her head, but an impressive pair of ram-like horns. With all that, people rarely seem to notice that she's Asian, until she cusses in Korean.

Kimera has incredibly fast reflexes, is able to see heat signatures, and yes, her bite is venomous. She was also now the oldest member of the Project, being about five years younger than Dynamistress and a year or so older than Bloodmoon.

"It was horrible," she said in a raspy voice. "We all ran after her, on the pier." Kimera licked her lips and took a deep breath. "She was hanging there in the sky, maybe fifty or sixty feet up. And then," she said, her eyes closing, "she screamed. Like no scream I'd ever heard. As though her very spirit was in agony."

Kimera opened her large eyes and looked at me. "I hear that scream every night, in my dreams. Sometimes I even hear it while awake." She took a shaky breath. "And then, still screaming... she just..." Kimera blinked, sending a tear down her scaly cheek. "She just... erupted."

I'd read on Metapedia of Dynamistress's ability to "explode" tremendous amounts of energy. "It wasn't like that," Kimera said. "It was more like something catching on fire. There was smoke. And licks of flame here and there. And the smell of burning flesh." Kimera paused again to collect herself. "And then she dropped into the bay."

Kimera firmed her jaw as she stared at her lap. Then she looked up, turning her big, snake-like eyes to mine.

"She burned the whole way as she sank."

Two

"What we have done for ourselves alone dies with us; what we have done for others and the world remains and is immortal."
~ Albert Pike

I've been feeling quite nostalgic, lately, my brain filled with memories of my time with the Bay Scouts. I realize I'm looking back with my rose-colored glasses firmly in place, of course. There's no question that the team was dysfunctional, to some degree, and that I wasn't much of a team player at the time. Yet, when I compare that tenure to my time with the Gatekeepers, it's obvious which team felt more like home to me. Had the Bay Scouts not been disbanded and their funding removed, or had Daniel not been so injured and/or remained willing to keep the team alive, I have little doubt that I'd still be with them.

I realize, too, that this is naïve thinking. We lost more than Valora's life and Daniel's career. I think all of us suffered psychologically. I know I would have recovered better if I'd had someone to talk with about it. The twins moved back to Texas, Esteban to San Diego. Song is not far away, but for some reason, we never talk about it more than superficially when we meet. And even if Val had survived, she wasn't the type to discuss her feelings about things, unless they were feelings of anger.

Jack is great, of course. He listens to me. His ability to relate is better than most, but still not quite the same.

I think that's a large part of why my time with the Gatekeepers was so rocky. The exchange experience messed me up even more than I realized, especially when including my unintentional killing of Dr. Gray. I look back on my journal entries in the years following, for example, and they feel so disjointed and superficial. They read almost like I was an outside observer to my own life, like I was just reciting events, rather than capturing how I felt about them.

My therapist told me I was suffering from PTSD. I told her that she has a gift for stating the obvious. At any rate, I think I've improved a lot over the past few months. I feel less scattered, more focused. It was, though, a less-than-optimal couple of years.

I don't mean to say that my time with the Gatekeepers was bad. Obviously, I met some fantastic people and am still friends with them, today. This is evidenced by the fact that several of them left the Gatekeepers to form the Pariah Project with me. I'm closer with them than I was with most of the Scouts.

One thing both of those teams had in common, though, was a leader who gained my deep respect. Granted, it took some time with Invictus, because I didn't work as closely with him at first as I had with Scoutmaster.

To that end, I spoke with both of them this morning about regular get-togethers, just the three of us. Sort of three generations of team leaders, since Scoutmaster had learned under the leadership of Invictus and I learned under both of them. They liked the idea and we've got plans to meet up next week.

As for the Project, I'm pleased with how it's coming along. Today, Caracara was accepted into the group by full consensus. She told me once that she never seemed to fit other groups, which made her an obvious choice for the Project.

I invited her mainly because of my encounter with her double in the other world. That woman nearly succeeded in killing Sinta. But that was before she knew the truth of the situation. When I spoke to her in the medical unit, I explained Valora's intentions and the reality of the inter-world swap. When she understood this, when she realized how she'd nearly shredded Sinta on helicopter blades, she was aghast. Her horror and regret were genuine.

I figured that, if her double from that terrible place had a good heart, the one from my own world had to be a wonderful person. Not a logical conclusion to make, of course, but so far my instincts haven't been wrong.

I worry about Vicky, though. It's been about four months since her ordeal in the U.K. I wish I could say she's recovered well from it, but I can't. Most of the time, she seems fine, but every so often, she'll have a sort of flashback and will crawl inside herself for a couple days. She's not the most open person at the best of times, even with me. But she still won't talk about it. She claims she doesn't remember much of it at all, due to being sedated much of the time. I can't tell if she's being honest about that. I wish she'd open up, but I can't force her to, obviously.

But it's not as though she doesn't think about it. Lately, she's taken it upon herself to learn every last detail about her father's activities as much as possible. I'm pretty sure she's been communicating with Probe, enlisting his help. No idea if Invictus is aware of this or not, and I'm certainly not going to ask.

In other news, it seems my last DNA tweak has succeeded wonderfully. For the past couple months, I'd been noticing that I always seemed overly amped. But now, it's clear. I'm eating less than I used to, but still have plenty of energy, even after fairly long flights. Couldn't have hoped for better results!

Since I'd gotten to know individual members of the Pariah Project, at least a bit, I wanted to see how the group acted as a whole. I mentioned this to Bloodmoon, but she said they only had full group meetings once a month, unless something urgent came up. "However," she added, "you can see the end result of some of our efforts."

She led me down to the kitchen, where a man was replacing a damaged hinge on the pantry door. He looked familiar, but it took me a moment to realize I'd seen his photo on the bulletin board in the office. He was introduced to me as Jeremy. At Bloodmoon's urging, he told me his story. He spoke awkwardly, with frequent glances at Bloodmoon.

"Was maybe nine, ten months ago," he said. "Been homeless for a lotta years. Dyna, she saw me bein' kicked to shit by some gangbangers. Was the Maltese Falcon who actually stopped 'em, but Dyna followed me to the hospital, paid my bill, gave me some cash. I was grateful, of course, but figured that was that. Never had reason to think I'd see her again. Then, back in September, she tracks me down on the streets. Offers me a job as handyman at this place here. Then she helps me get into a low-income unit over on Eddy Street." Jeremy shook his head, as though he couldn't imagine someone going to all that effort for a stranger. Then his face fell and he looked away. "What kind of world is it where someone like that has something like this happen to them?" Then Jeremy smiled weakly and excused himself before returning to his work.

Bloodmoon had prepared tea for us while Jeremy spoke. Now we sat in the corner armchairs to talk. "One of Dyna's ideas for the group was that each of us would have a particular cause that we would support by donating our time. For example, Dyna herself was a suicide prevention counselor. Jack has begun working with amputees in support groups. Bridget volunteers at a dog rescue. Jennifer..." She smiled suddenly. "Dyna loved poking friendly fun at those she cared for. One of her favorite targets was Jen. She called her 'Bat-Girl' the first time they met. Made jokes about her eating mosquitoes. It was always bat jokes. Always." She laughed a little. "And then Jen goes and volunteers at a bat rescue center up in Sacramento. She'd never told us this, before, but both of Jen's parents are chiropterologists in Texas. By the age of six, she knew more about bats than ninety-nine percent of adults ever do. Turns out she'd never minded the bat jokes at all."

It was nice to see Bloodmoon's mood lighten. The Pariah Project was, it was clear, a bit of a mess without their "leader who wasn't the leader." They were no longer a team, just a handful of individuals going through the motions, interacting only occasionally, almost as though seeing each other was too much of a reminder of how things really were. And it didn't help that they now had to deal with me. No wonder they were so uncomfortable around me.

I read her journals whenever I wasn't talking with Bloodmoon or the others. I'd made it from the earliest entries, when she was sixteen, up through her college years, then graduate school through receiving her doctorate, and finally her job at a genetics lab. With the exception of her resentment of her brother, these entries had less of the teenage anger of her earlier writings. There was almost nothing in them beyond work on her pursuit to become a meta. There was a lot of scientific talk in these passages, though just in generic terms. There was also mention of a roommate, and a couple pages about her brother's wedding, but that was about it.

Reading about her scientific pursuits got me to wondering about the actual process itself. Her personal journal only alluded casually to that aspect of her life. Her scientific records were probably in the lab.

I don't know why I felt such a burning desire to see her notes. It's not as though I expected to understand them. But surely they couldn't just be a bunch of formulae and equations in a book. There had to be commentary, too, and I thought that might give me another level of insight that personal journals couldn't.

One day, Bloodmoon took me out to dinner at an Indian restaurant not far from the Project's building. Since I'd never tried Indian food before, she recommended a dish called Butter Chicken. It was amazing!

As we ate, we talked about how she and Dynamistress had met. "It was when Kimera nominated her for admission to the Gatekeepers and she was interviewed by the leadership. This would have been just over two years ago. Kimera had spoken well of her, as did Scoutmaster, the leader of her previous team. And we'd heard about her role in the Nevada Incident, so there was no hesitation in offering her membership. Because I was one of the Prefects – that's the second-tier leadership in the Gatekeepers – I took it upon myself to get to know her and we got along well.

"I suppose the aspect of her personality that I was most drawn to," she said, "was her passion. When Dyna got something in her head, that was it.

She wouldn't think twice about doing whatever was necessary, including breaking rules, in order to do what she felt was right." Bloodmoon was quiet a moment, sipping her tea. "When she was thinking of leaving the group, with the idea of forming the Pariah Project, I was the only one of the Gatekeepers she told about it. And while I was content on that team, it was that same passion that drew me in."

After a minute of silence, I asked if she'd heard anything more regarding the weapons. Bloodmoon looked askance at me, a slight smirk touching her lips. I frowned and asked what she found funny.

"I just find it interesting that you're so curious about our activities." Bloodmoon absently tore at her naan as she spoke. "Arsenal received more of the weapons and has been asking for information about their source, without success. Vicky replied to my voicemail, by the way. I've put her in touch with Arsenal. With any luck, they'll be able to figure out where they're coming from."

I asked what the next step would be, assuming she could discover this. "That depends on what exactly she learns. If the weapons are being manufactured here, we'll want to know who's doing it and for whom. When there's some solid information, we'll reach out to our contact at the ATF and probably work with them, unless they tell us to butt out."

Then she switched the subject and asked about my reading. I admitted that I was having difficulty connecting the much-admired Dynamistress everyone had been describing to me with the person in the journals. Bloodmoon just nodded and said, "The Dyna who wrote the words you're currently reading is the one who was hurt by a dysfunctional family life. She was more prideful back then, I understand, so her passion took the form of defensiveness and a bit of arrogance." Bloodmoon shrugged casually. "Who hasn't been like that, at some point?" She pushed her empty plate aside. "But Dyna's passion doesn't just pertain to ideals. She cares deeply about others. According to her brother, she always did."

In the journals I was reading, Dynamistress and her brother were estranged. That had obviously changed, since he'd been staying with her.

"Oh, absolutely. By the time I met her, she and Dana were as close as could be." I asked when I would meet him. "I... really can't say," she said, her voice heavy. "Not until his condition improves. If it ever does."

I reminded her that she still hadn't explained how he'd come to be in a coma. She shook her head and apologized. "Dyna and her brother shared a mind link." Seeing my confusion, she said, "Perhaps 'link' isn't the best word. May I give you a small sample?"

I hesitated, but agreed, and a moment later, I felt her presence in my head. It was a feeling I can't compare to anything else. It wasn't intrusive. If anything, it was calming. Before I could even voice the question, I heard her say, *No, what Dyna and her brother shared was much more intense, much more intimate, than this. This is a superficial imposition on your mind. Imagine this, multiplied perhaps a hundredfold. And not just intentional communication, but all thoughts. Emotions, too.*

And then, she was gone. "What I'm getting at," she said as I recovered from the experience, "is that when Dyna erupted over the bay, that link – that complete connection – was active." She looked into my eyes, and I could see hers were pained. "Dana didn't just witness it. He *experienced* it."

That evening's reading was like a soap opera. Again, it astounded me that Dynamistress didn't think people would find her story interesting. I felt like I should have been eating popcorn while reading.

Dynamistress got romantically involved with her roommate. She'd also quite obviously developed a drinking problem. She completed her work on becoming a meta and, on the night when she injected herself with the altered DNA, the building somehow caught fire and was destroyed.

After the fire, she was sued and it went to trial. Dynamistress had a sexual tryst with her attorney and admitted it to her girlfriend, which effectively ended their relationship, though they remained living together. The trial finally ended, with Dynamistress being found culpable. Her roommate moved out and, after increasingly odd and obsessive behavior, committed suicide.

That seems to be what made her change. There were lots of entries where she wrote of feeling guilty about her ex. Not long after, she and her brother made up, as Bloodmoon had said, and went on a trip together to Europe, during which her meta abilities manifested, about three and a half years after her initial procedure.

I read with fascination the account of how she realized her experiment had worked. After casually slapping her brother, he developed a large bruise. And in the weeks that followed, she was able to focus energy in her fists, allowing her to punch through walls.

I looked at my hand. I made a fist and imagined energy suffusing it, putting up a barrier around it for protection, effectively making the fist a fantastic weapon. What would that feel like? Would it be warm? Tingly? Would it even feel like anything at all, once you got used to it? Or would you never get used to it?

And what about actual energy blasts? What would they feel like as they erupted? Hell, I thought, what would they feel like on the receiving end? My reading hadn't yet covered that, but in truth, she probably had little idea what it felt like to be struck by one of her blasts. Would it be like being hit with a bullet? A sledgehammer? A boxing gloved fist? Given the different types of blasts she could allegedly produce, probably all of the above.

I honestly didn't know what to think of this woman. I agreed with Bloodmoon, in that most of us have our periods of being self-centered, though that's usually during our teen years. For Dynamistress, it lasted until her early thirties. On the other hand, the way she was treated by her mother might make anyone prone to being overly defensive.

I couldn't help feeling bad for her. She was on the hook for a huge amount of money from the trial, and for something that might not even have been her fault. Worse, she blamed herself for her former lover's suicide. That's a lot for anyone to bear.

The next chunk of reading took Dynamistress to San Francisco, including her first outings in the streets. Here, I learned the origin of the bullet necklace, in an entry that was clearly written with a combination of horror and excitement.

Then there was the story of her joining the Bay Scouts, and then the events referred to as the Nevada Incident, where Dynamistress and several others on her team were somehow swapped between worlds with doubles who didn't exactly have our best interests in mind.

Tucked into the pages of the journal at this point was a letter, handwritten over several pages. The paper was dog-eared, with small tears where it had been refolded so many times. It was a letter to Dynamistress from her other-self from that world. Reading it was surprisingly moving, and I found myself feeling for this woman. And that I was even reading such a thing at all made my head spin.

This span of her journals also introduced me to some of the people I'd met, including Zero-Point, who was in the Bay Scouts. Kimera and Caracara were mentioned toward the end, though not in much detail. I took a break, then, with so much to think about. It was all still a jumble, though it was beginning to come together.

It was clear that talking with the team members about Dynamistress was uncomfortable for them, but it was also obvious how much love and respect they had for her. They weren't uncomfortable about that at all.

I wondered if she knew. So often in her journals, it was clear that she didn't have healthy self-esteem. She certainly didn't love herself and, at times, I got the impression she might not even like herself much. If she did know how much she meant to others, I suspect she thought this was more a character flaw in them than a reflection of her own good qualities.

The exception to this, it seemed, was her brother. She seemed aware of how much he loved her. Bloodmoon kept telling me that he was the key to my understanding, that once he was back to full health, I'd have no more questions. But that wasn't likely to be soon. Bloodmoon said his condition had gone from comatose to what's called a "minimally conscious state." What that meant was that he could track people with his eyes, return a hand squeeze, and so on. And of course, his telepathy didn't work, either. It could be weeks, yet, before I could talk to him.

Given this, my next request of Bloodmoon was to see if we could arrange for meetings with some of Dynamistress's friends outside of the Project. There was one in particular who figured large in her journals.

Captain Shepherd worked at the Coast Guard Air Station, near the San Francisco Airport. We met him at a café nearby. Shepherd was a distinguished-looking man, probably in his late fifties. His black hair was gray at the temples. He was quite friendly when we met, but it was clear that this meeting was still uncomfortable for him. Bloodmoon had warned me that he might be unable to answer certain questions, given the sensitive nature of government work, so I led off by asking about the evolution of their relationship.

"It's true," he said, "that we became friends over the years. I was the Coast Guard liaison to the Bay Scouts and had, of course, known about her from the day she joined that team. But we first met in person around the time of Project Echo – the Nevada Incident – and I know I don't need to tell you how pivotal her role was in that." He sipped his coffee and spoke wistfully. "After that, the Scouts were disbanded, but we stayed in touch during her time with the Gatekeepers. My girls – I have two daughters – just loved her. We'd have her over for dinner, occasionally. Picnics on holidays. That sort of thing."

When I asked why he thought a friendship developed with her and not with other metas, he was thoughtful for a moment. Eventually, he said, "I can only speak for me, of course, but I think it's because I was so impressed by her convictions. She wanted the existence of Project Echo to be revealed to the public, and was willing to break a government gag order to do it. She risked imprisonment for her beliefs. You've got to admire that." He smiled warmly, then said, "And she was just as dedicated to her friends – and strangers, for that matter – as she was to her principles." With a smile, he said, "I also liked that she wouldn't take crap from anyone, but would dish it right back. And that included me," he said with a chuckle.

We spoke for a short while longer, and he finally asked, "Is any of this helping?" I assured him it was. I needed to get a sense of who she was, I told him, and the best way to do that was to see her through the eyes of those who actually knew her. "Wonderful," he said, and looked at me with a gaze I can only describe as hopeful. "I look forward to seeing the end result."

THREE

"I am afraid of death, scared by it. I already don't know if I exist or not. So dying really terrifies me."
~ Stephen Rea

It's been a very good week. I was able to spend a full afternoon with Macy. I'm relieved to see her behaving more like her old self. She told me that her counseling sessions were going well, but admitted that she still has the occasional nightmare about her ordeal at the hands of her schoolmate. I'm glad she finally opened up to me about it all. As for Aaron, I was surprised to learn that he's being tried as an adult. This concerns me, honestly, because it's obvious the kid needs psychological help.

Macy was excited about doing a redesign of "my" website. I told her she's free to do whatever she wants with it. She also urged me, not for the first time (or tenth), that I need to become more actively involved with the fan club. I told her I'd try.

Yesterday, I bumped into Terry as I was out and about. He seemed troubled and, when I asked him about it, he vaguely alluded to some family issues. He assured me that he and Helena were fine. Naturally, I asked about Sydney and Layla. His eyes betrayed that this is where the issue lay, but he just smiled faintly and said I should come visit sometime. The girls wanted to see me. I promised I would.

Things with the Project are good. This morning, I pitched to the group the idea of each of us doing volunteer work as a requirement for membership in the Project. I personally want to renew my commitment to being a suicide prevention counselor. The hotline folks here have been exceedingly accommodating to me over the years, knowing that it's not easy for me to maintain a regular schedule on the phones. But I'd like to think maybe now I can, since our work with the Project won't be anywhere near as demanding as the Gatekeepers' was. We're not subject to being handed an assignment on short notice, since we choose what we do.

Happily, the others seemed to like the idea. Some even seemed excited about it and started tossing around ideas for what they might do. Bridget is a huge animal lover and immediately said she wanted to volunteer at a dog rescue. Others expressed interest in working with children in some fashion. Kit wants to work with deaf kids. Lily said she'd like to work with orphans.

In other news, I visited Dynasonic again. The band's fifth album, *Whine*, is coming out soon. She played me the title track of it in her studio. It's pretty wild. Really intense vocals, almost to the point of being an assault on the eardrums. She admitted that she used a tiny amount of her meta ability in the recording.

We talked more about the situation in her world that we'd just touched on during my last visit: the large-scale telepathic monitoring of society. Specifically, I wanted to find out her brother's role in things, since she'd been somewhat cagey about it, before.

I learned that the network of telepaths is controlled by one central figure (surprise, surprise), a telepath of tremendous ability referred to as "The Overseer." This is a *male* telepath, which she'd previously told me didn't exist. There's always an exception to such "rules." I put two and two together and didn't like the answer I came up with. But I asked her straight out: was The Overseer her brother?

Turns out, he's not. In fact, her Dana is sort of the opposite. He's a wild card, an undiscovered male telepath, working in deep secret to undermine The Overseer and restore true autonomy to the society. As with most totalitarian states – even ones as "nice" as this one – there is an underground movement of "power to the people" types.

Naturally, I asked if he operated with a name, like The Overseer did. Not officially, she said, but when necessary, he was referred to as Liberator. Fitting, I suppose.

I found it interesting that Dana is/was a proactive guy in both of the other worlds I've visited, but not in my own. I swear, I'll break down his resolve, one day.

As for my personal life, I haven't been sleeping well, lately. More accurately, I'm finding it virtually impossible to fall asleep. I have so much energy that I need to expend a lot of it before I can doze off. And even then, I find that if I've eaten anything past about six p.m., I'll just end up waking again in the middle of the night, fidgety and anxious.

Maybe my last tweak was a little *too* efficient.

The evenings were strangest. It was unusually quiet for being in the middle of a city. Maybe this was due to heavy insulation or something. The quiet was a bit disconcerting, but comforting at the same time, if that makes sense.

Bloodmoon created a guest account for me on their computer network and showed me how the whole thing worked. Their system was way more advanced than any computers I'd ever seen. I spent a lot of time browsing the internet while listening to Dynamistress's impressive digital music collection. I sorted the music to see what songs she played most often. There was a lot of classic rock, but also a lot of bands I'd never heard of. I listened to as much as I could, hoping it would somehow connect me with her.

I also found a folder of photographs. The earliest of them seemed to be of the trip to Europe she and Dana had taken. And nearly all of these were of Dana... of him crossing Abbey Road in London, drinking beer in Belgium, sitting in a camp chair looking over Cardigan Bay in Wales, and so on. In fact, in that entire set of photos, only one showed her. It was a picture of the pair of them, her head resting on his shoulder, both of them smiling. A floppy hat and sunglasses hid most of her face.

Surely, I thought, there must be printed pictures of her somewhere. After searching a while, I found a single photo album in her bedroom. I flipped through it, finding plenty of pictures of a young Dinah, but nothing from her later life. This was a woman who seriously didn't like to be photographed.

That night, in bed, unable to sleep, I tried to put together all the pieces of information I'd gained into some sort of whole. I couldn't understand why it was so difficult. Those who'd spoken to me seemed to be pretty up front about everything. Even though almost every one of them seemed uncomfortable when we spoke, I never felt any of them were holding anything back.

I was looking forward to her brother's input. I had to admit, though, that when Bloodmoon had explained to me about the mental connection the two of them shared, I started to wonder how I'd even approach that one. When I thought of what he must have felt as Dynamistress went into runaway, it sent a chill through me. How would I even broach the subject? Assuming, of course, that he made a full recovery.

For that matter, how would I bring it up to Nexus? It was difficult enough with her friends, but she had been Dynamistress's girlfriend. I sat up in bed and turned on the reading lamp.

I read from the journal again, learning of her sale of "DynaPaste" to a sports nutrition company, of how her mother had "killed" her in her hometown, of the disbanding of the Bay Scouts, and of the kidnapping and rescue of her then-girlfriend, Rachel. Then there was the bit that Captain Shepherd had mentioned, with Dynamistress pushing to reveal the truth about Project Echo to the public, followed by her capture by the other-world version of her teammate Valora, her escape, and then the final confrontation in Nevada with the other-worlders.

Following all that, I finally got a peek deep inside Dynamistress. She blamed herself for the death of her college mentor, even though he was basically one of the bad guys. She felt her actions hadn't been the right ones, that she could have escaped without having him die.

But it wasn't a simple case of regret. She wrote page after page about her guilt, questioning herself on many levels. She was clearly quite messed up by the experience.

The thing is, if she'd described it accurately, it seemed to me that her options were pretty darn limited. I doubted anyone could blame her for doing what she did. Anyone but herself, that is.

I put the volume aside and tried to sleep again. But the truth of the matter is that I had some anxiety regarding sleep. I'd begun having dreams about the events in Dynamistress's journals.

And not the happy parts.

The next night's reading covered her joining the Gatekeepers, being featured in *Supers* magazine, and the first mention of Macy, whom I'd seen on the photo wall. She was also the girl who maintained Dynamistress's website. I made a mental note to ask Bloodmoon to set up a meeting with her.

I also read about her growing feelings for K.T., the one who'd interviewed her for the magazine, and would later be the one to push for Dynamistress to write her memoirs.

Then there was a strange situation with the other-world portal in Nevada, where she was the only one who could pass through, and where she met and spoke to her other-self in the "in-between," as she called it. And then the other-Dynamistress betrayed her and stranded her there.

Obviously, she found her way back, and that's when she told K.T. how she felt. But it turned out that K.T. was straight. I couldn't help but feel for Dynamistress. That had to be hard. And in her heartbreak and embarrassment, she went to visit her brother, just as Bloodmoon had said.

And then I read her account of her visit, including how Dana put up psychic defenses in her mind. And in the morning, they discovered their actions had made the mind link. She went on about how awesome she thought it was, and how it freaked out her brother.

What really struck me, reading of how it happened, was how casually she wrote about it. I can't say I was overly surprised, given what I knew of her by this point. I understood why the others told the story they did. But I wondered if they knew it wasn't true.

Over breakfast the next day, I spoke to Bloodmoon about things from that morning's reading, including the crippling guilt Dynamistress seemed to have been suffering.

"Yes, she was definitely off her game for a good while, there. It was unfortunate, how she kept second-guessing herself. She got through it, but it took a while. To be honest," she continued, "she only started being back to her normal self about a month before... you know."

That morning's reading had also introduced Resonator and the girl who would eventually become Half-Life. "I think that was one of Dyna's proudest moments," Bloodmoon said, "figuring out what was happening with Lily, and how to cure her. Dyna empathized with Lily, who felt guilty about accidentally killing her family. That little connection of guilt, I'd say, is why Lily is alive, today."

Then there was the strange epidemic that broke out in the city, how Dynamistress was infected, too, and her inability to get rid of it. And amazingly, there was reference to yet another alternate Earth that she visited, where her other-self was the singer in a famous band. I asked Bloodmoon about Dynasonic's world.

She looked at me with a confused expression. "Dynasonic? I think she has some CDs by a band of that name, but I'm not clear on what you're saying."

So I told her about the portal discovered by her friend Ping Song, about her visits to that world, and about Dynasonic herself.

"That's... disturbing," she said. When I asked why, she said, "Because something that huge should not be done alone. She was still one of the Gatekeepers at the time. The leadership should have been informed." After a moment, she shook her head. "No matter. I can hardly be upset about it at this point, can I?"

She sipped her tea, then changed topics. "I'm heading over to the hospital to see Dana today. There's not been much change in his condition, but I figured a friendly presence couldn't hurt."

By the end of the day, I'd read the journals through Dynamistress's somewhat insane attempt to find a cure for her disease by deliberately going through the portal to bring her other-self here. Her plan had gone south when, before she could carry out her plans, she had a seizure, instead.

But in the end, it was her other-self who ultimately saved the day, when Sinta brought her to this world. The woman not only gave her life to destroy the bizarre creature that had been spreading the disease, but also got Dynamistress what she needed for a cure.

I read this passage twice, surprised that it wasn't as emotional as I expected. It's not every day someone makes that kind of sacrifice. I remembered her writing about the letter her "other-self" had left her, and how often she'd read it. Why didn't she write about how she must have really felt?

For that matter, the tone of the journals themselves had changed from the ones I'd read just days ago. The entries from her college days, up through her time with the Bay Scouts, were more thoughtful, more emotional. By comparison, the entries beginning around the time she joined the Gatekeepers weren't as personal. They seemed almost detached.

It was clear that the events that ultimately broke up the Bay Scouts had hurt her in a way she didn't realize, and it affected the way she wrote.

But the last passage I read focused a lot on Sinta, making me want to meet the girl even more. She had lived with Dynamistress, after all. She was clearly the third part of the trio of essential people whose knowledge I needed. It was like the universe was conspiring against me. Those three were the ones I couldn't get access to.

I decided to power through and finish the journals. There weren't that many pages left, after all. Less than a year's worth.

So I read, straight on into the wee hours. I read of the discovery that Nexus had been taken by her father, the head honcho of some weird, cult-like organization. Dynamistress organized a trip to the U.K. that was ultimately successful in rescuing her, though it didn't go entirely smoothly. Her brother had nearly been killed. Dynamistress blamed herself for that because of course she did.

Then an unfortunate call from Invictus, her boss. One of the Gatekeepers had died from an aneurysm, of all things. After the memorial, Dynamistress decided to visit home, where she was surprised by her mother actually seeming like a human being, for a change.

And then another surprise, in the airport, where she saw her college sweethearts for the first time in nearly two decades. The writing became quite emotional when talking about the women, and their daughter, who'd been named after her.

After returning to California, she left the Gatekeepers, bought the building I was now reading in, and formed the Pariah Project. And then another discovery: a stalker Dynamistress had paid little attention to had, in fact, actually been stalking Macy. And he had taken her and her parents hostage. Another rescue, though this one went well, all things considered.

The final few months of pages were really difficult to read. They covered how she learned that her DNA tweak was leading to a runaway event. She wrote only in the most general terms about the different things she was trying, in hopes of slowing and ultimately stopping it. She even referred to them only as Options A, B, C, and D. I think she did this because the lettered shorthand helped her be more detached, more objective.

Again, I wished I could see her scientific notes, to learn what these options really were. Option A seemed to have something to do with expending or depleting her energy, which is where Zero-Point entered the picture. Option D was clearly where she injected DNA from before the last tweak in an attempt to overpower the "new" DNA, or however that worked.

As for the other two, she seemed to have little faith in either of them. They were either too complicated, too time-consuming, or both. Whatever they were, they seemed to be too little, too late.

And she knew it. Her final entries showed that she knew she had no hope of surviving runaway. The tone of the entries reflected this. And yet, they weren't particularly sad, or regretful, or even hopeless. That sliver of a chance is what she clung to. She never quit trying.

I had to admire that.

Four

"He who doesn't fear death dies only once."
~ Giovanni Falcone

Thanksgiving is in just a few days, but I'm not feeling very thankful, at the moment. There's no question now that my last DNA alteration was flawed, somehow. My energy production is off the charts. I'm converting food to energy to a degree I didn't think possible, and it's problematic, to put it mildly.

My body is approaching runaway, and I find myself in a damned-if-I-do/damned-if-I-don't dilemma. The more I eat, the more my body wants. And if I try to starve myself in order to avoid runaway, my cells will begin to take energy from wherever possible. Meaning that my body will start to eat itself. In fact, it seems likely that this is already happening. I've lost five pounds in the past two weeks.

Others have commented on it. And I'm not happy to say that I've been lying, telling them I have the flu, which is why I've been reclusive. I don't want to get anyone else sick, I tell them.

Jasmine has taken over a lot of my duties with the Project while I "get over my bug." I should just tell her the truth. Vicky, too, since she doesn't believe me about the flu, anyway.

I've been considering several possible solutions to the problem, and have narrowed them down to the four most likely to work. But in truth, I don't have high expectations for any of them.

One is only a temporary measure. My late other-self had her weird thing where energy would leak out from around her eyes. I can't do that, but I can keep my shields at full during waking hours and expend as much energy as possible in other ways. Eventually, I'll need Jack's assistance. But at some point, this will likely become insufficient.

The obvious next step up from that is probably viable, though it's far outside my area of scientific expertise. Jack might be able to help. Maybe Kit, too. I'll speak with them about it.

One is just too damned complicated, with so many things that can go wrong at every stage of it, not to mention that it would be delving into scientific areas that haven't been even close to mastered, yet. Then again, the same could be said about my original experiment to become a meta. Anyway, it's intriguing enough to consider. But if I'm going to do it, I need to start right away. Hell, I probably should have started months ago.

The most logical treatment is one I've already implemented. But it'll take months to see any results, if it works at all. And I don't know if my body will wait that long.

If the runaway can't be stopped, I'll go up like a torch, with my cells literally eating themselves in their unending effort to convert "food" to energy. It looks like all those people who accused me of "playing God" will get the last laugh.

My emotions are all over the place. I'm angry, of course, at having screwed up. Terrified, because this screw-up will almost certainly end in my demise. And of course, there's a fair amount of self-pity going on.

Fortunately, there are things to think about other than my death. When I'm trying in vain to fall asleep, my mind keeps returning to Dynasonic's world. I wonder if she's more disturbed by the state of her society than she lets on. I suspect she is. I wonder about her brother, too, and his efforts. I wish I knew more about them.

But at the same time, I wonder why. It's not like I can do anything about it. Some might argue that, even if I could, it's not my position to do so. That's not my world. It's really none of my business. There's more than enough here in my own world to worry about.

Weatherford, for example. Not that we've seen any sign of him. Or at least, I haven't. Vicky isn't sharing anything she may have found out. And sometimes I wonder whether he's even worth worrying about. He and his group are such mysteries. I have no idea if they're even doing anything illegal. Dangerous, probably, but that's something the group has allegedly been doing for centuries, so I should probably just quit dwelling on it.

But since the alternative is to dwell on my death...

It was late when I finally woke the next day, and the sleep I was getting wasn't great. Twice, I'd had nightmares inspired by the journals. And it occurred to me that if just reading about them affected me this way, what must it be like for the metas who've experienced these things? Did Zero-Point have nightmares of losing his arm? Did Kimera have dreams about being ridiculed for her looks? Did Nexus relive the horrible things her father did to her? Probably. And this made me feel lame for being so disturbed by my nightmares.

By the time I'd showered and had breakfast, Bloodmoon arrived. She joined me in the kitchen, dropped a pile of mail on the table, and then made a pot of tea for us before sitting with me.

"I just met with Sinta," she said. "She seems to be doing a little better. I wouldn't say she's doing 'well,' but it's an improvement. The first we've really seen." I told her I was happy to hear that and hoped I'd get to meet her soon.

"What about you? How are things progressing?" she asked, sifting through the mail.

I wanted to tell her everything was going fine, but she would have known I was lying. So I told her the truth, that it was frustrating.

"Don't worry about that," she said. She took another sip of tea, then said, "Scoutmaster is willing to talk with you, by the way. He'll be over this evening. Jack will be with him. And I'll work on getting some other meetings set up, as well."

I thanked her and cradled the hot cup in my hands, looking blankly at nothing.

"Ah," she said, looking at the mail. "Maybe this would be of use to you." She slid a magazine across the table to me. It was a *Supers* magazine, a memorial issue for Dynamistress.

Later that night, I skimmed through the magazine. It wasn't particularly thick. Most of the photos were of her days with the Gatekeepers, though virtually none of them were close-up shots.

But it was interesting to read the magazine's history of her career, which provided a different perspective from her own journals. It lacked the personal angle, but in some cases provided more detail.

One unexpected entry was an interview with her, apparently done just in the past year, but not published until now. One question she was posed was about why the Pariah Project was formed.

Supers: As a member of the Gatekeepers, you were basically an A-list meta. What happened to cause you to walk away from that to the relative obscurity of the Pariah Project?

Dyna: I suppose the best way to put it is that I just became more aware of how complicated our society is. Look, there will always be a need for the A-listers. The Gatekeepers and other teams are fine groups doing good work. But as good as they are, they can't do *all* the work. Our society routinely fails the needs of many, and one such overlooked group is the victims of crimes. Their problems don't disappear once the crime is over or the perpetrators are caught.

Supers: And the Pariah Project provides what they need?

Dyna: In some cases, perhaps, but the real goal is to help them find the help that they need from the many organizations out there that exist to provide the help, most of which seem to be unknown to the general public. The Project helps by providing information, aiding them with applying for assistance, acting as their spokespeople, and so on.

Supers: This is obviously a very helpful service you're providing. But doesn't it seem somewhat mundane, compared to the work you were doing before? Don't you feel that you could or should be doing more of that sort of work?

Dyna: Well, none of us works exclusively with the Project, including me. I still help out the Gatekeepers on the rare occasions when they need me. The other members of the Project behave similarly. But to address your assertion of it being "mundane" work, what's wrong with that? "Mundane" workers are often the real heroes in this world. Just because what you do isn't flashy and shown on TV doesn't make it any less significant.

Scoutmaster looked just as Dynamistress had described him in her journals. Young, but old. He was walking with a cane, but seemed to be otherwise good.

"I am, thank you," he said after greeting Bloodmoon and me. "I've been doing speech therapy... and physical therapy... religiously, since my injury." He paused, seeming unsure of what to say next.

I told him that I'd read about Dynamistress's time with the Bay Scouts. I explained that I was getting a fairly good feel for the woman, but was hoping he could share something personal about her. Something insightful.

Scoutmaster nodded thoughtfully. "She was referred to me by... Maltese Falcon. And when we first met, I nearly laughed... at how she was dressed."

I told him that her brother described the outfit as being a cross between a biker and a hooker.

"Exactly!" Scoutmaster laughed as Zero-Point smiled. "Ridiculous... high heels. Leather. Lots of leather. I questioned Falcon's thinking... but he must have thought she was worth it. Said she was tenacious."

"There's an understatement," Zero-Point said.

"I gave her the same test I'd give anyone. Put her up against Sinta and Jack. And... well... she did okay."

"She did," Zero-Point agreed. "My energy-draining ability is touch-based. And she found a way, at least temporarily, to prevent me from touching her. It took me by surprise. And this was before she'd developed her blasting ability, otherwise I'd never have stood a chance."

Scoutmaster was quiet a moment, and when he resumed, his voice was soft. "Dyna presented as... tough. Feisty. But underneath, she was a sweetheart."

"Absolutely," Bloodmoon agreed.

"I'm sure Jack agrees," Scoutmaster said. "He was pretty sweet on her."

Zero-Point actually blushed. "Shut up, Dan," he laughed.

Scoutmaster's slight smile disappeared. "But Dyna... was not a happy person. She had pain... deep inside. She did her best... to hide it. Covered it with jokes. Sass." He looked wistful for a moment. "She never let me see what that was all about."

There was an awkward silence. Was he right? I found it hard to believe that this woman, who had achieved her dream of being a mega, was unhappy. Had it all been for naught? I shook the thought from my head. That wasn't where I wanted to focus my thoughts.

So I mentioned to Scoutmaster that it was clear from her writings that Dynamistress held him in high esteem, and definitely had hopes that he would one day return to active duty, so to speak. He gave a tired sigh. "She was always sending emails with links to... articles on spinal cord treatment and such. Urging me to consider stem cell treatments... and other things. I mean, that synthetic biology stuff worked for her, but..."

"Or not so much," Zero-Point said, "in the end."

"Well... yes," Scoutmaster muttered.

We ended up speaking for about an hour. Scoutmaster shared a lot of good stuff and I was pleased with it. Dynamistress was starting to come together.

The talk with Scoutmaster was possibly the most interesting one of all, mainly because he and Zero-Point talked about their missions, which none of the others had mentioned. I'd read accounts of them in the journals and the magazine, but it was fascinating to hear the others speak of them, and I said so to Bloodmoon.

"Dyna certainly saw a wide variety of missions," she told me as we sat in the living room in front of the fireplace. "The Gatekeepers, as you know, were given high-profile cases. The Bay Scouts, less so. And then with the Pariah Project, it was entirely different. For the first time since being solo, she was free to choose what to pursue. And of course, nothing we've done is anywhere near as high profile as the Nevada Incident or even the average Gatekeepers activity."

I brought up the rescue mission in the U.K. when Nexus had been kidnapped. Bloodmoon frowned. "Technically, the Project hadn't been formed, yet. Of course, it wasn't an official Gatekeepers operation, either, so some of us do consider it to be the genesis of the team. That was the exception to the rule, for sure. And it went far from perfectly. But we got Vicky back, and that's the crucial part. And yes," she said, anticipating my next question, "I do believe we'll encounter Weatherford again." She smiled wickedly. "Maybe I'll get to shoot him in the face again!"

I forced a chuckle at this somewhat unnerving statement. Then I asked her more about her weapons. "Arsenal and I met several years ago in Europe, working a job together. It was that job, in fact, that ultimately made both of us return to the States, where we turned to different lines of work. I ended up here, obviously, and Arsenal chose to become a specialty arms dealer. I mainly use non-lethal stuff, but there's the occasional call for something special. Like rounds that can change trajectory in mid-flight. Or for heavy-duty work, there's a grenade that can punch through a wall and *then* explode. Nasty stuff," she said with another smile that, I confess, disturbed me.

Feeling the need to switch subjects, I told her that Dynamistress believed Nexus was gathering data on her father, possibly enlisting the aid of the Gatekeeper named Probe, who'd helped them with information when Nexus had been kidnapped.

"Is that right?" she said. "Well, if anyone can help, it would be him. While the information he had at the time we contacted him was limited, he's the sort to continue researching something for its own sake."

I asked about other missions they'd had. "Keep in mind, the Project has only existed for a little over half a year. We're still finding our place, so to speak. But like most metas, we respond to fires and other disasters when we can be of use. And in truth, we're finding ourselves acting as sort of back-up for other groups, including the Gatekeepers, on occasion. We're the ones who linger when they leave, taking care of the wrap-up, helping the victims, dealing with the authorities. Definitely not spotlight activities."

I admitted to Bloodmoon that the Pariah Project seemed odd, to me. The purpose of groups like the Gatekeepers was obvious. But what the Project members were doing – wrap-up, as she'd said, and helping the victims – seemed to me to be a waste of meta talents.

"I can understand why you'd think so. To be honest, many of us felt the same way when Dyna first approached us with the idea. And, if you must know, most other teams consider the Project to be a bit of a joke. At least, until they see the results of our work. But keep in mind, for members of groups like the Gatekeepers, that's a full-time gig. The Project is most certainly a part-time thing. Several of us do solo patrols. Some, like Jack, have day jobs. And Bridget is a senior in high school. And then there's the volunteer work that we've all agreed to take on. For example, I do a variety of things for the Red Cross. Preparedness classes of different sorts."

We chatted about that for a bit before I turned the conversation back to the meetings with others. Since the group was still on good terms with the

Gatekeepers, I asked if we might arrange a meeting with their leader, Invictus. Dynamistress obviously held him in high esteem, too.

But Bloodmoon balked on that request. "That might be too difficult to arrange. I'll inquire, but I wouldn't expect much to come of it." At just that moment, there was an urgent beeping from the conference room.

I followed Bloodmoon as she dashed to the back wall and activated the big screen. It came to life instantly, and just as quickly, pulled up a map of the city. A flashing dot indicated the site of the emergency. Even as she clicked on it for details, Bloodmoon was opening a comm channel to the rest of the Project.

"We've got a crane collapse at a construction site," she said into the screen's built-in microphone, rattling off the address. "Reports indicate workers trapped. Injuries likely. Who's available?"

"En route," came a voice I recognized as Resonator's.

"Right down the block," said Zero-Point.

"Be there as soon as I can!" That was Bricky.

Bloodmoon said, "Kit, can you broadcast?"

"One drone camera, coming up."

A moment later, the screen changed, showing an aerial view of the streets as Resonator flew to the collapse site. This was the first time I'd witnessed the team's emergency alert system in action. I asked Bloodmoon how it worked.

"Our computer constantly monitors emergency channels for certain key words and police codes. Each of us also wears a tracker tied to our computer. We've designed the program to alert us when there is a suitable situation in a proximity convenient to wherever one of us might be, including all of our residences and workplaces, as well as the headquarters, here." She nodded at the screen. "This is an excellent arrangement today. Three of our physically strongest members, well suited for moving debris."

We watched as Resonator arrived at the site. His drone camera caught the action from a safe distance. We saw Zero-Point moving massive pieces of concrete with his mechanical "battle arm."

The team provided a commentary as they worked. Rescue personnel were on the scene, too. Bricky arrived not long after Resonator. It was almost comical, watching this skinny little girl lifting steel girders with almost no effort.

I knew that Bricky's strength was present whether or not she was in her brick-like form. But she was so tiny! How was it possible? "Much of it comes from her meta mutation," Bloodmoon explained, "but also it's because she's built like a chimpanzee." I looked at her stupidly until she elaborated. "As Dyna explained it to me, chimps have specialized muscles. They have more of what are known as 'fast-twitch' muscles for power than humans do. And these muscle fibers are much denser and longer than in humans. So a chimp is much more powerful than a human, despite being smaller. Bricky's musculature is built kind of like that, except to an extreme far beyond chimps. She's little, but she's got a lot more mass than you might think, due to the density of her muscles." Bloodmoon paused, with an amused smile on her face. "As to why her skin becomes like brick... we assume that's just a subconscious trick her brain is playing."

I knew Dynamistress had her natural strength enhanced by her energy abilities, but wondered where that placed her in the muscle rankings.

"That's an interesting question," Bloodmoon said. "And I really am not sure. Certainly, nothing close to Bricky's level. Even Jack and Kit can't compare to Bricky for brute strength. Jack's strength, of course, is from his mechanical arm, while Kit's comes from his armored suit. But in truth, Dyna could probably hold her own against either of them. At least, in a battle of punching. In lifting, I don't think so. But it's not like we've ever held a contest."

Other metas arrived on the scene of the crane collapse, helping out where needed. I can't say how long we sat there staring at the screen and listening to the chatter, but the next thing I knew, Resonator was signaling that all workers were accounted for. And best of all, there were no fatalities.

The next day, Bloodmoon took me on an overdue tour of the city. I'd been wanting to see the different places mentioned in the journals, including the neighborhood where Dynamistress and Sinta had lived, the club where she and Rachel had met, and Golden Gate Citadel, headquarters of the Gatekeepers.

The Citadel, it turns out, is open to the public. The ground floor of the building, anyway. The huge room is filled with statues of select members both past and present. Portraits decorate the walls. It's like a tourist attraction.

When we left the Citadel, I surprised Bloodmoon by asking her to take us to Kirby Cove. She looked at me strangely, before realization hit her. So we crossed the Golden Gate Bridge and, before long, we were walking on the beach at Kirby Cove. At the western end, I studied the rocky outcroppings, eventually finding what I was looking for – a rock with the word "Dinah" scratched into it.

We stood there in the cold, quietly paying our respects to Dynamistress's other-self until I felt chilled to the bone. Then I thanked Bloodmoon and we returned to the Project building.

FIVE

"The thing is to appreciate the fragile wonder of it all, down to the last breath, down to the dying embers of consciousness."
~ Maryam D'Abo

It goes without saying, but I don't want to die. All indications, though, are that it looks inevitable that I will, very soon. At times, I just want to cry over the unfairness of it all. But I don't. Because the truth is that it's perfectly fair.

When I look objectively at what I've done, at what I've accomplished, scientifically, I must admit that it's amazing. And as much as I dismiss those who believe synthetic biology to be "unnatural," I also have to admit that what I did is maybe something we shouldn't be able to do.

I fulfilled my wildest dreams, cheating death all along the way. And that's a damn sight more than most people get to do. So, yes, it's fair that it's finally caught up with me.

I'll fight like hell to prevent my early expiration, of course, but I'm also acknowledging that the odds are frightfully slim that I'll succeed. With that in mind, I've started putting my affairs in order. I spoke to an attorney and have given Jasmine the responsibility of taking the Project forward. She'll have access to my financial accounts, in order to pay the mortgage and team operating expenses. I've also written letters to my loved ones to be given out after I'm gone. I'll give them to Dana to distribute.

But there's one person he wouldn't be able to deliver a message to, someone I did want to see one more time. To that end, I risked a trip to Dynasonic's world yesterday. And what a freaky trip it was.

Upon arrival, I called her. She answered, but, as luck would have it, she was out of state. She had time to talk, though, so we did. I landed on the deck of "our" building and sat there while we talked. I told her everything, and she was predictably upset. I needed to tell her how much I appreciated having her in my life, even in such a limited way. It got a bit teary.

We talked for more than half an hour. When we finished, I decided to spend a little more time in her world. For all the disturbing aspects of the telepathic Big Brother network, I still loved seeing a San Francisco that was clean, safe, prosperous, and friendly.

Feeling a bit nostalgic, I went to the Mercury Café, the spot where I'd sat and read everything I could about this world, the first time I was there. And where I discovered "my" career as a singer.

This time, I had cash, thanks to Dynasonic. So I went inside, ordered a latte, then sat at a table outside to enjoy it. It was cold, of course, but lately I've been even warmer than usual, so I didn't notice it, other than having my drink cool off quickly.

I finished it and stepped over to a trash bin to toss away my cup. As soon as I had, however, I experienced a familiar sensation in my head. It felt like when Dana would mentally poke me to test my defenses, only stronger.

Reflexively, I concentrated on keeping those defenses up, but the attacker got through them in moments. Panic hit me as I felt his presence in my mind. I wasn't sure what to expect, but it certainly wasn't a firm voice saying, *Run!*

It was so unexpected that I just stood there. Who was telling me to run and why? I looked up and down the streets at the intersection, and then I saw them. Two men, about half a block away on Page Street, approaching from the east. One of them was looking directly at me. The expression on his face was surprise, at first, but then turned to annoyance. Maybe anger.

NOW!

This wasn't my world. I had no business with these men, even if they seemed threatening. So I blasted straight up, heading toward the bay and my way home.

Or fly. That works, too.

The voice in my head seemed to be on my side, so I thought back, *Thanks.*

Don't thank me, came the reply. *Thank my sister.*

My heart skipped a beat. *Dana?*

Take care, Dinah, he said, and then was gone.

I didn't get a good look at the other guy, but the pissed off dude was quite familiar. Evidently, Dynasonic's world has a Dane Weatherford, too.

I woke the next morning feeling like crap, with body aches and chills and the occasional stabbing pain in my head. When Bloodmoon arrived, I apologized, but told her all I wanted to do was stay in bed.

I slept a lot, though not well. Bloodmoon brought me soup and tea. She also sat and talked with me for hours. We didn't talk about Dynamistress or the Project, though. It was just friendly conversation.

This went on for three days, with each day worse than the one before it. But just as I was seriously considering a visit to the emergency room, it cleared up overnight. I woke the next morning feeling perfectly fine. I got dressed and, as I was about to head downstairs, I heard voices from below. One of them was Bloodmoon. The other was female, with a London accent.

Nexus was back.

"I dunno," I heard her say. "Bloody spinny is what it is."

"I know it's hard," Bloodmoon replied. "But I'm glad you're back."

"Yeah, well... let's do this thing."

"I'm not sure..." Bloodmoon trailed off as I descended the stairs. "Ah. Feeling better?"

I nodded, then Bloodmoon introduced us. Nexus looked at my outstretched hand, but didn't shake it. She crossed her arms in front of her as we all sat at the conference table.

She didn't look like the glamorous woman in the photos. She looked rough, with a severe expression. Her hair was pulled back in a ponytail and she kept her sunglasses on. She still wore her jacket, too. Clearly, she wanted this to be short and sweet.

I started by thanking her for speaking with me, and saying that I understood how difficult it must be for her. "Do ya?" she snapped. "Really?"

Bloodmoon glared at her as I apologized. Obviously, I couldn't know just how it was for her. I told her that the others had all been a great help, but that she herself had insights no one else could share. And I needed that.

Nexus rubbed at her forehead, one elbow on the table and her face turned aside. I didn't know how to ask what I really wanted to, so I asked her how her investigation was going, and if she'd figured out where the energy weapons were coming from.

Then she stared at me, jaw hanging open, before turning to Bloodmoon. "Seriously?" she said. "I mean... *seriously?*"

Bloodmoon shrugged. "Why not? And this is as good a time as any to give your update."

Nexus continued to stare at Bloodmoon for a few seconds, then sighed heavily. "Whatever. You're the boss."

"Vicky..." Bloodmoon admonished.

Nexus frowned, but spoke professionally. "I found the person who takes delivery at Port Hueneme. From there, the weapons follow the familiar distribution channels, including your friend Arsenal, ultimately ending up with a recipient here in the Bay Area."

"So they come in by boat?" Bloodmoon asked.

Nexus confirmed. "Boat. Not ship. Short-range vessels. But I can't tell you their port of origin."

"Anything else?" Bloodmoon asked.

"The interesting bit is that, once they reach Oakland, that's it. No trace of them going into public hands."

Bloodmoon frowned. "Stockpiling?"

"Maybe."

"All right. Thank you," Bloodmoon said with a frown. Then she looked at me. "Your turn."

Nexus turned to face me again. I hesitated, then said that I didn't have specific questions. I just wanted her to share whatever occurred to her, beyond what most everyone else knew about her.

She rubbed her forehead again and leaned back in the chair. She seemed to be looking down around my knees instead of at my face, but it was impossible to tell with the sunglasses.

"Dyna," she said, then hesitated. A small smile touched her lips. "She could always make me laugh. She could be total snark. And when she and her brother got going in on each other..." The smile faded and she fell quiet. "And she was quite lovely to others."

I mentioned that this was obvious, given the nature of the Pariah Project. "Just so," she said, nodding. Then she stiffened again. "Look, I know you want personal stuff, but I honestly don't know what to say. She was wonderful." Then she hastily added, "Not that she didn't get on my tits from time to time. But then, just about everyone does. Maybe more of a comment on me than them."

"Vicky..." Bloodmoon sighed.

"What? Oh." She smirked and said to me, "She doesn't like that expression. Means she got on my nerves. Kind of like people who get uptight about the word 'tits' in polite conversation."

"I'm not uptight!" Bloodmoon insisted.

Nexus just smiled smugly, but again, it faded quickly. She removed her sunglasses and rubbed her eyes wearily. They were bloodshot, with dark circles underneath. She looked exhausted, and I had to wonder what all she was going through. The journals were vague regarding Nexus's psychological state after the U.K. events, but I couldn't imagine that she wouldn't have lasting scars.

Given this, I told her we could talk another time, when she was rested and in a better mood. She raised an eyebrow and stared at me. "I might be more rested, but my mood won't improve. So maybe we should just get this done."

I looked over at Bloodmoon, who frowned sympathetically. Truth is, I didn't have any idea what to ask her. As I was about to say this to Nexus, her expression changed. "All right," she muttered. "Something personal. Okay." After a moment, her face softened. She licked her lips and, when she spoke, the harsh edge was gone. "Like most of us do, Dyna hid part of herself from people in general. The public saw her as... I dunno... stylish, flashy, very hero-esque. Her friends saw the snark, the kindness, and the brains." Nexus chuckled. "I'm not sure who, but someone dubbed her 'Dynapedia' because of her broad knowledge on many topics, as well as seemingly endless trivia." The smile faded. "But a few of us got to see the private bit. We got to see the vulnerable Dyna. The one who felt alone and lost, despite having friends who loved her. The one who wanted nothing more than to feel needed, to know that she mattered to others." Nexus turned her eyes to mine. "It always pained me to see that, just as I felt privileged to be allowed to." She was quiet a moment, then said, "That personal enough for you?"

I just nodded dumbly. Then Nexus put her sunglasses back on, said goodbye to Bloodmoon, and left the building.

Later in the day, I asked Bloodmoon if she'd had any luck in setting up other meetings. "I'm sorry," she said, "but I haven't. I called Macy on Thursday, when you were sick. She's on spring break from school for the next week or so. She and her parents left this morning on vacation. Hawaii, she said."

I asked how they were all doing, since the hostage drama. "Her parents seem fine. Macy, well... she's improved, but still has a way to go. From what Dyna told me, she's experiencing what's called rape trauma syndrome. She's in counseling, I understand, but I'm not sure how well she's progressing. She didn't sound excited to be going to Hawaii, for example."

We were quiet a moment, then I asked about others. "I have a message in to Invictus, but he hasn't called me back, yet. Same for Ping Song. Not sure what's up with them. I'm sorry."

Then, she brightened a bit. "I do have some good news, though. I visited with Sinta every day while you were ill. She's coming over, tomorrow."

The entire team was on hand for Sinta's return. I was expected to be part of her welcome, but I didn't think that was appropriate. I stayed upstairs, out of sight, though not out of earshot.

The welcomes were warm, all around, but Sinta herself was quiet. After a month and a half in a state of mourning, I guess I could understand that. From what I could hear, there was a lot of hugging, a good bit of laughing, and an abundance of happiness.

The welcome party lasted a couple hours. After the others were all gone, Bloodmoon yelled up to me that she was going to drive Sinta back to her apartment, and that she'd see me in the morning.

After they'd left, I made my way down to the kitchen for a snack and was surprised to see Neon there, making a peanut butter and jelly sandwich. "Oh, hi," she said. "How are you feeling?"

I told her I was fine, and explained why I hadn't joined the party. Then I complimented her pink-flamed hair.

"It felt like a pink day," she said, sitting at the table and taking a huge bite of her sandwich. I found an apple and some string cheese in the fridge and joined her at the table. "I know I can't help you much," she said, "but I'm happy to talk with you, anyway."

I thanked her, my eyes never leaving her hair. She noticed this and said, "Okay, I'll answer everything you're going to ask about my hair, since everyone asks the same questions. No, it's not really fire. Jack says it's what's called nonthermal plasma. So you can touch it, if you want."

I reached out and did so. She was right. It wasn't hot. In fact, it didn't feel like anything at all.

"Yes, I can make the stuff any color I want. No, I don't know how that works. Yes, the color change is easy." As she said this, the hair plasma changed to blue, then orange, green, red, and back to pink. "Yes, I can do it with my hands, too." She repeated the color change with a ball of fire in her hand. "Yes, this stuff actually *is* fire. No, it doesn't hurt, just feels a little warm. Yes, it *will* burn *you*. Yes, I can control the flames." The ball of fire grew, then warped into a pillar, then flattened and raced up her arm, across her shoulders, and down to her other hand. "No, I can't control other flames, just the ones I make. Yes, other fire will burn me. No, I don't know how that works, either." She took another bite of her sandwich, evidently finished with the Q&A session.

I couldn't help but smile. I wondered aloud if all metas were asked a standard set of questions by nearly everyone. "Probably," Neon said. "The flashier or weirder the abilities, the more likely. I mean, I don't mind. My abilities are pretty cool, if I say so, myself. But then there are metas where the questions are always – and I mean *always* – about how they look." She shook her head and frowned. "I can't even guess how many times Sinta gets asked if she's part cat. Like that's even genetically possible," she said, rolling her eyes. Then her brow knit. "'Least, I don't think it is. Anyway, for Kimera, it's even worse. The first question she always gets is, 'What are you?' or something equally as rude."

She paused in her rant and looked at me with wide eyes. "I'm sorry! I talk a lot. Too much." I laughed and told her not to worry. Given how little most of the Project members wanted to talk to me, this was nice. I understood how uncomfortable it must be for them, I explained, but it was frustrating. In fact, I noted, this conversation was the first one I'd had with anyone where Bloodmoon wasn't present, almost as though she needed to convince them to talk to me.

Neon gave an obviously forced smile and nibbled at her sandwich. "So, um... how's it all... you know... coming together?" I told her it was going okay, though I was looking forward to talking with Sinta and Dana. I was certain they'd be a wealth of information. "I'm sure. And I wish I had something to share with you, but like I said, I barely knew her."

Neon chewed the remainder of her sandwich, then said, "Y'know, maybe I do have something. It's about her and Lily." The journals frequently mentioned how gratified she was to be able to save the girl's life. "Oh, not that part," Neon said. "I mean, yeah, that's awesome. But it was something Lily told me, about how Dyna didn't let Lily give her any shit whatsoever. In fact, she gave it right back. Lily said it was that attitude of Dyna's that caused her to take a look at how she'd been acting, and that allowed her to open herself up to recovery."

Tough love, I suggested. "Yeah," Neon said. "Lily never understood at that point why Dyna cared." She looked at me intently. "Lily didn't care about herself, so she couldn't imagine Dyna could. Or Kit, for that matter." She was quiet a moment, lowering her eyes. "I didn't have the best self-image when I met Lily. She was the one who made me see that I wasn't quite as damaged as I'd always considered myself. All because Dyna showed her that she wasn't, either." She looked back up at me, a bit self-consciously. "So yeah... I guess that's my Dyna story."

SIX

"When one door closes, another opens. But often we look so long, so regretfully, upon the closed door, that we fail to see the one that is opened for us."
~ Hellen Keller

Christmas is coming. Dana has been trying to get me to go home to see the family, pointing out rightly that it could be my last chance to be with them. I told him the only way I could do so would be to have Jack come with us, to drain me at a moment's notice. And that clearly wasn't going to happen.

Of course, if Option B were to come to fruition, that would allow me to go home with my own little portable "Jack." He and Kit are working on it, but it's not looking good. It would be easy if we had one of those energy-sucking weapons that Jack's counterpart invented. We're trying to obtain the one the police took as evidence when we rescued Rachel after she was kidnapped by Hellion. For that matter, if we had the gun, we wouldn't need Option B. I could just shoot myself whenever necessary. But that weapon was turned over to the DHS and there's not a chance we'd be able to get it back. And its power has almost certainly been depleted by now, anyway.

Dana is still convinced that I'll find a way to stop the process, I guess based on my previous success in fending off a deadly disease. Even when our mind link is fully "open," and he can sponge off everything I know about it, he's resolute in refusing to accept it. I guess even psychologists can experience denial.

I told Vicky about my foray into Dynasonic's world and seeing another Weatherford there. She said she didn't care about her father's otherselves, just the "original," as she put it. Of course, "original" is subjective, but I knew what she meant.

It's hard, though, not to think of oneself and one's own world as being the "original" one. The public, after learning of the other world via Project Echo, tended to look at those from that world as "imposters," even though they are every bit as "real" as we are.

I have to admit, it was difficult for me to see that point of view, at first. But going to Dynasonic's world, where things are so different, made me change that view. From her perspective, my world would be as "sick" as my late other-self's world seemed to us.

To my disappointment, it wasn't until the beginning of April that Sinta was ready to talk to me. I certainly didn't want to rush her. Besides, it's not like there was a great hurry. I still had to wait for Dana's recovery. Even so, when the day rolled around, I was up early, eager to meet the girl.

Bloodmoon took me to Sinta's apartment and we got comfortable in her living room over a pot of tea, a passion Sinta seemed to share with Bloodmoon. It was a nice apartment, tastefully decorated in a rustic theme that didn't seem to fit Sinta's personality. Then I remembered being told that the apartment actually belonged to Scoutmaster.

As for Sinta herself, I couldn't help but stare at her dark gray fur and feline features. Except for the noted absence of a tail. I shuddered, thinking about how she lost it.

I began by thanking Sinta for agreeing to meet with me. She nodded, not making eye contact for more than a moment. Bloodmoon sat watching us, probably making sure I didn't cross any lines or push her too hard. So I decided to let Sinta take the lead. I asked her just to talk. Didn't matter about what.

As she sat there, staring into her tea, my heart ached for her. Sinta's looks were utterly deceiving. She was nineteen, though she didn't seem it. And though she looked like a fragile little girl, I knew she was anything but. Beyond that, she'd been through some awful stuff, coming out of it better than most people could ever hope. For her to have been traumatized to the point of seclusion for a month shows just how devastating it had been for her. Finally, she looked over at me and took a deep breath.

"When Jasmine told me about you and why you wanted to talk with us all, I didn't know what to think. I mean, it just seemed so..." She shook her head.

I told her I understood, so there was no need to worry about feeling awkward. She cast another glance at Bloodmoon. Then she looked back to her tea, but said nothing.

I told her that I'd read Dynamistress's journals, so I knew how much Sinta had meant to her. And I knew about the other-Dynamistress, and how close the two of them were. I hoped this would get her to open up. Instead, she tensed up. She closed her eyes.

She was quiet for several long seconds before opening her eyes again. "That Dyna gave her life for our Dyna," she said quietly. "For a while after, I didn't think our Dyna appreciated that. But she did. It was just hard for her to admit it. I didn't understand why. But I get it, now. Every time she looked at the other Dyna, she saw a version of herself that made her super uncomfortable, one who wasn't fully sane, to be honest. That would probably freak anyone out."

I suggested that perhaps we could talk about when she first met Dynamistress.

Sinta tilted her head with a faint smile. She sipped her tea and licked the moisture from her furry lips. "The first time we met was when she was trying out for the Bay Scouts. She had to fight me." I nodded, remembering both the written account of the event and Zero-Point's story. "She got in a good hit, which was what she was supposed to do, of course. But later, she came over and apologized to me, saying she felt terrible about it." Sinta giggled. "I knew right then I was going to like her." The smile disappeared, then, and she said, "But she didn't pay a lot of attention to the individuals in the group, really, including me. She was trying to prove herself, and even though she was part of a team, she was still acting as though she was solo."

She was still growing up, I offered. Sinta agreed. "Which was weird to me, 'cuz she was twenty years older than me, but sometimes it felt like I was more grown up than she was."

I asked when Dynamistress started to be an actual team player. "When we were in the desert, fighting against the other-worlders. That's when it started, anyway," she said. "She saved me from being chopped by a helicopter. She saved Bobby's life by bein' quick to inject anti-venom into him. And she helped Esteban by holding ice packs on his head to keep swelling down." She looked up at me. "The irony is that the Bay Scouts had already been disbanded by that time. I guess maybe it took losing a team for her to appreciate being part of one."

Sinta was quiet for a bit, then glanced again at Bloodmoon. I could tell she'd shared enough for our first talk, so I thanked her and said I hoped we could talk again, soon.

On April 5, WikiLeaks released two major items. The first was a classified military video from 2007 that showed a U.S. helicopter attack killing at least a dozen non-combatant individuals in New Baghdad, including a pair of Reuters war correspondents.

The second release was a number of documents that revealed how the U.S. government was secretly using metahumans for espionage and assassination, both domestically and abroad. This included evidence that those metas not belonging to a U.S. government-affiliated team were being closely monitored for any possible ties to anti-U.S. militants. Metas such as the Pariah Project's members.

Bloodmoon and I were having dinner in the kitchen. Resonator and Half-Life had joined us. "I wish I could say it surprised me," Bloodmoon said, "but I've had enough dealings with the government to view this as typical."

I wondered aloud about what sort of monitoring they were talking about. Bloodmoon explained. "Some metas have abilities that aren't what you'd call offensive. Mine, for example. That's why I have so many weapons. You could theoretically have telepaths capable of reading from a great distance, or with great control, or able to get past psychic defenses."

"There are metas who can do similar things with other methods," Resonator added, "such as electronics. Technopaths, for example, could read computer contents, able to bypass firewalls easily."

"And don't forget regular old spying," Half-Life said. "Some metas can render themselves nearly invisible, blend with their surroundings, or even control darkness, like Jen."

The entire situation made me think of the energy weapon trafficking investigation.

"Arsenal is going to help us," Bloodmoon told me, "by requesting a meeting with the source. It's not a common request, but these aren't common weapons. And Arsenal is a big enough name in the arms dealing community, so they'll probably agree." She said we should know more soon.

The rest of the week consisted of a few more talks with individual members, but mostly lots of thinking, on my part. I was understanding Dynamistress as a person, and I felt the only thing still missing was input from her brother. According to the doctors, he was steadily improving, but I certainly wasn't going to question him until he was discharged and back to his normal self.

That Saturday was Neon's twenty-first birthday. The party was held in the kitchen/bar area. And, unsurprisingly, I felt out of place. The whole team was there, though not everyone could stay for the entire party.

I wished Neon a happy birthday and apologized for not getting her a gift. She laughed and told me not to be silly. Even gave me a hug, which was unexpected, but nice of her.

I tried to mingle, at Bloodmoon's urging. But all I could think about was how almost all of them found me and my constant questions to be uncomfortable.

It was a nice party, as such things go. There were presents, of course. And there was pizza. Lots of pizza. And an ice cream cake. And, since it was her twenty-first, there was alcohol. Nexus played bartender. I sat to the side of the bar, out of the way, smiling when necessary, and wondering when I could go hide upstairs.

I was chatting with Vesper at one point and asked her a question I'd been wondering about ever since meeting her, which was how she got the scar across her eye.

"Happened when I was eleven," she said. "In fact, it was at another birthday party, of one'a my friends in school. At that age, my wings were tiny. I could hide 'em under a shirt. But one'a the parents there saw a little bulge underneath, I guess. Actually walked right over an' yanked my shirt up. He saw the wings, stood between me and his son, an' shoved me to the ground. Started quotin' scripture, callin' me a demon, and yellin' for the hosts to call the police or a priest or somethin'. Kids were screamin'. His son was freakin' out, mostly at his dad. An' when I tried to get up, the guy busted a beer bottle and attacked me." Jennifer idly rubbed at the scar as I said how horrible her story was. "Yeah," she agreed. "It was a pretty wide gash, 'cuz of the way the bottle broke. There was a lot of blood, and it made me afraid of people for a while. Not to mention bottles." She smiled, then excused herself to get more pizza.

Shortly, Bricky sauntered over to the bar. "I'll have a Scotch and soda," she declared. Her cousin raised an eyebrow, then set out a glass filled with ice. She poured in club soda most of the way, then topped it off with a pour from a bottle of butterscotch syrup.

"Aw, *maaan*," Bricky whined. "That's so lame."

"And you're so sixteen, ya daft little prat," Nexus said. I couldn't help but laugh.

Nexus glanced over at me as Bricky wandered off with her drink, which she clearly considered delicious. Her smile faded, and I turned away. I decided now was the time to leave, so I excused myself and got up.

"Hey," Nexus said, before I could step away. "You don't have to go." I turned back to her and mumbled something about not feeling comfortable there, but she ignored it. "Look," she continued, "I'm sorry I was rude to you. Had no cause for that."

I told her not to worry about it. I knew it had to be hard for her. Then she asked if I wanted a drink. Seeing my hesitation, she stepped out from behind the bar and urged me to fix whatever I liked.

I looked over the selection of bottles, remarking that many of them looked quite fancy. "Oh, yeah," Nexus said. "Dyna always said there were two things you don't buy cheap: shoes and booze."

I chuckled at the quip and figured, what the hell, I'd have a drink. Unlike Dynamistress, though, I knew nothing about making cocktails. So I looked for something interesting on the shelves.

As I did so, I told Nexus I'd been wanting to ask her about something that had been bothering me. I told her about the entry in the journals about

Dynamistress's final trip to Dynasonic's world. I wondered why she'd had such a dismissive reaction to hearing about it.

She shrugged and said, "She saw someone who looked like him, or maybe the other-world version of him. So what?"

But I explained that it wasn't just that she saw him. It was that he seemed to recognize her. Ever since reading in the journals about the encounter, I'd been bothered by the fact that Dynamistress wasn't more freaked out at being recognized.

"He obviously thought she was that world's Dinah Geof-Craigs," Nexus said, as though I were stupid.

But I reminded her that her friend's hair had turned white due to her energy abilities, while Dynasonic's was golden yellow. And the Dinah Geof-Craigs of that world also appeared younger than this world's Dinah.

Her eyes widened. Then I mentioned the other thing that had bothered me: the other-Dana's telepathic warning.

Nexus stared at me. "What warning?" So I related the journal entry to her, as best I could remember it. "I didn't know about that," she said, frowning. "Thanks for telling me," she said.

I'd just selected a bottle of something that smelled good and poured some for us. We sipped in silence for a moment until Bloodmoon walked over. Seeing me behind the bar, she said, "Now, Vicky, you're not making our guest *work*, are you?"

I glanced up, grinning, but saw that I was the only one doing so. The women stared wordlessly at each other, practically glaring.

I didn't know what was going on between them, but it was enough for me. I replaced the bottle, excused myself, wished Neon a happy birthday again, and headed upstairs.

I woke the next morning, still overwhelmed from the party, and tired from a lousy night's sleep. I didn't even want to think about Dynamistress and wanted something to keep my thoughts focused elsewhere.

I glanced over at the bookshelves, thinking that escape into a good novel might be in order. Something not too long. Then my search landed on *Brave New World*, by Aldous Huxley. I'd always wanted to read it, so it might be just the thing. I got comfy in the bed, ready to read. But as soon as I opened the pages, something fell out onto my stomach.

It was a key.

After a moment of questioning surprise, I picked it up and glanced over at the locked door to the lab. So much for not thinking about her, today. I stepped over to the door and slipped the key into the lock. It turned easily and a moment later, I was in Dynamistress's secret sanctuary.

I was amazed at how much equipment she'd jammed into the small, L-shaped room. I recognized certain things right away, as would anyone: a refrigerator, a separate deep freezer, a sink with a water treatment system attached, a computer, a centrifuge, and lots of standard lab stuff such as beakers, microscopes, and so on.

Many of the other items were, at first, a mystery to me. Luckily, some of them were labeled. A blue and white machine was an Applied Biosystems 3500 Genetic Analyzer. Beside it, an identically colored machine from the same company was a Veriti Thermal Cycler, whatever that was. There was what appeared to be a pressure cooker, which I eventually realized was an autoclave, used for sterilizing equipment.

The back corner of the lab was clearly the junk corner. Everything here seemed damaged or discarded. There was what appeared to have once been a large tank. Its glass walls had been shattered and there was a bit of residue on the interior that didn't smell good at all. One of the broken walls held ports with rubber gloves attached in such a way that someone outside could reach into the tank and handle whatever was inside.

Next to this stood a dialysis machine with a cracked outer housing. And beside it was a pile of tubes and things I couldn't identify, including one item that was like a rubbery pouch the size of a backpack.

Returning to the main area, I sat at the computer desk and went through the drawers, where I located exactly what I was looking for: Dynamistress's scientific notebook.

Curious to know what the different Options were that she was pursuing in finding a cure, I flipped to the back of the book and scanned the notes. But then I saw that the date of the last entry was more than a year past. It was the process for one of her genetic tweaks, possibly even the one that resulted in her going into runaway.

The notes I wanted to see must be on the computer, I figured, so I went to the machine and turned it on. But, of course, there was a password required and the guest password they'd set up for me didn't work on this computer.

With a disappointed sigh, I turned the machine off. Locking the lab behind me, I took the notebook to the bed. Huxley could wait. I opened the notebook and started reading at the beginning. It was thick, with sticky notes and index cards stuffed throughout.

The earliest entries were, of course, related to the processes she'd used in her original self-experimentation. It felt as though I was starting in the middle of that, though, so there was probably another journal elsewhere.

It was not an easy read. The notes were sprinkled with abbreviations I didn't recognize. And the ones I did remember from high school chemistry classes weren't sufficient for me to comprehend what was being said. Before long, my head hurt from reading. And from the dates on the entries, I was still reading notes from her college years.

I put the book aside and lay back on the bed, still in wonder at the commitment and drive she had, especially for someone whose sole motive seemed to be a shallow desire for fame.

After a couple more attempts at deciphering it, I just put the lab notebook aside. Her notes were all becoming a big mess in my head. No way was I going to pull anything meaningful from them.

SEVEN

"Do not go gentle into that good night. Rage, rage against the dying of the light."

~ Dylan Thomas

I've made it to 2010, thanks to Jack. He's been my lifesaver, literally. Or at least my life prolonger. His energy-draining ability is pretty much the only thing preventing my abilities from going into full runaway. Whenever I feel as though things are getting wonky, I send him a *911* text message and then fly to his location for him to drain me. Fortunately, I've only had to do that twice, so far, but I fear it'll become a much more frequent thing if my "correction" doesn't start working, soon.

Jack has been working hard on the portable treatment, saying that if his double could create something like the enervation weapon, so can he. Hope he hurries. Obviously.

As for Option C (for "crazy"), I started preparations last month and told Dana about it. He was suitably skeptical, but didn't hesitate to agree to help. Of course, it comes with its own set of issues if this is the path we eventually go down. Not even remotely sure how to address them, yet. But, against all odds, it's going okay, so far.

Speaking of enticing scientific things and runaway chemical reactions, I heard today of a terrible accident at a company down in Riverside County that was testing the viability of recycling ceramic materials originally produced from powders. Details were sparse, but somehow a large quantity of the melted material was spilled, dousing one of the workers. It covered the floor, making it impossible for anyone to get near the victim. By the time they could, the man was obviously dead, but – incredibly – a "statue" of him was left standing. There was a disturbing photo. The "statue," which looked like unpolished, pale bluish glass, was caught in a pose of agony, mouth open in a scream, and arms held out almost as though in supplication.

What a horrible way to be remembered.

The next day, I spent more time with Sinta, who seemed to be almost comfortable around me, though not completely. After a moment of levity, she would catch herself and sober quickly.

Bloodmoon, though, felt it was good for the others to have a lighter mood. She was always around, making sure everything was going okay for me. I asked her again about meeting with Macy, who was now back after spring break. She promised to see what she could do.

She did, however, arrange for a meeting with Ping Song on a Friday afternoon at U.C. Berkeley. We met her at a coffee shop just off campus. Bloodmoon and I arrived first and sat at a corner table with our drinks, waiting for her to arrive.

We passed the time by talking about San Francisco. I'm not a fan of crowds, but if you're going to live in a major city, you'd be hard pressed to find a more beautiful one than this. I asked Bloodmoon if she was a native.

"No, I'm not. I've lived all over, honestly. New York, Amsterdam, Berlin. A few others. Never for long."

I admitted my surprise. She didn't look old enough to have moved around so much. She said she was thirty-three and had moved to the Bay Area in 2000, so all those other cities had been in the first twenty-three years of her life.

"I was a military kid," she said, but didn't elaborate.

Ping Song arrived as I was in the rest room. When I returned to the table, she was talking with Bloodmoon, a cup of coffee in front of her. She greeted me politely. After a bit of preamble, I asked her to give me her impressions of Dynamistress.

She considered this for a moment, then said, "When Dyna first joined the Bay Scouts, she kept to herself. Perhaps it was the natural discomfort of being thrust into a group of strangers, but most of us had the impression that it was more deliberate. She was friendly, but made little effort to truly befriend anyone. Granted, some of us were more difficult to get to know than others. I am aware that my introversion is off-putting to many. And Valora was... gruff. To put it mildly." She sipped her coffee, then said, "But Dyna changed. It was when a few of us were exchanged with the other-worlders."

I told her that I'd read the account of that in her journals. "That experience was her crucible, I think. I don't know exactly why, but she came out of it much stronger, much more focused on others."

I asked about her involvement with Dynamistress in the years since the Bay Scouts ended. "Not as much as either of us would have liked, I think. About every six weeks or so, we'd meet here for coffee and just chat. She was always interested in my work at the university."

I mentioned the gizmo she'd given Dynamistress to detect the portal into Dynasonic's world. "She told me about her visits," Ping Song said. "Very disturbing, a society under constant surveillance."

Bloodmoon frowned as we discussed this, clearly still upset that Dynamistress hadn't told her about it. As for me, I was surprised Ping Song knew about the surveillance state, as it was mentioned late in the journals. I asked when she'd last spoken to her friend. "Near the end of January," she said. "She, Jack, and I met here. She didn't look well. That's when she told me about... about her condition." She hesitated a moment, then said, "Has Vicky learned anything?"

Bloodmoon and I both stared at her in confusion. "What do you mean?" Bloodmoon asked.

"She contacted me a few days ago, saying she needed to go to that world to look into something. Regarding Weatherford, she said. She needed coordinates to the portal."

Bloodmoon was still confused, but I knew what it had to mean, thanks to the journals. I explained to them both about how, since Dynamistress and Dynasonic didn't really look alike, Weatherford couldn't have recognized her on one of her visits unless he was the same Weatherford from our world. Bloodmoon, unsurprisingly, wasn't happy about this.

We spoke with Ping Song for another half hour. I appreciated her input, even though it ultimately wasn't terribly useful. As Bloodmoon and I drove back to the city from Berkeley, I wondered if I was wrong in expecting everything to just fall into place when I finally met with Dynamistress's brother. Even with all the information and opinions I'd gotten from her friends, I was disappointed that I didn't have a better feel for the woman. I was starting to think I never would.

Nexus returned the following day. Bloodmoon confronted her and Nexus confessed to the secret trip. "Didn't matter," she said. "I couldn't locate him. But I did do some 'net sleuthing. While I did find a Dane Weatherford, it wasn't the same guy. Nor were any of the Vicky Valentines or even Vicky Weatherfords 'me.'" She looked at me soberly. "I think you were right. I think the Weatherford she encountered was my father."

One Thursday afternoon, I spent time with Bloodmoon as she did her "monitor duty" for the Project. "What that means," she told me, "is that I'm actively monitoring the police bands and such. Yes," she said before I could ask, "our system does that automatically. But I also handle the occasional phone call and in-person visit."

For most of her shift, we just sat and talked. But late in the afternoon, the door opened, setting off an electronic bell, and a young woman entered. Bloodmoon immediately crossed the room to greet her.

I watched as Bloodmoon offered her a seat near the fireplace and the two sat and talked quietly for a few minutes. I couldn't make out what they were saying, so I just waited. Shortly, they rose and walked toward the office. The woman smiled faintly at me. I nodded in return.

From inside the office, I heard Bloodmoon say, "Help yourself to a drink. No money needed. Just hit your choice." A moment later, I heard the *kachunk* of a canned beverage being dropped into the machine's delivery chute. "Okay, have a seat and we'll go over the application process."

I tuned them out and wandered upstairs to the bedroom for a nap.

I woke around seven that evening and made my way downstairs. I was surprised to see nearly all the Project members in the conference room, staring at the monitor. On the screen, I saw an oil rig on fire at sea. The others filled me in. The *Deepwater Horizon* in the Gulf of Mexico suffered a catastrophic explosion. We'd eventually learn that eleven workers died, and a ridiculous amount of oil was spilling into the gulf.

Metas, I knew, often assisted when disaster struck. But there were few metas who could do much in this case. Still, they showed up. Those who could fly hung uselessly in the air, not having a clue what to do. There were those who were at home in the water, of course, but the leak was far deeper than they could safely go. They were limited mainly to helping to deploy floating booms to keep the slick from spreading across the surface. Fire-wielders helped with burning the corralled slicks. Even those metas who were strong enough to tolerate the great depths of the ocean were little help when it came to capping a spill that would, over the course of the next three months, spew close to five million barrels of oil into the Gulf.

"It was like this on nine-eleven, too," Bloodmoon muttered as we watched the live newsfeed. "Metas expected to help in the rescue efforts. Invictus took several of the Gatekeepers to New York. It was my first official Gatekeepers mission. A few other telepaths were there, too, but none of us were of any use. We detected no thoughts because there just weren't any survivors to locate," she said. "We ended up standing around, feeling absolutely helpless." She was quick to add, "Not that I'm equating the two events at all, but the feelings are similar. We're the ones who are supposed to help. And when we can't," she said, her voice catching, "it's as though we have no purpose."

Her words made me ask something I'd often wondered – what drives a meta to join a super team like the Gatekeepers, or to do the solo thing like the Maltese Falcon and so many others?

Zero-Point chuckled. "Ask twenty metas and you'll get twenty reasons. Some are just noble people. Some do it to help quench their anger. Some treat it as just another line of work, like being a firefighter or police officer. And of course, there are some who choose the other side of the law, obviously. And some who don't do either. Like Dyna's brother."

"Some people just need help," Sinta said, "and anyone able to give it should do so."

Resonator said, "My first efforts to do things with sound were aimed at making money. I sold plans to the government. But I kept developing different devices and decided to keep those for myself. Maybe that makes me selfish, despite using them to help others."

"Jus' seemed the thing to do," Vesper said. "I mean, some of us can't exactly pass as non-metas, so..."

"No kidding," said Kimera, her ram horns bobbing as she nodded.

Caracara agreed. "*Vraiment.*"

"I was inspired by Vicky," Bricky said, making her cousin smile.

"Not sure I know, myself," Nexus said. "Perhaps just to annoy my father."

"Guilt," Half-Life said frankly. "I wanted to make amends for killing my family."

I turned to Neon, who shifted uneasily as we awaited her response. "I spent most of my life being hated and regarded as a freak by my aunt. She was the one who raised me, if you can call it that." She frowned. "If you wanna get all analytical about it, I guess the reason I started doing it was because I wanted to feel loved. Like I mattered. Like I *wasn't* a freak."

There were nods all around, at that. Then we all silently continued to watch coverage of the disaster on TV until people began to leave.

The next morning, I went for a walk to clear my head. I'd had nightmares, again, which wasn't helping me sleep at all. I stopped in for coffee at a shop a few doors down on Post Street. It was a cute little place, with an eclectic mix of decorations. I got a caramel latte and took a seat on the sofa under the life-sized mural of Marilyn Monroe.

I like to watch people, and there was no lack of them there. A few were on laptops. An older gentleman sat near the window reading a newspaper. A woman and her toddler waited for their order. The woman was focused on watching the barista, but her little girl looked at me and smiled shyly when I waved at her.

I sat there for a long while, enjoying my drink, but lost in thought. Bloodmoon had told me that Dana was improving and could be discharged within the week.

Dana was the single most important person I needed to talk to, and I'd been wanting to do so ever since my arrival. But I was anxious because I feared where things would stand if his input ended up not helping, despite Bloodmoon being convinced it would.

For that matter, I didn't know what *would* help. Not only was this frustrating, but I still couldn't shake the feeling that I was intruding and unwelcome, even though I had no real reason to think that.

I'd gotten lost in thought so long that half the people I'd observed earlier were gone. I tossed my now lukewarm drink in the trash and headed back to the Project building.

As I walked through the door, I heard voices. One I recognized as Bloodmoon's, but the other was unfamiliar. I entered the conference area and saw Bloodmoon sitting with another woman at the conference table.

Seeing me, Bloodmoon interrupted their conversation and the stranger turned to face me. She was blonde and beautiful, with blue eyes and a warm smile. Bloodmoon said, "This is Arsenal."

I know my jaw dropped. I stood there in shock, causing Bloodmoon to smirk. "Call me Sharlisse," the woman said. Her handshake was firmer than expected and her voice deeper.

I joined them at the table as Bloodmoon brought me up to speed. "Shar was just telling me of her meeting."

Arsenal recapped for me. "The long and short of it is that I met with the supplier of the weapons, but he is not the manufacturer. He wouldn't – or couldn't – tell me where they were produced. Somewhere in the Channel Islands is what he thought, but that doesn't narrow it down, much."

After a moment of self-conscious hesitation, I told them I thought I knew how they could nail it down, causing both women to look at me in surprise.

"How?" Bloodmoon asked.

I reminded her of how the portal into Dynasonic's world had been discovered by Ping Song.

"Portal?" Arsenal said. "You don't think the weapons are being manufactured here?"

I admitted I didn't. After all, she herself had said these weapons were essentially identical to those that came from the first alternate Earth encountered by the Bay Scouts. But they obviously couldn't be coming from there, since that portal was destroyed. And as we had no indication that our world had the ability to produce them, it made sense to assume they were coming from elsewhere.

"Interesting," Arsenal said. "So you think Ping Song could help us locate a portal in the Islands, if there is one."

"It's worth a shot," Bloodmoon said. "I'll contact her tomorrow." She turned to me. "Good thinking. Thank you."

"Agreed," Arsenal said.

"I'll make up the guest room for you," Bloodmoon said to Arsenal.

I excused myself and headed upstairs, feeling rather good about my contribution. It was my tiny taste of being part of a super team.

EIGHT

"I took a deep breath and listened to the old bray of my heart. I am. I am. I am."

~ Sylvia Plath

Today was Dana's birthday, and I'm still here to celebrate it with him. We had a nice time, going out for dinner. I had salad. Minimal calories.

Jack and Aimee joined us. I'm glad Aimee understood why her boyfriend was holding my hand every so often. She's sweet. They make a great couple.

Dana's been staying here, helping out. Obviously, he's vital for this all to work, but I'm afraid it's all going to be for naught. The absolute soonest this could be done would be late March, but the way things have been going, I'll be lucky to make it to my own birthday.

I don't want to die. Obviously, since I'm grasping at the most fragile of straws. But if this fails, as is likely, I guess I can't feel my life will have been wasted. A large chunk of it was, yes, but I think I've made up for that. Any regrets I have are minor. I'm satisfied with who I've become as a person, and for me, that's been the biggest challenge.

I think the Pariah Project will be a good legacy. I know Jasmine will do an excellent job of keeping it going, assuming the money is there to fund it.

All my affairs are in order, all debts paid off, other than the mortgage, and that will be paid off out of my life insurance policies. PowerPaste residuals will go to my estate, to be used for the Project. Dana is executor, of course.

"Estate." That word always makes me think of rich peoples' homes, big mansions with lots of acreage, flower gardens, and staff. And I suppose for a while, at least, after selling all my stock, I was rich. Not that I ever felt it. Not financially, anyway. It's trite, but in recent years, I've come to realize just how rich my life has been, with amazing friends and incredible experiences. In the end, that really is the stuff that matters. But, damn it, is it so unreasonable of me to want a little more time to enjoy these things?

I didn't get the chance to speak more with Arsenal the following day, and she departed in the early morning. After she left, Bloodmoon told me that I needed to prepare myself. Dana's recovery had reached the point where he could be discharged.

The plan was for Bloodmoon to pick him up, once she got word from the hospital. But there were probably still several hours to pass while waiting for him. I spent the day trying not to think about it, just hanging out in the building, wishing others were there. Empty, the place seemed much larger than it was.

I prepared a nice lunch in the basement kitchen. Sitting at one of the tables there, the silence was unnerving. Every clink of my fork on the plate echoed in the room.

My thoughts were all over the place. There were a million things I wanted to ask Dana. Which should come first? Which were too personal? Did I really want the answers to some of them?

I had to stop thinking about it. I needed something else to hold my attention, something not related to him or Dynamistress or the Pariah Project. Then I remembered the book I'd planned to read, the one that had held the key to the lab. I went upstairs and retrieved *Brave New World* from the nightstand and brought it down to the main floor. I reclined on the sofa near the fireplace and began reading.

After the very first page of the book, something twitched at the back of my mind. With each paragraph, this feeling grew. By the time I finished the first chapter, I was completely on edge, and not because of the book's plot.

I was convinced that she hadn't just randomly selected this book to be the keeper of the lab key. She chose it because of its connection to the work in that lab. The sudden realization made my stomach turn. I put the book down and allowed my thoughts to run wild.

This book was, at the least, hinting at the truth. But it was a truth that just couldn't be. It was too crazy. But if it were true, it meant that Bloodmoon had flat-out lied to me.

There was only one way I was going to find out. I needed access to the lab computer. For that, of course, I needed the password. I remembered from her journal how she'd determined the password to her other-self's computer to be the title of an Alice Cooper song. Stood to reason that this password might also be one. Thanks to Huxley's novel, I had a good idea what it might be. I just needed to verify if my recollection of early 80s music was accurate.

I went to the office computer and accessed the music library, where a quick word search confirmed my suspicion. There it was, on Cooper's album, *Flush the Fashion*. I retrieved the key to the lab and entered, taking a seat in front of the machine.

When the login screen popped up, I typed in the title of the minor hit single. A moment later, I had access to her files.

I stared at the screen, my pulse racing as I scanned the directory. It read like a college course listing, with labels such as BIO, CHEM, MATH, and so on. I clicked on the one labeled META.

Subfolders galore, here, but I found one called "Runaway." In that folder was a notes file that explained in full what she expected would happen, should she go into runaway. And as I read it, despite my heart pounding like mad, the blood still drained from my face.

The description was straightforward and unambiguous. It allowed no chance of incredible survival and recovery. It spoke of total, rapid self-consumption. The reason no corpse had been recovered was because there had been nothing left to be recovered.

I took a moment, recalling the descriptions her teammates had given of her final moments, and couldn't help but shudder. But I shook it off and turned my attention back to the META folder.

It contained four subfolders, labeled Options A, B, C, and D. I read everything in them. The first two were different measures she could take to delay the progression of the runaway. The last one was a potential cure for it.

But the third one... the third one took the most time to read. It was the most scientifically complex, and it confirmed that I had, in fact, been lied to. This angered me, of course, but my feelings about being deceived were nothing compared to how I felt about the actual truth.

Bloodmoon and Dana arrived around nine in the evening. I was in the kitchen when they returned, drinking something from the bar. Lots of something from the bar.

I was surprised at Dana's appearance. He looked older than I'd expected. But then, everything he'd been through since February was likely to make anyone look a bit ragged.

After introducing us, Bloodmoon quickly said goodnight and left. I found this odd, since she'd never left me alone with anyone else upon first meeting. But then I realized there was no longer any need for her to be present.

After she'd gone, I looked at this man, thinking – as others had commented – that he didn't look like Dinah at all. Except maybe around the eyes, though his were brown. Then again, shave his face and slap a wig on him and maybe the resemblance would be clearer.

Dana saw my drink was almost empty and telekinetically pulled from the shelf the very bottle I'd poured from. As he refilled my glass, I prepared to berate him for lifting that from my mind without my permission. Then it occurred to me that maybe that wasn't how he knew.

He poured himself a glass, too, and joined me at the corner table. The first thing I did was ask him how he felt. "Still a bit rocky," he said. He thanked me for asking and smiled softly.

We drank in silence, exchanging awkward glances, for a few minutes. I wanted to grill him about what I'd found. I wanted to know everything, and I wanted to know it now. I needed answers to the impossible questions in my head. But Dana looked exhausted. Rocky, as he'd said. And even though I was dying to have this conversation, he clearly needed rest, so I pushed my curiosity down and told him we'd talk in the morning.

"Are you sure?"

I told him I was, but also said he should be prepared for an intense conversation the next day, since I'd read the notes about Option C on the lab computer.

His eyebrows lifted in surprise. "How did you get into the lab? And does Jasmine know?" he asked. I assured him that she did not, then explained where I'd found the key. He chuckled and shook his head. "Appropriate," he said. I agreed, but didn't find it amusing at all. "I'm sorry," he said. "And how did you get access to the computer?"

He smiled when I told him. "I guess you really have read the journals, if you knew to take that approach." After a moment, he said, "So... how are you taking that information?"

I told him I was still processing it.

"Yeah, I'd imagine you would be." He was quiet a moment. "Jasmine briefed me on the way over about your discussions with others. I'd like to know your thoughts."

I wasn't entirely sure how to answer that, and said as much. I told him how everyone was uncomfortable around me, though it had lessened somewhat over the six weeks I'd been there. At least now I understood why.

"But has it helped?" he asked.

I admitted that it hadn't helped as much as I'd hoped, and that I was afraid my talks with him wouldn't, either.

"Oh, don't worry about that," he said as he finished his drink. "Until tomorrow, then." He wished me a good night and headed up to the guest room.

As I watched him go, I realized I was utterly drained. It had been such a brief meeting, but I'd been anxious all day and tense the entire time we spoke. But, tired or not, I was in no way ready for bed. In fact, I suspected I'd be up all night.

I left the kitchen and made my way up to the deck. It was a cool night, but not cold. I stood leaning on the low wall surrounding the deck, looking out at the sea of buildings. The one next door had a large smokestack on its roof. It was non-functional, though, and a bit of an eyesore. Another building nearby had an advertisement for Owl Cigars on its brick wall. It was old and worn and I wondered how long it had been there. But the distractions of the neighborhood weren't helping much.

After a while, lost in thought, I went back into the lab. I sat at the computer again and went to the PHIL folder, out of curiosity. There were no journal entries referring to philosophy. Subfolders there were Aristotle, Baum, Heraclitus, Hobbes, Hume, Locke, Plato, Plutarch, and Socrates.

Baum? I knew that name, but not in association with philosophy. I clicked on the name. In the folder, unsurprisingly, was a PDF of *The Wonderful Wizard of Oz*. Assuming it was a filing error, I closed it and continued browsing.

I spent hours looking through all the folders while listening to music. Around four in the morning, I locked the lab behind me and went back into the bedroom. I stood there in the middle of the room, still a little drunk, but not ready to sleep.

I dug out her photo album and looked through it again, more carefully this time. The images were inserted chronologically in the album, beginning with baby pictures. There were photos of the siblings as children, including some of her dressed in a makeshift hero outfit, complete with a mask, a big letter "D" on her chest, and a white towel for a cape. Adorable, but I was looking for pictures of her at an older age, before joining the Bay Scouts. Before her hair had turned white. Before being Dynamistress.

All the photos of her post-teen years, though, were of others, of her friends and classmates. These were followed by pictures of her after she'd begun her career as Dynamistress. They went from teenager to mid-thirties, with nearly nothing between.

"Nearly" being the key word. One of those in-between pages held a graduation announcement from 1996. On a hunch, I peeled back the plastic page and pulled the announcement from the sticky board. Opening it, I found a photo. I stared at it, a chill spreading through me. Dinah Geof-Craigs, age twenty-four, probably, when the shot was taken.

So different from her high school pictures. Slimmer. More serious, lacking the broad smile that had graced her younger photos. Here, she looked determined, more than anything. And, of course, her hair wasn't white, yet. It was difficult to accept it to be the same girl at all.

I tucked the photo and announcement back into the album. The picture removed any lingering doubts. I looked at myself in the mirror, once more, feeling completely lost.

I'd been stupid. I'd been deceived.

I was angry... I was confused...

I was anxious... I was relieved...

I was Dynamistress...

...and I was a clone.

NINE

"We all have big changes in our lives that are more or less a second chance."

~ Harrison Ford

I despise the word "miracle." I bristle every time I hear someone say it or see it used in print. It's a common word in our language, used when referencing things that may greatly defy the odds, but are nevertheless still well within the realm of the possible. But "miracle" implies an event that can't be explained by nature, as being the result of divine intervention. And to the rational mind, anything we can't explain is merely something for which we don't yet have enough data to understand.

A person winning millions of dollars in a lottery when only buying a single ticket isn't miraculous, just highly improbable. A person being shot a dozen times and living through it isn't a miracle, either, but a result of the paths taken by the bullets and the skills of surgeons. The most improbable thing you can think of, so long as it's at all viable in the natural world, does not need to invoke the miraculous.

Despite our best efforts, some of our endeavors have lousy success records. For example, the first mammalian clone had two hundred seventy-six failed attempts (stillbirths and defectives) before Dolly the sheep came healthily to life.

This area of science has advanced quite a lot since 1996, of course, but there are still many fatalities and deformities that seem to be unavoidable. This is one reason why human cloning is off-limits. The idea of having so many embryos, fetuses, and infants die or be deformed is unacceptable to nearly everyone. Based on past experiences, we can't expect a complex cloning to be successful on the first attempt. It would be foolish for a scientist to begin with anything less than, say, fifty cloned embryos.

Of course, I didn't have fifty.

I had fifteen.

In the entertainment world, clone stories never address or, at best, are incredibly vague on how the clone possesses the memories of the original. DNA doesn't contain that sort of information, after all, any more than the blueprint of a house contains a list of the people who will live there. But then, most clone stories don't include powerful telepaths.

I glared at Dana as he, Bloodmoon, and I sat in the kitchen over tea. "For the past six weeks," I said bitterly, "I've been under the belief that I'd somehow survived the runaway event, with my body healed, but my mind stuck with a severe case of amnesia. I believed it because that's what you told me," I growled at Bloodmoon.

Jasmine avoided my gaze as Dana said, "I'm sorry. I never thought your death would–"

"*Her* death," I corrected him. "As I told Bloodmoon from the start, I feel no connection whatsoever to Dynamistress." I glanced at the woman as I said, "I didn't want people calling me by that name or telling me about things 'I' had done or what kind of person 'I' was." I shook my head. "There's just too much of a disconnect."

"And I made sure the others honored that," Bloodmoon said.

"How?" Dana asked.

"I was always present when she met with others," she explained, "telepathically reminding them not to use her name and to always refer to Dynamistress as another entity." She turned, her eyes meeting mine. "The last thing we wanted was more stress for you."

I had to admit that she'd kept her word, realizing now that she'd even gone so far as to mentally interrupt anyone who was about to violate the rule.

"Fine," Dana said, sounding a bit frustrated. "I never thought *her* death would cause such a pronounced psychic feedback in me. Probably should have. All this could have been avoided." He sighed deeply. "When I consented to take part in this absurd plan, I came here from Sacramento. We went on alternate sleeping schedules. I'd sleep while yo– while *she* was awake. And when she slept, I would telepathically 'copy' her memories, transplanting them into the clone."

"Into *me*," I said.

Dana didn't acknowledge the clarification. "Remember, the others knew nothing about this experiment, including Jasmine."

"And that still ticks me off," Bloodmoon said to both of us.

"As best I can figure out," Dana said, "when Dyna went into runaway, this caused not just the feedback that put me into a coma, but also resonated within you, causing your abilities to manifest."

"But I don't *have* any abilities," I said. "Don't you think I've tested that? I can't so much as make a finger glow, let alone punch through a wall."

"I think they'll return once the memories are fully intact," Dana said.

"Even so," I said, "how could her going all supernova cause anything within *me*? That makes no sense."

"I'll explain that in a minute," Dana said, nodding for Bloodmoon to continue.

"The blast ruptured the tank and set off the alarms in the lab," she said. "I was here on monitor duty, so I ran upstairs and broke in, finding a small lake of fluid puddled around a tank at the back end of the room." She paused for a moment, then shook her head. "Inside, a fully grown woman with an umbilical cord connecting her to this weird machine. You have no idea how much of a shock it was."

"I think I have you beat on shock," I said.

"Fair point," she admitted. "At any rate, it didn't take long to figure out what was going on, but I hadn't a clue how to deal with it."

"What *did* you do?" Dana asked.

"First, I pulled her from the tank and made sure she was breathing," she said to him. "And that wasn't as easy as slapping her on the butt. Mainly because she was unconscious." She turned to me, again. "Fortunately, you don't weigh much. Holding you upside-down as best I could allowed some fluid to drain. Eventually, you coughed up more and began breathing. I cut and tied the umbilical, then called my cousin Alex, who's a nurse for the Gatekeepers. She came over and made sure you were okay. Then we moved you over to their medical bay."

"Why not a hospital?" I asked.

Bloodmoon raised an eyebrow at me. "How would you suggest I explain to a hospital why a grown woman would have the stump of an umbilical cord?"

"Oh," I said. "Right."

"By the way, in case you were wondering if your fast healing abilities are still there, the stump fell off and was fully healed in less than three days."

"Um... I wasn't. And gross."

"Anyway," Bloodmoon continued, "once you were there, Dr. Stone took over. Mostly, this was monitoring vitals, but she did the transplant, too."

I felt my heart skip a beat. "Whoa, what? Transplant?"

Bloodmoon cleared her throat awkwardly. "Yes, the... um... stool transplant."

I stared at her, my mouth hanging open for several seconds. Finally, I said, "I had a *shit* transplant?"

"As she explained it to me," she said, "a newborn's intestinal biome is essentially established at the time of birth. If a child is delivered vaginally, the baby's biome will resemble the bacterial composition of the mother's uterus. If by a C-section, it tends to resemble that of the mother's skin."

Dana caught on quicker than I did. "But she had neither," he said.

Bloodmoon continued. "The artificial uterus had something of a biome, but Ashley felt it would be insufficient, so she... rectified it. If you'll pardon the expression."

I felt my stomach flop. "You're saying I have someone else's *poop* in me?"

"Well, not by this point, no. But yes, you had several administrations of the stool solution."

"Administered... how?"

"Well... rectally, of course. Basically, an enema," Jasmine said.

Dana and I both cringed, and for the same reason. Our mother thought enemas were the cure for nearly everything. He looked at me and said, "Remember how mom–"

"Don't!" I said. "Just... don't go there."

"Then, one day, you woke." Bloodmoon shook her head in amazement. "And then you *spoke!*" She looked at me, as though I should understand how weird that must have been for her. "Alex was with me, and she literally jumped in shock. We were absolutely not expecting that. Obviously, that's when I realized Dana had been involved."

"And that's when the lying started," I said.

Dana ignored the jab. "While all of her memories had been implanted in you, not all of them were accessible. Only up through about high school."

"Again," I said to Bloodmoon, "you lied to me. You said I'd been in a terrible accident. Head injury and all that. Amnesia. You said I'd been unconscious for weeks."

"It was true, in a sense." Jasmine said, then frowned. "What would you have had me say? The truth? Do you think you'd have accepted that?" I grimaced. I hate being lied to. But she wasn't wrong. I probably would have freaked out. "Honestly," she went on, "I was surprised you accepted the explanation. I mean, one look in the mirror would show that you didn't look much like her."

I shifted uncomfortably in my seat. She'd brought up the one part of all this that was truly embarrassing to me. "Well," I said, "at first, I assumed that her white hair was a wig. At least, until I got to the part of her journals that described her hair going white from the energy affecting the follicles or whatever. Then, since it was clear that I didn't have any such energy – due to this alleged brain injury – I assumed the follicles must have healed and brought the color back."

"And how did you rationalize looking a lot younger?" Dana asked.

"I dunno," I said. "Because anyone would look older with white hair?" The others laughed. Despite myself, I did, too. "Besides, in all the recent photos, her face is covered either by a mask or those big damn sunglasses, and it's hard to judge someone's age when half the face is covered."

"But you knew your birth date," he said. "Did you think that face in the mirror looked nearly forty?"

"No," I said. "But photos I did find didn't show a woman who looked her age, either. And you don't look your age, for that matter."

"Our family does age well," Dana agreed.

"And then there's the stuff she said in her journals. I mean, first of all, my memories matched what she wrote as a teen. But on top of that, she wrote that the genetic modifications, combined with the accelerated healing ability you mentioned, would make her age slower," I said to Bloodmoon. "I mean, I'd read about Dynamistress being impaled with a spear, but my body has no abdominal scar. I assumed the healing factor was responsible for that, too." I shrugged. "Either way," I said, "it didn't matter. The point is, I had no reason to think I'd been lied to, so no reason to think I *didn't* have amnesia. I mean, what else *could* I believe?" I frowned. "Let's get to the meat of things. This whole implanting memories thing sounds impossible."

Dana stood and began gathering our cups. "Let's put a pin in that while I get us refills and take a potty break."

I wanted to argue, but realized I could, in fact, use a bathroom break. I trudged up the stairs, my brain buzzing with all this new information. Whatever Dana was going to say didn't really matter. I wasn't his sister. I was a clone of her.

The truth of this didn't sit well with me. I still had no attachment to my DNA donor. She and her world were utterly foreign to me. But even more than that, the idea of existing as a clone... well, it made my stomach turn.

I returned and took my seat just as Dana set refills out for us. Then, he said, "So... as you were getting at, the memory transfer process was quite complicated. But there's a factor that reduced the complexity for me. It's why I would never attempt such a thing with anyone other than you." He paused, then said, "I'm intimately familiar with your mind."

"Yeah," I said. "I read about the telepathic link. 'Intimately' is the right word." I saw a flash of something on Dana's face. Pain? Shame? "Sorry," I said. "I have to keep reminding myself that my memories are incomplete. In my head, I still resent you," I admitted. "The memories you say were up through high school are, to me, like yesterday. Convincing myself that it was two decades ago is hard. It just doesn't feel that way."

Dana was strangely quiet for several seconds, avoiding my gaze, before saying, "I know. And I want to fix that for you."

I stirred sugar and half & half into my cup. "Anyway, go on. You were saying how intimately you know my noodle."

He smiled faintly. "Yes. But it isn't just because of the link we shared. It goes back to when you were little," he said. "When I was a boy, my abilities would frequently become overwhelming. I often needed to escape from the barrage of thoughts from others, before I learned how to effectively block them out. I found that refuge in your mind. I'd dive in and just sort of... *be* you, for a bit. It allowed me to tune out the external thoughts." He smiled sheepishly. "I know your mind, in some ways, better than I know my own. That's why it was even possible for me to do the transference in the first place."

Bloodmoon and I listened raptly as Dana explained the process. He said the copying wasn't that difficult. The tricky part was placing them into the new brain in such a way that they'd be accessible in the same fashion that I was used to. He said that, since he was pressed for time, he planted lots of memories into the new brain somewhat less than perfectly, where he then "locked" them, making them inaccessible, while also "labeling" them.

"It's like settling into a new house," he said. "You're moved in, but are still living out of boxes. You know, for example, that you have a blender, and you know it's out in the garage in a box marked 'kitchen.' But until you physically open that box, take out the blender, and set it up, you can't make midnight margaritas." As Bloodmoon and I chuckled at the analogy, he continued. "By January, I'd finished the 'move' and had begun the 'unpacking.' I started with basics – language, math, and societal information – all the stuff you'd need to get by without feeling like a complete alien. After that, I went chronologically from infancy forward."

"But how?" I asked. "I mean, how do you 'see' a memory? How do you know when it was created? How do you 'label' them?"

"Obviously, I don't see an accurate visual of a brain, with a bunch of folded gray matter all over the place. It's more a subjective interpretation that puts an artificial structure over it all, making it easier to understand and navigate. For example, distinct categories have different appearances or sensations to me, and because of that, it's easy to gather them all up at once."

"Give me an example," I said.

Dana paused a moment, clearly trying to think of a better way to explain it. "Okay," he finally said. "Remember that big bag of marbles we played with as kids?"

I remembered the marbles, of course, being much "closer" to those days than he was. "Old drawstring bag," I said. "Had to be a couple hundred in there."

"Right."

"I remember one that was rough, and lighter than the glass ones, like it was made from clay."

Dana smiled. "I'd forgotten about that one, but you're right, it was clay. There were a couple of steel ball bearings, too."

I laughed. "Yeah, that always bugged me."

I sipped my coffee as he explained. "Okay. Now imagine spilling them out on the floor. They're all marbles – or ball bearings, as the case may be – and therefore all spherical. Let's say that spherical things are all memories... I dunno... about food. But, though they're all spherical, they're all different, sometimes in major ways, sometimes trivial. Different colors, sizes, designs. Say all the yellow ones are memories about cheese. All the cat-eyes are memories about meat. So the yellow cat-eyes are memories that might be about cheeseburgers."

"You're hungry, aren't you?"

"Maybe."

"Wait," I said. "So if you can identify all my memories like this, does it mean you know all the specific details of the memories?"

"No, it's like... It's like seeing a cheeseburger and knowing it's a cheeseburger, but not tasting it and truly experiencing the cheeseburger."

"I see... I guess."

"Anyway, that's kind of how it is. Everything has multiple categories, not just by subject, but by chronology, emotional attachment, and so on. So, yes, it's very involved. And time-consuming. Of course, it helps that your brain is physically so new."

"Why should that make a difference?"

"Because of what's called brain plasticity. Younger brains learn more easily. In this case, it made it easier for the implanted memories to take root."

"But, even if I let you restore everything, my memories will still be incomplete. I'll never have the memories of that last day."

Dana looked at me with a pained expression. "Here's where we get to the feedback issue. You see, once your body had matured to a certain point, I was able to set up a sort of real-time 'mirroring' in your brain. All the new experiences Dinah had during the day instantly copied to your brain, like a computer hard drive being automatically backed-up to a second drive."

I saw Bloodmoon's eyes widen at this, and her mouth hung open. "That's..." she began before pausing. "Just how powerful are you, Dana?"

"Oh, I wasn't even sure I could do it, honestly," he said, sidestepping her question. "And I'm sure it worked only because, in a sense, it was the same mind in two bodies. It was just a shot in the dark."

"So that link is what allowed the feedback that destroyed the tank," I said. "Just as the link with you put you into a coma."

"Exactly," he said, nodding and staring into his cup.

I let out a breath, feeling like I was in a weird science fiction movie. Whether it was a good one or bad one, I wasn't yet sure. "I read her notes on the whole cloning thing," I said. "I know she had some of her eggs harvested. And I know she kept some of her own tissues from different times. I read how she gathered somatic cells from a sample of her skin from before her last DNA tweak. And thanks to Wikipedia, I actually know what somatic cells are. Then she fused these with the eggs, fertilizing them."

"That's right," Dana said, as Bloodmoon listened intently.

"That rubbery, sack-like thing in the lab... that was the artificial uterus, right?"

"Yes. It was lined with endometrial tissue also developed from her cells. Once the eggs were well into cell division, they were planted into the tissue, which she then coaxed into producing an actual placenta. It worked fairly well, delivering the nutrients, glucose, amino acids, hormones, and such that a fetus would require, all of which were supplied to the tissue through a modified IV system. But it wasn't eliminating waste sufficiently, so the dialysis machine was brought in to help."

"Wait," I said. "I get that the placenta delivered these nutrients and whatnot, but where did they come from in the first place?"

"Some of what was needed came from medical supply. But the big thing was that Dinah had concocted an artificial amniotic fluid. Every day, she had to manage it all. I couldn't tell you the details. Probably in her notes, if you're that interested."

"So at a certain point, the fetus was moved to the tank, right?"

"Yes. Everything was transplanted for the growth to continue."

"Okay," I said. "But here's the thing that makes even less sense than all of that. Human gestation is about forty weeks. You're trying to tell me that this procedure produced *me* – a grown-ass woman – in a *fraction* of that."

Dana said, "That was the exact point I made when the idea was first proposed. But fetal growth is regulated by hormones. Control those and you control the growth rate." I stared at him in disbelief, a look he had to have grown accustomed to by this point. "You know," he said, "all this will be easier for you to grasp once I finish replacing your memories."

"No offense," I said, "but unless I can grasp it without you mucking about in my brain, I'm not going to be sure you're not just... you know... planting false memories."

To my surprise, Dana looked utterly stricken, as though I'd just deeply insulted him. And of course, I probably had. Bloodmoon frowned at me, as well. Then Dana nodded, avoiding my gaze, and continued.

"Anyway," he said, "she spent virtually all her waking time in here, really, monitoring the content of the fluid in the tank, controlling the temperature, holding and moving your body around, giving it the sort of sensory stimulation necessary. Lots of stuff well out of my area of expertise."

"The rest of us," Bloodmoon interjected, "assumed she was just resting a lot, which is why we weren't seeing much of her."

"Did you expect it to work?" I asked Dana.

"Nope," he said bluntly. "But I went along with it because it made her feel better. I was still certain I was going to lose my sister. This allowed me to spend more time with her."

I shook my head. "It makes no sense at all that it should have worked. I mean, it sounds impossible. No way she should have succeeded."

"No?" Bloodmoon said, as Dana and I looked at her. "Look, we live in a world where seemingly impossible stuff happens on a regular basis. You and I have telepathy," she said to Dana. "That shouldn't be possible."

"But that's a meta thing," I said.

"And you're assuming that your only 'meta thing' is the ability to produce and discharge massive amounts of energy? Did it never occur to you that perhaps your meta abilities also include an aptitude for the biological sciences far beyond normal? That this is what allowed not only the successful cloning, but also the success of your original experiment?"

I stared at her, so stunned by the idea that I ignored her use of "your" in her statement. I looked at Dana. It was obvious that it hadn't occurred to him. Whether it had ever occurred to Dynamistress, I didn't know.

Bloodmoon said, "I started thinking about this after getting to know Kit. He has an incredible aptitude with sound-based tech, with no formal training. He built a flying suit of armor! Again, without relevant education. How can you explain these things without invoking the meta factor?"

I mulled over her statement. She raised a good point.

"Anyway," Dana said, "we didn't tell anyone else about this. Neither of us had enough conviction that it would work, so why get anyone's hopes up?"

"Then after your premature 'birth,'" Bloodmoon said, "I kept it a secret because I was frankly not sure you would survive."

I snorted. "You might as well have told everyone. I don't know that they could have reacted any worse than they have to me being here."

"That's not fair," Bloodmoon said. "You have to understand–"

"No, I do," I interrupted. "They'd just lost their friend."

"Not just that," she said. "It's also that you *are* different. As you know, you look a fair bit younger. Your hair's a different color. Your skin is, if I may say so, freakishly pale, due to being exposed to so little sunlight."

"It's been a bit chilly for sunbathing," I said.

She smiled slightly. "And your voice is different, too."

"What?"

"This body hasn't had all the trauma of the old one," Dana said. "Not just from meta activities, but the normal wear and tear of everyday existence. Your skin hasn't had decades of exposure to the elements, so it's nearly flawless and soft. Your voice is a higher pitch than we're used to because your vocal cords are so new and, frankly, haven't suffered all the years of alcohol abuse." He smirked. "Now might be the time to pursue that singing career."

I rolled my eyes at his attempt to lighten the mood. Then we sat in silence for several minutes as I mulled over all this information. Strangely, there was still a tiny part of me that wanted to deny it, but I couldn't. Not only was the evidence overwhelming, but it all resonated, somehow.

"If you set up an automatic copying between the minds during the final weeks," I said, "why don't I have access to those memories?"

"They were copied to a section of your brain that I'd reserved," Dana said simply, "not yet integrated with the rest of the mind. You would have had no existing context for them, yet, so they would have just confused you more when you regained consciousness. Besides," he said, a pained expression again crossing his face, "you really don't want that final memory."

I sure couldn't argue with that.

It was late. Bloodmoon had long since gone home and Dana had been asleep for hours. I sat in front of the blazing fireplace on the main floor, wide awake, somewhere between midnight and sunrise. I sipped from a glass of aged rum that held a huge cube of ice that filled most of the glass.

There were so many things I had to wrap my head around, not the least of which was my age. In a literal sense, I was only a couple months old, but physically appeared to be in my mid-twenties. My memories stretched back nearly four decades, but they were just memories up through being a teenager. So I had no idea how old I *should* feel.

Regarding those memories, Dana was certainly right. There's no way I'd want to have the memory of going through runaway. But what about the rest? The memories I had were vivid and felt recent. High school graduation seemed like last month. Losing my virginity, just a couple years ago.

And I did still feel resentment toward Dana, just as I had at seventeen, though it had faded somewhat when I read in the journals her words of regret and accounts of the closeness they shared in later years. And talking with him today had helped, too.

The thing I was struggling with most was the question of all those memories that were hidden away in my brain. Did I want them back? Did I want the actual memories of all that I'd read? Did I want to experience again the heartbreak of Sharon and Jackie? Or K.T.? Did I want to relive the agony of being impaled by a spear, of being blistered over half my body, of broken ribs and a punctured lung? Did I want the grief of losing friends?

Or did I want to start over? I could have Dana unlock only specific memory sets, if they were all coded the way he'd described. Give me all the knowledge of history I had up to present day. All the understanding of technology, so that computers didn't seem so much like magic. I could be an entirely new Dinah Geof-Craigs. Since I didn't appear to have the abilities of Dynamistress, I could just go back to research. Or something else entirely. Maybe I *could* pursue that singing career. I could be this world's Dynasonic, if I had any musical connections, which I didn't.

I drained my glass and lay down in front of the fire. Then I laughed aloud in my tipsy state. Who was I kidding? I'd listened to current hits online and knew the kind of music kids were listening to these days wasn't my thing. Sure, I could understand why some was popular, but the appeal of rap or hip-hop or whatever was incomprehensible to me. Then again, it's not like all the music of my youth was fantastic. But at least it didn't have Auto-Tune.

The warmth of the fire and the effects of the alcohol finally brought a sense of weariness. As I welcomed it, I realized there wasn't any real question of what I was going to do. Maybe if I hadn't read the journals, I could have started fresh. But I had and, even though they didn't match up with the memories in my head, I knew those words, those experiences, were mine. I'd never be able to shake that fact and it would eat me up if I tried to ignore it.

In those words, I'd read about the people I'd just spent several weeks getting to know. They were people who'd worked with and, in some cases, lived with Dynamistress. They were words written with obviously very real emotions. How could I turn my back on that kind of friendship, that kind of love?

Yes, I thought to myself as sleep claimed me. I would be Dynamistress once again.

TEN

"Looking back, you realize that a very special person passed briefly through your life, and that person was you. It is not too late to become that person again."
~Robert Brault

"What is your earliest memory?" I'm always shocked that so many people seem able to answer this question. I have no idea how they do it.

I have many memories from when I was quite young, of course, but with few exceptions, I'm not able to sequence them chronologically. I suppose some are able to do this because they can place the memory in relation to significant life events: moving to a new home, a death in the family, etc. It's easy enough to place a memory as before or after such things. But I have only minor memorable events in my early childhood. It's not likely that I could place a memory as before or after any of them. Even so, if pressed, I do give an answer, though I can't swear that it's my earliest memory.

I was perhaps four years old and had been outside playing. A sudden storm rolled in, the sort that we don't get here in San Francisco. It caught me by surprise, and I was frightened. Not of getting wet, but of the scary lightning and booming thunder.

I ran to my house and, to my horror, found the door was locked. In a panic, I pounded on it with my tiny fists, yelling for my mother. I remember at one point fearfully looking over my shoulder at the huge, black clouds coming to get me. And then, of course, the door opened and I dashed inside, my mother shaking her head at what she perceived as me exaggerating my fear.

Of course, I now understand her attitude. She knew there was nothing to be afraid of. I was in virtually no danger of being struck by lightning, and thunder couldn't hurt me. And, as she would point out, I wasn't sweet enough to dissolve in the rain.

Today, I love thunderstorms. I miss the ones from back east, the energy and majesty of them. I know the benefits of them. Not just the provision of life-nurturing water, but the cooling effect they bring, how they remove pollution from the atmosphere, how lightning releases fertilizing nitrates into the soil, and how it sparks fires that are themselves beneficial to the overall health of forests.

But as a child, I knew none of this. Like most people, I didn't understand that things that are so destructive can be so necessary.

It was several days before the memory restoration could begin. Dana needed more time to recover from his own ordeal. During these days, I minimized my contact with others. I was trying to mentally prepare myself for what was to come. My anxiety about it increased with each day, but I didn't change my mind. I was still going through with it.

If it was going to be done, it needed to be done right, with nothing left out. I knew I'd been rude when I implied that Dana could plant false memories in my mind, but the truth was that he could do so at any point and I'd never know.

Logically, I had no reason to think he'd do anything of the sort. Dana was, by all accounts, an honest and honorable man. His love for "me" was obvious. But maybe that wasn't the best thing. Our natural instinct is to protect our loved ones. Parents lie to their children all the time, wanting to spare them pain. Wouldn't Dana want to spare his dear sister some of the pain of her past, even if only by tempering the memory a little bit? I made him promise that he'd never do so. Still, the worry didn't leave me.

Dana expected the restoration to take about a week. Finally, the day came to begin. As he said we'd done before, we went on alternating sleep schedules. In my room, Dana pulled his chair over to the head of the bed, in order to have better access to my mind. Proximity helped, he told me. Soon, I was nodding off. And as I slept, he did his thing.

I woke the first morning with a slew of new memories to process. I'd expected it to be jarring, but it wasn't. It was like remembering a dream, but instead of it fading as the day progressed, the "dream" only became more entrenched, growing from imagination to reality.

This initial batch covered my first few years of college, including the time with Sharon and Jackie. These memories hit me hard. I woke feeling as though the events had just happened yesterday, including every bit of the joy of being with them and the heartbreak when they left. It was so strong, so real, that I couldn't imagine Dana had eased the pain of that memory one little bit.

These memories didn't flood into me in chronological order. They were like puzzle pieces floating around in my head, connecting – albeit quickly – in no particular order.

I lay there in bed for an hour, just absorbing everything, allowing emotions to wash over me. I laughed. I cried. And of course, it's not as though I consciously assimilated everything. What I took in was a general overview. A CliffsNotes version of those years. Throughout the day, bits and pieces would float to the surface, say hello, then sink back into the folds of my brain.

I'd asked everyone to allow me some privacy during this week. I didn't need the questions that were sure to come from others during the process. It was going to be hard enough without that.

The most disconcerting thing, which I should have expected, was being able to experience these events while already having knowledge of them from the journals. Knowing what was going to come of them put certain things into perspective that was lacking when I'd read them. Of course, the journals didn't even begin to fully reflect the reality of the events.

Day two took me through graduating with my bachelor's degree, though my Master's, and to the beginning of my job at GACTech. During that time, I met Lee and she moved in, Dana got married, and I drank a lot. It was sad to see just how much I withdrew during those years. Obviously, I devoted myself to my studies, but I had no social life, nor did I seem to really want one. This stood out in stark contrast to my younger years, when all I wanted was to be popular.

Interestingly, the presence of these memories caused the ones from the day before to suddenly seem further in the past. No longer did it feel like Sharon and Jackie had left just weeks previously. Now it felt like it was a few years ago. This phenomenon would continue over the remainder of the week, with each day's reintegrated history pushing the last ones deeper into the past, although they were still quite clear in my mind.

Day three covered the rest of my education and up to the beginning of my relationship with Lee, in which alcohol continued to play a large role. This was a difficult day of assimilation for me, knowing what was coming with Lee. I couldn't help but feel like I was an utter failure as a human being during these years. I was still alienated from my family, utterly self-centered, and one bender away from full-blown alcoholism.

The journals didn't prepare me for the knowledge of just how good a friend Lee had been to me and how poor of one I was to her. I was focused only on myself and my work, too blind to see the problems she was having and how she was – for reasons I couldn't figure out, even with fresh memories – falling for me. Her admission of it was such a surprise. And my acceptance of it was devastating, since I knew what the future would bring.

Day four brought so much. First and foremost was the final experiment that would eventually bring about my abilities, and, of course, the fire at the GACTech lab. So much confusion in these memories. I felt like life was utterly out of control. I remembered feeling how, after I was sued, I honestly thought I'd end up in prison.

And I was so caught up in all of it that I didn't see the effect it had on Lee, how she was deteriorating almost daily. The trial took a lot out of me, and I didn't appreciate the support Lee gave me during that time. And I repaid her by cheating on her with my attorney.

What an utter shit I was.

Day five was the big one. I woke up overwhelmed by the events of these few years. There was the horrible deterioration of my relationship with Lee and her moving out. Then her behavior becoming irrational and stalker-like. Then nine-eleven, of course. And, a month later, Lee taking her life. The horror of that day, for me, far outweighed anything I'd ever been through.

Dana and I reconciled and took our trip to Europe, which seemed almost magical. It was clear that I'd latched onto him out of a desperate need to not be alone with my thoughts about Lee. But that was totally fine. That's what family is for, right?

Reliving everything, of course, was much different from reading about it in a journal. But this particular event forced me out of bed, even though I was still assimilating. I stepped down to the guest room and looked in on my brother, sleeping soundly. My heart was almost bursting with renewed love for him. I had an urge to jump into bed and hug him fiercely.

So I did.

Overwhelmed, tears began to flow. They were complex tears. They were from sadness over the loss of Lee, but they were from relief, too. This was my brother. This was the only person who had ever truly understood me. And now I knew again just how important he was to me.

He woke, of course, but one look at my damp and contorted face told him all he needed to know. He knew, after all, which memories I'd been dealing with this day. He held me tightly as I cried into his shoulder until he returned to sleep.

A while later, I went back to my own bed, so as not to disturb him further. I continued processing my new memories, which went up through my move to San Francisco, where I began my career as a crime fighter while trying to pay my rent. Obviously, this included the period when my abilities were growing, and this seemed to trigger something within me. I remembered how it felt to be more aware of the energies inside me.

It was as though this recollection itself kick-started them again, just as Dana had predicted. I sat on the edge of my bed, feeling the energy inside me, remembering how to let it flow into my outstretched fist. I grinned stupidly as I felt the warm tingle as it suffused my flesh.

That evening, I went out. Probably because of this day's memories, I felt the urge to dress as I had when I first became Dynamistress. I pulled the old leathers out of the bottom drawer of the wardrobe and put them on. There was a strong sense of nostalgia as I did so, which I found a bit disconcerting. They were a bit loose. I still had muscles to build up, after all.

It would soon be dark outside, but I wore the sunglasses, anyway. I also added something else. I pulled a certain necklace from my jewelry box and put it on. The pendant hung over my sternum, appropriately.

Then I hit the streets of the Tenderloin, hoping for some action. My "biker/hooker" outfit drew the attention of men who obviously were hoping for action of another sort, which amused me a good deal. Eventually, I encountered a mugging. And the mugger encountered an energy-enhanced uppercut.

It felt good. For me, anyway. Probably less so for him.

After ensuring the victim was all right, I asked him to call the police and waited with him until they arrived. As one officer took his statement, I took his partner to the mugger, who was now regaining consciousness.

We loaded the guy into the back of the patrol car and they took off. I smiled to myself and figured that was enough for my first evening out. I turned to head home, when I saw a familiar figure step out of the shadows.

"Well, hi," I said to the Maltese Falcon. He said nothing, but moved closer. I couldn't see even his mask under the hood, but could guess what was going through his head. "Yeah," I said. "It's me."

"Not convinced," he said in his low, gravelly growl.

I couldn't blame him. "We first met at a convenience store hold-up on Hyde Street." I held up the pendant. "Here's the souvenir you gave me."

He was silent a moment as he, I assumed, stared at my face and hair. Finally, he said, "One day, you'll have to tell me how you survived what I hear was a rather spectacular demise."

I tilted my head, surprised that he knew about it. "Yeah, fun story. We'll do lunch," I said. I waved as I jogged off, pleased with myself for having confounded the notoriously enigmatic protector of the Tenderloin.

The following day, the memories brought me up through my tenure with the Bay Scouts, and with it, my earliest memories of people who would go on to become some of my closest friends. Unfortunately, this batch also included the other-world exchange, Valora's death, and the disbanding of the team.

I pulled up my nightshirt and looked at my torso, touching the area that once had a spear protruding from it. The memory was so fresh that it took me a moment to remember why I had no scar there.

The memories included my development and sale of "DynaPaste" and the visit home to learn that my mother had "killed" me, all in order to not have to talk about me with her neighbors. They also brought with them the recollection of how to blast. And how to fly.

That night, I tested that memory. High in the air, away from the noise of the city, I could think without distraction. Flying without a destination, I was surprised to find myself across the Golden Gate. Such an iconic structure, and the one most identified with this city. It wasn't hard to see why.

I landed on the pedestrian walkway, inside the security gates, which were locked at this hour. It was about a mile and a half across, and I was in no rush.

I unslung the small backpack I'd brought and pulled out my shoes. I'd remembered enough to know that I had so many shoes because I liked shoes, not because I'd destroy them when I took to the sky.

My thoughts were all over the place as I walked the bridge. Naturally, I was still absorbing the previous night's influx of memories. With each restoration, I came to see people more fully. They weren't just names in a journal, anymore.

And of course, neither were the events. Now they were real experiences, real emotions, inside me. Now I could see and feel what the words described.

I still had more than two years of memories to come, and I knew some of them would be painful. I was especially eager to recover the memories of the final months. From what others have said, she... *I*... wasn't thinking too clearly, then. I couldn't help but wonder if, once I was "current," I'd think differently about the last visit to Dynasonic's world. I wondered if I'd make some connections I hadn't, then. And I wondered how soon I could go back there.

In twenty-four hours, according to Dana, I'd have all my memories, with the exception, of course, of dying. The journals chronicled the events of those few years, and I knew it would be a hard day. They were all hard, in one way or another, just as they were all good. But this batch would include more bad than good, if I remembered the journals accurately.

Before I knew it, I was nearly the whole way across the bridge. I shook my thoughts back to the present. Then I flew home and landed on the roof deck. I entered, descending the stairs to my room. "Getting a late start, tonight," Dana said, rising from the bed.

"Yeah," I said. "Sorry." I felt bad, because I knew every night was worse than the last for him. There were so many more connections he had to make for every memory. It was like building a database, he told me. The more categories, the more relationships had to be made between items. My only response to that was to ask when the hell he'd ever built a database.

"Everything okay?" he asked. I nodded as I headed toward the bathroom. "Not the most convincing nod I've seen," he said.

"Just a lot to think about, y'know?"

"Yeah," he said. "I imagine so."

I entered the bathroom, washed up, changed into my nightshirt, and returned to the bedroom.

"You look nervous," he said as I crawled into bed and pulled up the blankets.

"Yeah, well... tomorrow is the defining day."

"You're worried that it won't feel right?"

"Maybe," I said as he settled in.

I felt myself growing weary. Dana's doing. "Well," he said. "I'll try to do an especially good job tonight."

I smiled. "You better."

Morning came, and with it the fresh bloom of memories I'd grown used to. It took me until three in the afternoon to assimilate enough to function. But Dana had finished it. I was "current."

I'd gone through Rachel's kidnapping and final encounter with Hellion, followed shortly by my own capture by the otherworld Valora, and my escape, which killed Dr. Gray.

It was clear, now, that this messed me up more than I'd realized. It haunted me during the years that followed, through joining the Gatekeepers, the debacle of falling for a straight girl, the establishment of the mind-link with Dana, my near-fatal illness, the second exchange with my other-self that ultimately led to her sacrifice, meeting Dynasonic, the U.K. trip to get Vicky back, Transcendant's death, Macy's stalker, leaving the Gatekeepers, forming the Pariah Project, and so much more.

My last memory before waking up in the Gatekeeper's med-bay was of being out with the gang on my birthday. I remembered the beginning sensations of runaway: the heat, the needle-like stabbings over my entire body, and the feeling that everything inside me was coming loose. I remembered running away from the others and taking to the air over the water. Most of all, I remembered panic, the awareness that this was *it*. This was the *end* of me.

And that was all.

Just reviewing the memory made my heart race. It took a while to clear it from my head. But throughout the rest of the day, which I spent at home, it would rush back, unbidden. I'd tense up and hold my breath until I could shake it.

Unsurprisingly, these bad memories made it difficult to focus on the good ones, like the unexpectedly decent visit with my parents or seeing

Sharon and Jackie again. But most upsetting was that it wasn't as satisfying to be "complete" as I'd hoped.

I didn't do much of anything that day other than allow it all to sink in. I checked in on Dana and watched him sleep for a while. I owed him for this, so much more than I could ever repay.

But it wasn't quite over. That night was for "tidying up." Dana spent the evening putting strays into place, fixing missed connections, and whatnot. He did some of this at the end of every session, but this was the "deep cleaning" on top of the casual dusting and vacuuming. I woke around quarter of six the next morning, relieved that I didn't have a deluge of new memories to assimilate. What I did have, though, was the feeling of being less scattered. Whether this was from Dana's "tidying up" or just having another day to process everything, I didn't know. But I felt better than I had the day before.

I got out of bed and dressed quickly, before descending to the kitchen. To my surprise, Dana was awake, waiting for me. We sat over tea and talked, mostly of how everything had gone better than we had any right to expect. And I thanked him again for agreeing to it.

"I know you struggled with it," I said.

"Well," he said, "I wasn't ready to lose you any more than you were ready to die."

"Even so," I said, "I couldn't have done this without you."

"Oh, I know. I'll collect my payment later." He smiled, but it seemed forced.

"What is it?" I asked.

His smile faded. "I just had a phone call with the parental units."

"Oh, shit," I said. "How'd that go? Or don't I want to know?"

"About as well as you'd expect. Word of your death had gotten to them. That's your fault, by the way."

"*My* fault? How?"

"Hey, you're the one who went home and patched things up. After that, they actually started paying attention to news about metas. They even got a subscription to *Supers*."

"You're joking."

He shook his head. "Nope. So they were pissed at me for not contacting them after you blew up."

"So you had to tell them you were in a coma."

Dana frowned at me, staring at my forehead. "I clearly missed some connections in there. Do you not remember our parents?"

I laughed. "Okay, so what *did* you tell them?"

"I told them that reports of your death were, as the saying goes, greatly exaggerated. I said you had been in the hospital, but were now fine."

"But all that was months ago. Aren't they used to hearing from you at least every week?"

"I told them I was out of the country again, visiting Bronwyn. They seemed to buy that."

"You're lucky they're Luddites. Otherwise you'd have a hundred emails waiting for you."

"Well, I had a slew of voicemails on my phone," he said. "Anyway, I had to promise to visit as soon as possible. And to bring you with me."

"You didn't."

"I didn't commit us to a particular date or anything. But you better start thinking of how to explain to them why you look fifteen years younger."

"Surely, they must be senile enough by now not to notice." I paused as Dana chuckled. "Speaking of Bronwyn, what did you tell her?"

"Ah... well, I told her the truth. Or part of it, anyway. I mentioned being in a coma, but not the cause of it."

"She must have been freaked after not hearing from you for so long."

"Oh, yeah. She thought I'd lost interest." He smiled sadly. "Anyway, I'm headed to bed."

"Sleep well," I said as he left.

I thought about going back to sleep, but there was something I'd been wanting to do for the past day. I headed up to the deck and took off. The sun was not quite up as I flew to Kirby Cove. I'd been here with Jasmine before Dana worked his mental magic on me, but now it was different. Before, I'd only had the journals. Now, I had memories of the woman, including being present for her death. I swooped down and landed at the western end of the beach.

It wasn't difficult to find the stone marker, even in the low light. It was cleared of all brush, which looked to have been done recently. There were the remains of some flowers in a tiny vase buried in the dirt next to the stone.

Then I remembered that the anniversary of her death was just over a month past, the day I first spoke with Sinta at length. I understood now that she'd wanted to talk to me that day *because* it was the anniversary. Not to take her mind off of it, but because she needed a Dyna around. Even a broken and unfinished one.

I stayed there for several minutes, paying my respects more sincerely than I had in the past, and regretting that I'd been so closed-minded about her when she was alive.

After a time, I blasted into the sky again. Minutes later, I knocked on the door to Sinta's apartment. It was only about seven, and judging by the squinty eyes and yawning, I'd woken her. She stood in the doorway, her Team Dyna shirt hanging nearly to her knees, looking up at me in surprise.

I knelt down and hugged her, squeezing her against me. Sinta hesitated, but returned the hug. Before letting go, I whispered, "I love you, kitten." Then I smiled and told her to go back to bed, leaving her standing in the doorway, probably still confused.

Throughout this entire week, I hadn't been in communication with anyone in the Project. I didn't want to be expected to give daily updates to anyone, even Jasmine.

To make my reintegration easier on everyone, she and Sinta threw together an *ad hoc* "Welcome Back" party at the Project HQ. Over the course of the day, the entire team appeared, but I spent most of the time with the non-Project folks. Some of the Gatekeepers came, for example. It was great to see Lumen, Speed Freak, Miss Fire, and Starburst. "You simply *must* tell me who your plastic surgeon is," Miss Fire said in her Georgia accent. She was one of the Gatekeepers I didn't know very well. She was a tall, busty woman with flaming red hair in a long perm.

"It's all natural, hon," I said with a smile. In response, she just rolled her eyes, grinning as she moved on.

I greeted others just as casually, but it was Invictus I cornered. After pleasantries, I asked point-blank, "Why did you never agree to see me before I regained my memories?"

To my surprise, the big man's face displayed inner conflict. He was quiet a moment, then said, "I remember seeing you in our medical bay. You were all fresh and new. Different-looking. Not the woman I'd become friends with. Jasmine informed me of what all had taken place, stressing that we didn't yet know what would happen with you."

"Okay," I said. "But others dealt with that and still acted okay."

He gave a half smile. "Dyna, I may be able to lift a truck, but when it comes to that sort of thing, I'm pretty weak." He looked me in the eye, then said, "It was just too uncomfortable for me. I knew I couldn't pretend, as Jasmine said we needed to when talking with you."

I smirked, then gave him a chuck under the chin. "Aww, ya big softie."

"Of course," he said with a small smile. "Why do you think I wear armor?" He smiled as I chuckled, then he said, "What are you telling people? Not the full truth, I assume."

"It's funny," I said. "So far, no one has asked."

"I asked the team not to," he said. "They all understood."

"Thanks for that," I said.

We chatted for a few more minutes before I moved on.

Daniel and Ping Song were there, and Dana invited The Golden Bear down from Sacramento. Marcus wrapped me in a bear hug, since he doesn't know how to give any other kind. He had a ton of questions and, as he was one of those I trusted, he got the full story.

Somehow, the Maltese Falcon heard of the event and made a brief appearance, in time to hear me relating the story. It was odd, watching him interact with other metas. He just seemed out of place. But I was honored that he'd come. I owed him a lot for introducing me to Daniel.

Non-metas were there, too, including Dr. Stone, Nurse Alex, Jeremy, and Captain Shepherd. This was the first time any of these people had interacted with the "new and improved" me. It was as wonderful as I'd hoped and as awkward as I'd expected. None of them particularly knew how to act around me. Some, in fact, kept interaction to a minimum.

Most of the interactions were okay, especially with those I didn't see often. Most of the awkwardness, perhaps unsurprisingly, came with those to whom I'd been closest. Not Jasmine, so much, because of the great deal of time we'd spent together over the past couple months. It was a bit strained with Jack, but I imagine it would have been worse if he'd still been as infatuated with me as he once was. Sinta wasn't so bad. I knew she'd adapt pretty well. It was a defining characteristic of her personality.

The worst was with Vicky. We went up to the deck, away from the crowd, to speak privately. We stood there, leaning against the low wall and staring over the buildings, for at least a minute. "So," I finally said, "is this too uncomfortable for you?"

She shook her head, but didn't look at me. "I'll manage," she said. Then, after a pause, "It's just bloody weird, y'know?"

"Believe me, I do."

Now she looked at me. "Don't misunderstand. It's wonderful to have you 'back,' so to speak."

"But...?"

Vicky turned her gaze to the deck. "But I don't know if... I mean, I had to accept that you were..."

"Yeah," I said, reaching out to clasp her hand. "I hope you can get past that."

Vicky looked at my hand. I knew it felt differently in her grip than my "old" hand did. Softer, for one thing. "I hope so, too," she said, then squeezed before letting go and turning to look again out across the rooftops. "Of course, it doesn't help that now you look younger than I do."

"You're saying you have a thing for older women?"

I caught the slight smirk as she said, "Don't judge me."

We laughed together, breaking some of the tension. I had to appreciate the irony. I'd always been the hesitant one when it came to relationships. And now that I was eager to resume one, it was the other person who needed time. We stayed on the rooftop for another few minutes before returning to the kitchen, where most of the partygoers were.

Not long thereafter, Jasmine escorted Macy down the stairs. She was clearly anxious about seeing me. I stepped forward and scooped her up in a hug.

"It's great to see you, Mace," I said.

As I put her down, she looked at me with wide eyes. "What's with your hair?" was the first thing she said. "It's not white."

"Neither is yours," I said, causing her to roll her eyes.

"And you look different. Sound different, too." She said this with a frown.

"I know. Can't do anything about that, I'm afraid. But it's really me."

She smiled awkwardly, and I could tell she wasn't sure if she should believe me or not. "So... is the hair gonna stay that color?"

"I don't think so," I said. "The roots are pale, as you can see. And since it grows so quickly, it won't be long before the old lady jokes start again."

Macy chuckled and asked, "What causes it?"

"As best I've ever determined, the energy in my body is somehow disrupting the ability of my hair follicles to produce melanin."

Macy nodded, but still seemed uncomfortable. I guided her in the direction of refreshments and we loaded up plates with goodies and grabbed a couple bottles of root beer.

"Tell me how you're doing," I said as I twisted off the caps.

"Good," she said, taking a bottle from me.

"Counseling going well?"

"Yeah. I mean, I still have bad dreams sometimes, but I'm a lot better than before."

"Glad to hear that," I said. We stood drinking in silence for a minute, as I searched for a way to ease her anxiety. "How was Hawaii, by the way?"

"Nice," she said. "Very pretty."

I frowned. "That's all you've got to say about it? What did you do there?"

She shrugged. "Well, we went snorkeling. That was cool."

"Pictures?"

"Oh, sure. Uploaded a bunch to Facebook."

"I'll have to take a look," I said. "Glad you had a 'nice' time. And tell your parents hello for me, please."

"I will."

"How goes the revamp of your website?"

"Good, but *your* website, you mean."

"You created it. You maintain it. I consider it your website that happens to be about me."

"You should blog," she said, nodding. "Make it more your site, then."

"Blog," I said. "You're joking."

"People will love it!"

"I dunno, Mace."

"Oh, shut up. You know I'm right." She smiled, and I was relieved that she was easing up.

"Yes, boss."

She asked for a tour of the building, since it was her first time there. I obliged, playing tour guide with as much humor as I could. Ultimately, we ended up on the rooftop deck, by which point she was in good spirits.

"This is a really cool building," she said, her chest up against the wall, looking out over the neighborhood.

"I fell in love with it at first sight," I said.

Macy frowned slightly and looked sideways up at me. "What's it like?" she said. "The memories, I mean."

"They're just... you know... memories."

She was quiet for a minute, then said, "I really missed you." Then she punched me in the arm. "Don't do that again, okay?"

I smirked. "I won't if you won't."

Macy rolled her eyes again. "So, hey... when will you be letting the world know that you're not dead?"

"Does the world even care?"

"Are you kidding? Of course!"

"As far as I'm concerned, the people who need to know already do. I don't need some grand announcement."

Macy was quiet for a moment, then said, "You should let *Supers* know, at least. They did a nice memorial feature on you."

"I'll think about it," I said. "Now let's head back downstairs. I need another root beer."

As I prepared for bed that night, I reflected on the party. It was interesting to me how I looked upon my friends and teammates with fresh perspective due to my untimely demise and unlikely rebirth.

Things seemed clearer to me, now, but in a way I wasn't sure I could identify. I felt as though I was seeing the bigger picture, rather than my old, somewhat tunneled view.

I thought, too, about Macy's suggestion. It didn't particularly matter to me whether readers of *Supers* magazine knew I was alive or not, but the girl had a point. The magazine itself had always been good to me. I could call the editor-in-chief, but that would only raise questions. What happened? Why do you look different? Will you give us an exclusive?

I didn't look forward to those questions, but the ones from my parents would be even worse. Would they even be able to accept the cloned me as their daughter? The party gave hints that this acceptance might not even be something I could take for granted with some of my teammates. With my conservative parents, I expected the odds were pretty heavily against me.

But then, when have the odds ever *not* been?

ELEVEN

"The more things change, the more they stay the same."
~ Jean-Baptiste Alphonse Karr

I'm not truly OCD, but I do have some areas where my behavior could be interpreted that way. I'm what you might call a "completist." If I discover a band I like, for example, I feel compelled to own every album they ever put out. And even if I end up thinking any of them are terrible, I'll still keep them, just so I can say I've got the whole set, as though that were somehow important. And if one I don't like happens to get damaged or lost... yes, I'll buy another copy.

Dana once explained that this is likely due to my attachment issues. Because my childhood was tainted by the lack of love from my mother, and a father with a decidedly hands-off approach to parenting, my subconscious tries to make things "whole" to compensate for the fact that my family wasn't. I suppose there could be something to that. But in the end, it doesn't matter what the reasons are. All I know is that it makes me keep several CDs that I will almost certainly never listen to again.

But I suppose this trait has a positive side, too. It causes me to do everything I can to make things work, to keep things together. Including relationships.

I woke the next morning with Macy's words in my head. She was right, of course. I needed to let the world know I was alive. I didn't feel ready to make those phone calls, mainly because I didn't know what I was going to say. But I had a good reason to make at least one call today. Taking a deep breath, I dialed the number to my childhood home.

My mother answered and I said, "Happy Mother's Day!"

There was a pause and perhaps a gasp. "*Dinah*?"

"Yeah, it's me."

To my shock, she began sobbing. "The magazine said you were dead!"

"Clearly not," I said. "I didn't even know about that until recently."

"They put out a memorial edition!"

"Um, yeah. I saw that."

"But what *happened*?"

My mind raced, then grasped at something. It had worked once, why not twice? "It was nothing, Mom. I was deep undercover on an assignment and was injured. Was in the hospital a while, then was a recluse for even longer. I wasn't checking voicemail or anything. I'm sorry you were so worried. How's Dad?" I said, before she could continue her line of questioning.

"Oh, you know your father," she said. "He never changes." She hesitated, then said, "You need to let us know when you're doing that undercover thing! We were worried!"

"I'm sorry about that. In the future, I'll make sure to have one of my teammates get in touch with you, if needed."

With a little further placation, she accepted this. We chatted about general things back home for several minutes, until I hinted that I needed to go. "Now, you and your brother are coming home for Christmas this year," she said. "I won't take no for an answer."

"All right," I said. That gave me seven months to figure a way out of it. "But now I've gotta go. We have a team meeting today and I need to get ready for it."

We hung up and I let out a breath. It had gone better than expected, but I didn't have the nerve to call anyone else. Besides, I wasn't lying about the meeting.

Hours later, I sat at the conference table on the main floor, waiting for the others, feeling nervous and out of place.

Jack and Sinta were the first to arrive. I greeted them as they sat, and we chatted idly while we waited. Jack tried not to stare, but I could feel his eyes on me. Fitting, since this was one reason why I'd called the meeting. I made a point to "catch" him more than once, so that he'd focus on what Sinta was saying to him.

Eventually, everyone was present and seated around the conference table, looking at me expectantly. I took a deep breath. "Well. Now we've proven that we can, in fact, hold twelve people around our table." The others waited politely. I'd hoped for at least a chuckle to break the tension.

"Anyway," I continued, "there are three reasons for this meeting. The first is because..." I hesitated, still unsure how to put it. "...because some of you are still pretty freaked out. So let's talk about it."

There was an awkward silence as my teammates avoided my gaze and glanced at one another. Sinta was frowning. "Dyna, nobody's freaked out."

I smiled softly at her. "I have always loved your unfailing optimism," I said, "but I don't think I'm mistaken." Before anyone could confirm or deny, I continued. "When I was seven years old, there was this baby born in England. Her birth caused quite a stir. Well, not her birth, exactly, but rather, her conception. Because she was the first child born who'd been conceived via in-vitro fertilization."

The younger members looked at me with raised eyebrows. It was Nena who spoke up. "What's the big deal about that?"

"Today, nothing," I said. "It's a quite common method of conception. But the reaction to that first one was crazy. Being the very first such birth, it was all over the news. She was born in the summer, and I remember talking about it with my classmates when school started up again. Being kids, of course, we were mainly parroting whatever our parents were saying about it. And in almost all cases, in that small town, what our parents said about it leaned negative. That it was an affront to God. That such babies wouldn't be "normal" in some way or another. And so on. As you say, Nena, it's not a big deal, today. But, at the time, the general reception of it was an uproar. Even today, you'll find some people who find it to be wrong."

Kit spoke up. "I had a friend in high school who was an IVF kid. He said one of his classmates in elementary school told him that it meant he didn't have a father. Another said he should be 'tested' for abnormalities." He shook his head. "And more than one told him it meant he didn't have a soul and would never go to heaven."

As the others absorbed this, I said, "I bring this up because it's important that you understand that what I've done is *way* more extreme than in-vitro fertilization. As far as we know, I am the world's first human clone. The reaction to that child's birth in 1978 would be nothing compared to the chaos that would occur if news of my cloning success got out."

"I don't know," Lily said. "I mean, it's a really different society now than it was in the seventies. We're way more accepting of many things that would have freaked people out back then. Sure, some will get their panties in a bunch at first, but in a week or two, it'll pass. They'll turn their attention to whatever offensive thing is trending in social media that week."

Jack spoke up, next. "Lily may be right about the public, but not about the scientific community. Some of you remember how it was when it was revealed that Dyna was the first 'self-made' meta."

I interrupted him. "And that would have been much worse if not for the fact that there are still so many out there who don't believe that's what I did."

"Right. And this would make that look like nothing, by comparison." Jack paused, then said, "Plus, there's also the legal aspect. Reproductive cloning is illegal."

"It is," I said. "But therapeutic cloning isn't, at least in California."

"But that's defined as creating an embryo for the purpose of retrieving embryonic stem cells," he said. "Implanting a cloned embryo into a uterus is illegal."

"Into a *woman's* uterus," I said. "I didn't do that."

"I don't know that the law will accept the distinction."

"Definitely a gray area," I agreed. "But so long as word doesn't get out, we'll never need to worry about it."

"Dyna," Kim said, "we metas are used to keeping secrets. You don't need to fear that any of us will reveal anything."

"I know, and I don't have that fear. I just felt it needed to be emphasized."

"Anyway," Jennifer said, "what's this got to do with us? Like Sinta said, none of us are freaked out."

I looked across the table at Caracara. The others followed my gaze, to see Cara shift in her seat, her eyes looking from one person to another. "*Je suis désolé*," she said, looking around the table. "But she is correct."

"But why?" Sinta said.

"Because of *son âme*," she said. "Her soul."

Sinta's jaw dropped. "But it's *Dyna*," she said.

"It's okay, kitten," I said. "Cara, I personally don't believe in the concept of a soul, so we're simply not going to agree on that one. But I'd hope that, unless you consider me some sort of abomination, you'll be able to accept me."

She frowned slightly and said, "It will be *difficile*."

"Why?" I asked, hoping I did so with a calm voice, despite the pang in my chest at her words.

"Memories alone do not make a person. You are not the woman we knew three months ago."

"None of us are," I said. "We all change from day to day, from moment to moment."

"*Oui*, changed by events of our lives, *growing* daily. But that is not my meaning," she said. Then she gestured at me. "Your body is all new and different."

"True," I said. "But almost every cell in our body dies and is replaced, at varying intervals. Red blood cells live about four months. Cells in our stomachs live less than a week. Epidermal skin cells, a couple/few weeks."

Cara shook her head. "But you were *détruit!* Destroyed! You did not heal. You grew a new body, completely. In a tank!"

"From my own existing cells," I pointed out.

"Even so... It is not the same. It is not natural."

I gestured toward Jack. "Last year, our friend here lost an arm." Jack looked at me with a raised eyebrow. "He's replaced it with a robotic version. A few of them, in fact. Is he still Jack?"

"*Bien sûr*," Cara said.

"What if he were to lose his other arm? Both legs?"

"It would not matter," Cara said.

"It would kinda matter to *me*," Jack said, causing some chuckles.

"And let's say," I continued, "that, twenty years from now, his organs begin to fail. By then, we should be able to replace them with synthetically grown versions. Heart, lungs, liver, pancreas, and so on. Still Jack?"

She hesitated, before saying, "*Oui*." I could tell she knew where I was going with this.

"And let's say that he was in a terrible accident that damaged his head, forcing us to give him robotic eyes and a metal skull."

Cara frowned at me. "Still Jacques," she said.

"What if it were possible to take Jack's brain out of his head and transplant it into the recently deceased body of someone better looking?" Jack flipped me off, bringing more needed levity to the conversation. "Would he be Jack, or would he be the other person? Or a hybrid of the two?" Cara stayed silent, so I said, "The brain is just another organ. Far more complex than the others, yes, but still an organ. And if other synthetic organs are acceptable, then a synthetic brain must also be, provided all the memories are there." I let that sink in, then said, "Jack is our Ship of Theseus, our Tin Woodsman of Oz. No matter how much we chop off and replace, he is still the same person."

"*C'est vrai*," Cara said. "Pieces of the body do not matter. The soul is what matters. And that, you cannot replace."

"Let me ask you this, Cara, and I mean absolutely no disrespect. If the body is okay, and the memories are all the same, then what difference does it make – from the standpoint of our working relationship or even our friendship – whether I have the same soul, or whether I have one at all? Shouldn't you view that as something between me and God and, frankly, none of your business? Or do you, in fact, consider me an abomination? And if so, how do you differ from the many people in the world who would consider you yourself to be one? Or Kim or Sinta or Jennifer? Or *any* meta? When it comes right down to it, what makes your views different from those of the people who viewed an IVF baby as unnatural?"

The room was dead silent as everyone waited for Cara's reply. She stared at me alone, to avoid everyone's gaze. A long moment passed before she finally said, "God has chosen to express his creativity in many ways." She absently stroked one of her wings as she spoke. "You, however, are a creation not of God, but of your own vanity."

There were gasps and protests from some of the others and I admit her statement caught me off guard. But before I could say anything, there was a loud bang on the table. We all turned to see Bridget standing and staring at Cara, her fists clenched on the tabletop. "*Vanity*? Are you *kidding*?" she spat. "Is that what you think when we use advanced medicine to prevent people from dying?"

"It is not the same," Cara said.

"It's *exactly* the same!" Bridget shouted. "Do you know what a 'micropreemie' is?" When Cara shook her head, Bridget said, "It's what they call a baby born way, *way* early. A baby born at twenty-two weeks has a ninety percent chance of dying, even with the *best* medical care. There are a *ton* of medical problems these babies can have. Some of them life-long."

Bridget's skin had mottled and begun turning to its brick-like state as she ranted. Vicky reached out a hand and placed it on her cousin's arm. "Take a breath, love."

Bridget fought down the transformation, then turned back to Cara. "I was born at twenty-one weeks. I weighed nine and a half *ounces*. The *only* reason I'm here is because of the 'vanity' of doctors in cheating death. In any earlier time, it would have been considered 'God's will' for babies like me to die. Any attempts to prevent it would have been considered unnatural, an act *against* God. Even today, lots of doctors *won't even try* to save a baby born at less than twenty-three weeks. If my doctors had held to the 'against God' belief, I wouldn't be here." She continued staring at Cara, but pointed across the table at me. "Dyna just did the same thing. She prevented the loss of her *self* at all costs. That it required a new body is beside the point."

Bridget plopped back into her chair and silently fumed, while the rest of us sat in shock at her speech. Vicky tried to hide a proud smile, but mostly failed. Just about everyone else was, I knew, looking at Bridget with new admiration. I certainly was. Not to mention wondering what lasting problems she had due to her premature birth.

Cara had been quiet through Bridget's speech, and I was worried that she felt as though her beliefs were being challenged. Especially since they basically were.

"The skills of doctors and our advances in life-saving ability," Cara said softly, "are due to the grace of God. That we are able to prevent death in cases such as yours, Brigitte, is a wonderful thing. But this was not a case of preventing death. Dyna *did* die. And she *created* life, which is something only God should do."

Before I could point out the inaccuracy in her statement, Jack spoke up. "As Bridget said, not so terribly long ago, today's life-saving techniques would have been considered an affront to God. As would my mechanical arm. And while you view the physical extremes of some metas to be examples of divine creativity, you must admit that you would have been put to death, not so long ago, by the same church whose tenets you follow."

Cara frowned. "The understanding of God's word has changed over the centuries, it's true. But there is still a line we cannot cross."

"Oh, please," Nena sneered. "Ignoring the fact that divine words shouldn't be subject to various 'understandings,' there are *dozens* of lines your religion says we're not to cross, but people do, every single day. Eating pork or shellfish. Wearing cotton with wool. Working on the Sabbath. And on and on. Every one of those is considered a sin in the Bible."

"If I can say somethin'?" Jennifer interrupted. When she had everyone's attention, she said, "I grew up in Texas. Bein' the oversized buckle on the Bible Belt, there's a lot of religion. My folks, bein' more progressive than most, urged me to study different religions and make my own decisions. An' one of the things I learned is that the Bible doesn't explain what a soul actually is. An' there isn't even agreement among Christians about what it is, either."

"That's not true," Cara said.

"It absolutely is," Jennifer said. "One view is that humans don't *have* souls, but *are* souls, simply by virtue of bein' alive. Another view is that the soul an' body are the same thing, not separate. Meanin' that the soul is not immortal, but can and does die."

"No. The soul is immortal," Cara said flatly.

Jennifer shrugged, her bat wings rising with her shoulders. "So you believe. But lots of equally religious folks will disagree with you. An' even among those who believe as you do, some say the soul's immortality isn't automatic, but only comes through grace. In fact, if ya read what modern theologians have to say about it, consensus is that the Bible never refers to the soul bein' immortal at all. Heck, even within your Roman Catholic Church, there's disagreement about it."

That statement got Cara's attention. She frowned, but said nothing.

"You do know we're not attacking your beliefs, right?" I asked. Cara nodded, but didn't make eye contact. "There has always been, and always will be, disagreement within religions. If there weren't, there would only be one religion. Or at the very least, one version of each, instead of the multitude of sects and denominations we have. I mean, how many different Catholic churches are there? More than two dozen, if I'm not mistaken."

Cara was quiet for a long moment, then softly said, "I will... give more thought to this."

"Thank you," I said, relieved. "That means a lot to me."

Cara nodded again, still avoiding eye contact.

"Okay," I said. "So the second reason for this meeting..."

"Hang on," Lily said. "While we're on this whole cloning thing, there's something I've been wondering. If you'd found a way to stop the runaway, what were you gonna do with the clone?"

Everyone looked at me in anticipation. I'd wondered the same thing, at one point. "In that event, I would have stopped the accelerated growth of the clone and allowed it to be 'born.' Dana would have adjusted her memories to whatever physical age she appeared to be. But from that point on, she would have her own life. And I'd basically have a little sister."

"Really?" Lily said. "That would have been... kinda cool, actually."

"And I'd have *another* Dyna!" Sinta said.

I smiled at Sinta's excitement as others chuckled. After a long silence, Kimera spoke up. "What's the second reason we're here, Dyna?"

"Right," I said, after the others quieted, then nodded to Jasmine, turning the meeting over to her.

Jasmine stood and addressed the team. "As you all know, we've been trying to determine the point of origin of the energy weapons that Arsenal brought to our attention. We suspect these weapons are not being manufactured here, but are coming to us from yet another parallel world through a third portal located off the coast of Southern California on one of the Channel Islands."

"*Wau*," said Kimera. "*Third* portal? Did I miss the memo about a *second* portal?"

Jasmine looked at me with a tiny, you-should-have-told-everyone smirk. I took a breath and explained to them about how Ping Song had discovered the portal over the Bay with a device she'd invented, and that I'd been through it a few times. I told them about Dynasonic, though I didn't go into detail about her world.

Naturally, there were reactions of surprise and questions of why they hadn't been told of this before. Jasmine waved them off. "Dyna and I were able to convince Ping Song to loan the device to Arsenal and show her how to use it, hoping she'd be able to discover another portal in the area where she believes the weapons are coming from. Last night, she contacted me to confirm that this is, in fact, the case. Another portal exists on San Nicolas Island."

The others were obviously concerned by this bit of information. Then I proceeded to make it worse. I related to them my last visit to Dynasonic's world, in which I encountered a Weatherford and received a warning from that world's version of my brother. "I'm convinced, though, that the man I saw wasn't from that world, but was, in fact, Vicky's father."

"Whoa, what?" Jack said, looking between me and a somber Vicky. I explained how the man seemed to recognize me and how the Dyna of that world doesn't look a lot like me.

"That's not much to go on," Kit said.

Vicky spoke up. "I went there, myself, to do some research." And she told them what she'd told Bloodmoon and me before, that there were no search results for either her or her father.

Jack cleared his throat. "If it is the same Weatherford, that adds a disturbing context to things we've dealt with." He frowned as the group gave him their attention. "We were told that the Jack Fullerton from that first world created the energy weapons. But what we don't know is whether it was his idea or if someone suggested it to him. I only mention this because the idea of creating such a device never crossed my mind before I met him. I don't know that it would have occurred to him, either, without outside influence."

"It also could mean that the idea of invading our world might have been suggested to that world's Valora. That she wasn't the mastermind behind it, after all."

"Further complicating matters in our own world," Jasmine continued, "is the fact that San Nicolas Island is under the control of the Navy. It's a weapons testing and training facility."

"Are you suggesting that our government is part of this?" Jack said.

Jasmine frowned. "No, but if they're not, then this is taking place right under the Navy's nose. My reason for mentioning it is just to point out that the island has no public access. Reaching this portal won't be remotely easy."

"Unlike the portal in Area 51," I said, "we can't count on Captain Shepherd for help with this. Although I will, of course, inform him of it." As the rest of the team looked at each other and muttered their misgivings, I said, "On the other hand, maybe we won't have to access that portal at all." All eyes turned to me, so I said, "Arsenal said the weapons aren't actually entering the population here, right?"

"Not that she's seen," Jasmine said. "Our assumption is that they are being stockpiled for some reason."

"And where did she say was the last place they could be traced to?"

"Oakland."

"That's more than a little coincidental," I said. "The weapons that came through a few years ago also ended up at a shop in Oakland. Worth paying it a visit."

"Okay," Jasmine said. "But what are you thinking?"

"You could be right about them being stockpiled," I said. "But I find it suspicious that they're coming in way down south, but ending up here – near a portal into Dynasonic's world – where I saw Weatherford."

"If there were more of them, I'd consider the possibility that it was being used as a staging area," Jasmine said, "as preparation for an incursion into that world."

"But at the rate they're coming in," I said, "it would take a hell of a long time to amass enough for that sort of thing."

Jasmine nodded in agreement, but no other ideas were forthcoming.

"Final agenda item," I said. "The Project has been selected to test a prototype of a potentially life-saving device." From my bag, I produced what looked like a large hypodermic, a bit over an inch in diameter and close to five inches long. It had no needle, but the end was scored to break open when the plunger was depressed. Through the clear plastic housing, we could see that it was filled with what appeared to be several dozen white tablets. I sat it upright on the table.

Eyes widened around the table. "Wow, Dyna. That's hardly appropriate," Jack said, causing chuckles from the others.

I sighed. "Go ahead. Get all the dildo jokes out of your systems." I sent others around the table, enough for everyone, then waited for the laughter to stop before continuing. "Several teams around the country were chosen to field test these."

"Uh... that seems even more inappropriate," Lily said with a smirk, eliciting more sniggers.

"Yeah, yeah," I said. "Trust me, you don't want to use these in that fashion." I asked Jasmine to explain.

She pointed at the plunger. "This is a hemostatic device designed to stop bleeding in gunshot wounds. These small tablets are actually highly compressed sponges. They have an absorbent coating that contains a coagulant. Shove the cylinder into the wound and inject the sponges. Within twenty seconds or so, they'll expand, soaking up blood and applying internal pressure These, along with the coagulant, should stop the bleeding until the victim reaches the hospital."

"So, not a dildo, but a huge tampon applicator," Nena said, bringing yet another dose of laughter.

I said, "Actually, I've heard of using tampons for similar purposes. With mixed results."

Jasmine continued. "Tampons really aren't big enough for many gunshot wounds. Plus, they're designed to soak up more than just blood. These will be much more effective. Now, severe or especially large gunshot wounds may require more than one application. Each of our crisis kits will be stocked with these. Anyone on patrol should carry a couple with them, too. If and when any are used, we're to fill out a questionnaire, which will go back to the manufacturer."

As there were no follow-up questions, we adjourned. The others filed out, but Cara remained, still obviously deep in thought. I walked over to her as she stood to leave. She avoided looking at me, but I impulsively gave her a hug. "Take all the time you need," I said, then headed upstairs.

"Okay," Dana said as he joined me on the deck after the others had left, "what's wrong?"

I stared out over the neighborhood. "That's what I've been trying to figure out. Although right now, it's that I'm feeling more than a little bit like a hypocrite."

"Why's that?" he said, standing next to me.

I was quiet for a moment, then looked up at my brother. "I essentially just lectured Cara on why she was wrong to feel that I'm not really 'me.' But is Cara right? Did I do something I shouldn't have?"

"Dinah..."

"I don't mean for religious reasons, of course, but..."

"Then why are you questioning it?"

"I don't know," I admitted. "I meant everything I said to her, but the truth is that I still don't feel quite right."

Dana frowned "Your memories should be intact, Dinah. I was quite thorough. But if you think I missed something..."

"I don't think it has anything to do with memories. I can't define it. I just feel... incomplete."

"That's a little ironic, since, if anything, you're more complete than you were before."

"Physically, I suppose," I said. "But this isn't a physical thing. I think..." I hesitated, because I knew the effect my words were going to have. "I think what's missing is our telepathic link." I could literally feel my brother stiffen as he stood next to me. "I know," I said. "I know you were never comfortable with it, so it's just something I'm going to have to get used to."

"Are you certain that's what it is?"

"No, I'm not, but it's the one thing I can definitely say is missing from before. Whether that's the entirety of it, I have no idea."

Dana didn't respond to that. We stood looking out over the neighborhood for a minute, enjoying the afternoon breeze. Then I playfully bumped my hip against him. "I don't suppose you'd want to–"

"Dinah..."

"Wow," I said. "Was it that bad for you?" He turned to face me, a horde of emotions competing for the right to show on his face. I laughed and elbowed him in the ribs. "Let's get pizza."

Exasperation won the facial battle. "Sure," he said.

One thing definitely not missing was how much I loved messing with him.

Arsenal contacted us the next day and told us she'd received another small shipment of the energy weapons. We confirmed that a courier would deliver them that same day to the same shop in Oakland where I'd paid a visit more than three years earlier.

So I was waiting atop a roof next-door as the courier arrived in a small U-Haul truck, pulling up in an alley at the rear of the shop. He rang a bell at the back door, then lifted the gate of the truck. The door soon opened and a man came outside with a manual forklift to transfer the heavy crate to the shop's stockroom. I smiled to myself as I saw the tattoo on the man's arm: Animal from the Muppet Show. This was the same loser I'd dealt with before.

I hopped down from the roof and waited for the courier to depart. Once he drove off, I rang the bell at the back door. Animal soon opened it, obviously surprised to see me. He looked around, probably for the courier who'd just left.

"Wrong door, lady."

"I don't think so," I said, easily pushing him back inside.

"Hey!" he said. "Get the hell out of here!"

I removed my sunglasses and hung them from my bullet necklace chain. "Look," I said. "I may not be in as big of a rush as the last time I bitch-slapped you, but I'm willing to do it again, just for fun." As he squinted at me in confusion, I smiled sweetly. "I know," I said in a light, matter-of-fact tone, "I was older then, with white hair. And you shot me. Let's not go through all that again, okay? Especially since you don't have a super-strong Valora to sic on me, this time."

Realization finally dawned on him and he held up his hands in front of him. "Look, I'm a legit dealer. Everything on the up and up."

"Not with this crate sitting here, you're not."

He blinked in surprise. "Honest, I don't even know what's inside. I swear. I don't know what I don't know, you know? I like it that way. That whole thing with that Valora freak..." He shook his head. "Never again."

"Whatever," I said. "I'm not here to bust you. I'm just interested in these," I said, gently kicking the crate.

"Look," he said, with a resigned sigh. "I can't tell you much."

"How many more do you have?"

"Just these, I swear."

"You're not stockpiling them?"

"I just hold 'em for a few hours until another courier comes to get 'em. Where they go after that, I dunno. And I don't care."

"Who does the other courier work for?"

"I don't ask. I'm just a drop point. I get a couple hundred bucks for every crate that comes through here. All I gotta do is take 'em from one and give 'em to another. Nothin' else. Easy money."

"Right. So when will they get picked up?"

The Animal lover hesitated. "Dunno."

"Sure you do."

"Not tellin' you, even if I do," he said, puffing himself up.

"That's fine. I can hang for a while." I nearly laughed at the look on his face. "If I'm right about who's behind this, he'll know you received delivery today, and he'll pick them up as soon as possible. Which means today, sometime. And since you close in about three hours, it's not that long of a wait." His expression told me I was right.

I pulled out my cell phone and hit the speed dial for the Project HQ. When Jasmine answered, I said, "Delivery made. Will be picked up within the next few hours." I tucked the phone back into my pocket. "One of my colleagues will be following the other courier. Enjoy your extra pocket money while you can, because that revenue stream is about to dry up."

He sighed, deflated. "Yeah. Okay."

I knelt down and easily tilted the crate up to reveal the bottom, smiling to myself at his shock. The thing easily weighed two hundred pounds. I'm not remotely considered among the strongest in the meta community, but I'm certainly above average, and far beyond what my appearance would imply.

I pulled a tiny tracking device from my pocket and jammed it between the wooden slats on the bottom. I lowered the crate to the floor again and verified that it showed on my phone. Then I said, "It would be a shame for you if the courier was somehow alerted to the fact that this shipment is being tracked."

"I don't know nothin' about no tracking," he said as I walked him out to the sales floor. "What'd you mean you were 'older' last time?"

I ignored his question and joined him behind the counter, taking a seat next to him. "So," I said, "got a deck of cards around here?"

The second courier arrived right at closing time. To his credit, Animal said not a word. He got his pay and the crate went on its way. Outside, Resonator tracked the shipment to a self-storage facility about a mile away. And there it stayed, until three in the morning, when my phone beeped me awake.

I was up and ready in seconds. Grabbing a satchel I'd prepared with a change of clothes, toiletries, and a few other things, I dashed upstairs to the deck, alerting Jasmine by comm as I took to the air.

I followed the blip on the tracking application as it moved toward the bay. Minutes later, my suspicions were confirmed, as I spotted a figure in the distance rising into the sky. I flew far enough below that I was unlikely to be noticed. And sure enough, the person was headed straight up to where I knew the portal to Dynasonic's world to be.

The figure was clearly a telekinetic, given that the crate floated nearby, but I didn't recognize the energy signature of whichever meta it was, and this bothered me. I thought I knew all the telekinetics in the city, given how many of them we'd needed the previous year in our attack on Neukölln. Before becoming a meta, myself, I'd gorged myself on information about them. But in the years since, I'd not had time to maintain such a base of knowledge. Or possibly, my memories weren't restored as fully as Dana believed.

The thought of the attack on Neukölln caused a twinge inside me, a reminder that another "me" had sacrificed herself on my behalf.

The flight to the portal was long, since this meta's movement rate was slower than my own, and the portal was about three miles up. But we eventually made it. I watched as the figure and the crate disappeared. I spoke into my comm. "Okay, they're through. I'm headed in." Jasmine acknowledged and I blasted up and through the portal.

On the other side, I descended behind the meta-courier's line of sight as he or she dropped toward the city. Interestingly, the final destination was this world's corresponding storage unit in Oakland. I watched covertly as the crate was placed in storage and the telekinetic took off for the portal back to our world.

Since it was still only about four in the morning, I found a hotel nearby. I pulled some of this world's cash from my bag and paid for the night.

After a few hours of sleep, I checked out of the hotel, then called Dynasonic on the pre-paid phone she'd given me. She answered quickly. "Hi," I said. "It's me."

There was a pause on the other end. "Holy shit," she said. "Given the way you talked last time, and how long it's been, I didn't expect to hear from you again."

"Yeah. I'm a bit surprised, too."

"What's with your voice? You sound different."

"I'll fill you in on that. Can we meet?"

"Yeah. Come on over. I was just about to make breakfast."

"Wonderful," I said. "See you soon."

I flew across the bay, and soon was ringing the bell to her front door. When she answered and looked me over, the confusion on her face was obvious. We sat in front of the fireplace as I explained once again what had happened over the past several months.

She stared at my face for a minute after I finished explaining. I couldn't blame her. I knew I looked and sounded different. Finally, she spoke. "Cloning," she said flatly.

"Yeah."

"I can't..." She fell silent again, staring, until she let out a chuckle. She shook her head. "And you think *I'm* the one who leads an amazing life."

"Different category of amazing, altogether."

She stared again. "What's it feel like?"

"Being a clone?" I asked. "I feel the same as I remember feeling." I paused. "Well, no, that's not accurate. Honestly, I feel better. This body is physically much younger and healthier."

"I guess that makes sense," she said. "But... you're never going to know for sure that your brother's memory work is fully accurate, right?"

I tensed up. "True. But it's one of those situations where I'm just going to put my trust in him. He's never let me down, before."

"Anyway, you hungry?"

"Always," I said. "But... where's your kitchen? Your entire downstairs is a recording studio."

"Just up here," she said, and led me to the room that, in my building, was an office.

"Oh, wow," I said as I entered. "Love it!" The décor was classic fifties diner, complete with red and chrome chairs, black and white tiled floor, and retro signs for food and coffee.

"Thanks," she said. "I love old-style diners."

"Me, too," I admitted. "I'm sure that comes as such a surprise." She chuckled as she began making pancakes and eggs for us. "How's the new album doing?"

"Great! Our most popular, yet. It hit number two on *Billboard*. I have a copy for you. Don't let me forget."

"Thanks. And that's great to hear. Are you working on another?"

"We are," she said, pouring the pancake batter onto the griddle. "And it's pretty exciting. We're going to be working with the San Francisco Symphony for the recording. We're trying to secure them for the tour, too."

"Wow!" I said. "That would be awesome!"

"The album has a sort of twisted Alice in Wonderland theme. We're calling it *Wanderland*. Hoping to release it in about a year."

"Can't wait to hear it," I said. "You guys must have sold a lot of your other albums for you to be able to afford this place."

Dynasonic shrugged. "Up until *In the Clear*, we made more from our shows than record sales. We've always had a solid following here in California."

I remembered just how different this world was from mine in certain ways. "How much did this place cost, if you don't mind me asking?"

"I got it a few years ago for three hundred thousand," she said as she cracked eggs into a skillet. As my jaw dropped, she said, "You bought the same property in your world, right? How much did you pay?"

"A million five," I said flatly.

She turned to stare at me, eyes wide. "Oh, my god! Are you kidding?"

"Nope. In my world, San Francisco has crazy expensive real estate." Not for the first time, I wondered how this world could be so similar to mine in so many respects, but so different in others.

I remembered, from my initial visit, how our worlds had paralleled until the mid-40s. After World War II, the U.S. in this world pulled back from military endeavors, investing much of the military's previous tax allocation into education, infrastructure, and so on. I mentioned this to her as she flipped the pancakes.

"Yes," she said, "that was a turning point. Things started to change almost immediately, from what I understand. I've never known our society unlike how it is now, but my grandparents are old enough to remember what it was like before and during the transitional years."

"Are they still living?"

"My father's parents are. Both in their eighties, now. Mom's folks passed within the last few years."

When the food was ready, I carried our plates to the table. Dynasonic followed with a pot of coffee and mugs. I sat and immediately placed my sunny-side-up eggs on top of the stack of buttered pancakes before pouring syrup over it all. Dynasonic laughed and I looked up to see her staring at my plate. I laughed, too, when I saw she'd done exactly the same thing. We'd both broken the yolks, allowing the golden goodness to soak into the cakes.

As we ate, she got to the point of my questioning. "What you really want to know about is the telepath network, right?"

"Right," I said. "At what point did it become part of your society?"

She sipped at her coffee, frowning. "As best we can estimate, it began around twenty-five or thirty years ago."

"Do you know how it began?"

"Keep in mind, everything I know about it is just from word of mouth. There's never been any official explanation, so I can't swear to how accurate this is. As I heard it, it began here in San Francisco. The mayor at the time was allegedly told that it would make San Francisco the safest city on the planet. I have no idea what was said to make it a convincing argument, but I suspect it didn't involve telling the mayor that the population would be telepathically monitored."

"The Overseer is a telepath, too, isn't he?" I asked.

"Yeah. That's not common knowledge, however. For that matter, his very existence isn't common knowledge."

"Something I've been wondering," I said, wiping syrup from my lips, "is how much the public knows about the monitoring."

Dynasonic smiled mysteriously. "As I told you before, when a telepath is born, nearby telepaths know it. Don't ask me how. And once the ability manifests, that child is taken into service. Or maybe it's the power manifesting that alerts them. We don't really know for sure."

"How the hell is the public okay with this?" I asked.

"With the child conscription? Most people don't know about it."

"But how's that possible? It doesn't matter how powerful a telepath this guy is. People don't ask questions when the neighbors suddenly have one less child? Teachers don't notice?"

"There are all sorts of explanations given. They went to live with their grandparents. They transferred to a different school. Or other such things. And before you ask, people believe these excuses because there aren't a huge number of telepaths to begin with. No neighbor or teacher is likely to ever experience more than one instance of this happening. I mean, the only reason I know about it at all is because of my brother."

I let that soak into my head. Was it plausible? "And what's his involvement?"

"The people in Dana's resistance group try to spread the word, but it's not terribly effective. Again, because telepaths are rare and people don't see this happening a lot, many regard the actual truth as being a conspiracy theory."

"What does the public think about the network itself?"

"Again, they don't know about it." She poured us more coffee. "Sorry that seems to be the reply I always give, but it's the truth."

"But..." I began, then frowned. "Last year when we talked about it, the impression you gave was that it was common knowledge and people were generally cool with it."

Dynasonic hesitated and sipped at her coffee. "Yeah... I'm sorry. Halfway through our conversation last year, I regretted telling you at all. So I gave you just the quick and dirty, and generalized things quite a bit."

We were quiet for a moment as I absorbed all of this. Finally, I said, "Even if this network does do some good, these telepaths don't have any choice in the matter. It's slavery."

"Yes," she agreed. "It's reprehensible."

I stirred sugar and milk into my coffee. "You told me before that the network was nation-wide."

"Well, technically," Dynasonic said. "Again, I gave you the watered-down truth. It spread to other cities, some of which are on the east coast. That's the definition of 'nation-wide' that I was using. It's not in every state and certainly not in rural areas."

"Then it's likely that there are plenty of telepaths who haven't been detected by the network?"

"Yes, in regions where the network doesn't have a presence," she said.

I frowned "Another thing you said last year, which is clearly not the full truth, was that the system was designed to keep everyone safe."

"That's how it's justified, in those cases when it needs to be."

"But the single biggest factor affecting the crime rate is poverty. And you have a very low poverty rate. Why don't people realize this? Why do they think such a network monitoring the public is even necessary?" Before she could respond, I continued. "This sounds more about control than crime prevention. And it probably doesn't matter that it isn't totally widespread. Control the majority and you don't have to worry much about the rest."

"Dana has said similar things," she agreed.

I sipped my coffee and looked at her. "Do you remember the last time I came here? You were out of town." Dynasonic nodded, and I told her about what had happened, then.

"Wait, Dana actually contacted you?" she said, surprised.

"He didn't give his name, but it had to be him," I said. And then I told her about the weapons shipment, now sitting in a storage unit in Oakland.

"What's so special about these weapons?"

"Bullets are of limited use against certain metas," I said. "The super-tough. Powerful telekinetics. Ones with armor or other types of shielding. Instead of firing projectiles, these guns drain energy. A non-meta would be knocked unconscious right away. In fact, quite a lot of metas would, too. Someone like me, with a much higher than normal amount of energy, can tolerate a few hits, but that's about it. If you're going up against metas, this is the sort of weapon to use."

"So you think this Weatherford guy is trying to take over our world or something?"

I frowned. "That's where I'm having a disconnect," I said. "He's never seemed like the world-conquering sort. Although," I said, "maybe the weapons aren't for him. Maybe they're for the Overseer." I frowned, shaking my head. "But that doesn't make sense, either. If his telepaths are so powerful and in such control of the populace, what possible use would he have for them?"

Dynasonic finished her breakfast and looked at me thoughtfully. "You say these guns are especially useful against metas." I nodded, and she continued. "While it's true that our meta teams are primarily there to help with disaster relief and other things of a non-criminal nature, there *are* other metas out there."

I looked at the woman, hearing an unspoken "and" in her words. "What aren't you saying?"

Dynasonic hesitated a moment, looking at me over her mug. "For years, my brother has been recruiting metas to help him unravel the telepath network. As you say, it's slavery, and he's passionate about ending it."

"And you think the Overseer is aware of this?"

"He is. At some point in the past, he learned of Dana's existence and his telepaths are under orders to find him."

"So he could need the weapons for defense against Dana's forces. Okay, that tracks," I said. "But it doesn't shed any insight on Weatherford's role in all of this." I was convinced that he was behind the supply of weapons, though I had nothing more than my own hunch about that. But what was he getting out of it? "What else can you tell me about this Overseer guy?" I asked.

"His name is Ben Michaels," she told me. "He runs a place called the Access Institute over at Gough and Page. It provides counseling services, as well as training for counselors. It's all quite legit and provides some much-needed services for the community. But Dana also believes this is where the telepaths are trained. Or at least some of them."

That location placed the Access Institute at only a block from the Mercury Café, which is where I was when I saw Weatherford in this world. He and the other man had been walking down Page Street from the direction of Gough. They could easily have been coming from the Access Institute. Which means that other man could have been the Overseer himself. This would explain why Dynasonic's brother gave me the warning he did. Not to warn me about Weatherford, but Michaels.

We cleared the table and then, to satisfy my curiosity, used her computer to repeat Vicky's searches. I looked up Dane Weatherford and Vicky Valentine. As Vicky said, there were some hits, but none of them were the people I knew by those names. I was convinced that the man I'd seen was the one from my world.

Back in the living room, I opened my satchel and removed the tracking unit and charger. I turned on the screen and indicated the display. "This will allow you to track the crate of guns that came in today. Assuming they're not removed from the crate before being moved, you'll be able to follow them. You, or one of your associates, that is."

Dynasonic frowned. "That's a problem."

"Why?"

"Because if this Weatherford person is working with Michaels, they'll have the city's telepathic web at their disposal. I can't imagine this would go unguarded."

"Right. Well... what about your brother?"

"Maybe," she said, without elaborating. "Since you're not sticking around, how will we communicate?"

"That's part of why I asked about other metas. If you've got someone you trust who can fly up to the portal over the bay and slip through, they can call me on this." I pulled a phone from the satchel, a pre-paid one like the one she'd bought for me. "My number's programmed into it, of course." I also handed her the tiny scanner Song had given me to detect the portal. I had the coordinates programmed into my comm, so I no longer needed it. "This can detect the portal and will allow you to home in on it."

"Got it," she said. "And while you've got your bag open, let me grab your CD."

"Do you have any pictures of your brother?" I asked as she headed into the living room area.

"Of course!" As she returned with the disc, she snagged a frame from the mantel over the fireplace.

"Wow," I said.

"Look just like your brother?" she asked as she stashed the disc into my bag.

"No," I said. "I mean, yes, but..." I stared at the photo of a man who looked like my Dana, but with a full head of long hair. "My brother's bald." I handed the photo back to her and we talked for a while longer before I said goodbye and headed home. As I flew back to the portal, I couldn't help but wonder how much danger this world was in. And whether I'd just put it at even more risk.

TWELVE

"In the kind of world we have today, transformation of humanity might well be our only real hope for survival."
~ Stanislav Grof

As children, we're exposed to the concept of transformation by looking at animals. We're fascinated when we watch tadpoles become frogs and toads. And we marvel at the rebirth from caterpillar to butterfly.

In my field of science, though, transformation is one of a few different processes where genetic material from an outside source is taken in by a cell. Some species of bacteria do this naturally, but of course, my studies always took me into areas where "natural" was just a boundary to be pushed.

Even so, at its most basic, the transformations I was able to induce were small. Cumulatively, they resulted in something tremendous, but the individual changes were just the other side of trivial.

But all through my years of education, I remembered how fascinated I was by butterflies as a girl. My little mind couldn't grasp how a worm-like bug with a bunch of pudgy, sticky feet could become an elegant creature with ornate, delicate wings. The entire body of the caterpillar essentially disappears, to be replaced by something utterly different. It was like magic.

Even today, after years of studying biology, it still seems that way.

Having already gotten the most difficult phone call out of the way, I now felt ready to tackle the rest of them. I started with *Supers* magazine. I wasn't about to fly to New York for an in-person appearance, of course. It took a while, but I was able to eventually get connected by phone to Malcolm Goodman himself, publisher and editor-in-chief. For what felt like the fiftieth time, I told the story of my "accident," but this time leaving out the "deep undercover" lie. He agreed to print something along the lines of a "greatly exaggerated" death.

He asked about the book deal and if I was still willing to publish excerpts in the magazine. I told him that it was still in the works, and that I would still do so. If he wrote the foreword, anyway. He happily agreed.

Since the book was now on my mind, my next call was to K.T. After the fifty-first explanation, with somewhat fewer details than the fiftieth, she shared some news of her own. She was engaged.

The news hit me like a brick. After a moment of silently mourning a love that never was, I forced a smile into my voice and congratulated her. I didn't ask anything about her husband-to-be. She seemed to sense how the news affected me, and said she had to get to a meeting. I was relieved to end the call.

I went from the not-girlfriend to the ex-girlfriends, Sharon and Jackie. However, it was Michael who answered, being the only one home. In a way, I was glad of that. I gave him recitation number fifty-two, even less detailed than the last. "Listen," Michael said after the story, "We're going to be in San Diego in July for Comic-Con. Maybe after it's over, we can swing up to San Francisco. I'd love to do a shoot with you." Knowing how much little Dinah would like that, I agreed. Before we hung up, I told him to give all three girls a big hug for me.

From girlfriends to old friends. I phoned Rhonda back at home. Fifty-third, with only vague detail. We talked for almost an hour. It was nice to hear how her kids were doing and just catch up with someone from my life before it became what it was, now. By the time we said goodbye, I felt like a weight had been lifted.

My next battle was with paperwork. "You have no idea how glad I am to turn all this back over to you," Jasmine said as we sat in the office. She sorted through the pile, telling me what we had. Grant renewals. Proposals for upgrades to our security system. Bills. And more bills. All the fun things.

"Wow," I said, looking at the receipts for completed improvements to the building interior that I'd commissioned after buying the property. "That was more expensive than I'd figured."

Glancing at the receipt, Jasmine said, "You wanted every square inch of wood stripped and refinished. Including that fancy fireplace. What did you expect?"

"Thanks for taking care of things while I was... you know."

"Of course," Jasmine said. "Oh, meeting notes are up to date in the computer."

"Okay." I sighed as I looked back at the stack.

"Well, have fun." Jasmine smirked as she left, closing the door on her way out.

I handled the bills, first, since they wouldn't take long. Then, for two hours, I dealt with grant renewals, a much more tedious activity. The Project received four grants: one as a general non-profit, one as a non-government meta organization, one for being a social support organization, and one for being a disaster relief organization. Collectively, they paid the paltry salaries of the other members and provided a modest fund for equipment and so on.

Not for the first time, I reflected on how good it was that the Project members accepted such measly compensation. Because of that, we were doing okay. Still, I wanted to pay them more. One day, maybe, but it would never approach what they'd make with a government team.

In the paperwork was a residual check for PowerPaste. I was shocked to see that it was nearly double what the previous one had been. I was confused, but welcomed it.

My personal finances were a bit tight. Income from the sale of PowerPaste was enough to cover my bills, including the mortgage on the property. But my savings account was nearly empty. I'd built it up during my time with the Gatekeepers, but drained it in financing the cloning procedure. I had been at a loss as to how I was going to bring in more money. This increase, so long as it maintained, would certainly help.

I glanced into the corner behind the desk and was unsurprised to find three large boxes there. Every month, I was sent one box of each flavor of PowerPaste, which was part of the arrangements I had with the manufacturer.

I opened the box and smiled. I'd received notice from them that they'd added a larger size offering. The meta community had apparently been major purchasers, so they added a full three-ounce packet in addition to the half-ounce version. This was what I'd initially suggested, but I understood why they went with a smaller size to begin with. Non-metas generally don't want to consume three thousand calories at a pop.

I closed the box and turned back to the last of the paperwork. It was Jasmine's proposal for security upgrades. Reviewing it was just a formality. I trusted her implicitly. And I knew little about security matters. Normally, suggestions had to be run by the entire group, but since the building belonged to me, this was my decision alone. I signed off on it.

When I was finally finished, I sat back in the chair, resting my eyes and reflecting on my status. The team, generally speaking, accepted the "new me." I'd evidently handled the "not being dead" thing adequately. My memories were intact, as far as I knew, and felt comfortable. But I still had an awkward feeling of being out of place.

It was stupid, of course. I couldn't expect a complete and seamless return to my old life right away. It would take time. But I was impatient. Then I laughed at myself for thinking how unfair it was that dying had disrupted my life so much.

But the truth is, despite the long discussion we'd had at the team meeting, I wasn't as comfortable with being a clone as I'd let on. Oh, I had no regrets. It beat being a corpse. But there were aspects of it that still felt off.

The biggest thing was that I still felt "unfinished." I'd told Dana that I thought it was the lack of our telepathic link. And that was true, but I was beginning to think it wasn't the whole truth. There was something else. I had an inkling of what it was, but I needed to think about it further.

In a way, I was struggling with who I was, and who I was supposed to be. In some ways, the identity of Dynamistress just felt alien. I clearly remembered when Dynamistress felt like the "real" me and Dinah Geof-Craigs was more of an adopted persona. But I didn't really feel that way, anymore.

When I'd read in the journals about the cloning idea and the reasoning that led to the decision, it felt so weird. Such thinking was so far out of my reality. Even now, I question it. I know it was the result of desperation. Today, in my non-desperate state, I can't imagine even considering such a thing. This difference in thinking added to my feelings of self-estrangement. Even with all my memories (to the best of my knowledge), I found it hard to believe I was the same person.

Aside from that, the most immediate concern was what I'd warned my team about: being "outed" to the public. I could probably handle the ostracism, I told myself. I didn't give a damn about being thought of as an abomination. Or a hero, for that matter. My real fear was what Jack warned about. The scientific community would go nuts. They'd want to know everything. They'd want to study me.

As a scientist, I understood. I'd want to know everything, too. In fact, there was a part of me that felt guilty for *not* revealing myself to the public. And no, the irony of this situation was not even remotely lost on me.

Vicky and I spent increasing amounts of time together. We weren't romantically involved, though I certainly was hoping to rekindle something with her. She, however, showed little inclination to reciprocate. We spent most of our time talking, often over drinks in the kitchen bar. Mostly, we talked shop.

It had been more than a week since we'd tracked the crate of weapons to Dynasonic's world. And unless the tracking device had been found and left to sit there, the weapons hadn't moved an inch.

"I sometimes wonder why he hasn't tried to snatch me again," Vicky said one day.

I finished my drink. "Because now we know where his base of operations is, probably," I said. "We'd just come get you again."

She shook her head. "No, he could hide me anywhere. Pretty much literally."

I nodded at the truth of her statement. Weatherford could be anywhere, in any number of worlds and dimensions, which was a fact I simply had no idea what to do with. How do you defeat someone who could, at any moment, retreat completely out of your ability to even detect?

"What I often wonder," I said, "is why you aren't completely pissed off about what he did to you."

"Like I've said, I probably would be, if I hadn't been so doped out the whole time. It's like it was just a bad dream I had, long ago."

"So the hell what?" I said. "I mean, Jesus, Vick!" But she wouldn't go further into it. We sat in silence for a bit, before I said, "The other thing I wonder about is why it wasn't more difficult getting you back. All in all, it wasn't that hard to beat your father and the others."

"That's because they're not fighters, Dyna. They're a group of mystics, basically, not an army." Then she said, "Tell me again why you think the weapons are going to Dynasonic's world."

With that, the subject was changed, and I had no choice but to accept it. "She thinks it's because of her brother's resistance efforts. The weapons would be of good use against the metas he's recruited. But I think there might be more to it than that."

Vicky pondered this for a moment. "Like exchanging weapons for telepaths."

I stared at her stupidly, my mouth hanging open. "I'm an idiot," I finally said. "It never occurred to me that he might have been using the weapons as barter. And I assumed that, since those telepaths were held in thrall by the Overseer guy, they would be of no use to anyone but him. But maybe that's not the case. Maybe it's not a matter of constant mind control. They're taken as children, so they've been programmed their whole lives."

"That's really twisted," she said as she finished her drink.

"I agree," I said. "As you just said, the group isn't made up of people accustomed to combat. It's possible that our rescue of you last year might well have been the first time a group of metas had gone against them," I reasoned. "I'd wager that, if we were to do so again, we'd find ourselves facing both energy weapons and telepaths."

"Well, it's not as though we have any cause to go after him, anyway."

I frowned, but she was right. We had no standing. Legally, the most we could do would be to alert the proper authorities, but we didn't even have justification for doing that. Arms trafficking charges would never stick. The weapons were coming from one world, going to another, with only ours as a temporary stopover point. It would take a lot to even prove that.

Going after Weatherford as a kidnapper and rapist was morally justifiable, of course, but what would the point be? Not only could he create a portal and disappear, but even if we did somehow capture him, it seemed like Vicky wouldn't even press charges. Like it or not, I couldn't see anything we could do other than monitor him and act defensively, if it came to that.

I'd have to let Dynasonic know what we determined was really happening. There wouldn't be much need for her to tell me about any movement of the weapons. Rather, her brother was the one who'd need to know about them, since they were likely going to the Overseer. Dane Weatherford was my problem; Ben Michaels was hers.

Daniel and I sat with Invictus in his office in the Citadel, sharing a pot of tea and some mini scones I'd picked up before our regular get-together.

"It's disturbing to me that talk of multiple worlds is being done so casually," Invictus said, "as though they were commonplace."

"To me, they almost are. I've been dealing with them so often," I said.

Daniel snagged another pastry and nibbled on it thoughtfully. "It does make me wonder," he said slowly, "just how often it's happened... how many there are. For all we know... it *could* be commonplace."

"At any rate," I said, trying to return the conversation to the real point, "what would you do? I mean, is there anything we *can* do?"

Invictus set down his cup. "Has Probe turned up anything further on Weatherford and The Nexus?"

"A bit," I said. "Apparently, there is some unrest within the group. From what he's been able to learn, it seems that they've been growing tired of Weatherford's long-standing promises of the ultimate portal thing without any results. Weatherford himself has been keeping a low profile."

"Interesting," Invictus said.

"What I always wondered," Daniel said, "is why he was... Director of the Office of Metahuman Affairs. That was... a completely legitimate position."

"I think it was a way for him to learn a lot about metas," I said, "including the Bay Scouts. And maybe a way for him to locate Vicky."

"Have you ever considered that Weatherford... may have been the one ultimately responsible for the exchange between our worlds?"

"It's crossed my mind, yes," I said. I finished my tea and toyed with the cup. "The thing that worries me the most," I said, "is just how powerful the guy is. I mean, we got insanely lucky the last time we took him on. We had the element of surprise, and Jasmine nailed him with a tear gas round. But that won't happen again, especially if he's got a team of telepaths guarding his place." I shook my head. "How do you fight a guy who can open a portal to anywhere in the universe?"

Invictus frowned. "Dyna, are you sure you're not exaggerating the danger Weatherford poses to our world?"

"Well," I said, gathering my thoughts, "that's not quite what I've been thinking."

"Then what?" Daniel asked.

"I'm actually more worried about his association with the Overseer."

Invictus raised an eyebrow. "You think there's more going on than a simple exchange of weapons for telepaths. That they jointly are planning something."

"If so," Daniel said, "and you can supply evidence... we need to notify the authorities. Have all teams... put on alert."

"Truth is," I said, "I think it's clear that Weatherford wanted the telepaths for defense of his group's little burrow in the U.K. But why does Michaels want the energy weapons?" I let out a breath, knowing how my friends were going to respond to my words. "I think Michaels is planning a more thorough method of being in control of his own world."

As the others exchanged glances, I barreled forward. "So far, he's convinced the powers-that-be that his telepaths helped to establish a peaceful society. But doing so by monitoring the thoughts of every citizen? That's abhorrent. Doing it with telepaths who are slaves? That's even worse. But adding the energy weapons could very well mean that he's planning a domination of another sort."

"Dyna..." Invictus began.

"I know!" I interrupted. "You're going to say that I'm sticking my nose where it doesn't belong. That Dynasonic's world needs to deal with it on its own. But I disagree. Someone from our world – Weatherford – is meddling in their business. I just want to balance the scales a little."

"Of course."

I paused. "What?"

"I agree with you."

I blinked stupidly and turned to Daniel. "Did he just..."

Daniel chuckled. "Why so surprised? I agree, too."

"You've said," Invictus continued, "that there are few metas in that world, and virtually no groups, as there are here. Providing such support is a good idea."

"If someone from here is making trouble there," Daniel said, "it's our responsibility to make things right."

"Well," I said. "I'm relieved to hear that."

"However," Invictus cautioned, "right now, you have little to go on. You need something concrete before you can act."

Daniel agreed. "You need to know a lot more... about Overseer."

"I'm on it."

Invictus continued. "Further, you need to be asked to help. And though you're free to offer as many suggestions as you want, any action must be done under their direction."

"Of course." Once more, these men surprised me. I looked at them with more respect than I thought possible.

Then I poured another cup of tea.

The next day, I paid Dynasonic a visit. She answered the door, surprised to see me. We hugged and she invited me in. "So what's the occasion?" she asked.

"I have news, but I'd like to share it with your brother, as it concerns him even more than you."

"I figured you'd want to meet him, eventually. Let's see what we can do," she said, and pulled a disposable phone from her purse. Surely she wasn't just going to call him.

"Even those phones are traceable, you know."

"It's a virtual private network, connected to about a dozen different nodes around the world before it reaches his own VPN connected phone," she said as she tapped out a short text message. Then she looked up at me. "I told him to expect this message, so it won't take him long to get here."

"Where's he coming from?"

"The underground," she said. "There's an entrance to the old tunnels not terribly far from here, north of Civic Center."

We sat in her kitchen chatting over coffee while waiting for him to arrive. I wasn't sure why, but I was nervous about meeting him. About half an hour later, we heard the front door open.

"In the kitchen," Dynasonic called.

I looked him over as he joined us. He was about the same height and build as my brother. But, as the photo had indicated, he had a full head of hair, pulled into a long ponytail. He was dressed in jeans and a T-shirt under a black hoodie and a red NASA baseball cap.

Dynasonic greeted him with a hug, then introduced us. Dana shook my hand. "Pleased to meet you," he said, joining us at the table and pouring himself a cup of coffee. "It's not every day you get to meet someone from another world."

I smiled faintly. "I dunno. It's a lot more common an occurrence for me than I'd have ever imagined."

Once we were all seated near the fireplace, he got straight to business. "I take it you have information," he said.

"I do. What I think we need is an info swap. I'll tell you everything I know about Dane Weatherford and you tell me everything you know about Ben Michaels."

"That would be great," he replied, "because I haven't been able to find out a thing about that guy."

I gave them my history with Weatherford, then proceeded to fill them in on everything, from Vicky's assumption that Weatherford was trading energy weapons for telepaths and all the hypothesizing about why the Overseer might want the weapons in the first place. I could practically hear the wheels turning in Dana's head. I finished by asking, "What can you tell me about the Overseer?"

Dana frowned. "Precious little," he said.

"So what's his background? Where did he come from?"

"That's the frustrating part," he continued. "We have no idea. Hell, we don't even know what he looks like."

"Why not?"

"Well, you saw him. He always looks like that."

I shook my head. "I was focused on the guy with him. That was Weatherford."

"He has a bushy beard that obscures everything below his nose. He always wears reflective sunglasses and headwear of some sort."

"But surely others have seen what he looks like. And I'd be surprised if you hadn't encountered these people. Couldn't you lift that information from them?"

"Oh, I've tried that any number of times. But it seems like everyone who's seen his face has had that particular memory wiped. Well, everyone except me."

"You've seen his full face?"

"Not completely," he said. "I've met him only once, about four years ago. Completely random encounter. I didn't know who he was until I considered it in retrospect. We looked straight at each other for a couple seconds, until he looked away. And then, it was as though I'd only caught a glimpse of him, even though I knew I'd stared right at him."

"He tampered with your memory."

Dana frowned, and I could sense how much this upset him. I knew how much it would upset my brother, so it must be at least that disturbing to this man.

His sister spoke up. "He's one paranoid dude."

"And he evidently was able to get past my defenses and lift information, since it became clear soon thereafter that he knew who I am and what I'm doing."

"And how go your group's efforts against him?"

"We're making progress," he said. "I'm getting better at freeing the telepaths from his control, but there's still a ways to go."

We talked for about another hour before he departed. I left, too, after more conversation with Dynasonic. All in all, the trip wasn't nearly as productive as I'd anticipated.

The following day in the news, there was a small blurb about the "Glass Man" I'd read about earlier in the year. The crystalline corpse had been purchased by the California Academy of Sciences and was now on display.

I found this extremely odd. Granted, there was nothing left of the man's actual body, and the remaining figure may have had a face, but it was not recognizable as the man who'd died. Even so, I can't imagine his family could be happy about having it there for anyone to see. Of course, one of those people was going to be me, so I was glad they were okay with it.

I took Sinta with me, and we stopped for pizza in the Haight before heading into Golden Gate Park.

"Thanks for inviting me," Sinta said.

"I'm sorry we haven't spent more time together since... you know."

She balanced the pizza on her fingertips, protecting her fur from the sauce and cheese. "It's okay. You've had a lot of adjusting to do."

I couldn't argue with that. "Been a while since we've eaten here, huh?"

"Well, yeah," she said. "We mostly had them deliver, before."

More than a few people stared at Sinta, as we sat there, but she didn't seem to notice. That is, until one jerk forced her to.

He was a big guy with scraggly hair and a crooked sneer. "I didn't think animals were allowed in here," he said as he saw us. He laughed at his joke as he passed, heading to the front to place his order.

Sinta saw the anger on my face, but shook her head. "It's okay, Dyna."

"No, it's not," I said. I hopped off my stool and followed him to the front, but before I could accost him, the petite girl behind the counter held up a hand.

"Out," she said.

"The fuck?" He stared down at her, clearly not intimidated by her green hair, black lipstick, and heavy eye liner.

"You harass our customers, you don't get served. Out. Now."

With a condescending laugh, the man stood his ground. "Fine. Your pizza sucks, anyway. But I think I'll stay."

"Not happening," she said.

The big guy laughed. "You gonna call the cops on me, little girl?"

She glanced at me standing behind the man and smirked. "No need."

The man turned around to see me. And since he greatly outsized me, he laughed again. "You kidding?"

"Nope," I said, gripping him by his belt. I lifted him off the floor until his head bumped the ceiling. "Now, you want me to carry you, or will you split on your own?"

In his shock, he flailed and nodded frantically, so I put him down.

"Apologize," I said.

He looked at Sinta as he sped past. "Sorry!" he said, and was out the door.

"That was fun," I said as I returned.

"Still, you didn't need to do that," she said. "I'm used to it."

"It shouldn't happen often enough for you to get used to it."

We looked around at the other customers, many of whom were staring at us. But now they were staring just as much at me as they were at Sinta. Some with fear, but a couple with smiles. One with a big thumbs-up.

"You lifted him with one hand," Sinta said. "You seem stronger."

"I've been thinking so, too," I said. "It might be because this time my abilities developed along with my body, rather than being jump-started when I was thirty." The words came easily enough, but I wondered if they sounded as bizarre to Sinta as they did to me.

My thoughts were interrupted by the green-haired girl bringing us two more slices of pizza. She set the plates down in front of us. "On the house," she said. Then, "Sorry about that, Sin."

Sinta smiled. "It's okay, Ali."

I was surprised that they knew each other. Then she looked at me. "Thanks, Dinah," she said with a smile. "That was awesome." Now I was even more surprised, and she noticed. "I know you don't remember me," she said. "I delivered to you guys a bunch, but Sin usually answered the door. Plus, I was blonde, then. Haven't seen you in a while."

"Yeah," I said. "We moved."

"Heard you died," she said, tilting her head.

"Really? That's weird."

She laughed softly and said, "Well, it's great to see you. Thanks, again." She turned to go back to the counter, but her coworker loudly cleared his throat and stared pointedly at her. I watched as Ali paused, hanging her head. Then she turned and timidly came back to us. She avoided looking at me while reaching for the notepad in her pocket.

People didn't often ask for my autograph, but I was always happy to oblige. She tore a sheet off the pad. "Um," she began, then saw my smile. "In case you wanna grab a drink or something, sometime." She dropped the paper in front of me, then hurried back to work.

I stared at the phone number on the paper. Sinta was grinning at me and making suggestive noises. I glanced toward the counter, but Ali was avoiding looking at me, her cheeks obviously flushed.

"So," I said to Sinta, trying not to stare at the girl, "'Sin'?"

Sinta rolled her eyes. "Yeah." I expect she blushed, too, under her fur.

"Should I call you that?"

She shook her head, with more embarrassment. "I like it when you call me 'kitten.'"

I smiled. "Me, too."

After we finished, we waved goodbye to Ali, then stepped outside. "Since we're in the neighborhood," I said, "I want to say hi to someone."

My old hair salon was just across the street, so we went inside. I saw Fabian sitting at his station reading a magazine. I walked over. "Slow day?"

He looked up at me, a confused look on his face. He looked at my hair and his eyes widened. Standing, he reached out and took a lock of it in his hand. "You're yellowing. Using too much product." Then he took stock of my face. "Wow, girl, you've had work done."

I laughed. "Not exactly."

"You move back to the Haight, or did you make a special trip to see me? Because, damn, girl, you need a cut."

I looked over at Sinta. "Go ahead," she said, picking up a magazine.

So I let him escort me back for a wash. And as he chopped and styled my hair, I had to explain what had happened. This man had seen my face close up more times than I could count. He deserved the full truth.

I finished my story at the same time as he finished doing my hair. He stepped back, hand on his hip. "That is the biggest load of bowel movement I've ever heard," he said. "Just admit it. You had work done."

"Fine," I said as we walked to the front. I pulled out my card to pay for the cut. "I had work done."

"I knew it," Fabian said.

"But I did it, myself," I said with a grin. Then I gave him a hug before Sinta and I left for the park.

Outside, she said, "It's cute. And you're all white, again."

I smiled at her. "Okay," I said as we walked to the Academy. "So tell me how you think it's going."

"How what's going?"

"Are the others okay with me? I mean, aside from Cara's issues. I'm just not sure where their thoughts are."

"I think they're fine, Dyna," Sinta said in a tone that told me she didn't understand why I was even asking. "You worry too much about it."

"Do I? I mean, if I hadn't been the one at the center of it, I'd have a hard time swallowing it."

Sinta looked up at me with a puzzled face. "Because traveling through portals to other worlds and encountering other versions of yourself is easier to swallow?"

That made me pause. "Point taken," I said.

"It's only Cara's religious beliefs that made her react that way," Sinta continued. "I think the group discussion showed that no one else feels the same. And I think it really had an effect on her."

"Oh? Have you spoken to her since?"

"No, but... she had that look people get when they've encountered a view that is against their own, but makes sense."

"Cognitive dissonance."

"I think she'll come around, Dyna. After all," she said, "you're awesome. And who wouldn't want to be around you?"

I snorted. "You're way too kind." I decided to switch topics. "So how are things for you?"

"Good."

I waited for an elaboration, but there wasn't any. "Well... good," I said.

Sinta pulled out her phone and texted as we walked. After a few minutes, she said, "Jen's working today. I told her we were almost there. She can take a break and see us."

The Academy currently had an exhibit on bats. Jennifer impressed them with her knowledge and was working as a volunteer docent exclusively for the bat exhibit.

She met us at the Academy Café and we sat for a while over drinks and pastries as she told us about her experiences there. "Me bein' a docent is a bit of a distraction," she said. "People tend to wanna stare at me instead of the bats. At least, at first. But it seems people tend to get more outta the exhibit when they're bein' told about bats from–"

"From Bat-girl," I said.

Jennifer glared at me, but said, "Well... yeah."

"I think that's cool," Sinta said. "I know it would make it a lot more interesting for me."

"One thing I do is let people touch my wings," she said. "Feels just like a reg'lar bat wing, just thicker."

Sinta frowned. "You're okay with that?"

"Yeah," Jennifer drawled. "It only gets uncomfortable when they want to feel where the wings connect to my back. I draw the line at that."

"I hate it when people come up and want to pet me," Sinta said.

An awkward silence fell. I broke it by saying, "So have you seen the Glass Man exhibit?"

"Yeah, it's cool, but kinda disturbing," Jennifer said. "There's somethin' about it that..." She frowned, then shook her head. "Well, you'll see." She gave us directions to its location, then said, "I gotta get back. Y'all have fun." She hugged me, then gave Sinta's head a scratch before walking off.

Sinta laughed. "I don't mind when *you* do it!" She waved as Jennifer left, then we followed her directions through the building. It turned out that the "statue" was part of a side exhibit on metals, since aluminum was one of the elements involved in making the material forming the statue. At first, I was surprised that visitors were allowed to touch it. But then, this wasn't glass, but an incredibly tough transparent ceramic. It was too bottom heavy to tip over and no kid was going to break off even the little finger of the thing without a sledgehammer. Or even with one, probably.

The photo I'd seen in the news didn't do it justice, mainly because it had shown the figure only from the chest up. The mouth hung open, as though screaming. The arms were extended, reaching for a salvation that never came.

The photo had not shown the stomach. Or rather, the lack of one. Where a person's midsection would be was nothing but air. It seemed to me as though the hot ceramic had burned away all flesh and organs, leaving only the portions of a body with skeletal support. So the face had small sockets for eyes, and no nose or ears. The chest area looked "normal," in that it was a solid mass. The arms and legs were thin, like bones thickly coated with the substance, but still looking almost normal. The spinal area was thicker – again, as though heavily coated with the ceramic – and a large mass of the solidified stuff was around the figure's lower legs, covering the feet and calves, acting as a base for the statue.

Jennifer's assessment of it was accurate. It was cool, but disturbing. And, in its own way, quite beautiful. Sunlight from a nearby window struck the figure, causing it to brighten. It would be at home in an art museum every bit as much as a science exhibit.

I ran my fingers along its surface, around the torso, admiring the color of the substance. The sunlight had warmed it. I pressed my forehead against its chest and looked deep inside, surprised to see tiny flecks of red inside. As was my frequent habit, I expanded my perception. Switching to this energy-sensing view seemed much easier than before. I barely had to concentrate at all. It took just a thought. But as I did so, I recoiled in shock.

It was faint – and barely active – but there was an unmistakable pattern of organic energy. Incredibly, the "Glass Man" was alive.

THIRTEEN

"Conviction is worthless unless it is converted into conduct."
~ Thomas Carlyle

Even as a young girl, I realized that most people only give lip service to their beliefs. I first saw this in my mother, a devout Christian who never hesitated to denigrate those who didn't follow the teachings of Jesus, all while being oblivious to or ignoring the fact that she wasn't doing so, either. After that, I couldn't help but see this hypocrisy everywhere.

In social media, I see countless people making posts about how much they care about an issue, but that's the extent of their devotion to it. You can be appalled at the poor treatment of animals, for example, but unless you're doing something about it – volunteering at a shelter, donating to rescues, or whatever – you're not truly addressing the problem. Spreading "awareness" of something that's already common knowledge doesn't make you an activist.

This is why all members of the Pariah Project do volunteer work for causes important to them, such as Jennifer's work with the bat exhibit. And it's why I found myself shelling out a bundle of money for a big chunk of aluminum oxynitride.

Because, naturally, no one believed me. The Academy thought I was delusional, which was understandable. After all, there was absolutely no reason to think that a man doused in liquid ceramic could possibly be "alive" in any sense.

I urged them to subject the Glass Man to testing, but they refused. It had all been done, they told me. The statue was utterly inert. I told them they needed to do different tests. But they wouldn't.

After my repeated pleading failed, I finally just put my money where my mouth was and offered them considerably more than the amount they'd paid for it, as well as the promise of a lifetime membership to the Academy at their Platinum Circle level.

I don't know if it was the money, or the fact that parents were complaining that their children were disturbed by the thing, but that's how Glass Man came to take up residence in my lab. Dana positioned him in a corner, where I put him under high intensity lights, with sensors attached and cameras aimed to capture different angles of the figure. I wasn't sure there was anything to see, really, but until I had other ideas, this would have to do.

Jasmine could detect no emotions within it. Dana could detect nothing, either. If there was any sort of activity in the thing's head, it was ridiculously faint. In all likelihood, there was nothing at all. But what if there was something, just too faint for Jasmine and Dana to detect?

What would be the right thing to do?

The first week of June brought a momentous occasion: Bridget's high school graduation. Vicky and Bridget lived in the Inner Sunset neighborhood of the city. Vicky said the fog there reminded her of home in the U.K. Bridget attended the Woodside International School, where about half the students were from other nations. Bridget's parents felt this would help their daughter appreciate other cultures.

Mr. and Mrs. Mason flew up from Los Angeles for the ceremony, which was held on a Wednesday evening in the school's auditorium. To my surprise, I was invited to attend. It was a typical graduation ceremony, and reminded me of my own, more than twenty years past. Afterward, the five of us went out to dinner at Lavash for wonderful Persian food. Bridget's appetite nearly rivaled my own, which endeared her to me, for some reason.

After dinner, we returned to their apartment. The Project would later have a graduation party for Bridget, but this night was for family. And me, evidently.

Vicky had purchased Bridget's favorite dessert, Nutella bamboloni from Heartbaker. We sat in the living room, eating the decadent pastries and drinking coffee. Mr. Mason challenged his daughter to an arm-wrestling match. Even with him using both arms against her off-hand, she kicked his butt. I admit, I envied the relationship she had with her parents.

As Vicky had told me I would, I found the Masons to be great folks. Their pride in their daughter was obvious. There wasn't a shred of shame over her being a meta. I enjoyed talking with them.

I couldn't help but ask them something that had been nagging at me ever since learning of it. "Bridget mentioned that she was considerably premature at birth," I said.

Her mother smiled stiffly. "Yes," she said. "It was quite frightening."

"I'm sure," I said. "If you don't mind, I was wondering what lasting effects, if any, came from that."

"She had Bronchopulmonary dysplasia," her father said.

Her mother nodded. "Her lungs had developed oddly and were inflamed. It cleared up on its own over time, but she has breathing issues, even today. Almost like asthma."

"She has some vision problems," Mr. Mason added, "a form of retinopathy, which hasn't progressed, thankfully. Moderate hearing loss, too, in her right ear."

"But the worst was her heart," her mother said. "They detected a murmur almost right away. They determined it to be a PDA."

"I'm guessing that doesn't mean public display of affection," I said, to lighten the mood.

"Patent ductus arteriosus," her father said. "It's when there's an opening between two blood vessels in the heart, meaning that the blood wasn't circulating properly."

"The doctors said such things often clear up on their own within a year or two for preemies," her mother said, "but in Bridget's case, it didn't. Even with the drug treatments they gave her. So when she was about two and a half, she had a procedure."

"She had heart surgery?" I said, shocked.

Her father shook his head. "Not open heart, no. It was done with a catheter, through her veins," he said. "Went off without a hitch."

"She still has a murmur," her mother said, "but the PDA is gone."

"Pretty remarkable history she has," I said.

Then the conversation took a turn I'd been dreading. "Speaking of remarkable," her mother said, "Bridget had told us that you'd died. But... here you are." I smiled nervously and prepared myself for a grilling. "And amnesia! That must have been awful, waking up on the shore like that, not knowing who you were!"

I glanced over at Bridget, who of course was aware of everything being said, and looked back at me with an expression at once apologetic and goofy that nearly made me laugh. "Yeah, it was disconcerting," I said. "It wasn't complete amnesia, though it may as well have been. But it's all good now."

"Bridge talks about you all the time," Mr. Mason said. "Though, I have to say, I expected you to be older."

"Well... I'm older than I look," I said with a smile back at Bridget. "Good genes."

And that was the end of the dreaded conversation.

At home that night, my emotions were a mess. As much as I'd been pretending, as much as I'd been trying to make it so, things weren't "all good," as I'd told Bridget's mother.

Seeing them together, how well they all got along, and the total acceptance and obvious love that Bridget's parents had for her only reminded me of how incomplete I felt.

It had been nearly a year since I'd been home to visit my parents. And while that visit was overwhelmingly positive when compared to previous visits, I still didn't feel close to them. My mother's evolved views couldn't erase the decades of abuse and neglect.

Bridget's wasn't the only graduation. Layla Shepherd was graduating from high school and her sister Sydney was graduating from UCLA.

This reminded me of the last time I'd seen Shepherd before my untimely demise. He'd alluded to some sort of problem with the girls and said I should visit.

I thought about doing so, but had no idea what their father had told them about my situation. Besides, this was an exciting time for the girls. I didn't need to be there distracting from it. I made a mental note to send them some gifts and to follow up with a visit in a few weeks.

"Just you and me, now, Henry," I said to the Glass Man in my lab. His name had been, hilariously, Henry Glass, according to the Academy. And he had no family in California, which was why they had little problem obtaining permission to purchase and display the figure.

I'd taken to talking aloud when around him. And since I was spending more time in the lab – mostly to keep my mind occupied than for any scientific reason – I was around him a good bit.

"My brother went back to Sacramento," I told him. "It feels weird not having him here." I looked up from my desk, staring into those eye sockets that were as empty as the building felt without Dana around.

As I stared at the figure, thinking about his horrible accident, I thought about my own. I remembered clearly how I'd felt upon realizing that runaway was likely. I could still feel the desperation that led to coming up with the cloning idea in the first place. And it seemed like yesterday that I pleaded with Dana to help me, since I couldn't do it without him.

My last memories before coming to awareness in my new body were of the moments leading up to my death. Not just the fear and the panic. There was also profound sadness. Wanting to do nothing but embrace my brother and my friends, to tell them how much I loved them all. It was something I hadn't done because I was in such denial about my predicament. And now it was too late.

I was actually bothered that Dana had taken the final memory only to a certain point, refusing to allow me access to all of it. He wouldn't take the risk of the memory traumatizing me. When I protested, he said he didn't mean trauma in the form of nightmares, but actual physical/mental trauma. I gave in, then. I didn't want that any more than he did. Besides, it wasn't like I could change his mind on it.

I shook myself back to the present, took a deep breath, and turned my attention back to the article I'd begun reading before getting caught up in my thoughts.

"Hank, listen to this," I said, then paused. "Do you prefer Henry or Hank?" Then I shrugged. "Anyway, this says they've been able to use gene therapy to restore day vision and cone function in young dogs with achromatopsia." I looked up at him. "That's complete color blindness, by the way." I turned back to the computer screen. "The day is coming, my friend, when gene therapy will be the cure to most of our ills. Not to mention a preventative. And, honestly, all those life extension folks who think there are ways to effectively live forever... they might not be too far wrong."

I looked at my new friend, shining under the light of all the lamps. "I know a little about that, in fact. Many of the tweaks I made to my own DNA were designed to allow for cellular replication less prone to error."

Back on the computer, I pulled up the programs I was using to analyze the Glass Man. I studied the sensor recordings, graphing them over the time he'd been with me. I didn't know what I was expecting to see, but there had been nothing out of the ordinary.

"And yeah, my telomeres are kind of obscenely long," I said as I studied the readouts. "They're what keep the DNA replication in our bodies going properly. With every division, they become a bit shorter until, eventually, they don't work, anymore. And no, I didn't figure out how to make them longer. It was just a strange side effect of what I was doing. Not sure I could do it intentionally if I had to."

The sensors weren't detecting what I knew to be true: there was some sort of organic life in this thing. True, the heat sensors noticed a minor uptick in temperature, but that could easily be from the prolonged exposure to the lighting.

"You, sir, are a puzzle," I said, looking at the shape with my energy-sensing sight again. I wished there was some way to record what I saw, and to chart that. Because I could swear what I saw was intensifying. I admitted, though, that this was probably just wishful thinking. "Gene therapy won't help you, I'm afraid. And y'know, my friends think I've got a screw loose for even thinking there's anything going on with you. They don't understand what I see." I frowned. "Hell, *I* don't understand it. But there's something going on with you. I'm certain of that. I just wish I knew what, if anything, was going on inside your head."

I did have one idea. The next day, I'd pick up a few of the hottest parabolic space heaters I could find. I'd move him up to the roof, since I didn't need that kind of extra heat in my lab.

I didn't know what I was expecting. I was just certain something was going on inside there and heat was the only thing I could think of that might affect it.

That weekend, I found myself sitting nervously at the curved bar at Zam Zam. I was halfway through a Finlandia martini, alternately looking admiringly at the beautiful Persian mural behind the bar and anxiously at the front door. Against my better judgment, Sinta had convinced me to make a date with Ali.

I'd chosen Zam Zam because it would be fairly quiet on a Saturday afternoon. It was probably my favorite bar when we'd lived in the Haight, and it was close to where Ali worked, so I assumed it would be convenient for her.

She arrived just as I finished my drink, saw me immediately, and walked over. She was undeniably cute. I was surprised that I liked the green hair. She still had the heavy eye liner, but was lacking the black lipstick. She was dressed in faded jeans, a Velvet Underground t-shirt, leather biker jacket, and Doc Martens. I'd anticipated that sort of wardrobe and, wanting to make her feel comfortable, I'd worn pretty much the same thing, though my t-shirt was of Alice Cooper and my leather was a stylish blazer, distinctly lacking in both zippers and buckles.

"Hey," she said, sitting on the stool next to mine.

"Hi."

"Sweet Docs," she said, admiring my calf-high boots.

"Thanks," I said. "My first pair. I love 'em."

"Better than the stiletto boots you usually wear, I'm sure," she said.

Ali eyed my empty glass. "What's good here?"

"Everything," the bartender said, smiling at Ali. "ID, please?"

Ali pulled it from her pocket, handing it to the man. An uncomfortable feeling washed over me. "Thanks," he said, handing it back. "What can I get you?"

After she ordered a Captain and Coke, we sat quietly for a moment. Then I cleared my throat. "So... how old *are* you, Ali?"

"Twenty-three."

I know she saw the surprise on my face even before I muttered, "Oh, geez." What on earth was I doing here with her?

"Oh, come on," she said. "I'm not *that* much younger than you."

I forced a weak smile. "I have good genes."

She frowned and assessed me. "Twenty-seven, tops."

I laughed. "I wish."

The bartender returned with her drink and, to my relief, another martini for me.

"Hey," Ali said to him, "Did you card her when she ordered?"

"No," he said. "She used to be a regular, 'bout a year ago."

"How old would you say she is?"

The bartender appraised me, looking closely at my eyes and hands. "Twenty-eight, give or take a year."

Knowing they wouldn't take my word for it, I produced my ID and handed it to the bartender. "*Daaamn*," he said. "Well done." Then he turned back to other customers.

Ali's eyes widened as she looked at the ID, then up at me. "*Thirty-nine?*"

I took a healthy sip of my drink. Setting the glass down, I forced another smile. "*Really* good genes."

Ali lifted her drink, avoiding my gaze. Finally, she said, "So... is this too weird for you? I mean, I don't care how old you are, but if it bugs you..."

I'd been thinking of nothing but that since she told me her age. I generally don't have an issue with large age differences, but sixteen years definitely made me stop and reconsider. "Ali, why me?" I asked.

"Jesus," she said, rolling her eyes. "Don't psychoanalyze it, okay? I just think you're cool and goddamn pretty, okay?" Despite myself, I blushed, which seemed to amuse her. "I'm not looking to move in together, y'know. Don't get hung up."

I sipped my drink again, looking at her over the rim of the glass. "Okay."

She smiled, and I couldn't help but do the same.

I hadn't been to see my therapist for close to a year. I had a growing need to talk, though, and found myself confiding in someone I knew would never reveal any of my inner thoughts: Henry Glass.

Of course, being unable to speak meant he couldn't offer any real counseling, even if he could hear me, but that wasn't what I was after. Sometimes just talking aloud to myself is therapy enough. It forces me to focus on my issues more than just thinking about them does, allows me to hear just how stupid some of my thoughts truly are.

I looked at the big, faintly bluish guy on my deck, parabolic heaters assailing him from three directions. I leaned against the low wall as I spoke to him. "There's a part of me that is honestly embarrassed to be standing here. And not because I'm talking to a man-sized chunk of polymer. I mean..." I sighed deeply. "I mean standing here at all. Alive. As a clone." I shook my head and looked away. "Sometimes I think Cara is right, that I've done something that should never have been done. Not because it was immoral or anything, or against some deity's wishes. But I can't shake the feeling that it was, as she said, an incredibly selfish thing to do. On the other hand, no one was hurt by it, so I shouldn't feel guilty, right?"

I looked at the face, frozen in its death agony, and my stomach dropped. I wondered if that had been what I looked like, in those last seconds. I looked away, again, feeling self-conscious.

"And then there's my life expectancy. I'm just estimating, but barring anything unexpected, I'm likely to live for a couple hundred years, due to all the tweaks to my DNA. Again, that wasn't planned, but it seems to be what's likely." I sighed heavily. "On the one hand, it's great, because our time on this earth is tragically short. On the other, though, it's going to be really difficult to watch my friends and loved ones die before I'm halfway through my own life."

Voicing that fact aloud was somehow much more sobering than merely thinking it. I felt a lump form in my throat and shook my head, trying to dislodge the thought.

"It's been hard, with the others," I continued, shifting my position on the wall. "Some of them treat me the same as before. Sinta, of course. Dana. Jasmine. Bridget. The rest, though, act differently to one degree or another, Cara being the most extreme example. And I get it. It's fine. But it's hard. Especially with Vicky.

"I do want to try again with her, y'know? But even though she hasn't outright rejected that idea, she hasn't embraced it, either. I get that she needs time. I just feel like the more time she takes, the less likely the result will be one I like."

I decided to switch topics. "Dana's planning a trip back to the UK next month," I said. "He's been sort of virtually dating this girl named Bronwyn that we met there. I guess they Skype a lot or something. Has to be tough with it being eight hours later there. And, I mean, she's nice. And gorgeous. I like her, I guess." I glanced up at the Glass Man. "Don't look at me like that," I said. "I'm not jealous. Or I'm trying not to be, anyway."

I switched to my energy-sensing sight. The energy readings I'd detected inside the form were a little more pronounced, I was certain of it. And the red specks I'd seen inside it were now brighter.

"Speaking of dating, I had one yesterday. Ali. She's... young." Before setting up the heaters, I'd taken as many photographs as I could, especially of the areas with hollows, such as the eyes, the abdomen, etc. I'd carefully measured the depths of them with precision tools. I wasn't sure what I was expecting. But it seemed that now, after so long in the heat, the pits weren't quite as shallow. The diameter of the spinal area was ever-so-slightly larger.

"She's cute. Clever, too. And we did have a fun time. We haven't set another date, but I suspect we will."

I stared at the figure, deep in thought. The heat was working, but it was like feeding a starving man nothing but lettuce. I needed more heat. "Okay, buddy," I muttered. "Let's get you a smorgasbord."

Back in the office, I went online and researched metal fabrication in the Bay Area. After nearly an entire day on the telephone with the heads of various companies, I finally found a facility with an electric arc furnace that would be open to a science experiment. With financial compensation, of course.

So it was that, a week later, I loaded Henry into a rented truck and drove him to the facility. The plant manager met me. The man frowned, staring at the figure. "You're sure this won't melt?" he asked.

"Not unless your furnace is a lot hotter than I was told over the phone."

He rubbed his chin, never taking his eyes off Henry. Finally, he nodded. "Okay," he said. "Let's do this."

He summoned a forklift and I watched with fascination as his workers maneuvered Henry into the basket of the furnace. A layer of shredded metal lay underneath him, more was piled on top of him, and the basket was closed before being moved into the melt shop. The plant manager went along, but I wasn't permitted to follow, so for the next hour or so, the CEO and I sat in his office and chatted.

After I wrote a check, I answered his questions about the "hero biz," as he called it. As requested, I'd brought with me some autographed photos for his children, feeling both flattered and awkward doing so. I posed with him for a selfie. Finally, his office phone rang. The basket was leaving the melt shop.

By the time we got there, Henry had been decanted, so to speak. The manager looked the figure up and down. "That what you were expecting?"

Henry looked virtually the same as when he entered the basket, with the exception that the red flecks inside were now much brighter and more numerous. I shifted to my energy vision. I smiled and said, "Yeah. Yeah, it is."

As the Glass Man cooled, the red specks dimmed. Some remained quite visible, but the majority were only detectable upon close inspection. The exciting thing, though, was that Henry never cooled to ambient temperature. The polymer felt warm to the touch, even without the parabolic heaters pointed at him.

I continued to take measurements on a daily basis, but kept the results to myself. I didn't need more weird looks from my teammates.

Speaking of my teammates, it seemed the only ones I saw at all were Jasmine, Sinta, and Kim. Most of the rest had legitimate excuses to be away from the base. Jennifer had her docent job with the bats. Jack was busy at Wonderland Robotics. Kit and Lily were in the process of moving. Nena was helping them. Bridget was on a vacation with her parents. Cara was still "thinking." And Vicky... well... I didn't know. In the two weeks since Bridget's graduation, I hardly heard from her. Her replies to my texts were short. She always had a reason to end phone calls quickly. In other words, she seemed to be avoiding me.

Certainly, I had enough to keep myself occupied. Beyond the normal duties of running a team, I had my project with the Glass Man. I had regular visits with Daniel and Invictus. I'd had a fun date with Ali. And now I had a dinner invitation from the Shepherd family.

Unlike my previous visits to their home, the mood was a bit on the tense side. Helena brought us iced tea in the living room as Terence and I talked.

"Where are the girls?" I asked.

"They'll be home soon," Terence said as Helena joined him on the sofa. He smiled as he said this, but there was a quality to his voice that spoke of some anxiety.

"What's going on?" I asked.

Helena waited for her husband to speak, but he just shook his head. "Last fall," Helena said, "the girls suddenly began acting... oddly." She frowned, reaching for words. "They've always been close, thankfully. But they became inseparable."

"Their grades dropped," Terence put in.

"Yes, they weren't focusing as much on schoolwork," Helena agreed. "But I was more concerned with their social lives. Sydney and her boyfriend broke up and she didn't seem all that upset by it. She and Layla started spending so much time together, going out all the time, whispering to each other when they thought we might hear them, locking themselves in one or the other's room and talking all evening."

"What were your suspicions?" I asked.

"Terry didn't allow for much speculation. He confronted them."

This didn't surprise me. He was a no-nonsense kind of guy, after all. "And?" I prompted.

"Well, it turned out they'd each been keeping secrets from the rest of us. And from each other," Helena said. "At some point, one of them found out the other's secret and revealed her own."

"That's when they became joined at the hip," Terence said.

Helena nodded. "So we sat them down and demanded to know what was going on. And... well..."

"They're metas, Dyna," Terence said, looking at me with a pained expression.

I blinked. "Wow, really?"

"To say the least, we were shocked," Helena said. "They'd each discovered this around the normal time one does, from what we've read. Which meant that Sydney had been keeping this secret from us for about a decade."

That sounded about right, I thought. "What are their abilities?" I asked.

Terence shook his head. "They'd kill us if we didn't let them show you, themselves," he said with a faint smile.

I smirked. "Yeah, okay. So... has this been causing problems with you all? The last time we talked..."

"Well," Helena said, "for my part, I was most upset that they felt they couldn't tell us. We've always been close, so it hurt that they didn't think they could confide in me. As for Terry..."

He looked at me, apologetically. "I'm having a hard time with it. When we had girls, I was relieved. I figured the likelihood that either of them would choose a dangerous career – military or law enforcement, for example – was pretty slim, compared to what boys might choose. But now..."

Terry knew how dangerous the life of a meta could be. As our Coast Guard liaison for the Bay Scouts, he shared in our pain when Valora was killed and Daniel was crippled.

Just then, the front door burst open and the girls came rushing in. "Dyna!" they yelled in unison a moment before Layla jumped on me. Sydney was a little more restrained, but sat beside me and gave me a hug.

I hugged them back, then they both took stock of me. "Wow," Layla said. "Dad wasn't kidding. You do look different!"

I spent a few minutes answering their inevitable questions about all of that, before finally saying, "Okay, enough about me. What about you two?"

The girls exchanged glances and grins, both of them seeming suddenly to be much, much younger. Together, they each grabbed one of my hands and hauled me through the house, their parents following.

The Shepherds had an above-ground pool in their back yard. Sydney led us to the edge, then extended a hand toward the water, twirling her fingers around. In moments, a waterspout shot up from the pool.

"Nifty," I said.

She then plunged her hand into the pool, pointing it along the wall. The water began to churn, turning into a pool-sized whirlpool. A beach ball and other pool toys zoomed around and were eventually sucked down.

"Nice! Can you form a vortex in the air, too?"

"Sure can!" she said.

"How hard can you hit me?"

Sydney looked cautiously at her father. "Go ahead, kiddo. She can take it."

"Um, okay," she said. We moved to face each other, several yards apart. "Are you sure?" she said to me.

"Give it your best shot," I said.

And she did. Planting one foot in front of the other, she leaned forward, both arms outstretched toward me. Her hands were a blur, to the point of it seeming as though she didn't have any. And the wind blew me backward so hard that I nearly plowed into the wooden fence.

I walked back. "Okay," I said. "That was pretty good. What else you got?"

"That's about it," she said.

I frowned, looking at her. She smiled awkwardly, then avoided my gaze. "Seriously," I said. "What else?"

Sydney glanced between her parents, who clearly believed their daughter. "Um," she said.

"Go ahead," Layla said, causing Terence and Helena to stare at her, then back at Sydney.

With a sheepish smile at her parents, Sydney lowered her arms to point at the grass. The next thing we knew, she was lifting into the air. Then she pointed her toes at the ground and her feet, too, began to rotate faster than we could follow. She shot into the sky.

"Oh, my god!" Helena cried. Terence just stared. Layla cheered.

Sydney performed some impressive aerobatics, making her mother's jaw drop. "Get down here!"

"Do it!" Layla yelled.

At her sister's command, Sydney stopped her flight and came plummeting to earth. As her parents gasped in horror, Sydney stopped her fall by engaging her abilities again, landing softly on the lawn with a bow. She again smiled awkwardly at her parents.

"So, yeah," she said. "There's that, too."

Her parents struggled to find words. Before they could go all apoplectic, I said, "That was great!" I hugged her tightly. "I guess you've had quite a bit of time to practice." As Sydney nodded, I turned to her sister. "And what about you, Layla?"

The younger sister shrugged her shoulders. "Nothing as impressive as that," she said.

"Oh, baloney," Sydney said.

Layla looked behind me, toward the pool. A second later, the beach ball bounced off the back of my head. I chuckled. "Telekinesis," I said. "That's awesome!"

"Well, not so much," she said. "Like, I can push things around, but that's it. I can't lift them."

"What kind of weight are we talking about?" I asked. The next thing I knew, I was hurled across the yard again. I picked myself up with a grin. "Not bad."

"But I can't pick you up," she said. "And you don't weigh that much."

"Can you lift yourself?"

Layla shook her head. "Not... no."

Then her sister spoke up. "Show her what you *can* do."

Layla smiled shyly. "Okay. Meet me in the front." Her father wore a resigned expression; Helena looked worried. I knew this had to be hard for them, but there was no stopping it, now.

As the rest of us walked around the house, Layla dashed inside, meeting us in the front a minute later wearing a pair of roller skates. "Okay," she said. "Here I go." She skated to one end of the block and around the corner.

"Okay, now look this way," Sydney said after her sister disappeared from sight. We all turned to look toward the corner at the other end of the block. A few seconds later, Layla came tearing around the corner, shooting past us like a rocket.

"Whoa," I said, my eyes popping.

"I just know she's going to fall and rip every bit of skin from her body," Helena said, frowning.

"Still," Terence said, "I don't think that's the most impressive thing she can do, though it's certainly the showiest."

"What's the other bit?" I asked him.

"I believe you guys refer to it as a technopathic ability."

"Like Ping Song," I said.

"She can't control machinery like Song can, but she's able to interfere with electronics. As long as she's in proximity to them, anyway."

"Interfere how?"

Sydney laughed. "She can make the TV go all staticky."

Terence grimaced. "I called the cable company *three times*," he said. "*Three. Times*. Never understood why the girls found it so funny."

"That's because you're a fuddy duddy, Daddy," Sydney said.

"It's still not funny."

"It's kind of funny," I said. And even though Terence scowled at me, I could tell he was pleased that I was siding with his girls.

Layla came rolling to a stop near me. "So what did you think?" she said with a grin.

"I think you'd be a terror on the roller derby circuit," I said.

Layla laughed. "That's what Mom said!"

"Okay, you two," Helena said. "Come help me with dinner and let Dyna and your father talk business."

The girls hugged me before heading off with their mother. Terence and I went for a walk. "So what do you need from me?" I asked.

"Advice, I suppose."

"I can't be the first you've told."

"No," he confirmed. "I confided in Daniel."

"I was going to suggest that. He's a great choice for helping to train the girls."

"Train them," Terence said flatly. "Dyna, I just..."

"Look, you know what's going to happen. You've seen their faces whenever I answer their questions about stuff I did with the Scouts and the Gatekeepers. They're going to want to establish themselves in the community."

Terence shook his head. "I know, but I just can't–"

"What you *can't* do," I interrupted, "is prevent it. So your choice is only whether you get them some training or let them go their own way." He smiled faintly and looked into my eyes. "Which is the other reason you asked me over," I said, "isn't it?"

"I trust you, Dyna. Aside from Daniel, there's no meta I know better. Daniel is willing to help with training, but when it comes time for them to join a team, I want them with you."

I raised an eyebrow. "I'm flattered. But don't you think you should leave that decision up to them?"

"You think they *won't* want to be with you? They practically idolize you."

"That's because I'm the only meta who comes over to visit."

"You know that's not why," he said. "They like you because you're genuine. You clearly care about them, and they know that."

"Even so, they may decide that the Project isn't the right kind of group for them. They're young and will likely want the full experience. We act out of the public eye, generally. Joining my group won't get them noticed."

"My girls may have started acting differently once they learned each other's secrets, but I don't think their personalities have changed. They've never sought the spotlight. Never wanted to be the star of the show. I don't think they've turned into glory hounds."

"If they're interested, I'll certainly put my vote in."

"Your vote?"

"The girls would need to be approved by the rest of the team," I explained.

"I thought you were the leader."

I shook my head. "Just the founder and primary paper pusher. We're not a dictatorship. Nor a democracy. We operate by consensus." When he frowned, I said, "But don't worry. I can't think of any reason they wouldn't get complete support from the team. In a way, they're just the sort we look for."

He smiled faintly. "Thanks. I appreciate that."

"But do have Daniel work with them. That's a great start."

"I will," he said, turning back to the house. "Hungry?"

I laughed. "If you have to ask, you don't know me as well as you think."

That night, my brain was fixated on the Overseer. If the man was strong enough to erase, or at least muddle, someone's memory of meeting him, he was definitely powerful enough to remain mysterious if he wanted to.

The thing I was most curious about was how the telepaths were controlled. Surely, he couldn't be strong enough to keep them all in line by himself, could he? Dana had had some success in removing individual telepaths from the network in that world, but until he knew how the control was done, he couldn't break it.

Giving up on sleep, I got out of bed, intending to see what I could pillage from the fridge. But I never made it to the stairs. Two steps across the floor, an intense pain slammed my body, all over. Every bit of me felt like it was burning up, even my bones. It had no point of origin, feeling as though it erupted everywhere simultaneously. It took my breath away and I collapsed, gasping, too shocked to even moan.

It stopped as abruptly as it had come on, leaving me panting on the parquet floor. As I recovered, I continued to lie there, a dread of suspicion slowly growing in my mind.

I got no sleep that night.

Fourteen

"Nothing is perfect. Life is messy. Relationships are complex. Outcomes are uncertain. People are irrational."
~ Hugh Mackay

My relationship with my family (as is overwhelmingly obvious) has always been a bit of a mess. Sometimes it was my own doing, but my parents were largely at fault. Fortunately, all of us matured over the years and things improved.

It was after this improvement that I began to understand just how complicated my relationships were in the first place. To my surprise, I discovered that, no matter how much I hated my mother for what she'd done and how she'd treated me, there had still been some love there, all along. It wasn't until then that I truly understood the idea of a "love/hate" relationship. And of course, if such a thing was true for me, it certainly could be true for others. Including Vicky.

She had been avoiding me for weeks, and I'd been allowing it, since I knew how hard a time she was having with me being "back." But I shouldn't have, because we needed to understand Weatherford's motives, and I believed she had more to tell us. So I called her to come in for a chat.

I was downstairs in the kitchen when she arrived. She entered, seeing me sitting at a table with a pot of coffee and a pink box of donuts.

"You said this was about business," she said.

"It's a business breakfast."

She sat and poured herself a cup. "That works."

"Still, if you wanted to talk about non-business things, such as why you've been avoiding me, I'd be open to hearing it."

"I haven't been," she said.

"Then why haven't I seen you since Bridget's graduation?"

Vicky added milk to her cup. "Does it matter? I heard you're seeing some teenager, anyway."

I contained my surprise. "Not a teenager," I said. "And it's only been one date." Then I smiled a little. "Was that jealousy?" I smirked as Vicky frowned at me, her gray eyes narrowing.

"So what did you want to discuss?"

"Your father."

"Fucking hell. Again?"

I swallowed a bite of apple fritter. "Don't take this the wrong way, but I have the feeling you've been holding back."

"On what?"

"About his goals, for one thing. About your relationship with him, for another."

"If this is about the abduction again..."

"It really isn't," I said. "Though, now that you bring it up, I also get the feeling there's more behind your somewhat indifferent attitude about it than you having been drugged." Vicky didn't respond. "Let's start with this: how old is he?"

She chuckled, snagging a custard-filled from the box. "I'll defer to Probe's research on that one. I honestly have no idea."

"Okay," I said. "And what about you?"

Now she frowned. "You know bloody well that I'm thirty."

"Do I? I mean, that's what you tell me. But for all I know, you could be a *hundred* and thirty."

Vicky looked at me like I was an idiot. "Seriously?"

"Vick, I don't know!" I said, and regretted the exasperation in my voice. I changed the focus of the conversation. "Look, you told me once that the so-called Nexus Prime would be able to tap into all the dimensions, right?"

"In theory."

"But why is that such a big deal? I mean, both you and he can tap into all but one, allegedly, if there are only as many planes as you've told me. And you said that he thinks the addition of that one extra will allow *time travel*, of all things."

Vicky wiped custard from her mouth. "Right. He's a nutter."

I frowned. "You've never described him as crazy, before. And he's never struck me as delusional," I said. "So are you sure that's what he honestly thinks it will do?"

"Christ, Dyna," she snapped. "I'm not sure of *anything*! You should know that." She collected herself and said, "About the only thing I'm certain of is that he's desperate."

"Oh?"

She took a deep breath and explained. "He's like a politician. He tends to make promises at the drop of a hat, whether or not he can fulfill them. So he's been grasping at straws for years in order to fulfill his promise of this big breakthrough."

"And what's the big deal if he doesn't have his breakthrough?"

"Honestly, it's probably not a big deal at all. The rest of the group most likely wouldn't care. Hell, many of them don't even believe there's anything left for the group to discover. They think all possible planes have been reached. But he's obsessed. And that's made him do things that he otherwise wouldn't," she finished quietly.

I was a bit shocked by what she was implying. Was she actually defending him?

"Vick... Do you still care about him?"

She let out a chuckle. "I don't think that's the right word."

"Then what is?"

Vicky gazed into her coffee mug and spoke without looking up. "Whatever else you can say about him, you have to understand that he's not evil."

"How can you say that?" I blurted. "After what he did to you?"

"There's a difference between evil and amoral," Vicky said. "Believe me, part of me wishes he *were* evil. It would make it easier. But he's not out to conquer the world. He's not out to deliberately hurt anyone, for that matter."

"Except you, evidently."

Now she looked up, with a smirk. "Yeah, well... that's just the nature of our relationship. We hurt each other."

"How have you hurt him?"

Her expression changed, her eyes showing pain. She hid it with a casual shrug. "I tried to kill him." I know the shock showed on my face. I wasn't expecting that kind of admission. "Thought I'd done, too," she continued, "but I didn't stick around to find out. Guess that cheesed him a bit."

"And what had he done to warrant that?"

Vicky stared into her coffee. "Honestly... probably nothing," she said. I waited for her to explain. Vicky placed the remnants of her donut on a napkin. "About seven years ago," she said quietly, "I learned that my mother was dead. She hadn't been sick or anything, and she wasn't that old. The person who told me said no one was sure how she'd died, but there were suspicions and rumors. I guess I just assumed those rumors were true."

"You thought he killed her? Why?"

"Because she had helped me escape. I assumed he learned this and took it out on her." She was quiet for a moment. "If I'd given it serious thought, I'd have realized this was wrong. He had to know she'd done this as soon as I went missing. Why wait? If he was going to kill her, he'd have done it then. But I didn't think about it. I just reacted."

"What did you do?"

"I showed up at his office in London and confronted him. Accused him of it. He denied it, of course. Said it was a brain aneurysm. But I didn't believe him. I called him a liar, opened a portal behind him, and shoved him through."

"A portal to...?"

Vicky shook her head. "Doesn't matter. He didn't stay there." She frowned. "Thing is, he even expressed his sympathy and seemed genuinely sincere. Had I not been so angry, I'd have seen it sooner."

We were quiet for a moment, then I asked, "You still want him dead?"

"No." Frowning, she said, "I have no desire to see him again, of course. But I know that's unlikely, especially given these developments with him and that Overseer guy."

"Whatever those developments might be," I said bitterly. Then I sighed. "But you're probably right. Your old man doesn't seem evil. I have no idea what his goals really are. But at any rate, they don't seem as insidious as the Overseer's actions."

"And what's happening with that?" Vicky asked as she finished off her donut. "Anything new?"

"Not that I've heard. Dynasonic's brother and his group are doing all the covert stuff. When they need our help, they'll send word to us."

"What kind of covert stuff?"

"As I understand it, they're trying to undo the Overseer's work. They've successfully deprogrammed some of the telepaths, removing them from the network. But so far, they've had no luck in getting to the political leaders the Overseer has psychically corrupted."

"And you think they're going to need us?"

"I don't know," I said. "They don't have much of an established meta presence, and it's unlikely that the Overseer's telepaths will encounter much resistance from the locals."

"Yeah, I would imagine that's true," she said. Then, after a short silence, she asked, "And how was the date?"

I laughed. "So it *was* jealousy," I said.

Vicky snorted. "As if."

I grinned. "Well, it was fun, actually."

Vicky stared into her coffee. "Gonna see her again?"

"Is there a reason I shouldn't?"

She ignored my question. "Is she pretty?"

"Right... you're not jealous," I teased.

"I'm not," she insisted. "Just curious."

"She's a green-haired, impish, emo sort of thing who dresses in leather. With a dimple. So, yeah. She's cute. But that's not why I'm dating her."

Now she looked at me. "Oh? Why are you?"

"You seriously don't know?" When she shook her head, I said, "Vick... she works in a *pizza shop*!"

Vicky stared at me, then burst out laughing. "Oh, my god."

I grinned at her. I love Vicky's laugh. Then I stood and cleared away our empty mugs. Vicky fell silent as I did this. When I returned to the table, I stepped up behind her and ran my fingers through her hair.

Vicky stiffened. "Um..." she breathed.

"Hm?" I said as I pulled her hair aside and kissed her neck.

"I don't think–"

"I don't want you to," I interrupted.

I kissed down to her shoulder, feeling her shiver. But then she pulled away and stood. She gave me an apologetic smile, but only looked in my eyes for a moment. "I should go," she said. "Sorry." And then she turned and headed up the stairs to the street.

Because I'm an obstinate woman, I didn't tell anyone about the sudden, overwhelming pain I'd had a couple nights before, but I couldn't stop thinking about it. As a formality, I'd gone online and tried to find a description of what I'd experienced, but found nothing. Other "all over" pain descriptions were about joints or muscles, mostly. But mine was literally everywhere. All the joints, all the muscles, but also every inch of my skin. Anything that could feel pain did. And maybe some things that couldn't, since I'm pretty sure my hair hurt. Had it gone on for more than a few seconds, I was certain I'd have passed out.

I thought about this as I studied the readouts from my monitoring of the Glass Man. It had been more than a week since his stint in the electric arc furnace. I was pleased with what I saw. According to the readouts, his body temperature was still above ambient temperature. And it was even a degree warmer than it had been five days before.

But as exciting as the readings were, the real stunner was with the physical measurements I took daily. There could be no denying it, now. The "glass" was flowing.

His eye sockets were filling in. His spine was thickening. And while it was difficult to measure, I was certain that the large mass at the bottom was shrinking.

If this "growth" stayed at the same rate, I expected that Henry's body would look more or less normal within three months. Of course, the rate could change, one way or the other. But there was no question something amazing was happening.

This, too, I kept to myself.

That Saturday, Kit and Lily had a housewarming party at their new place in San Bruno. It was a nice place. Three bedrooms, two baths, and a full basement. This, of course, would become Kit's workshop. I wondered yet again just how much money the kid had gotten for selling his sonic weapons to the military. The house had to have set him back lots of zeroes.

Most of the team was there, bringing gifts and congratulations. And food. Lots of food. I brought a childhood favorite: red beet pickled eggs. They got strange looks from just about everyone, which just added to my pleasure.

After getting the tour of the house, I wandered into the dining room, where I found Nena sitting in a corner. Her hair was burning blue. Sitting next to her, I said, "I know your plasma isn't reflective of your mood, but you do seem a bit down," I said.

In reply, she put on a fake smile and changed her plasma to a sunny yellow. "Better?"

"Nope," I said, and the smile vanished, though the yellow remained. "You're upset about them moving."

"Just got to the point that Lily felt like family. And now she's leaving."

"It's not that far," I said.

"It's like an hour," she said.

"What? No, it's..." Then I realized what she meant. Her mode of travel would be public transportation. "Oh," I said. "Right."

"It's fine. I'm used to not having anyone around."

Lily wandered into the room just as Nena said this. Her hairline glowed with lilac flames, reacting to the sweat she'd worked up by running around visiting guests. "What are you guys talking about?" she said, grabbing a handful of sesame sticks from a bowl on the table.

Nena looked up at her. "Just... you know... this."

Lily stood next to me, her hand on my shoulder. "Neen," she said, "just do it."

Nena shook her head and said, "It's nice of you, but Kit–"

"Kit is cool with it!"

"He's just saying that to be nice."

I frowned. "What are we talking about?"

Nena said nothing, so Lily replied. "We invited her to live with us. We totally have the space."

It was a nice gesture, I thought, but I could certainly understand Nena's hesitation. Such arrangements often sound great at first, but deteriorate. "Where do you live now?" I asked, embarrassed that I didn't know.

"I share a house with some other girls," she said. "It's fine."

"It's *not* fine," Lily insisted. "Dyna, it's six of them in a duplex with three tiny bedrooms and one bathroom. Very cramped. No privacy."

"Doesn't matter," Nena said. "I'm almost never home."

"Yeah, but don't you want to be comfortable when you are? Don't you want to have a room of your own? Hell, a bathroom of your own! And with the money you save in rent, you can buy a car," she said.

Nena sat on her hands, staring at the floor. It seemed to me that she wanted to do this, but felt like she couldn't. I elbowed her gently. "Seems like a great offer, kiddo."

"Please," Lily begged. "You're my best friend. I really want you here."

I stood and left them to their discussion. Sinta pounced on me as I stepped outside into the yard. "What do you think?" she asked. "Like it here?"

"I do, yeah. It's much quieter."

"That's the part I don't like," she said. "I've lived my whole life in the city. I'm so used to noise that a quiet neighborhood like this feels weird. Even though it's pretty."

"Kitten," I said, a thought striking me, "how much travel have you done outside of the city?"

"Just whatever missions we've had that took me there."

"Seriously? You've never traveled for fun?" She shook her head. "What about local sights? Muir Woods, maybe?"

"I think one of the foster families took us there once, but I was really little."

"Wow. Okay, we're going to remedy that," I said. "There's so much to see just here in California, alone. And you're going to see some of it."

Sinta smiled, then went back inside for more food, leaving me alone in the yard. Their new home was on Crestmoor Drive, with Crestmoor Canyon practically in their back yard. You could look over the fence into the trees.

I stood there, admiring the greenery, and was soon lost in thought. Truth was, I understood how Nena felt. In a way, I was feeling the same way in the team.

Sure, most of the members claimed they were accepting of the "new me," but there was a part of me that didn't fully believe them. At least Cara made her feelings clear. Were the others really being honest?

Then there was my family. I knew I shouldn't worry about it, since they weren't exactly a large part of my life. But I'd spent so long feeling unloved and unaccepted, and lately things had been better. Would our relationship revert to how it was before? Or be worse?

How would Sharon, Jackie, and little Dinah react to seeing me? Or Rhonda and her family? I'd promised all of them that I'd bring them out to visit. But my stomach knotted whenever I thought about those reunions.

I already tended to hide from situations that made me uncomfortable. The last thing I needed was to use this as an excuse to become a recluse.

I exhaled heavily, then turned to return to the party, only to find Cara walking toward me. "*Pardonez*," she said. "Am I interrupting?"

"Not a bit," I said. "I'm glad you were able to come."

"It is a nice house," she said.

"Very," I agreed. "But that's not what you came to say to me." I braced myself for her words.

"*C'est vrai,*" she said, standing next to me. She gazed out at the trees. "You and the others gave me much to think about," she said quietly. "I wanted you to know that I have been."

"And how's that been going?"

Cara hesitated, then said, "After speaking with *Père* Laurant, I have concluded that perhaps my views are too *rigide*. I have been thinking about our experience in the other world. That event itself shook my beliefs, if I am honest."

"Hell, it shook mine, too," I admitted. "Sometimes, I still find it hard to accept."

"What bothered me most is that there is no mention of such worlds in the Bible. How could such an important thing be omitted?"

That was a rabbit hole I wasn't about to go down, so I just shrugged. Instead, I said, "Have you changed at all how you view what I did and what I am?"

Cara turned to face me, a gentle smile on her face. "I still believe what you did was sinful. But we are all sinners, and all worthy of forgiveness. As for what you are... It is, I've decided, not my place to judge. You have never been anything other than kind to me. And it would be wrong of me not to return that kindness."

She said this with trepidation, but I smiled and hugged her. "That's enough for me," I said.

She seemed surprised, but hugged me back, gently, then said, "And you are very forgiving."

I released her from the embrace and said, "Is there anything else on your mind?"

"*Oui,*" she said after a brief hesitation. "I am worried about returning to the team. The others were quite upset with me."

"Was anyone rude to you, here?"

"*Non.* They were quite friendly."

"And that's how they'll be with you on the team. If you're okay with me, they'll be okay with you."

Again, the gentle smile. "*Merci,*" she said, then we headed back inside to socialize more before heading our separate ways.

Before going home, I stopped at Wonderland Robotics. Jack had been unable to attend the housewarming due to being neck-deep in a project at work. He was surprised to see me when I arrived.

"Can you afford to take a break?" I asked.

"Yeah," he said. "I was thinking of lunch, honestly."

The facility had its own cafeteria, so we ate there. The food was surprisingly decent. "So what's on your mind?" Jack eventually asked.

I hesitated, idly dragging a French fry through a puddle of mustard, causing Jack to wrinkle his nose. "Cara was at the housewarming," I said. "Things between us are good, but..."

Jack waited for me to complete the thought before saying, "...but you're questioning things?"

"Most of the time, I'm fine. Other times, though... I sort of feel like..."

"Like what?"

I shrugged. "Like I don't belong." To my surprise, Jack laughed. I stared at him. "What's so funny?"

He collected himself and said, "You mean you feel like a pariah?" And he laughed again.

Despite myself, I snorted, hanging my head. "Ugh. Okay, I appreciate the irony," I said, looking back at him. "Chuckles aside, though..."

"Yeah," Jack said. "Dyna, I don't know what to say, honestly."

"How does it feel having me around? Is it different from before?"

"Well... yeah. I mean, the obvious things, like your appearance and your voice. But to me, anyway, you're still the same friend I've had for six years."

"Has it really only been six years? It feels so much longer."

"Well, they've been pretty full years."

"That's for sure," I agreed.

I looked around the mostly vacant cafeteria. It was mid-afternoon, after all. But as I watched, an attractive woman entered, looked around, and headed to our table.

"Hi, Aimee," I said, causing Jack to turn.

"Hi, Dyna."

"Hey," Jack said.

"Cheating right in the open," she teased, ruffling his hair before sitting with us.

"Working him even on a weekend?" I said. "You taskmaster."

"He volunteered!"

Our conversation effectively over, I stood. "Thanks for the chat, Jack. I need to get going." As the pair bade me farewell, I carried my tray to the trash, then headed home.

As usual, Dana came to visit over the Fourth of July weekend. We spent Friday night relaxing at my place over a couple large bottles of Duchesse de Bourgogne that he'd brought. We sat in front of the fireplace, talking idly about different matters, including the Shepherd girls, my plans to take Sinta on a trip or two, and the "statue" upstairs.

"This beer is wonderful," I said. "Kinda has a hint of balsamic vinegar."

"One of my all-time favorites."

"How are things with you and Bronwyn? You guys getting serious?"

Dana looked at me with a curious expression at the sudden change of topic. "Would you be okay with that?"

I looked away from him. "Of course. Why wouldn't I be?"

"I don't even need telepathy to tell you're lying."

I've never been good at hiding my feelings from Dana. "I like her," I said. "Honest. But she's five thousand miles away!"

He gazed into his glass. "That may not always be the case."

"Really? She'd move here?" Dana hesitated, and I felt my stomach drop. "No!"

He shrugged and said, "I'm not inherently opposed to the idea."

I couldn't look at him in that moment. I turned my head away and fought down a nasty stab of anxiety.

"Look," he said, "it's too early to talk about it."

"But you're considering it!" I said, turning to face him again.

"Can we not talk about it?"

I let out a breath I didn't realize I was holding. "Yeah, okay."

After several seconds staring at the fireplace in uncomfortable silence, Dana said, "So... Sinta. Where will you take her?"

"Um... I was thinking Monterey, first. I think she'd like the aquarium."

"I'm sure."

"Of course, if I wait until later in the year for that, we can go over to Pacific Grove to see the butterflies."

"I've always wanted to do that."

"Well, you won't be able to do it if you're in Wales," I said with more snark than I'd intended. And I regretted it as soon as it was out of my mouth.

To his credit, Dana ignored it, asking instead about the Project and how it was going. We ended up talking only for another half hour or so before he said he was tired and needed to go to bed.

I couldn't blame him. After he went to the guest room, I sat there in front of the fire, angry with myself. I was being selfish, I knew, but I couldn't help it. The thought of Dana moving to another country made my stomach knot. Hell, I didn't even like it when he was in Sacramento. I'd even given serious thought to asking him to move to San Francisco, to take the guest room as his permanent residence.

Why was my relationship with my brother so complicated? Was I still making up for all the time lost due to my own stupidity? I turned off the fireplace and began clearing up the empty glasses. But halfway to the stairs to the kitchen, I was wracked with pain again. Just like the previous time, it was sudden and seemed to cover every inch of my body, inside and out. It was so intense that I couldn't breathe, let alone scream. Then I blacked out.

By the time I came to, Dana was there beside me, his face white with worry. "What happened?" he practically yelled.

I looked around as he helped me up. Broken glassware littered the floor. One of the conference chairs was on its side. As Dana guided me back to the sofa, I told him about the pain, both occurrences of it. We looked into each other's eyes, and I could tell, even without a psychic link, that he was thinking the same thing I was.

The memory of my death was becoming unlocked in my brain.

FIFTEEN

"It has been said that time heals all wounds. I don't agree. The wounds remain. Time - the mind, protecting its sanity - covers them with some scar tissue and the pain lessens, but it is never gone."

~ Rose Kennedy

I think nearly everyone has experienced a feeling of hopelessness at some point in his or her life. It can be debilitating, and once you've experienced it, you never forget it. Students in danger of failing a class have a taste of it, assuming they care about passing. Someone suddenly losing a loved one will often feel hopeless. An individual diagnosed with a terminal illness certainly feels it.

There have been moments in my life when I have felt hopeless. Like when it seemed as though my years of research into triggering a meta mutation in myself were totally wasted. Like when I nearly died from cryptococcal meningitis. And, though I wasn't about to admit this to my brother, his warnings about my death memory definitely reminded me of that feeling of despair. But, like the other instances, I wasn't about to give up.

I woke the next day to see Dana sitting next to my bed. "Hey," he said.

"Mmph," I replied, rubbing the sleep from my eyes.

"How do you feel?"

I thought about that for a second. "Like I have to pee," I said, pulling back the blankets.

"Aside from that," he said.

"I'm fine," I said as I walked to bathroom. After relieving myself, I quickly brushed my teeth, then yelled out to Dana, "I'm gonna shower. Come talk to me."

In the huge, walk-in shower, I turned on the water. It's heated by a built-in propane-fueled heat exchanger, which makes it instantly hot. I stood there, being sprayed from multiple angles. Dana entered the bathroom a moment later and took a seat on the toilet lid, facing away from the shower.

"So," I said as I soaked my hair and began shampooing, "I've been thinking a lot about this, even before the first episode. I've told you before that I've felt something's been missing, that I've felt incomplete."

"Right," Dana said. "The link."

"I do still think that's part of it, but more and more, I've been thinking it was actually the death memory."

"That isn't possible. That memory – that experience – was never *part* of you. It's what *ended* you."

"Right. It *completed* me," I said. "Literally."

"But the 'you' that you remember being was not in any way shaped by that."

"I know it makes no sense, but it just *feels* like the answer," I said as I rinsed out the shampoo.

"Oh, good," Dana said. "I'm glad you're approaching this like a scientist."

"Shut up," I said with a laugh. "But seriously, what could be the result of unlocking that memory completely?"

"Doesn't matter," he said. "I won't do it."

"Just humor me," I said as I worked conditioner into my hair. "Hypothetically, what could happen? Worst case scenario."

Dana was silent a moment. "It's impossible to say," he finally said. "Any way you look at it, it was a traumatic event, so we could expect you to be... well... traumatized."

"Lots of people suffer deep trauma, but deal with it," I said.

"And lots don't," he snapped. "If everyone did, I wouldn't have my career."

I picked up my body wash and squeezed it onto the bath pouf. "Yeah, and maybe then you'd be out there with the rest of us metas."

"Point is," he said, ignoring the jab, "you don't have a great track record of handling trauma well. You spent the entirety of last year trying to get past the death of Dr. Gray."

I frowned as I washed. "That was more guilt than trauma. I've dealt with physical trauma pretty well."

"Well, not to point out the obvious, but you've never dealt with physical trauma of this scale."

"Dana, you know what I'm asking."

He was quiet long enough for me to finish my shower. I turned off the water, squeezed the excess from my hair, grabbed a towel from the rack, and began drying off. I looked at Dana, seeing a hint of a frown teasing at the corner of his mouth. Then he said, "Yes. It's conceivable that it could kill you."

I absorbed that for a minute. "Then I guess you should unlock it pretty soon."

Dana stood, backing up to the doorway. "I already told you I won't."

"Well, it's coming unlocked by itself, whether you like it or not. I figure it's better to do it under your control than otherwise."

I wrapped the towel around myself, and we walked back into the bedroom area, where Dana sat on the end of my bed and said, "If I go into your head, I'm going to erase it, not reveal it."

"No," I said. "You won't." I sat at my vanity and combed out my hair before pulling it into a ponytail. Dana sat silently on the bed, evidently not wanting to argue with me. Probably because I tend to win our arguments. Or think I do, anyway.

I finished at the vanity, tossed my damp towel aside, then stepped over to my wardrobe, pulling out a pair of white jeans and a hot pink blouse. I tossed the shirt into Dana's lap as I closed the wardrobe. "Pink?" he said. "Really?"

I pulled on the jeans. "Rare for me, I know." Dana handed me the blouse. I slipped it on and buttoned it.

"Do you even own any bras?" Dana asked.

"Just sexy ones," I said with a smirk. "Seriously, do I have enough there to require daily support?"

"That question is a trap," he said.

"And they look even better with this new body, wouldn't you say?" Dana blushed and said nothing. "Now come on. I'm hungry."

On the walk to the restaurant, he tried arguing more against unlocking the memory. I ignored everything he said. As far as I was concerned, the conversation was over. He just had to accept it.

As we approached the venue, he saw the painted sign on the wall of the building. "Moulin," he said. "Shouldn't there be 'Rouge' there?" He pointed to the space where the word had clearly once been, but was painted over. "And there, and there," he said, pointing to the signs over the door as we reached our destination.

"Yeah, well, seems there's a cabaret in Paris that got wind of this place and became a little pissy."

Dana shook his head. "Because the two places are so easily mistaken for one another."

"Well, I *was* disappointed not to find dancing girls here," I said.

"And hordes of Parisians are wondering why they can't get waffles as they watch the ladies."

I laughed as we entered. A moment later, an elderly Korean man greeted us, picking up a coffee pot when he saw it was me. "Dinah!" he said. "Good morning." He indicated a small table near the door.

"*Joeun achimieyo*," I said. "Lee Jong, this is my brother, Dana."

As the men greeted each other, I waved at his wife, Janet, busy cooking. She smiled and waved back. Then we took our seats.

"Friendly fellow," Dana said as we looked over the menus.

"They're both very sweet," I said.

"You come here a lot, obviously."

"Mm hm," I said, pushing my menu aside. "And you'll see why."

"And you speak... was that Korean?"

"Kim taught me some basics."

After we placed our orders, Dana grew serious again. "I mean it, Dinah. Unlocking it is just too dangerous. I won't do it."

"So you'd rather it just come back by itself?" I said as I sipped my coffee.

"No! We need to get rid of it entirely. I don't know why I didn't do that from the start."

"Right. So, since I don't want you to do that, does that mean you're going to do it against my will?"

Dana stared at me, clearly unable to comprehend why I was being so obstinate about this. Finally, he said, "Yes."

I laughed. "You're a poor liar."

"I would," he insisted.

He avoided looking at me, which was good, since I didn't want him to see the smile I couldn't quite hide. We sat in silence until our food arrived. Dana looked at the huge portions on the plate before him.

"Now I see why you eat here. You might actually get full."

I laughed. "No, but it does come close," I said as I dug into my cream cheese-stuffed French toast.

"And it's good," he said with his mouth full. "I approve."

We chatted idly as we ate. Finally, I decided to put our ongoing conversation to rest. "Dana, I know you're worried about this. I've been waiting for you to realize how wrong you are about it, but if I have to prove it, I will."

"I do know how much you love doing that, but tell me why you think I should 'realize' this at all?"

"Because the evidence is right in front of you."

He frowned. "What do you mean?"

I pointed to my head. "Because this brain experienced that death, in a manner of speaking. Twice, now. And I'm clearly not dead."

Dana sighed, and I smiled, satisfied.

"No," he said.

"No, what?"

"No, your brain did not experience that. Remember, I told you that the daily experiences were being fed into a part of your mind that I'd blocked off. The death 'experience' was recorded there, in that separate area, away from your consciousness. Even so, it was so strong that some of it leaked through, out of the blocked area. That leak is what you've experienced, not the full thing." He waited for a response from me, but I had none. "If it had broken through completely – if you had *actually* experienced the full thing – then you would have the memory. Your own memory. Not 'hers.' What you got then was a mere taste of it, so what you're experiencing now is just that – the memory of that small taste."

I shook my head. "If that was the case, wouldn't I have that memory all the time? Of the bit that slipped past?"

"People often repress bad memories," he said. "Could be that's what you subconsciously did. And now it could be resurfacing. I won't know for sure unless I go inside and look."

I was quiet as I took this all in, a cold fear forming inside me. He waited for a response from me, but I just stared at him, my stomach now no longer appreciating the breakfast. I'd been so *sure*.

"So," he said, "tell me again how you want to experience the *full* power of that memory."

Though the rest of the weekend was tainted with that particular concern, Dana and I still had fun. Sinta and Jasmine joined us for dinner on Saturday. And Sunday night, we went out on a cruise of the bay.

As we stood on the deck, waiting for the fireworks to begin, Dana noticed I was a bit quiet. "You seem preoccupied," he said. "Still thinking about the death memory?"

I shook my head. "A little, but... I'm thinking more about your upcoming trip."

"I thought you were okay with it," he said, pulling me closer to his chilly chest.

"I am," I said. "Mostly."

I felt Dana shiver next to me. It was cold out on the water and he hadn't dressed appropriately. I asked if he wanted to go below deck, but he declined. So, since I tend to run hot, I acted as his personal space heater, snuggling into his arms as the fireworks began.

"Damn... I don't remember you being this hot," he said.

"Aw, thanks... you're kinda cute, yourself."

He snorted. "Seriously, though."

"Yeah, it's a trick I learned a while back. If I 'power up,' as though I'm about to do some blasting, but then 'power down' slowly, the energy dissipates in the form of heat."

"Well. That's handy."

"Mm hm," I agreed. "Bath water never goes cold on me."

He laughed, then asked, "Do you think you have any other undiscovered abilities? Do you expect more to develop?"

"Normally, I wouldn't think so. I mean, there's only so many ways to expel energy. But then I developed that weird vision thing. So... anyone's guess."

We were quiet for a time, watching the fireworks and snuggling against the cold. Finally, he said, "You never elaborated about the trip."

I pressed myself more firmly against him. "That's because you started telling me how hot I am."

"Very funny."

"Hey, you're the one with your hands all over me."

I looked up to see him glaring at me. I grinned and winked at him. And that broke him. He laughed. "I give up. Make all the sexual innuendo you want. I can't fight it, anymore."

I clapped my hands. "Yay, I win!"

"You're still avoiding the subject, though." I frowned. Yes... Yes, I was. "You're worried about me possibly moving to the U.K."

"Of course," I said. "I remember our first trip there. It was great."

"Especially because no one was trying to kill us."

"Yes, *that* trip," I said with a chuckle. "It was obvious how much you loved it there. I mean, so did I. Hell, I could see you wanting to live there, even without Bronwyn." I was quiet a moment as a couple massive bursts lit the sky. "I just... I feel like we're still making up for lost time, you know?"

"Really?"

"Yes!" I said, turning to face him. "We were estranged for fifteen years!"

"Yeah, but since then, we've spent an awful lot of time together."

I looked into his eyes, my stomach sinking. "Are you saying that I should get over it, that I should consider all that time to be compensated for? Or are you saying that we spend too much time together?"

He shook his head. "I'm not."

"Then what *are* you saying?"

Dana sighed. "I don't know."

He gently turned me around and pulled me closer, wrapping his arms around me from behind. I couldn't blame him. After all, I wasn't sure what I was saying to him, either.

I returned my attention to the fireworks. Dana shivered against me. I smiled and snuggled closer... and turned up the heat for him.

✧ ✧ ✧

Dana returned to Sacramento the following day, then flew to the U.K. that Friday. I spent the days in between mostly as a recluse, analyzing the measurements I was taking of Hank, giving Jeremy some fix-up projects around the kitchen area, and dropping in unannounced to visit Daniel and Invictus.

That weekend, I was at Peacock Meadow, looking for possible prospects for the Project. I spent less than an hour there before deciding I wasn't in a recruiting mood, anyway. I'd been in a funk all week and needed to snap out of it. I had an idea of what might help, so I left the park and headed out to Haight Street.

Seeing me enter, Fabian said, "I almost forgot just how fast your hair grows." As he gently shampooed me, he grilled me about my love life, as was his habit. I gave noncommittal answers as well as I could, until he got more pointed with his questions. "Vicky and I aren't together, anymore," I said.

He finished rinsing and draped a towel over the wet locks. "Oh," he said. "Sorry."

"It's fine. We're fine," I said as I sat in the chair. "We both just have our own issues, right now."

I considered my words. I'd spoken them reflexively, but it was true. Vicky and I both had things to work through before we could be good for each other. It didn't make sense to get hung up on the fact. It's not like we'd had this great romance, after all. It was fun, sure, but neither of us had any illusions that it was a perfect match.

"You're uncharacteristically quiet."

"Yeah. Sorry." I smiled apologetically. "So what about you?"

"Oh, same old," he said, working his magic with the scissors. "Well, not entirely. I'm an uncle, again. My sister had her munchkin."

"Yeah?"

"Mm hm. A girl, this time, to go with the two boys."

"That's nice. Congrats."

Fabian hummed to himself as he entered "the zone" in his work. I gladly resumed my silence, waiting for him to finish. When he finally pronounced it done, I gave him a hug and thanked him. As always, my hair looked great. And it would continue to do so until I got tired of maintaining it, which would be in about three days, if history was any indicator. After paying, I stepped out onto the sidewalk. Without hesitation, I crossed diagonally to the other side.

I entered the pizza shop and stepped up to the counter. A lanky young man greeted me and asked for my order. I smiled as I looked past him. "I'd like two slices with mushrooms and black olives, a Dr Pepper, and the girl at the oven."

He stared at me, then turned to look at Ali, who glanced over to see me. Her surprise was obvious. She closed the oven door and walked over to the counter as the young man made himself busy preparing my slices.

"I'm not on the menu," Ali said, crossing her arms.

"Don't you guys have a secret menu, like In-N-Out Burger?"

Her eyes narrowed, but I saw the hint of amusement. "We do, but you have to know how to properly order from it."

I nodded soberly. "I see. In that case, can I have the Ali Special?"

She shook her head. "That's not how."

"The Green-Haired Monster?"

Ali snorted with laughter. "Strike two. One last try."

I looked her in the eye. "Could I please get the Sorry-for-Not-Calling-You-in-Weeks-Because-I'm-an-Idiot Special?"

"Hmm... That's a big order," she said. "Are you sure you can handle it?"

"I'll do my best."

She was silent a moment, looking intently at me. Then she glanced at the clock. "Special menu items take a while to prepare. It won't be ready for about forty-five minutes."

I smiled. "Totally worth the wait."

"We had coffee and talked," I said to Hank a few days later, as I looked over the readings from the past week. "I felt bad, honestly. Ali had assumed I'd gone out with her in the first place just to be nice, not because I wanted to, and so she wasn't surprised not to hear from me again. Of course, I assured her that wasn't true."

I typed some notes into my laptop and could swear I felt Hank's big, eye sockets staring at me. I looked up, frowning. "No, I didn't tell her the real reason. Are you kidding?" I looked away. "I dunno. I can't really call it a rebound from Vicky. There's not enough there to rebound from, right?"

I looked up at his face again, unable to shake the feeling that he was judging me. I made a mental note to see my therapist soon, then frowned. "No. Just leave him out of it, okay?"

As if on cue, my phone buzzed with a text message. It was Dana. *Aug. 12*, his message said. *The Joy Formidable are playing at Popscene. Get us tickets.*

Who? I texted back.

Welsh band, he replied. *Bronwyn is friends with the singer.*

OK, I sent back, then put the phone aside and returned to studying the numbers on my screen. The distraction of the phone must have allowed me a fresh look, because I noticed something I hadn't, before. There had been a jump in the recorded temperature levels that was proportionately much higher than the previous week's average had been. A couple other measurements were higher than predicted, as well.

I stood and walked over, pulling out my calipers for physical measurements. I started with the eye sockets, then the spine thickness. A few calculations later, I realized I had to change my earlier estimates. I looked up again. "Getting impatient? You're filling in faster, now." I frowned. "Looks like I might need to figure out how exactly to explain you a bit sooner than I'd expected."

Sinta and I stood at the western end of the beach at Kirby Cove. She had called me early that morning, asking if I'd join her. She felt like visiting my other-self's grave, and wanted company.

It's a surreal thing, looking at a grave marker for "yourself." I know there's no reason to think of the Dinahs from the other worlds as "me," but it's sometimes hard not to. To me, they represent what I could have become, had I made different decisions in life.

After a time, Sinta said, "When you died... they tried to recover your body."

"Jasmine told me."

"I was gonna bury some of your ashes here. So you could be with her."

Despite myself, her words choked me up. "Thank you, kitten. I would have liked that."

We spent another ten or fifteen minutes there, mostly in silence, before deciding to leave. Sinta dusted the sand from her knees as we began our walk back to the city. And it didn't take her long to ask what I knew she was going to.

"I hear you and Ali went out again."

"Just for coffee," I said.

Sinta snorted. "Sure," she drawled. "Coffee and *lips!*"

I laughed. "What are you, ten?"

Sinta giggled. "Dinah and Ali... sittin' in a tree..."

"You've got to be kidding me," I muttered, shaking my head. "Okay, yes! There was k-i-s-s-i-n-g. Satisfied?"

"Oh, I know there was."

I frowned at her. "Just how often do you and Ali talk, anyway?"

"Often enough."

We walked in silence for a while, making it to the Golden Gate Bridge, before curiosity got the better of me. "So... what else did she say?"

Sinta grinned up at me. "She said the coffee was good." I glared at her, causing her to laugh again. "And so was the kissing."

I smiled slightly, but tried to hide it. "Well, to be fair, she's the one who kissed me..."

"Yeah, and you just pushed her away, didn't you?"

I chuckled, then asked, "So what about you?"

"I've never kissed her."

"I mean, you never talk about that part of your life. Are you seeing anyone?"

Sinta shook her head, but said nothing.

"Why not? I know there are guys interested in you."

With a sidelong look that seemed doubtful, she said, "I'm just not really interested in that, right now."

"Any particular reason?"

Sinta frowned, staring ahead, down the length of the bridge. I turned to see what she was looking at, just as our comms beeped. "Dyna," came Jack's voice. "I've got you placed on the Golden Gate Bridge. Confirm."

"Yes, with Sinta," I said. "What's up?"

"Potential jumper. Midpoint."

"Dyna, go!" Sinta yelled. An instant later, I was blasting along the bridge toward the city.

I flew straight up the middle, eventually seeing a group of people gathered on the eastern side. I landed next to the rail and looked over to see a young man sitting on "the chord," the single beam past the safety railing, a few feet below the sidewalk. His face was pointed down at the water, but his eyes were shut tight.

I quickly hoisted myself over the rail and lowered myself to the chord. Then I took a moment to assess him. He couldn't have been more than nineteen or twenty and looked like he'd been sleeping on the streets, given the grungy clothes, greasy hair, and dirt smudges on his face. He was scrawny, with a runny nose and red-rimmed eyes.

"Hi," I said. His head spun and he looked at me in alarm. "Sorry. Didn't mean to startle you."

"Who the fuck are you?" he said, his gaze whipping back and forth, looking for others who might have approached. "What are you doing?"

"My name's Dinah," I said. "And believe it or not, I'm a suicide prevention counselor." He looked at me like I'd spoken gibberish. "I don't normally do this in person, but since you didn't call..." I smiled at my poor attempt at humor. "Can I join you?"

"Stay back," he warned. "I mean it."

"Okay. I'll keep my distance," I said, sitting down. He stared at me warily for a few seconds, then turned to look at the water again, ignoring me. "From here at midspan, it's around two hundred seventy feet," I said, causing him to look at me, again. "In case you were wondering."

"I wasn't."

"You were wondering if it'll hurt."

The look in his eyes told me I was right. But he shrugged and said, "I'll die on impact."

"Maybe," I said. "I mean, you'll hit the water going about eighty miles an hour. That's a pretty sudden stop for that speed. But not everyone dies immediately. You might survive a few seconds or a few minutes, and you could be conscious the entire time. You'll probably drown. Of course, about two percent survive completely. Not unharmed, obviously. Want to hear about what happens to your body?"

"No!" he yelled, looking at me in anger. "Shut the hell up!"

"Yeah, you probably don't," I said quietly. I watched him for a bit, to see if his resolve was faltering. "How about the sharks?"

He looked at me wide-eyed. "What?"

"Well, there are about a dozen different shark species in the Bay. Most are harmless, of course, but..." I paused for a moment. "The crabs and fish will go for the eyeballs and your cheeks."

"Why are you doing this?" he demanded.

"Why are *you*?" I countered.

"Because life fucking sucks!"

"Yeah. Sometimes."

Staring at me, he said, "You're not very good at this."

I laughed. "Well, like I said, I'm supposed to do this on the phone. Face-to-face isn't my specialty."

"I can tell."

I leaned toward him, conspiratorially. "I'm a bit nervous." I waited for him to say something. I had a feeling that he wanted to talk, but his anger was getting in the way.

His words, when they came, were bitter. "So, you gonna go on about how life gets better, how I have so much to live for, and all that shit?"

"You want me to?"

He snorted. "No."

"I mean, it's usually true, but I don't think that's what you need to hear, um..."

He hesitated, then evidently decided it didn't matter if I knew his name. "Nathan."

"Nice to meet you, Nathan."

"Whatever."

"Do you know what's interesting about those people who survive the drop?"

He sighed heavily. "No, but you're gonna tell me."

"Almost every single one regretted it immediately." Nathan gave me a skeptical look. "Seriously," I said. "In interviews, that's the common thing between them. I mean, it takes about four seconds to hit the water. That's plenty of time to regret it. But they usually say that the moment they went over, they wished they hadn't."

"Yeah, well, I won't."

"Won't what? Survive? Or regret the jump?"

"Either!"

I heard sirens from above and turned to look. "Looks like the cops are here. News crews can't be far behind." I saw Sinta at the rail, staring down at us. I gave her a smile and nod.

"I don't care. They can't stop me any more than you can."

I chuckled. "Nathan, I'm not here to stop you."

He looked at me, confused. "Isn't that your job?"

"No, not really. That wouldn't accomplish much in the long run. I mean, if I could grab you and haul you out of here, what's to stop you from just coming back?" I shook my head. "No, my job is to help you stop yourself."

Nathan was silent a moment, then said, "Well, if life didn't suck ass, you'd have a better chance."

"Does it suck right this moment?" I asked, gesturing around us. "It's a beautiful day. And we've got one hell of a view, don't you think?"

Despite himself, he looked around. After a moment, he said, "That's why I didn't just jump right away. Thought I'd at least have something pleasant as my last experience."

"That's Angel Island, over to the left," I said. "And I'm sure you recognize Alcatraz."

I watched his face, hoping his stern expression would look more relaxed. Instead of softening, though, I saw his pain. His head dropped slightly, and his gaze turned to the waters below.

He shivered a little. Despite being July, it could get chilly out there over the water. "Are you cold?"

He shook his head. "Nah. I'm from northern Idaho. This is fine."

"Idaho? What brought you here?"

He hesitated. "The bridge, I guess."

I nodded. "People come from all over the country to jump off this bridge. Maybe someday, the powers-that-be will get off their asses and approve a safety net." I waited a moment, then said, "So tell me why."

Nathan was silent again, but I waited. A minute went by. Then he spoke. For the next several minutes, I listened as he told me in detail about his deeply dysfunctional home life, including extremely strict and disciplinarian parents. He told me of how this already bad relationship effectively ended after he came out as gay, at which point they kicked him out. He told me how his boyfriend... *ex*-boyfriend... somehow "forgot" to tell him he was HIV positive. So now Nathan was, too. He told me how he lost his job, had no insurance, and was therefore unable to afford treatment. He talked about the deep depression he'd plunged into, and his hitchhiking trip to San Francisco with the intention of jumping, because it was just all too much. He couldn't handle it and was tired of trying.

"That's a lot to carry," I said. "Thank you for sharing it."

He nodded and mumbled, "Thanks for listening, I guess."

"That's what I'm here for," I said. "But I wouldn't be doing my job if I didn't point out that these aren't insurmountable things."

He snorted and said, "Getting full-blown AIDS is."

"But that's not inevitable. Many people live with HIV without it becoming AIDS."

"Yeah, but they're getting treatment."

"And we can get you treatment, too," I said.

"You'll say anything to get me back up there."

"I won't say anything that isn't true," I said. I saw a flicker of hesitation in his eyes. "Do you really want to die?" I asked. "Or would you rather get the help you need and have the chance of a good life?"

Nathan snorted. "Like that's even possible."

"Look at me."

With a frown, he did so. I locked eyes with him and said, "I guarantee that we can, in fact, get you help. You have my word."

He was quiet for a moment, but kept looking at me. "Why should I believe you?"

"Because even though you're tired of the struggle, you know the only truly insurmountable thing would be to jump off this bridge. And possibly more importantly, Nathan... because you *want* to believe me."

Immediately, his entire demeanor changed. His body slouched, his eyes welled with tears, and he began sobbing. I took the opportunity to slide closer to him.

A minute passed as Nathan cried, then composed himself. He noticed my proximity, but said nothing about it. "How?" he said. "I have no job, no insurance, no money..."

"There are programs," I explained. "They can help you find work, get you insured. There are programs to subsidize your medications. And there are plenty of people out there who'll help you navigate it all."

He looked doubtful, but said nothing. He closed his eyes and rubbed them. As he did so, I slid even closer to him. I was now close enough to touch him. But I didn't.

When he looked up again, he frowned. "I told you not to come near me."

I didn't apologize, just looked out over the water with him in silence. Finally, I said, "Look, you came to San Francisco because of this bridge. Because it's a symbol, right?"

"I guess."

"Well, this is San Francisco! The whole city is a symbol! But not of death... it's a symbol of hope. I grew up in a small, conservative area, and moved here for a number of reasons. One of them was because the city is so friendly to those of us who aren't heterosexual. I bet you've never lived in an area where you felt comfortable being gay, have you?"

He shook his head. "That would be nice," he mumbled.

"Damn right, it's nice. Why don't you find out? It's not like this bridge is going anywhere."

Nathan seemed to think about that for a minute. "Guess that's true."

"And," I said, "I predict the next time you come to it, it'll be to enjoy it, not to jump off it." I smiled at him. "You about ready to get back up there?"

He looked me in the eye. "You swear you're not bullshitting me?"

"You have my word, Nathan. No bullshit." I smiled weakly. "Now, can I come over to you?" He hesitated only a moment before nodding. So I slid the rest of the way and put my arm around his shoulder. I pulled him into a hug. "It's gonna be okay," I said into his ear.

"I thought you weren't gonna say that," he replied.

I laughed and broke the hug, but kept my arm around his shoulders. "Sorry. Habit."

Nathan glanced up at the gathered crowd of police and gawkers. Probably a dozen people had their cell phone cameras trained on us. "Oh, God," he said. "I can't face that. Shit, they'll put my face on the news. Hell, they'll probably just take me and throw me in a psych hospital."

"Yeah, probably," I said. And I don't know what possessed me to do what I did, next. Given a do-over, I'd at least give it more consideration. But once an idea is in my head, it's hard to dislodge. So I smiled at Nathan and said, "You want to avoid all that?"

Nathan frowned. "How?"

I looked down at the water. "We don't go up. We go down."

He frowned. "We what?"

"Trust me." I firmed my grip on him... and pulled us over the edge.

"FUUUUUUUUCK!" Nathan squeezed me and kept screaming for two eternal seconds. All the while, I kept watching his eyes. He was terrified. Both of us were certain, now, that he didn't want to die.

So I started blasting, taking us out and over the water in a low arc. His screams faded as we flew, and stopped entirely as we skimmed over the water. "Fuck, fuck, fuck!" he roared as he switched from staring at me to staring at the water, then back at me.

Slowly, the terror disappeared from Nathan's face, and his eyes lit up as he allowed himself to enjoy the sensation of flying. He laughed, then, tears flowing from his eyes as he blinked from the wind. I knew that look, of course. My own face held it, the first time I flew. And every person I'd ever taken on a flight had that expression, too. I couldn't help but smile back.

Eventually, we came to a landing on Torpedo Wharf. "That was amazing!" he yelled. "But you are fucking crazy!"

"*I'm* crazy?" I laughed. "You're the one who wanted to throw away his life a bit ago." Nathan looked back at the bridge, saying nothing. "I wasn't sure, earlier, but given all the screaming, I'm guessing you're serious about changing your mind."

He looked me over. "You could've flown me over the railing back to the road any time you wanted."

"Yeah."

"Why didn't you?"

"Like I said, my goal was to get you to stop yourself. And I guess I wanted you to experience that regret that you said you wouldn't have. And given your reaction..."

He was quiet for a bit, just looking at me. "I take it back. You *are* pretty good at this."

I smiled. "Thanks. And, um... I'm sorry for scaring the shit out of you. Literally."

Immediately, his face flushed in embarrassment, as he realized that he had, in fact, crapped his pants. "Oh, fuck."

"Don't worry about it," I said as I keyed my communicator. "Jack? Jumper is safe."

"I know," he responded. "I was listening to the chatter. Someone's already uploaded cell phone footage to YouTube. Hope you're ready for the bad press."

"I'm used to it," I said, and keyed off.

Nathan looked at me, his brow knit. "Who are you talking to?"

"A member of my team," I said. "The one who alerted me to your presence on the bridge, in fact."

"Jesus. Who *are* you?"

"I told you," I said. "My name's Dinah. It's my real name, but sometimes it's short for Dynamistress." I waited for recognition to dawn on him, but he just looked at me blankly, clearly never having heard of me. I cleared my throat and shook the anticipation of recognition from my thoughts. "You really will be okay, Nathan."

"You gonna promise me that life gets better?"

I shook my head. "Nope. But the chances are a hell of a lot better than you surviving that drop, anyway. Now, let's get you into some fresh clothes."

I lifted him into the air again and, less than a minute later, we were walking into the Golden Gate Citadel, home of the Gatekeepers. Despite himself, Nathan gaped at the tall statues of Gatekeepers members, past and present, as well as the paintings on the walls.

"Geez, it's like a museum," he said.

"The ground floor sort of is," I said. "It's open to the public. There's a viewing room where a documentary about the group plays every half hour."

"Gift shop?"

"Yeah," I said.

"That's... kinda tacky."

"A little," I agreed. "But all the proceeds go to charity. And for some reason, people think it's cool to have little meta-mementos." Just as I would have loved as a kid, I reminded myself.

"Hey, is that you?" Nathan asked, pointing to a statue I'd not seen before.

And it was. Larger than life in blue and white. I admit I was shocked that it existed. "Um... yeah," I muttered.

"Very cool."

I turned away from the statue and quickly ushered him to the restroom to clean himself up. While he did so, I dashed out and flew to the nearest clothing store where I picked up some things for him, as well as new shoes for me, since I'd shredded mine when I blasted. As I hit up an ATM for cash, I also called Jack and asked him to check the homeless shelters to find him space.

Returning to the Citadel, I was met by Miss Fire on her way out. "Nice save, sugar," she said, and pulled me into a hug.

"Thanks," I said.

"Where is he, now?"

"In the bathroom, freshening up," I explained, showing her the bag of clothing. "How've you been?"

She smiled, "Can't complain! Always something keeping me busy."

"It's good to see you," I said.

"You, too, darlin'. Don't be a stranger, okay?" she said with a smile.

She continued on her way as I moved over to the restroom. I walked in. "I'm back, Nathan."

"Jesus," came Nathan's voice from one of the stalls. "You just walk into men's rooms, too."

"I announced!" I said as I handed him the plastic bag over the top of the stall.

He took the bag, then said, "So... what should I do with..."

"Just put them in the empty bag."

My phone buzzed and I looked to see a text message from Macy. *Wow, D! That video is going on your website! It's totally trending on YouTube!*

How did you even know? I replied.

Someone recognized you and hashtagged it. I have auto-searches for #dynamistress, so I got an alert.

You scare me, sometimes. Take care. Talk soon, I replied and tucked my phone away. Then I leaned back, my butt against the sink station, and crossed my arms.

The door opened and a man walked in. Seeing me, he paused, probably questioning whether he was in the right place. Then he noted the urinals on the wall and looked at me like I was a pervert. I raised an eyebrow at him. "Problem?" I said. He turned his back to me as much as he possibly could and went about his business.

I heard Nathan stuffing the smelly clothes into the bag. A few seconds later, he stepped out. "Much better," I said.

I took the bag as he washed his hands, knotted it closed against the smell, then stuffed it to the bottom of the trash can. We left the rest room together, getting strange looks from other visitors. Nathan was staring into nothing, his brow knit.

"Everything sinking in?" I asked as we stepped outside.

"Yeah," he said. "I don't know what to do," he said. "I mean, I don't want to kill myself, anymore, but that doesn't mean I feel any better about my life."

"You will, though. In time." He looked doubtful, but I continued. "First things first. Let's get you off the street." I keyed my comm and said, "Jack? Where's our boy staying?"

"Hospitality House can let him use one of their emergency beds," he replied.

"Thanks. Can you put together an info packet on HIV med programs, please?"

"Will do."

Nathan stared at me. "What are you doing?"

"My job," I said. I flagged down a cab and we rode to the shelter.

When we arrived, I tipped the driver, then followed Nathan out of the cab. "I used to live at the other end of this block," I said.

Nathan looked around. The Tenderloin was an eyesore, even in bright daylight. Maybe especially so. "Really. And where do you live, now?"

"About six blocks from here. Five north, one west." I handed him one of my business cards. "I expect to see you there tomorrow morning."

Nathan stared at the card. "The Pariah Project?"

"Yeah. We'll have some information for you." I handed him some cash. "In case you need anything."

He looked at me, a concerned look on his face. "I'm not looking for charity, you know."

"Whether you're looking for it or not, you need some, right now. But don't worry. That's not the goal. The Project will help you find your path, Nathan."

"Gosh, that didn't sound cultish at all," he said with a raised eyebrow.

I laughed. "*Your* path. Not *our* path." We stood in front of the door of Hospitality House. "Okay, these guys can give you temporary shelter. They can also help you find work. Great organization. They're expecting you."

He looked again at my card, then back at me. "Dinah, I..."

"Oh, don't get all sappy," I said with a smirk. "I'll see you in the morning." He hugged me and entered the shelter.

Arriving home, I found Jack there, waiting for me. "Info you wanted is on your desk," he said tersely.

"Thanks. What's up?" I said, concerned at his tone.

"You've had visitors," Jack said. "The police want to talk to you about that stunt you pulled."

I chuckled. "Of course they do. What did you tell them?"

"That you hadn't been back and you weren't answering your comm."

"Did they want me to go down to the station, or what?"

"Well... yeah." He handed me the business card of one of the cops. "Dyna, what were you thinking?"

I cocked my head at him. "I was thinking he needed a good dose of reality."

Jack shook his head and packed up his laptop. "I believe the police will consider that to be reckless endangerment, at the very least."

"Show me the video," I said.

Jack pulled up YouTube on our screen and quickly found the video. "There are several," he said, "but this is the one that shows the most."

The angle of the observer was such that the camera never caught Nathan's face clearly. I watched as it replayed the events, showing me with my arm around his shoulder, then us plunging over the edge. The camera followed us down. We disappeared from view for a second as I blasted us away. By the time the observer focused on us again, we were rapidly dwindling into the distance.

"I don't see what the big deal is. How do they know it was me? Wait," I said before he could reply. "It's the hair, isn't it? It's always the hair."

Jack ignored my attempt at levity. "The video shows you pulling him off the edge, Dyna."

I shook my head. "Nathan knew who I was and asked me to take him flying."

Jack's eyes narrowed. "Are you serious?"

I smiled. "Can't prove otherwise."

With a shake of his head, Jack said, "I wonder about you, sometimes."

"Just sometimes?"

"Bye, Dyna," he said with a smile as he headed to the door.

I called the precinct house after Jack left. As I expected, the police didn't like my story, but there was no evidence to the contrary, so it was a short conversation. I told them where Nathan was staying, in case they wanted to talk to him.

The online video got all sorts of comments, most of which were positive, but some of which claimed I acted irresponsibly. I got a couple nasty emails via the website, which I allowed Macy to answer with a canned response to the effect that I did what I felt – in my opinion as a trained suicide prevention counselor – would be effective in that situation. And all indications were that I was correct. Good or bad, right or wrong, hits to my website soared.

I sent Dana a text, asking if he'd seen the video. When he hadn't replied after an hour, I called him. The call went directly to voicemail. I frowned. It wouldn't even be late, yet, in the U.K. I looked up the number for the Hen & Chickens and called there.

"Hi," I said when they answered. "I was wondering if Bronwyn was working now."

There was a pause at the other end. "Who's calling?"

"Um... a friend of..." I sighed. "I'm her boyfriend's sister. Is she there?"

"No. No, she isn't."

"Okay," I said. "Would you happen to have her phone number? Or can you get a message to her?"

"I could do," the man said, "if anyone knew where she'd gotten to. We've not heard from her in two days. Bronwyn's gone missing. She and your brother both."

SIXTEEN

"Memory is deceptive because it is colored by today's events."
~ Albert Einstein

Our brains play tricks on all of us. Everyone, of every age, misremembers things. It doesn't matter if the memory was of thirty years ago or thirty days. We often get things ever-so-slightly wrong. Ask any couple about an event in their joint history and you will hear details that are different, if not outright contradictory.

My brother and I have disagreements on events we both experienced, largely because our memories were shaped by our attitudes about the events themselves. And maybe because of alcohol.

In my memory, back in 1998, I acknowledged the possibility that I might die as a result of my initial self-experimentation. I'd considered it, but decided it was highly unlikely, and that the worst that could happen would be a simple failure.

Today, I have to admit that I never took seriously the possibility of dying as a result of mucking about with my own genetic code, not that first time or from any of the subsequent tweaks. It was always in the back of my mind, but I brushed it aside as not worth thinking about.

Which means, of course, that I was undeniably arrogant. Or maybe just stupid. In retrospect, I should have given it more serious consideration, as evidenced by the fact that my last tweak did, in fact, kill me.

It's still disturbing to put that in writing.

Just as disturbing was the fear that the actual memory of the event was surfacing, despite my brother's assurances that it was locked down.

Naturally, his first reaction, once I voiced the thought aloud, was that he should go back into my psyche and either erase that memory entirely or at least do a better job of blocking it.

But I'm stubborn, people tell me, so I was against the idea. This lack of feeling "complete" ate at me, becoming stronger as the weeks went by. I wanted that feeling. I needed it. I was desperate to have it.

"Desperate" didn't begin to describe what I felt now. I immediately called Vicky, because, rational or not, my only thought was that if my brother had disappeared while in the U.K., Weatherford had to be behind it. Dana could handle himself against almost anyone, so this had to be a deliberate trap. And if I was going to be going up against Weatherford, I needed backup. Vicky was the logical choice.

But I felt we needed more than just the two of us. So I put out a general call to the team, announcing departure for London within the hour. No passports needed. Ultimately, in addition to Vicky and myself, Sinta, Lily, Cara, Nena, and Bridget confirmed.

It was midnight by the time all had gathered at our headquarters, luggage in hand. After I thanked them for coming, Cara asked the question everyone was thinking. "Why might they have been abducted?"

All eyes turned to me. Except for Vicky's. "Possibly," she said, "to get me to come to them." When the others looked confused, Vicky explained, in vague terms, the relationship between her and her father's group, and the long-running antagonism between them. When she finished, she looked at me with apologetic eyes. But I was sure she knew I didn't blame her for this.

When we were ready, Vicky opened a portal to her flat in London. One by one, we filed through. For the rest of the team, except Bricky, it was the first time they'd used one of Vicky's portals. Caracara was hesitant to do so, but seemed intent on proving she was still part of the team, and stepped through. Vicky herself was last. She told us to make ourselves comfortable in her home while she picked up the rental.

"We're going by car?" Neon asked. "Why can't we just teleport there?"

"'Cuz 'porting takes a lot of energy," Bricky answered.

"But Aber-whatsit is way closer to here than San Francisco," Neon countered.

"Yes," Vicky said. "But it's not about distance. I can only 'port to a location I know is safe. In most cases, this means anything within my line of sight. But I've set up a sort of permanent landing spot in my flat. I can 'port straight to it in one hop from anywhere because of this."

"I still don't' get it," Nena said. "You can't see your flat from San Francisco."

Sinta spoke up. "How does a blind person get around their home without tripping over everything?"

Nena looked at her. "Because they know where every... oh." Her face flushed. "Gotcha." She dropped into an armchair, her hair glowing orange with plasma, her lanky legs jutting out in front of her.

"That was... disconcerting," Cara said. "Too much like being taken to that other world."

I nodded at Cara and gave her a consoling look. It didn't physically feel exactly like the portal into that world, but yes... I couldn't help but make the comparison, myself.

Vicky stepped out into the morning sun, after which I filled in the others about Weatherford as best I could, including every encounter I'd had with him. I didn't go into any further detail about Vicky's relationship with him, of course, as that was her personal business. I did wonder, however, how an encounter with him would go, considering their history.

After briefing them, I got us lodging in Abergavenny. The hotel where I'd stayed before was booked, as were the next four places I tried. I got lucky on my fifth call, though. A place a few miles outside of town had just had a large group cancel on them, so I was able to secure four rooms for four nights. Vicky and I would share a room, as would Sinta and Bridget. Lily and Nena would share another, leaving the last room for Cara.

Then I pulled out my phone and sent a message to one of the few people I knew in this country. *Kate*, I typed, *Dana and Bronwyn are missing. I'm here with some of my team. We'll be in Abergavenny probably by noon. We're staying at the Llanwenarth Hotel. Would appreciate help from you and Bill, if possible.*

Almost immediately, my phone buzzed. *We'll meet you there.*

Thanks, I replied. *See you soon.*

About half an hour later, Vicky returned with our vehicle, a SEAT Alhambra. Vicky and I took the front, Cara and Sinta took the back, and the middle row was for the other girls.

"I'd bet good money," Nena said, "that other superteams never travel by minivan."

As I expected, the others fell asleep almost as soon as we left. It was, after all, nearly two in the morning, California time. About halfway through the trip, we stopped at a Welcome Break rest stop near Oxford.

I woke the girls. After potty breaks, we grabbed drinks and fries. We sat at two tables, Sinta and Bricky joining Vicky and me, the rest sharing another. Other patrons stared at the more visually striking in our group, but no one said anything.

As we ate, Vicky noticed my sour mood and inquired. I frowned as I picked at my fries. "I'm mad because Dana's so hung up about the mind link," I said. "We had something like a fifty-mile range. It would be a lot easier to locate him, if we still had that."

"True, love. But he has his reasons."

"Yeah," Sinta agreed.

"*Stupid* reasons!" I snapped.

Bridget jumped at my outburst. Vicky held up her hands, palms toward me. "Just saying. They're obviously not stupid to him. We've had this conversation before. You know I don't judge, but..."

I grumbled to myself, then apologized. "Sorry. I'm just on edge."

Sinta said, "For someone to take Dana, they'd have to be either really lucky or really powerful."

My stomach sank as she said this. I'd been thinking the same thing, of course, but having someone else say it just made it more real. I sat in silence while the others finished eating, then we hit the road again.

We drove mostly in silence from that point on, crossing into Wales and arriving at the hotel earlier than I expected, around eleven-thirty. It was too early for us to get our rooms, since they needed to be cleaned after the guests who'd checked out that morning.

While waiting for Kate and Bill to arrive, we gathered in the open patio area between the buildings. There were a few other guests there, but they didn't stick around long.

The Llanwenarth Hotel sits on the bank of the Usk River. As the others sat around the tables, chatting, I walked to the edge of the bank and looked down at the water and into the pasture across the river. It was idyllic and, had it not been for the regular noise of traffic on the A40 right in front of the hotel, it would have been relaxing.

I don't know how long I stood there, but my reverie was interrupted by the arrival of Kate and Bill – Vulcana and Atlas. I returned to the group and made introductions, then we went inside for lunch.

The restaurant was fairly empty, and we were able to push tables together for all of us to sit as a group. "What the heck is 'gammon'?" Lily asked.

"That would be ham," Bill said. He and Kate answered other menu questions from the girls.

Once we'd ordered, Vicky and I briefed the pair on what little we knew, then they shared some information of their own. "After our experience last year with the Nexus," Kate said, "we started paying more attention to them, and have enlisted aid from some of our companions."

"Weatherford himself," Bill continued, "spends most of his time in London. We have him under watch."

Vicky shook her head. "You really don't. He can enter his office in the morning, 'port to anywhere, then back to his office to leave the building at the end of the work day. He's probably aware that you're watching him."

As Kate and Bill frowned, I said, "Do they still operate out of that facility under The Skirrid?"

"We believe so," Kate said. "As you remember, the entrance we found wasn't one they actively use."

"Portals," Vicky said.

"Then what makes you think they're still there?" I asked.

Kate and Bill exchanged glances. Bill spoke up. "We've seen a number of people on the hiking trails near the entrance. We inquired of the local hiking groups, and no one seems to know these women."

"Women?" I asked. "All of them?"

"Yes," Kate said. "Is that significant?"

"It could be," I said. "Have you spoken to any of them?"

"No," Kate said. "They seem a bit anti-social."

"They keep to themselves," Bill said. "They walk the trails and that's it. Back and forth."

"Like guards," Vicky said.

"Keep your distance from them," I said.

"Why?" Kate asked.

"Because if my hunch is correct, they're telepaths. And they're working for Weatherford."

When everyone but Vicky looked at me in confusion, I explained about Dynasonic's world, the Overseer, his network of telepaths, and the arrangement we presumed existed between them.

Our meals arrived and, as we ate, I answered as many of their questions as I could, and we made some tentative plans. Kate and Bill left us after we finished. Not long thereafter, our rooms were ready.

The sleeping rooms of the Llanwenarth are in a separate building from the rest of the property, on the other side of the patio area. The key to enter that building is an old-fashioned skeleton key, which we all found charming. The room keys were metal keys, too, rather than electronic key cards.

The rooms themselves are fairly modest, but pleasant. The room Vicky and I shared had a balcony on the river side.

Inside, I collapsed on the bed. Though only mid-afternoon in Wales, I'd been up for about twenty-four hours. I was exhausted, physically and emotionally.

I could feel Vicky's eyes on me as she exited the bathroom. After a couple minutes, she joined me. "We'll find him," she said, placing her hand on mine.

The following morning, we sat in the courtyard again over coffee and pastries, brainstorming ideas of what our next move should be. I was disturbed by the presence of the assumed telepaths. But of all of us, the only one remotely qualified to go up against them was me. Dana's training had given me the ability to resist casual telepathy easily and, with effort, some protection against directed telepathy.

Today would be for planning and preparation. The actions themselves would wait until the wee hours, when we were most likely to catch our targets off-guard.

Just as we were about to leave the hotel to run our various errands, my phone erupted with an urgent beeping. At first, I was confused, since the only time I'd ever heard this particular noise was when I first set it up on my phone, many months earlier. It was the home intrusion alarm.

The others gathered around to peer at my phone as I activated the access program for the home security system, including the video feeds. One showed that the front door had been compromised. Another, on our monitor in the meeting room, revealed four intruders, three of whom were shading their eyes from the floodlights that lit up when they broke in.

"What time is it, back home?" Bridget asked.

"About two-thirty in the morning," I said.

"Who the hell are they?" Lily asked.

Three of them, I didn't recognize. The obvious leader, though, was large. And muscular. And red.

"Hellion," Sinta growled.

"Ex-boyfriend of a girl I used to date. He doesn't like me, especially since I put him in jail."

Audio came through the phone's tiny speaker. "Oh, Dyyyynaaa... Wakey, wakey!"

I punched a couple menu items on the phone, then positioned the phone's camera. "Hello, Oscar," I said.

Hellion turned toward the team monitor, which had come to life and now showed my face. "Well, there you are," he said, moving toward the monitor while his flunkies held back.

"Bit late for a visit, isn't it?" I said.

"I wanted it to be a surprise."

"Sorry to disappoint, but I'm not at home."

"Obviously, since it's daytime where you are. And it's a shame," he said. "I was looking forward to torching your ass."

"And I was looking forward to beating yours. Again. When did you get out?"

"Yesterday," he said. "Good behavior."

I laughed. "I thought Rachel was the actor, not you."

"I'm a man of many talents," he said. He looked around, and I could see his smile as he saw all the beautiful oak panels around the room. "This is a real nice place you've got here. Much nicer than the dump you used to live in."

"Thank you," I said. "I'm pretty fond of it."

"I don't blame you," he said. "I think I'll burn it."

We all watched as Hellion stretched out his arms to either side. Flames rolled down his forearms and burst from his hands into the walls.

"Oh, my god!" Bricky blurted, as some of the others gasped loudly. I calmly entered another code into the phone.

A few seconds later, one of the thugs said, "Uh, boss? How come the walls ain't burning?"

Hellion stopped his flame jets and looked to his left, then his right, clearly surprised that the wooden walls weren't so much as scorched. "What the hell?" he said, stepping over to verify the lack of damage.

"Hey, Oscar," I said. Hellion spun and glared at my face on the screen. "Look up."

All of them looked toward the ceiling to see that hidden panels had slid open and gun barrels now targeted all of them from the revealed recesses. Before they could react, I fired three of the guns.

The girls looked on, eyes wide, as Hellion's pals were hit by Taser rounds, which stuck to them and delivered five long seconds of electric current.

As Hellion stared at his allies, writhing on the floor and moaning in pain, I said, "The police will be stopping by shortly to pick you up."

Hellion growled at the camera. "Fuck you!" He prepared to send another blast of flames, this time at the monitor with my smirking face on it. But before he could, I triggered the last gun. Seconds later, he was just as docile as his buddies.

"Give him one more, from me," Sinta said.

"I'm surprised that big dude is still down," said Lily. "I thought big guys could recover fast from Tasers."

"Newer Tasers work differently from older models. The charges literally interrupt the neuron communication between muscles and brain. Doesn't matter how tough you are. You're going down."

A minute later, Jasmine entered the scene, taking it all in.

"Hey, there," I said. "That was quick."

She looked up at the screen as she stepped around the would-be arsonist and his goons. "I was in the area."

"At this hour?"

"I do have a life, you know. I was on a date."

"Ah. Sorry to interrupt. How are the walls?" I asked.

After examining them, she said, "Might need to refinish, but the wood is fine. I guess it was worth the expense to treat it with that fancy flame retardant." She continued looking around. "No damage other than the front door. And the gate at the entrance of the block."

"Not for lack of him trying," I said. "Your Taser rounds worked beautifully. Well, the entire system did. Thanks for that."

"I'll have the door fixed before you return. Our insurance should pay for the street gate, too." She stopped examining the lack of damage and faced me. "Any progress at your end?"

"We think Weatherford has some of the Overseer's telepaths here acting as lookouts. Beyond that, not a lot."

She looked toward the door. "Police are arriving. I'll handle everything."

"Thanks, hon. Talk soon." I keyed off the video and turned to my companions.

"So that's what all that refinishing was all about," Vicky said. "Flame retardant."

"Yeah. Top of the line stuff. I figured Hellion would show up, at some point."

Sinta grinned. "The expression on his face... that was great!"

"Hard to believe that loser nearly killed both of us," I said, causing the others to look at the two of us, shocked.

"Anyone can get lucky," Sinta said.

"I was the lucky one," I said. "You were there to save my ass."

Sinta shook her head, embarrassed. "Aw, you'd have won, in the end."

"You and I both know that's not true," I said.

Is that what had happened with Dana? Had someone just gotten lucky? I hoped that was the case, rather than the alternative.

"Okay," I said. "Let's get on with it."

We spent the day making preparations. Vicky "mapped" teleport routes in the area. Her familiarity would allow us a convenient escape, should it come to that. The rest of us picked up supplies, including some snacks. We could be out there for a while.

By late afternoon, we returned to the hotel. We had tea at the restaurant's outdoor tables overlooking the river. The younger girls were excited by the finger sandwiches, *bara brith*, scones with clotted cream, and so on. Despite being a worried wreck, I couldn't help but smile at their obvious pleasure. Afterward, we talked for a bit, then went back to bed.

We met in the courtyard at midnight. I was, for some reason, pleased that everyone had chosen to forego civilian attire and were in their own "uniforms." Each of them had incorporated our "drum" emblem into their suits in some way. They were treating this as an official Pariah Project mission.

As for me, I was wearing my leather suit and trench coat. I didn't feel comfortable wearing the blue and whites. That suit still seemed like it belonged to a different person. The trench outfit was darker, almost militant, which rather fit my mood.

The plan was fairly straightforward. We would travel to the north side of The Little Skirrid. There was a hedgerow leading from the road to the edge of the heavily wooded area in which we'd found the hidden tunnel entrance a year ago. Atlas and Vulcana would meet us at that spot on the road. We'd travel along the hedgerow and enter that way, rather than from a footpath. I wanted to avoid the probable telepaths at all costs.

Vicky opened a portal for us, and we hurried through. When we stepped out, we found Atlas and Vulcana waiting for us, just off the road next to a gate, mostly overgrown. It was about a hundred yards to the edge of the woods. Hopping over the fence, we walked with the hedgerow on our left, a sheep field on our right, and no sign of telepathic women. But I kept my mental guard up, nonetheless. Who knew what kind of range they had?

Kate and Bill took the lead once we reached the woods. They knew the location of the entrance well. It took us only a few minutes to reach it. Bill reached down to the side of the metal plate and pushed the recessed button that caused it to lower into the ground, revealing the hidden tunnel. One by one, we entered, closing the door behind us.

"Well, this isn't at all creepy," Nena said as she stepped out ahead of the group. We had flashlights, but Nena acted as our guiding torch, creating balls of flame that rolled in front of us as we walked. "How far is it?" she asked.

"About four kilometers," Bill replied.

"Which is...?"

"Two and a half miles," I said.

"Okay," Nena said. "That, I get."

The mood was tense as we made our way between the two Skirrids. Even Nena gave up trying to lighten the mood. As we walked, I regularly looked to the ceiling to see if there were any recent additions, such as cameras. But there were none. I found it odd that they would leave themselves open to us entering the same way we had, last year.

But of course, they hadn't.

Last year, when we'd arrived at the end of the tunnel, we'd found a brick wall, which we'd easily taken down. This time, the wall was a familiar swirl of colorful energy. The Nexus had blocked our way with a portal.

"Well, bugger," Vicky said.

"Ooh, pretty!" Nena gushed. "So cool!"

"Any ideas, Vick?"

"Many," she said. "None of them good." Then she stepped forward and thrust her head through the portal. Before I could even react, she jerked back out. Her head was soaking wet. She wiped water from her face.

"That wasn't smart," I said.

In reply, she sent a stream of water from her mouth onto my chest, causing the others to laugh. "You, my dear, are not one to be lecturing others about doing things that aren't smart."

"Can you just...*unmake* a portal?" Lily asked.

"Not unless it's one I created."

"Is this permanent?" Kate asked.

Vicky hesitated. "I can't say that, but some of them can be quite long-lived. The simpler the portal, the longer it can last. This one is just a conduit to the bottom of a river. Tasted like the Thames."

As the others chuckled, I felt my heart drop. "What now?" I muttered aloud.

"Now we go around," Bridget said.

We all turned to see her transforming her body into its brick-like state. Then she turned to the earth wall beside her and, using her flattened hands as spades, began plunging them in with abandon, tearing out chunks of earth.

"Clever lass, isn't she?" Vicky said.

"Yeah," I said. "I think we'll keep her."

Bridget cleared a deep hole before she needed a break. "We'll take over," Bill said.

"Hang on," Lily said. "Let me take a crack at it." As she stepped inside the hole, she said, "Y'all might want to back up."

We all did so, and then plugged our ears as Lily created small explosions. Debris flew out, landing in front of the portal. After the third explosion, she stepped out, brushing dirt from her clothes.

"That was super loud," Nena said.

"*Oui*, but quite effective," Cara pointed out.

"And we're through," Lily said.

We all followed her inside, prepared to meet any resistance. But there was nothing. The room was vacant and dark. Immediately, I looked around using my energy-sensing sight. But that, too, revealed nothing.

"All for naught," Kate sighed.

I frowned. "No. I don't believe that."

The year before, Jasmine had planted in my mind an image of the floorplan of the place, which she'd extracted from one of the Nexus members we'd fought. I tried my best to pull up that memory.

"Okay," I said. "We've got two hallways. Kate and Bill, take Cara and Neon and explore that one. The rest of you are with me."

The other group began moving away, but Cara hesitated. I stepped over to her and spoke quietly. "What's wrong?"

"I... should not have come," she said.

"What? Why not?"

She glanced toward the hallway. "I am of no use in such cramped spaces."

I frowned. "It's true that you won't be able to fly in there. But you're not defenseless, either. I remember well what those claws of yours can do."

Cara looked shocked. "*Quoi*? But I never–"

I held up a hand. "I know. But your other-self..."

"Ah. *Oui*," she said. "I had forgotten."

"Look, when we get back home, I'll have you work with Sinta on improving your close combat abilities, okay?"

She smiled softly. "Thank you. I will do my best." She jogged off to catch up with the others.

Then I took my group down the hallway to the west, into the area where Vicky had previously been held. Whenever we encountered a side passage, one of us would take it, exploring the many rooms each held. As for myself, I just used my energy sight, my mood deteriorating with each minute. There was no life there. The base was abandoned.

Why the portal, then? Why protect an empty facility? Unless the protective portal was set up immediately after we left a year ago and the place was vacated later. That would make sense.

We spent a solid hour exploring the base. Our two groups met up somewhere along the way and eventually we made our way back to the main room. Everyone, I'm sure, was thinking the same thing, which was that we were back where we started, in more ways than one.

"All right," I said, defeated. "I guess we can head back." The others followed me toward our makeshift entrance.

"*Attendez*," Cara said. "Please. Wait."

We stopped and went over to her. "What is it?" I asked.

"Something does not make sense to me." She pointed toward our exit route. "We entered from the south, *non*?"

"We did," Kate confirmed.

"And those doors are east and west," Cara continued. "When we met, it was to the north, was it not?" There were murmurs of agreement from the others. "Then–"

"Why is there no door to the north?" I concluded.

Immediately, we all converged on the north wall of the room and examined it for any sort of hidden entrance. But the walls showed not even the slightest crack where a door could be.

"Here!" Lily yelled. We turned to find her crouched down, looking at the floor, rather than the walls. She pointed to what she'd found: a thin line running perpendicular from the wall. Another ran parallel to the first about four feet away. They were connected at the back.

"I figured, since the outdoor entrance was in the ground, why wouldn't they do the same thing in here?" she explained.

Suddenly, there was a grinding noise, and the floor began to swing downward. Bill crouched nearby. "Found the switch," he said.

Our flashlights revealed a short drop of maybe five feet. I hopped down first, finding just what I expected: a short doorway under the north wall of the main room. I stepped through, the others following me.

Just a few feet farther were stairs leading up. They came out into what appeared to be a small library. There was a desk at one end, and the walls were lined with bookcases, stretching back perhaps twenty feet. It wasn't a wide room, however, and felt decidedly cramped with all eight of us inside.

"Why would someone hide a library?" Nena asked. "Is it all porn, or what?"

Vicky had pulled a book from a shelf and was looking it over. "Could be. Anyone read Russian?" She swapped it out for another book. "Or... um... some Nordic language?"

"Son of a bitch," I said, mainly to myself.

"What is it?" Kate asked.

"This place isn't abandoned." I was looking at the floor, cursing myself for not thinking to use my energy sight on the ground. But this was Weatherford we were talking about. Before the others could even ask, I strode to the far wall and looked at the single bookcase that stood there. I swung it out away from the wall, revealing a steep staircase going down.

"Okay, you're kinda freaking me out," Nena said. "How...?"

"He did the same thing in Nevada," I said. "Maybe... seven down there. Hard to tell, since some of them are close together. Be on guard."

"Let me go first," Vicky said.

I didn't argue, but fell in step behind her as we descended as quietly as we could, with flashlights off. There was light coming from below. Our stealth wasn't going to matter, shortly.

As we neared the bottom, it became clear that the light was from electric sources. Three figures were moving into position near the bottom. "They know we're coming," I whispered. "Vick, be ready."

"Let me go alone."

"Why?"

"Because they'll recognize me," she said.

"That's what worries me," I said.

She just shook her head. I did as she asked, though. We held back and let her step out into the room.

"Wait!" came a man's voice from deeper within the room.

I could only see Vicky as she faced them down. There was muttering I couldn't make out. Then Vicky said, "Okay, Dyna," and the rest of us filed into the room.

The three men, dressed in ceremonial type robes, as last time, stared at us with concerned expressions. One of them seemed twitchy. I stared at him and said, "You know why we're here. Just bring them out and we'll leave peacefully." This seemed to calm him down, but he looked to the others for guidance.

At that moment, I noticed that two of the remaining four figures were approaching. "Company coming," I said. The three robed men seemed surprised that I could tell this. "And one of them is Weatherford."

"Lovely," Vicky said.

I desperately hoped the remaining two were Dana and Bronwyn, but they were so close together, I couldn't distinguish their energy patterns. So I watched the doorway in the direction of the approaching figures. Weatherford was the first to step through. He stopped when he saw Vicky. But then the next figure stepped up and stood beside him. He was about six feet tall with a bushy beard and wearing a hoodie that kept the upper half of his face in shadow. But I didn't need to see it to know who he was. Immediately, I concentrated on the psychic defenses I'd developed with Dana's help.

"Ben Michaels," I drawled.

Weatherford half-turned his face to Michaels. "I told you she would know you."

I felt him probing in my mind and raised an arm toward him. "Get out of my head, unless you want to learn what my blasts feel like."

"As you wish," he said in a breathy voice that gave me chills.

Weatherford faced me and said, "Ms. Geof-Craigs, if you insist on visiting us, I do wish you would stop damaging our property."

"Where's my brother?" I demanded.

The men ignored me completely. Michaels shook his head. "Only one male in your group." He said it with a sneer in his husky voice.

"So?" I heard Bridget say. "You got a problem with women?"

Vicky seemed about to shush her cousin, but then Michaels said, "They have their purposes, but they are weak." At which point, Vicky shut her mouth.

I felt Michaels again probing my mind and shot a small blast just above his head. "Next one won't miss. Now where is my brother?"

My blast was perhaps not the best idea. It caused everyone to be ready for battle. To my surprise, Weatherford calmed his allies, motioning for them to stand down.

"To answer your question," Michaels continued in his creepy, phone sex voice, "the truth is that Mr. Weatherford assured me that borrowing your brother would bring you here, thanks to his lovely daughter."

"If you've hurt him..." I said, only to be interrupted by his laughter.

He turned to Weatherford. "You're right," he chuckled. "She's so cliché."

For his part, Weatherford just stared at me. "Do not underestimate her," he said quietly. "But never fear," he said to me. "I have no reason to wish your brother or his feisty lady friend any harm."

My stomach lost some of its knots, but I tried not to show my relief. "Super," I said. "So you lured us here. Why?"

Michaels smiled, I think. It was hard to tell through the beard. "You have been poking your nose into our business, and I wish you to stop."

I wasn't the only one who chuckled at that. "If wishes were fishes..." Nena muttered. But before she could finish her aphorism, she fell silent. Then she walked out in front of us all, turned to face me, and fell into an attack pose. Her hands ignited with bright yellow flames and she glared at me with pure hatred.

As I stood there in shock, the remaining members of my team, as well as Atlas and Vulcana, surrounded me, each of them looking as though to attack. Lily's hands were forming an explosive ball of energy, and Vicky had opened a small portal in front of her, though nothing yet came shooting out. Even Sinta looked like she was about to disembowel me with her claws.

A cold sweat overcame me. Each of them looked like they'd do their level best to kill me if Michaels told them to. I thought for a moment that this all seemed a bit excessive just to warn me to stay out of their business. But that thought paled beside my very real fear of his abilities. I had no doubt whatsoever that he could punch through my mental defenses with ease. And if he could control seven other metas this casually, he was clearly someone not to be taken lightly.

Then, to my surprise, Sinta leapt at me with a snarl. I was too slow in reinforcing my defenses, and her claws raked down the arm I'd put up to protect my face. I was thankful that the sleeve of my trench coat took most of the damage, but I could feel blood trickling.

To my horror, all the others began converging on me. I had only one way to defend myself without hurting them. My personal "force field," incorporated into my body, could be expanded outward with effort. I rarely used this ability, and it had become more difficult over time, probably from disuse. But I was able to get it started by the time Sinta attacked again. I pushed it outward, keeping the others at bay. But it wouldn't last long once the stronger members began pummeling it.

"That's enough," Weatherford said quietly. Immediately, my friends came to their senses, standing in shock as they realized what they'd been doing. I could see the fear in their eyes as they turned to look back at Michaels.

"No!" Sinta yelled, staring at the blood dripping from my arm. "Dyna!"

"It's okay," I said, glaring at Michaels.

Weatherford said to him, "That was uncalled for."

"It was not," he replied. "It was to show the consequences of disobeying me." He turned to face me. "Should you choose to interfere again, you will unquestionably regret the decision."

"Now who's being cliché?" I asked.

Weatherford glanced at his three allies and nodded. They disappeared into the hallway from which Weatherford and Michaels had emerged.

Suddenly, a searing pain hit me. I gasped and doubled over. "Get out of her head!" I heard Vicky yell.

Fortunately, the agony passed as quickly as it had come. Breathing heavily, I stood up. Both Weatherford and Michaels looked puzzled.

And then, Michaels was inside my mind, poking around. I tried to push him out, but it was no use. I could feel him going through my thoughts, and knew he was doing the same thing Dana could do. But Dana did so gently. Michaels was basically raping my brain.

He chuckled. "Well, that's interesting," he said. I kept trying to push him out, but he was too strong. Suddenly, he said, "How extraordinary!" Turning to Weatherford, he said, "Did you know she was a clone?"

Eyes widening, Weatherford stared at me. "No," he said. "No, I did not. But it explains much."

I could feel Michaels continuing his probing. And suddenly, I had an idea of what might drive him out. I focused my thoughts on the death memory that continued to threaten me. Eventually, my focus piqued his curiosity. And he took the bait.

"What's this, now?" he muttered. I felt him as he opened the memory. The agony hit me, as I knew it would. And, as I'd hoped, it hit him, as well. He staggered, and I felt him jerk out of my head.

I took advantage of his disorientation and hit him with a blast that sent him hurling back into the wall. He fell to the floor, but quickly jumped to his feet, rage contorting his face. But before he could retaliate, Weatherford stepped in front of him. "Enough!" he spat.

Michaels glared at me, then at Weatherford, but did not try to get into my mind again. He straightened himself, his gaze never leaving me. "I do not envy you when that wall fails," he said.

Just then, the three acolytes returned, supporting Dana and Bronwyn, who were obviously drugged and barely able to stand. Kate and Bill rushed forward and took them, easily hoisting them into their arms.

"Come on," Vicky said. "Let's get out of here." I hesitated, still staring at the two men who now had information I'd sworn to keep secret. For his part, Michaels didn't seem to care. Weatherford, however, had a glint in his eye and the smallest of smiles on his face. "Dyna, come on," Vicky urged. With a final glare at Weatherford, I turned and followed the others out.

We retraced our steps in silence. I knew my friends were stunned by how easily they'd been manipulated by Michaels. I was, too, but I was more concerned about the flashes of death memory that hit me.

We made it out into the woods and then to the road. From there, Vicky opened a portal and we all stepped through, back to the spot where we'd first entered the woods.

"Should we take them to the hospital?" Lily asked.

"Of course!" Kate said.

"No," I countered. When everyone looked at me, I explained. "To determine why they're unconscious, they'll do a toxicology test and drug screening, which will reveal whatever was used on them. And that will just raise questions that can't be answered without creating all sorts of trouble, not the least of which would be having the two of them arrested for illicit drug use."

Kate frowned, but nodded. She knew how messy that would quickly become. "Back to the hotel, then?"

"Yeah. Vick?"

Moments later, Vicky had a portal opened. "Thanks for your help," I said to Kate and Bill. "We'll be in touch." Then the rest of us filed through, me carrying Dana and Bridget hoisting Bronwyn in her arms.

We got them settled into the bed in the room Vicky and I shared. As the others headed to their own rooms, Vicky and I sat on the balcony, where she began treating my injured arm, cleaning it with alcohol and bandaging it from elbow to wrist. My faster-than-average healing eliminated any need for stitches.

Then she sat back in her chair. "Now that's taken care of, tell me what happened back there," she said. "It wasn't Michaels mucking about in your head, was it?"

I hesitated before replying. Should I tell her? I wanted to explain, but it was too complicated. I didn't have it in me to lay it all out for her. I smiled weakly. "I'll tell you later, okay?" Her concern vanished, replaced by annoyance. "The others need to know, too," I explained, "and I don't want to tell this story twice."

Her face softened. "Okay, then."

Hours later, I woke, disoriented. I was still on the balcony. The faint glow of dawn was teasing on the horizon off to the left. I glanced right and saw that Vicky was awake.

"Hey," I said. "Are they...?" I turned to look into the dark room.

"Still out of it," she said. Then, "Is this even any of our business? In our world, they're not really doing anything."

I didn't answer her. I knew she was just speaking out of frustration and fear. I reached out and put my hand on hers. She yanked hers away.

"Stop it!" she said, turning angrily to face me. "Will you take this seriously?"

"What do you think I'm doing?" I said, my own anger rising.

"I have no bloody idea what you're doing! Do you?" She stood and turned her back to me. "Everything with you seems to be near shambles. I'm amazed more things don't go all pear-shaped."

"Look, you knew the Project was a different sort of group from the Gatekeepers."

"I'm not talking about the Project! I'm talking about *you*."

I stared at her, hurt by her words. "Oh."

Vicky shook her head. "Sorry. That was harsher than I intended."

"It's fine," I said after a moment. "Harsh or not... you're right." My heart throbbed as I forced out one of my personal shames. "I go through life hoping that nobody notices that I don't know what I'm doing, half the time. I've gotten by mostly by luck."

Vicky snorted. "Thought you sciencey types didn't believe in luck."

"Luck. Chance. Law of Averages. Call it what you like. My point is that my successes haven't always been the result of planning and skill. And right now, I haven't the slightest idea what to do."

"That's my point, though. Should we do anything? Is this even our fight? Didn't you tell me, once, that you didn't like how America was always sticking its nose into other nations' business?"

"For the most part, I don't. But sometimes," I said, "when there's very clearly a bad guy and a good guy, it's right to step in when the good guy can't put up a defense."

"Is that how you see this situation?"

"Don't you? Michaels is clearly a bad guy."

"It's honestly not that clear to me. Though working with my father doesn't earn him any points."

"He's trying to take over Dynasonic's world."

"Are you sure? What's your evidence? And you're saying that her world can't put up a defense? What about her brother and his group?"

I rubbed weariness from my eyes. "You and the others experienced a small taste of what Michaels can do. He controls people. Dynasonic's brother is convinced that he's manipulating political heads, including at least the mayor of San Francisco and the governor of California, but she's sure he has much larger goals. Probably the president."

Vicky was quiet for a while, then said, "We need to work more closely with Dynasonic, then."

"Not the easiest thing," I said. Then I frowned. "Hell, if what I fear is about to happen actually does, I may just move to her world." Now Vicky turned to look at me, but she knew what I was going to say. "Your father is going to ruin me."

"You don't know that."

"Are you kidding? Did you see that gleam in his eye when Michaels told him I'm a clone?"

"I did, but it's not like he can prove it."

"That's just it, Vick... he doesn't really need to," I said. "Assuming Michaels got enough information from me, he'll be able to feed your dad enough detail to make some reporter sit up and take notice. There are a ton of people out there who'll believe anything. Even totally false rumors have destroyed peoples' lives, you know."

"Sure," Vicky said, "but this is such an outrageous claim that it should be easy to brush it off, yeah?"

"I'd like to think so. But a reporter could easily discover that I had eggs harvested and obtained. They could investigate purchases I made, all around the same time, as it happens. And it wouldn't be hard to take this evidence to any number of scientists who would confirm that all these things could be used for a cloning procedure. Add to that my public demise back in January and recent reappearance and that's enough 'proof' for the public."

"That's a lot of research to do."

"Sure, but can you imagine being the reporter who revealed the world's first successful human cloning? That's Pulitzer material."

"But couldn't you just deny it? Explain that all those purchases were for different things?"

"I could," I agreed. "But that might not work if the reporter put together a solid argument."

Vicky was quiet for a moment. "What are you going to do?"

I sighed. "Ignore it and hope it never happens."

We sat in silence for a while before Vicky finally spoke. "Listen, I want to apologize. I've not been the most accepting of... well, of your 'return.' And I'm sorry."

"It's fine," I said. "There were a lot of things I didn't fully consider before doing what I did."

"Like how your friends would take it?"

"Among other things. But yeah, as far as others were concerned, I assumed it would all work out. Which it did, but I certainly could have set things up so it would have gone more smoothly."

"Again, sorry about being the way I've been."

I waved it off. "Forget it." I thought more about my lack of foresight. "When I came up with the plan, I didn't expect I'd feel any differently, being a clone. I was mostly right. Physically, I feel better than I remember. Mentally, though... I gave myself too much credit, thinking that it wouldn't bother me."

"And you didn't consider the possibility of someone outside our group discovering the truth?"

I shook my head. "Not a lot, no. I was more concerned about dying than about being a clone or any repercussions of it."

We were interrupted by a noise in the room. We both got up and headed in, turning on the light. Bronwyn blinked at the brightness, then looked around, confused.

"How do you feel?" I asked.

She seemed surprised to see me, but it passed quickly. "Like shite," she said. She pursed her lips, her brow knit, as she looked at the still unconscious Dana. "Where are we?"

"At the Llanwenarth," I said.

She raised a red eyebrow, then pulled back the blanket and tried to get out of bed. I went over to help her up, then supported her as we walked to the toilet.

Back in the room, I checked on Dana. Vicky poured Bronwyn a glass of water. When she finally returned, she stood in the doorway to the bathroom, leaning against the door jamb. "I don't even know what to ask first."

"I can imagine," I said. I helped her back to the bed, where she sat and listened as Vicky and I told her all about her abductors and everything that had happened since they were taken. She drank the water as we spoke.

When we were finished, she just shook her head. "I should take Dana's warnings more seriously."

"What warnings?" I said.

"About the danger of being with him," she said, looking at me. "You know, since he's related to you." I felt like I'd been gut punched by Bricky, and this must have shown on my face. "Oh, I didn't mean it badly," Bronwyn continued. "I mean, it's not like it's your fault, after all."

"Right," I said, frowning.

In the awkwardness that followed, I moved to Dana's side to check on him again. It was certain that he'd been more heavily drugged than Bronwyn. I held his hand as my mind raced. So many thoughts were competing for dominance. The threat of being revealed as a clone was winning, for the most part, but the two main challengers were fear for Dynasonic's world and, thanks to Bronwyn, guilt about innocents being in danger just because of who I am.

When I looked up, I saw an expression on Bronwyn's face that I couldn't read. She was staring at our hands – mine and Dana's. When she saw that I'd noticed this, she cleared her throat and looked away. "I think I'll lie down a bit more," she said. Vicky and I took the hint and left the room.

We retreated to the patio and sat in silence. Eventually, I must have nodded off, because when I opened my eyes, Vicky was standing next to me. "Dana's awake."

We went back to the room, where Dana was just leaving the bathroom. He looked like Bronwyn said she felt. I hugged him and helped him back to the bed. Then, as we'd done with Bronwyn, we brought him up to speed on how we learned of their capture and everything that followed. When we were finished, Bronwyn said, "I should be getting home. People are worried."

"I'll drive you," Vicky said.

Bronwyn smiled her thanks, then sat next to Dana. "I'll call you later," she said. She kissed him, then left with Vicky.

As soon as they were gone, I said, "There's more."

Dana listened as I related how Michaels revealed my clonehood to Weatherford. Then he frowned. "Well... that's..."

"A nightmare," I said.

"Yeah."

We sat quietly for a moment, then I said, "I think Bronwyn doesn't like me much."

"Don't be ridiculous," Dana said, yawning.

I let it go. Then I laid back on the bed. Dana did the same, and we were soon asleep.

An hour or so later, we woke and decided to head to the restaurant for breakfast. The entire group was in the patio area when we stepped outside. As they all greeted Dana, Vicky told me that Bronwyn was home, safe and sound.

"Hey, guys?" Vicky and I turned to see Lily looking at us.

"What's up?"

"The others and I were talking... and we were wondering if we had to go back right away, or if we could do some sight-seeing. I mean, aside from Vicky and Bridget, none us have been to the U.K. before."

Vicky and I exchanged glances. "Fine with me," she said.

"Sure, I think we can spare a day or two," I said.

"Sweet!" She headed back to the others to share the news.

When she was out of earshot, I turned to Vicky. "I'm about to ask a huge favor of you," I said.

"Are you, now?"

"Would you mind playing tour guide for them? Dana and I have some things to discuss."

Vicky raised an eyebrow and smirked. "And would Bronwyn be the subject of discussion?"

"What? No!"

"Right," she said. "Because you're not at all upset about their relationship."

"That's of secondary significance," I said. "You know what it's about."

Vicky's joking demeanor vanished. "That thing you promised to explain to us all?"

"Guess now's as good a time as any to do that," I muttered.

Vicky gathered the others around the patio tables as Dana went into the restaurant to grab some food for us. I sat there, not knowing how to start. The group looked at me expectantly.

For the next several minutes, I explained to them about the death memory, including everything Dana had warned me about it, as well as my belief that it was important for me to remember it fully. "So," I concluded, "while Vicky takes you to see some of the sights, Dana and I will be deciding how to approach the situation."

As expected, the others mainly just gaped at me, expressions of shock and concern on their faces. "I do not understand what is to discuss," Cara said. "You will let him remove it, *non*?"

The others seemed to agree with her, given how many nods I saw. I smiled faintly. "That's what we'll be discussing," I said.

It wasn't entirely a lie.

Dana and I sat on the balcony of my room overlooking the river. He'd picked up a pot of coffee and pastries at the restaurant. Between bites, he said, "So what's on your mind?"

"Death," I said.

Dana paused in his chewing. "Oh?"

"More specifically, the death memory," I said, and told him about the flash I'd had back in the underground and how I tricked Michaels into tapping into it. "

Dana raised an eyebrow. "That was... ingenious," he said.

"Thanks, but... I can't risk going up against him in the future and having him incapacitate me by poking at that memory. He won't be affected by it the same way, again, since he'd be ready for it," I said. "So it's time to do something about this."

Dana leaned back in his chair, cradling his coffee cup between his palms. "And by 'do something,' you mean...?"

I hesitated before replying, watching the slow current of the river. "I'm still not convinced that removing it completely is the right move."

"You honestly can't still be thinking about unlocking it," he said.

"Look, I haven't the slightest idea what to do," I said. "On the one hand, I do still think I'll feel incomplete without that. On the other, I do take your warnings about it seriously."

"Well, I'm glad of that, anyway," he said. "As I told you, I don't see how experiencing that horrible memory would in any way make you feel complete. And I don't think you're convinced of that, either."

"I'm not," I admitted. "It could just be that I feel incomplete because we don't have our telepathic bond, anymore. But since you've made it pretty clear that you're not open to that..."

Dana snorted. "I'm more open to that than I am to unlocking that damned memory."

"You are?" I said, surprised.

He looked at me warily and said, "Now, wait a minute..."

"No, that's the answer, Dana. You agree to the telepathic bond and I agree to you obliterating that memory."

"You should agree to that, regardless," he insisted, "instead of using it as a bargaining chip."

We were interrupted by Vicky's arrival. She stepped through to the balcony and said, "Okay, we've got an itinerary planned out. Are you sure this is okay?"

"Dana and I have a lot to discuss," I said. "Besides, it would just be wrong not to take advantage of being here."

"Where all will you go?" Dana asked.

"All of them want to see Stonehenge, so we'll head over that way. Cara would like to see a cathedral, and since Salisbury isn't far from there, that's where we'll go. A couple castles, of course. I chose Caldicot and Caerphilly. And Cardiff, of course, since we'll spend some time there."

"Bronwyn and I spent time in Cardiff. I like it a lot," Dana said.

"That's a solid couple days of sight-seeing," I said. "Sounds like fun."

"All right, then. I'll get the girls checked out of their rooms. We'll be leaving shortly. Be back here Monday afternoon."

"Perfect," I said. "We'll head back to London when you guys return, if that's good for you."

"Sure," Vicky said.

"Have fun," Dana added.

"Will do!" Vicky said, then grabbed her bag and left.

We were quiet for a minute after she departed, looking back out at the countryside. I broke the silence with a chuckle. "Vicky thought the reason I needed to talk to you was about Bronwyn."

"You're changing the subject," he said, then added, "though I imagine that is something you want to talk about."

"I don't really know what to say about that," I said. "You know I want you to be happy."

"But..."

My words caught in my throat. I couldn't say what I truly wanted to. It would hurt him too much. And it was too selfish of me. I gave a small smile. "But nothing. I want you to be happy. Bronwyn is lovely. I really like her."

Dana frowned at me. "I know you do," he said. "But you still don't want us to be together."

"That's not true," I said.

"Yes, it is," he said. "I don't need to read your mind to know that."

I glared at him. He could be so infuriating. Then I softened. "Look, it's not that I don't want you to be together. I just don't want you to be together *here*. I don't want you eight time zones away."

Dana nodded slowly. "I know that's a huge thing. But is that the only reason?"

I decided to ignore that particular question. "So about that telepathic link/death memory thing..."

"Right now, it doesn't matter," he said. "My head is still messed up from being sedated for so long. I wouldn't trust myself with removing the memory until I'm back to a hundred percent."

"And the other part?" Dana frowned and looked away, but I pressed him. "Come on," I said. "We had our link for a year and a half and nothing went bad with it. You kept thinking it would become like it was with you and Elizabeth, but it didn't!"

Dana avoided looking at me. "That's not the problem," he muttered.

His simple reply stopped me from getting more upset. Instead, I just stared at him. "But... you always said..."

"Yes, that *was* a concern, at first. But, as you said, it proved to be a non-issue."

I hesitated. "So... there was an issue that came up later?"

Dana shook his head. "No."

"Okay," I said. "Then I'm lost. What's the reason?"

"Seriously? You have to ask that?"

I thought about it some more, then shrugged. "Apparently so."

I waited for a reply, but he stayed silent. It occurred to me that this wasn't the first time Dana had refused to tell me something and acted all pouty about it. Years ago, we'd had a conversation in which I'd finally explained to him the reason for our long estrangement, which was still going on, at the time. He'd been surprised that the reason was because of my childish resentment of him and his abilities. Evidently, he'd always thought it was something else. But he would never tell me what it was, no matter how often I asked. So I quit asking. Until now.

"This is because of what you thought was behind our estrangement, isn't it?" When he didn't deny it, I said, "Will you finally tell me? Please?"

Dana took a deep breath, still looking away from me. He said softly, "Because of what happened when you were fifteen."

For a moment, I had no idea what he meant. Then I stared at him in surprise. There was only one significant thing that happened when I was fifteen. "You don't mean..."

"Oh, come on," he blurted. "What else could I possibly mean?" He practically jumped from his chair to stand at the railing with his back to me.

"You can't be serious," I said. "Why on earth would you think that was the reason I didn't talk to you for so long? And turn around. If we're finally having this conversation, the least you can do is look at me."

He reluctantly turned. "How could I *not* think that was it? It made perfect sense for you to be pissed off! In fact, I'd been expecting it."

"You... what?" I was more confused about this than ever. "You expected me to stop talking to you?"

"No, I expected worse," he said. "What I did was so wrong, on so many levels."

"Whoa, hang on," I said. "What *you* did?"

Dana hesitated. "Well... yeah. Obviously."

I tilted my head as I looked at him. "What exactly do you think you did?"

He frowned at me. "You know what happened."

"Yes, but I don't think *you* do. You were drunk, after all."

He flushed in embarrassment. "Well, that much we agree on." He shook his head, staring at his feet. "For years, I blamed the alcohol, but always knew that didn't excuse what I'd done."

I laughed out loud. "It wasn't the alcohol, Dana. And it wasn't you. It was *me*." He started to refute this, but I continued. "It was *me* who came to you. It was *me* who saw that you were drunk, and hurting, because that stupid bitch ripped your heart out."

"She wasn't a bitch."

"She hurt my brother, so she was a bitch." I said, dismissing it. "My point is that what happened was *my* doing. Entirely. It was deliberate. Hell, it was even planned."

Dana looked at me in disbelief. "What are you saying?"

"I'm saying that I'd already decided that you would be the one to take my virginity."

"For fuck's sake, Dinah, don't put it that way!"

"Why not?"

"Because it makes it even worse! You were *fifteen*! So, not only was it incest, it was also statutory rape!"

"Oh, give me a break," I said.

"Dinah, there are reasons it's wrong to have sex with a minor. Scientific reasons."

"I know, I know," I said, rolling my eyes. "Teens don't have a fully developed frontal lobe. The wiring isn't complete, yet, so their decisions are ruled by emotion, rather than reason."

"Exactly. They're much less likely to think about the consequences of an action."

"Right. Now, Mr. Psychologist, tell me why that scientific argument is bullshit."

"It's not bullshit!"

"It's complete bullshit, and you know it. At least regarding the age of consent. Our frontal lobes aren't fully developed at eighteen, either. Some women might hit that point by their early twenties. And some men might not hit until near thirty. If our laws were based on science, they wouldn't vary from state to state, and the age would be much higher than eighteen."

"That's beside the point!"

I snorted. "It's exactly the point you were making!"

Dana waved it off with a scowl. "The bigger point is that you could have gotten pregnant! It's not like you were on birth control."

I chuckled. "I put a condom on you."

Dana's frustration turned to surprise. "You did?"

"You think I was an idiot? I told you I'd planned it. So, of course, I thought of that. But get back to the point. You were saying how you thought this was the reason for our estrangement."

Dana sighed deeply. "I was terrified that you were going to tell someone. For months, I was a wreck, just waiting for the cops to knock on my door."

My stomach dropped at his words. "Are you serious?"

He nodded. "But time went by, and it was clear that you hadn't told anyone, and probably wouldn't, so I relaxed a bit."

I stood and joined him, reaching out to put my hand over his on the railing. "I had no idea," I said. "I'm so sorry." I hesitated, then said, "Why didn't you ever talk to me about it?"

He clasped my hand. "At first, I thought bringing it up would make it worse. I don't know if you remember or not, but I didn't come home again that year until Thanksgiving. And I expected everything to be awkward. But you acted like it had never happened. So I figured, why bring it up?"

"Well, you should have," I said.

"Maybe. But we had other things you wanted to talk about."

For a moment, I was confused. Then I remembered. "That was when I told you I was interested in girls."

"Yeah. And, of course, I couldn't help but wonder if this was because of what I'd done to you, that you didn't trust men because of me."

I just stared at him. "Dumbass."

"Anyway, once you started being cold toward me, I was afraid mentioning it would put you over the edge. That you'd tell someone."

"You know... I'd smack you for thinking I'd ever do such a thing, but to be fair, I was kind of a bitch toward you, then."

After a moment, he looked me in the eye. "Why, Dinah?"

"Well," I said, "I was already confused about my sexuality. I was leaning toward girls, but had yet to fully accept it. I figured that, since I'd never been with a guy, I needed to make sure they weren't my thing. Or maybe it was just to find out what I'd be missing. I don't know."

"But why me?"

"You were the obvious choice! I mean, for one thing, I knew I could trust you. You'd never hurt me. And you certainly weren't going to tell everyone at school that I was a slut, which just about any other guy would have."

"Okay, but–"

"Besides," I said, and I'm pretty sure I blushed, "I'd had a crush on you since I was little. I practically thought you walked on water." I glanced at Dana and saw the surprise in his eyes. "So tell me... if this bothered you so much when I was fifteen, why did you let it happen again a couple years ago, when we formed the bond?"

"Well, you got me drunk, again..."

"You got yourself drunk, that first time!" I punched him in the shoulder. "It is weird, though, that both times were after you'd broken up with someone. Guess I was your rebound girl."

"That's not funny. And if you remember, the reason you came to Sacramento was because *you* were heartbroken. Just coincidental that I was, too."

"That's true. But be honest. You *weren't* drunk that time, so why were you okay with it?"

Dana shrugged as he stared at the river. "I guess I figured that so much time had passed... and you were an adult... and we were both hurting... and..."

"And what?"

He frowned, as though the final reason were distasteful. "And because you weren't the only one with a crush."

Now it was my turn to be surprised. "Um... what?"

"Don't make me elaborate on that."

I didn't. Instead I just squeezed his hand tighter, put my head on his shoulder, and watched the river flow for a few minutes. Then I said, "If you don't mind me getting all analytical again, there's a scientific reason why we should re-establish the link."

"Do tell," he said, skeptically.

"To make the facts of my 'new' life match my former one." He looked at me without comprehension. "Technically, I'm a virgin, again."

Late that evening, I was soaking in the tub as Dana slept. I knew I should feel happy, or at least satisfied – and I did – but it was tempered by other concerns, especially Dana's relationship with Bronwyn. He was right, of course. It wasn't just the idea of him moving to the U.K. that bothered me. But when I thought of what it truly was, I felt like a hypocrite. I'd once been in a multi-partner relationship and still believed such things were totally natural and viable. I prided myself on not being a jealous person. But I couldn't deny that I was feeling it, now.

The water was cooling, so I let some energy flow out of me. Soon, it was hot, again. I enjoyed its warmth as I thought fondly about what had transpired a few hours before.

You done, yet? I need to pee.

I still vividly remember the first time Dana used his "inside voice" to speak to me, on my sixteenth birthday. It was such a thrill, and the second most amazing thing ever. The most amazing thing was being able to "talk" back to him when we had a telepathic bond.

Don't wet the bed, I replied.

May I come in?

Of course, I replied.

I couldn't help but smile warmly at him as he entered. Dana stood at the toilet. "Are you going to look away," he said, "or do your kinks include this, too?"

I laughed and allowed him a hint of privacy as I closed my eyes and relaxed back in the tub. When he was finished, he flushed the toilet, lowered the lid, and sat down.

I glanced over and saw the look on his face. It didn't take mind-reading to tell what was going on in there. I matched his frown. "You're not thinking of telling her, are you?" I asked.

He hesitated, and I could see the conflict on his face. "No," he eventually said.

"You seem unsure."

He frowned. "I don't like keeping secrets." He glanced at me, but continued before I could say anything. "I know, I know... there's no way she'd take it well. But part of me thinks she deserves to know."

I understood what he meant. "Just because someone deserves to know something," I said, "doesn't mean they should."

Dana looked up at me. "I mean, it was just to re-establish the link. She might understand that. No need to make it into more than it was." I stared at him and had to admit I was hurt a little by his words. He couldn't help but notice. "What?" he said. "That was our agreement, right?"

"Yeah," I said. Then I looked away, staring at the water. "I guess I thought..."

"Thought what?"

I just looked at him as though that were the stupidest question he'd ever asked. Then I sighed and shook my head. "Never mind."

"Wait..."

Suddenly, the bath was no longer enjoyable. I leaned forward to drain the tub, then stood and grabbed my towel. "I didn't realize that idea was so distasteful to you," I said as I dried myself.

"It's not distasteful, just... wildly unrealistic. And..."

"And what?" I demanded, glaring at him while drying off.

Dana gave me the look that said he realized he'd stepped in it and nothing he could say would fix it. "I'm sorry," he said.

Despite the soothing bath, I found myself becoming angry. "Don't be sorry," I snapped. "Obviously, I'm the one being wildly unrealistic and... something else." I threw the damp towel at him and strode into the bedroom.

"Look," he said, following me, "can we just talk calmly about this?"

"I *am* calm!" I yelled.

"Yes, clearly," he said as I pulled panties and a camisole from my bag. "Any calmer and you'd be asleep."

"You know what?" I said, pointing at him. "How about you take your sarcasm and shove it–" I froze, then, and gasped. I staggered, trying to steady myself on the dresser. I looked at Dana in alarm and saw panic on his face.

And here it was. The memory... the heat, the needle-like stabbings over my entire body, and the feeling that everything inside me was coming loose. Panic gripped me. I didn't know what to do. But then I felt Dana's mind inside my own. He was trying to contain the memory, but wasn't succeeding. I tried to push him out, afraid of what could happen to him if he was "inside" when it all blew up.

I heard him scream. Or maybe it was me.
More likely, it was both of us.

Seventeen

"I grew up with an older brother, and the bond between siblings is unlike anything else, and it can be a real journey to accept what that bond is once you both mature into it. Because it's not always what you want. It's not always what you expect. It's not always what you imagined or hoped. But it's one of the most important things in the world."

~ Ben Schnetzer

My brother's meta abilities manifested when I was four years old. Obviously, as a little girl, I knew nothing about them. It would be another twelve years before he'd reveal them to me, and quite a lot longer before he admitted to me how he would often seek refuge from the mental chaos of his world by diving into my prepubescent mind.

What I did know, throughout my young childhood, is that I seemed to be closer to my brother than any of my friends were with their siblings. It was a shock to me to learn that not all siblings were as super-close as I was with Dana. It surprised me that, when they'd tell me about what they did at home, it didn't include spending every waking hour with their brothers or sisters. And when they looked at me funny when I told them that my evenings were spent with my brother, seven years my senior, I regarded it as an indication that something was broken in their relationships, rather than there being anything even remotely unusual in my own.

When the day came, many years later, that Dana told me about his regular excursions into my noggin, I was shocked. But as soon as I gave it any thought at all, everything now made sense. I realized that the feelings I had – of him being almost like a part of me – weren't just my imagination. I accepted that my friends' sibling relationships were the normal ones. It was mine that was the unusual one. The abnormal one.

The *better* one.

Over the years, of course, his mental visits became less and less frequent. And once he went away to college, they stopped entirely.

I often wonder if my overblown reaction resulting in our long estrangement was exacerbated by the fact that I missed him in ways I didn't even know I *could* miss him. I also wonder if that intense childhood closeness was why I chose him as my heterosexual test subject.

One thing I don't wonder about, though, because I'm certain of it, is that our psychological closeness was responsible for our feelings being considered "unnatural" to most.

I came to with a gasp, jerking bolt upright. My heart was racing, and I was disoriented, as though I wasn't able to shake whatever nightmare I'd been having. I squeezed my eyes shut against the painful brightness in the room and waited for my breathing to slow before I assessed my situation. I carefully opened my eyes again.

In college, it wasn't terribly rare to find myself waking up naked on the floor with a throbbing headache, not knowing where I was. At thirty-nine, though, it was an unfamiliar experience. I took stock of my surroundings, noting something in common with the occasional college experience: I'd pissed myself.

I shakily stood, intending to clean myself and the floor, and that's when I saw Dana. He was on the floor, too. I could see that he was breathing. And by the look of his jeans, his bladder hadn't waited for him, either.

First things first. I entered the bathroom and wet a washcloth. As I shakily wiped myself down, I tried to parse what had happened. Once it came together, though, my heart began pounding again.

The death memory. It had come unlocked in my head. This meant that it was now like any other memory. It was accessible and, frighteningly, able to pop into my head without warning, like an annoying jingle from a chewing gum commercial. Even thinking about this caused it to flash back into my mind, and it was everything I could do to prevent it from overwhelming me.

Dana. I remembered him trying to contain it. I had panicked, though, afraid it would overpower him, and tried to push him out of my head.

I finished up and returned to the bedroom and took care of the puddle on the floor. Then I made my way over to Dana. I tried to rouse him, but couldn't.

The pain of the memory just wouldn't abate. Unless I consciously pushed it away, I could still feel the burning. I could smell the charring of my flesh, hear my own screams.

My heart raced again as it all washed through me. I sat on the floor next to Dana, holding my head in my hands as the pain grew and grew.

An eternity later, Dana's voice was in my head. *It's okay. We made it.*

I opened my eyes. I'd passed out again and was now lying on the bed with a blanket over me. Dana sat next to me, stroking my hair. *Thanks to you,* I thought to him. I reached out and clasped his hand.

No, he replied, squeezing back. *Thanks to you. If you hadn't insisted on re-establishing our link, I wouldn't have been able to share the brunt of that memory.*

I sat up and leaned against him. *How long were we out?*

No idea. I'm not wearing a watch.

Me, neither.

You're not wearing anything at all, he pointed out. He stood and fetched his phone. I noticed he was wearing a bathrobe, so he'd obviously cleaned up, as well. "Two missed calls and five text messages from Bronwyn." I waited as he quickly tapped a quick reply to her.

"So... how long?" I asked.

"Nearly fourteen hours," he said. "It's almost noon."

"Geez," I said. "No wonder I pissed myself."

Dana smirked. "Yeah. We won't be telling anyone about that when we talk about our trip."

I was silent for a moment, then said, "You warned me that the memory would pack a punch."

"I did," he said. "And honestly, it's probably a good thing that it knocked us out. Remaining awake and aware through that experience..." He shook his head.

"Yeah," I said, frowning. "I keep having to fight it down."

Dana was quiet for a moment. He didn't need to say it. I knew he was probably having to do the same thing. "Much as I'd love to continue discussing this, I've got to get some actual sleep."

"You mean half a day unconscious on the floor doesn't refresh you?"

"No more than it improves your sense of humor," he said, removing the robe. I pulled the blankets up to my chin. I was asleep before Dana even got in.

My sleep was, however, disturbed. Yes, there were intrusions of the death memory, in the form of muted dream flashes. But there were also dreams of Weatherford, of the Overseer, of a future in which the world knew I was a clone, and I was reviled even while being hounded by reporters day and night. And there were dreams in which Dana treated me as I'd treated him for so long, where he resented me, stopped talking to me, and moved to the U.K.

I woke, blinking away tears. I calmed my breathing and realized I was alone in bed. I heard Dana's voice, though, and saw him on the balcony, phone to his ear.

I slid out of bed and located my own phone. It was after four o'clock. Nearly twenty-four hours since I'd eaten. No wonder I felt so weak.

Dana must have seen me, because no sooner had I finished dressing than he came inside. "How are you feeling?" he asked.

"Starved."

"Good," he said. "Bronwyn's on her way over to join us for dinner."

"Oh?"

"Hope you don't mind."

I shook my head. "No... just... surprised. And you don't seem too excited by the idea."

He toyed absently with his phone. "Well, obviously, she wanted to know why I didn't respond for so long."

I frowned. "What did you tell her?"

"I told her I'd explain everything over dinner."

"And by 'everything,' you mean...?"

"Well, that's why I want you there. Because in order to tell her the truth, it'll require a lot of explanation of your situation. She's already commented on you looking and sounding differently from when you met last year. I told her she must be misremembering, but she's not stupid. She knows something's up."

"Right," I said, unsure whether the knot in my stomach was hunger or dread. "Okay, so, how much do you *want* to tell her?"

"I... don't know."

I took a deep breath. "Okay. I haven't straight-up asked this question before, because I'm afraid of what the answer will be, but... are you planning to move here?"

Dana hesitated. "It probably won't matter, once we've had dinner." Seeing my confused expression, he said, "She'll probably never want to see me again."

I studied my brother's face, seeing the pain in his eyes, along with... something I couldn't identify. I took a deep breath. "Then she *is* stupid."

Dana smirked, but said, "You know what I mean."

"Then don't tell her anything that's going to alienate her."

"Well, first we have to get past the lie I've maintained for the past several months about why I was in a coma."

"Did she know about our telepathic bond from... before?"

"Yeah," he said, nodding.

"And did you tell her how it was formed?"

"Oh, sure! I told everyone that!"

I nodded. "The idiocy of my question is duly noted," I said.

"Before we talk to her, you need to tell me how much she can know."

I'd been thinking about that for a while. But until this moment, I hadn't decided. "I guess... she can know the truth. She's been a major help to us, and now she's been sucked into the drama. So let's tell her about the cloning. The world will probably know soon enough, anyway."

I got dressed and we walked over to the restaurant. We were seated at the back end of the mostly empty room, again, and Dana's gaze frequently drifted to look out at the river. I could tell he was nervous.

Bronwyn soon arrived. Spotting us, she came over to our table, greeting me with a quick hug and a smile that I couldn't help feeling was a bit forced. She kissed Dana quickly and sat with us.

We skipped over small talk altogether. After we ordered, Bronwyn told us about how she had been inundated with questions from friends, family, and customers about her disappearance. Not to mention the police.

"What did you tell them?" I asked.

"Well, I lied my arse off, didn't I?" she snapped.

Oh, this will go well, I thought to Dana.

"I told them we went on spontaneous holiday and turned off our phones," she continued.

"Did they buy that?" I asked.

"Well, the police accepted it," she said. "Friends and family, not so much. But I got them to just leave it alone. Now," she continued, "let's get down to it. You owe me an explanation."

"More than one," he said. But he hesitated, seemingly not knowing where to begin.

So I took over. "We need to start several months ago," I said. "You need to know why Dana was in that coma."

Bronwyn frowned at him. "I never did believe the tale of you cracking your head on a piano."

I couldn't help myself. I snorted. "*That's* what you told her?" I said, laughing.

Dana pouted. "Shut up." He rubbed the scar on his forehead as he said this. It was only noticeable when he raised his eyebrows, so people thought it was just another forehead wrinkle.

"To be fair," I told her, "he did knock himself out in just that way, once. But that was before I was born."

"So the truth is...?" she insisted.

Dana and I exchanged glances, and I knew that most of the explaining was going to come from me. So for the next few minutes, I told her the truth about how Dana had come to be in a coma, which, of course, included telling her about my spectacular departure from the land of the breathing.

Dana explained, then, that his coma had been a direct result of my death, due to the link we shared. Then, together, we explained about the cloning procedure and Dana's restoration of my memories.

To my surprise, Bronwyn just nodded. There was a look of sympathy in her eye as she said, "I knew you looked different from when we met last year."

Our meals arrived and, as we ate, we brought her completely up to speed, explaining why she and Dana had been nabbed by Weatherford and Michaels, and then the reason for Dana's recent silence. To Bronwyn's credit, she took it well. But over this part of the conversation, I noticed that she seemed to grow... I guess "sad" is the only word that applies. And finally, she said, "You have your telepathic link again, don't you?"

Whoa, I said mentally to Dana.

"How did you know we didn't have it?" I asked.

She glanced at Dana. "He mentioned that it would've been easier for you to find us if you'd still had it." She looked back at me. "But you do have it now, yeah?"

I nodded, and the confirmation seemed to deflate her. She lowered her eyes, staring at her plate. "So you're... you..."

"What?" I said.

Bronwyn was silent for a while, just staring at her plate. "Look, I'm not an idiot," she finally whispered, looking back up again. "Do you not think I did all the research I could into meta telepathic abilities, once your brother and I started seeing each other?"

Oh, shit, Dana's voice said in my head, making my stomach drop.

What? I replied. I had no idea how much was out there that she could learn. *Is there a For Dummies book out there on this?*

"I know such bonds can form in times of trauma or... other strong emotions," she said, confirming the worst. Then she gave a sardonic laugh, still avoiding looking at us. "See, I knew it when I met you. I knew you were a couple. Even said it and you denied it."

"You said we were just pretending to be siblings," I corrected.

Now she stared at us. "Which is what makes this so awful!"

"Bron..." Dana began.

"I need to go," she said. And before Dana could stop her, she was out of her seat, heading for the door. Dana went after her, but was back at our table a minute later. He sat, staring at the remains of his half-eaten meal.

"I'm sorry," I said after a moment, but Dana just shook his head without looking at me.

This is my fault, I mentally told him.

I waited for him to deny it.

He didn't.

Dana left the hotel later that evening, in an effort to make peace with her. I felt just awful about it and wanted to help, if possible. But it was clear that he wanted me to stay out of it.

While he was gone, I called Jasmine, bringing her up to date on everything that had happened in the U.K. I was glad to hear that things were going well back home, including with Nathan, who evidently asked about me every day. I thanked her for dealing with him and told her to expect us home the next day.

I spent that night alone with my thoughts, which weren't the best company. Since I didn't want to dwell on the situation with Dana and Bronwyn, I instead focused on the bigger picture. When I wasn't fighting down death memories, anyway.

I found myself returning to what Vicky had said, about whether we should even be meddling in whatever was going on in Dynasonic's world. I understood her position, and even agreed with it a bit, but I couldn't convince myself that we should ignore it.

But everything was scattered. I felt like we had no firm grasp on anything. We'd tracked weapons, for all the good that had done. We had a good idea where they were coming in, which seemed equally irrelevant. Was Vicky right? Was Weatherford, despite being a scumbag, not doing anything we should spend our time worrying about?

This led to a massive wave of self-doubt: I began questioning all sorts of things, including the very existence of the Pariah Project. I blamed myself for everything, not the least of which was what was looking like the end of Dana's relationship with Bronwyn, and felt tremendously guilty for being a bit relieved about that.

I resisted the urge to speak with him telepathically. I knew he wouldn't reply, anyway. The later in the evening it grew, the more difficult it became, and the worse I felt.

I woke to a knock on my door. I'd passed out on the bed without even undressing. It was Dana, of course, who looked like he hadn't slept at all.

"Hey," I said, stepping aside as he entered. "Should I ask how it went?"

"Not particularly well," he said, plopping onto the bed. "Can I crash here for a while?"

"Of course." I looked at the time. It was just past six in the morning. As Dana kicked off his shoes and reclined on the bed, I said, "Want company?"

He was silent for several seconds, long enough for me to decide just to leave him alone. I put my hand on the door handle.

"Yes."

✧ ✧ ✧

I let Dana sleep until it was time to check out. Dana was so quiet that it eventually got on my nerves.

"Are you planning on telling me what happened?"

Dana sighed. "It went about as well as you'd think," he said. "I tried to tell her it wasn't like she was imagining. But it doesn't seem to matter. She's open-minded, but she has her limits, and it seems you and I crossed that line."

"Yeah. I get it. I'd be shocked if she didn't react this way, really." I hesitated, then said, "Were any decisions made?"

"None other than that she didn't want me staying there with her."

"So there's still hope for salvaging the relationship?"

"Can't say how much, but maybe." Then he shook his head. "Enough about me and Bronwyn. What about you? Are you still seeing the pizza girl?"

"Ali," I said. "I mean... I guess? We've only gone out a few times, so it's not serious. I doubt it really can be."

"I mean... not all relationships have to be serious."

"True," I said.

"Are you still trying to mend things with Vicky?"

"Honestly, no. I think it's best to just let that go."

Dana frowned. "Well, that conversation didn't last as long as I'd hoped."

I smiled. "Not all conversations have to be long."

Dana smirked. "True enough."

We spent the rest of our morning relaxing. Vicky and the others arrived in mid-afternoon, bearing gifts: a bagful of pastries from a bakery in town. We ate in the courtyard as they told us all about their tour. I was happy they'd had a good time.

Before long, though, it was time to head home. We all squeezed into the car and left, dropping Dana off at the Hen & Chickens, before heading to London and Vicky's portal.

Back in San Francisco, I stepped inside my home. I was exhausted, physically and especially mentally. All during the drive to London, I'd had to fight off the death memory. It wasn't as difficult as it had been, but it still wasn't easy. And it was draining.

On top of that, I'd had to explain to the others how the whole thing had played out. I did this without revealing the return of our bond, which meant hiding some of the truth and stretching the rest a little.

Inside, Kimera greeted me from the conference room. It was her turn on monitor duty, and she seemed to welcome the interruption.

"How's it been?" I asked.

"Not so busy," she said. "A few hold-ups stopped. One assist at a car accident. Two cases of violence toward homeless stopped. That just seems to be increasing," she said.

"I know. It's awful."

"Jasmine updated me on your trip," she said as I dropped my bag and sat at the conference table across from her. "I'm relieved that your brother is unharmed." Before I could thank her for the sentiment, she continued, "But she also said that Weatherford has learned you are a clone. Do you expect him to spread that information?"

"Probably. Or he may just keep it in reserve as a sort of insurance policy, a threat that we should leave him alone."

Kim was quiet for a time. A frown touched her golden lips. "Dyna, you may not wish to hear this, but some of us have been wondering why we are making Weatherford a priority."

"I know," I said. "We'll need a team meeting to discuss it, I think."

"Perhaps."

"What else did I miss while we were gone?"

She shrugged. "Not a great deal. You did, however, have a pair of visitors drop by."

"Nathan being one of them, I assume."

"Not counting him. Two girls. Layla and Sydney."

"Oh, really? That's unusual. Did they say what they wanted?"

"Kit was on duty when they came. He didn't mention anything to me."

"Thanks." I stood and lifted my bag, heading toward the stairs. "I'm going to unpack and grab a shower."

In my room, I tossed my clothes in the hamper. After a relaxing shower, I stepped into the lab.

"Hey, Henry. Miss me?" I said, with a brief glance. I pulled up the readings from the days I'd been gone and gave them a quick review. Then I read them again, to make sure I'd read them right.

Turning from the computer, I stepped over to the figure. I put my hand on his torso, which was noticeably warm, confirming the readings. The surface temperature had increased dramatically, and appeared to be continuing to rise faster than before. Since aluminum oxynitride is only about one-tenth as thermally conductive as aluminum itself, the internal temperature must be considerably higher.

I changed my vision focus and looked at Henry's energy signature. It, too, was much more pronounced than before.

Out of habit, I looked at his face, where I got the biggest shock. A nose had begun to form. And the eye sockets had filled in. Completely. He didn't have eyeballs, but what resided there was quite smooth and could, I supposed, work as a kind of lens, if it were clearer. A look at the floor confirmed that the excess slag there was being absorbed by the figure.

I grabbed my calipers and placed the inner jaws in Henry's mouth, expanding them until they touched his lips. One look at the readout confirmed it. His mouth was closing. A tape measure also confirmed that his hands were lowering, being a half-inch closer to the ground than before.

Henry had been busy.

I went to the office and took care of some Project business. Meaning, paying bills. Then curiosity got the better of me. I stepped down to the main floor.

"Kim, I'm going to go visit Layla and Sydney. I've got some things I need to discuss with their dad, anyway."

Kimera waved as I headed out.

I arrived at the Shepherd home just as Terence was pulling into their driveway. As he got out of the car, he said, "It's amazing how you always show up at dinner time."

"See, that's why we're friends," I said. "You just get me."

As we walked to the door, he said, "The girls are dying to talk to you."

"I gathered as much. They stopped by while I was away."

In the living room, Terence called to his wife. "Honey, I hope you're planning to feed an army, tonight. Dyna's here."

"Not to worry," Helena said from the kitchen. "Hi, Dyna!"

As I replied, the girls came bolting down the hall, practically jumping all over me with excitement. After a couple minutes of them talking over each other, Terence finally summed it up.

"They started meeting with Daniel last weekend."

"I see," I said. "No wonder you guys are excited."

They pulled me to the sofa and told me all about their meetings with him, the things he was teaching them, and so on. Their excitement was infectious, and I found myself grinning at everything.

"And our assignment," Layla said, "is to come up with our meta names."

"And have you?" I asked.

Both girls nodded. "Mine's pretty obvious," Sydney said. "Vortex."

"Yup," I said. "Perfect. What about you, Layla?"

"So you know how I can sort of 'jam' electronics signals?"

"Yeah."

"Well, did you know that one of the positions in roller derby is the jammer?"

I smiled. "I did."

"After you and Mom both mentioned derby..." She grinned. "It fits!"

"It sure does," I agreed. "Have you told Daniel?"

"Not yet," Sydney said.

"Well, you'll get the lesson from him, too, that your outfits must be professional."

"We got that speech, already," Layla said. "He mentioned a guy..."

"Jasen," I said. "Yeah, he's great. He'll get you suited up just fine."

"Another thing he told us," Sydney said, "was that we should find mentors who can help us with our specific abilities. He said you might be able to recommend some."

I thought about that for a minute. "Well, I can certainly hook you up with some telekinetics, Layla. A couple of my former teammates in the Gatekeepers," I said. "Booster and Newton. Both telekinetics."

"Sweet!"

"And I'll ask Invictus if he knows of anyone with abilities like yours, Sydney."

"Thanks, Dyna," she said with a big smile.

Helena soon called us to dinner, and I gratefully joined them. Conversation around the table was mostly about what Daniel had been teaching the girls. Their parents smiled politely throughout, trying to be encouraging, but it was obvious to me that they were still scared to death for their girls. I couldn't blame them. But Captain Shepherd's girls were as tenacious as he was.

I helped Helena clear the table before joining her husband in the back yard. We relaxed in lawn chairs with mugs of coffee. "What's on your mind, Dyna? I know you didn't come here just to see the girls."

I took a deep breath and exhaled slowly. "Terry... Weatherford has learned about me being a clone."

He looked at me, frowning. "How did that happen?"

I waved it off. "Doesn't matter. The point is, I'm afraid he's going to leak that information. And I can't even imagine what's going to happen, if he does."

"You think the public backlash will be that bad?"

"I honestly don't know. But even if it isn't, scientists around the world will be on me like nobody's business. I've succeeded in doing something no one else has, as far as I know."

"Aren't you the only known person to self-induce meta abilities?"

"Well, yeah..."

"You seem to have survived that scientific scrutiny."

"Yeah, but that's different."

"So what were you hoping I could do for you?"

I shrugged. "I dunno. You're military. You guys are used to keeping secrets and preventing them from getting out. I guess I was hoping for some tips."

"If I worked in the intelligence end of things, I might have some advice, but..."

"Yeah. I figured it was a long shot. I'm just stressing over it, and it hasn't even happened, yet."

"And maybe it won't. It would take more than just Weatherford's word for the world to believe it."

I gave a weak smile. I knew he was just trying to raise my spirits. He knew as well as I did that millions believe things without a shred of evidence.

"Yeah," I said. "Maybe."

A few days later, I dropped by the Gatekeepers Citadel, toward the end of the team's weekly briefing. I loitered in the hallway until the meeting ended. As the members filed out, many of them greeted me, some with hugs. Eventually, my targets appeared. I pulled them into an adjacent room.

Booster and Newton were both in their mid-twenties. They'd become fast friends after joining the team. Booster was tall and gangly, always with a smile. Newton was on the shorter side, friendly, but somewhat intense. Both greeted me warmly.

"Good to see you guys," I said. "You've been well?"

"Yeah," Booster said. "Things are good."

"How's your team doing?" Newton asked.

"We're fine, thanks. That's sort of why I'm here." Seeing their hesitation, I quickly added, "No, I'm not trying to recruit you."

They relaxed, then. "What's up, Dyna?" Booster asked.

"I was hoping the pair of you could take a young meta under your guidance."

"Another 'kinetic?" Newton asked.

"Yeah. She's eighteen. Her abilities seem to be somewhat limited, but of course, that could just be because she needs training."

"Limited how?" Newton asked.

I explained how Layla couldn't seem to lift objects, just propel them sideways. "Oh, wow," Booster said. "When my abilities first manifested, it was the exact opposite. All I could do was push things up." He grinned. "That's why I took the name Booster."

"That's encouraging," I said.

The pair exchanged looks. "We'd be happy to help, Dyna," Newton said. "I take it you're planning on bringing her into the Pariah Project, which is why you said this sort of related."

"I've been friends of the family for a while. The girls are pretty attached to me."

"She has a sister?" Booster asked. "Another meta?"

"Yeah. In fact, I came by to talk to Invictus about her."

"We'll be available on Saturday, if you want to send the kid to us," Newton said.

I smiled. "Thanks, guys. I'll do that."

I found Invictus in his office. After pleasantries, I explained to him about Sydney and her abilities. He looked thoughtful, then said, "Just vortexes? Not wind in general?"

"Not to my knowledge," I said.

"Perhaps Silver Storm," Invictus suggested.

"I thought she had ice powers."

"Technically, her ability is – as her name suggests – to produce a storm of freezing rain, the end result of which is often an icy mess, yes. However, I believe creating vortexes is part of it."

"Okay. More importantly, though... Isn't she one of the bad guys?"

Invictus smirked. "I agree that poses a bit of a challenge."

"You seriously have no other suggestions?"

"Plenty. Zephyr, Windstorm, Sirocco, Tempest... But none of them are local."

"Right," I said, disappointed.

"How have you been, Dyna?"

I chuckled. "I don't know how to answer that."

"Want to talk about it?"

"Not right now," I said. "Maybe the next time we get together with Daniel."

"I look forward to it," Invictus said as I rose to leave. "Take care."

Back home, I tapped into the meta database and searched for abilities similar to Sydney's. I'd gone to Invictus because I trusted his judgment, but hoped he was wrong about there being no one else locally who could train Sydney. Unfortunately, he was right.

River Smolts, age twenty-two, resident of Hillsborough, California. At nineteen, found guilty of being an accessory after the fact in a jewelry store burglary. She'd made the roads icy, making police pursuit largely ineffective. She was fined and received sixteen months' probation. Currently, there was a warrant out for her arrest as a person of interest in another burglary. As Invictus had said, she leaves a fairly incriminating trail.

All in all, she was far from a saint, but wasn't really a villain. After a while, I closed the database with a frown. Not a chance I'd trust her to train Sydney. I'd have to figure out some other way to help her.

My phone vibrated with a text message as I left the computer. It was from Dana and consisted of only three words. *Coming home tomorrow.*

✧ ✧ ✧

"You sure keep busy," Nathan said to me the following morning, as we sat in the Project's reception area (also known as my living room).

I set down my iced tea. "My life is a 'when it rains, it pours' kind of existence. Most days, it's sunny or overcast, though."

We sat in awkward silence for a minute. "I don't know how to thank you," he said, avoiding my gaze.

"You don't need to," I said.

"But I want to," he said, facing me again.

"Just promise me you won't throw your life away. That's thanks enough." Before he could protest, I continued. "How are things going for you?"

"Better than I expected," he said, and told me that Jasmine had helped him a lot in my absence. Nathan had no health insurance and didn't qualify for Medicaid, so she helped him apply for one of the AIDS Drug Assistance Programs. He was on the wait list for an affordable housing unit, but was staying at the shelter in the meantime. And he had several job interviews lined up. "They're just retail," he said, "but money's money." He smiled and said, "The folks at Hospitality House seem to like the Project a lot."

"That's nice to hear. We're pretty fond of them, too. They do good work."

We chatted for a while longer before he had to leave for one of his interviews. I wanted to get out to clear my head, so I walked with him up to the corner of Post and Larkin, where we parted ways. I wished him luck with the interview, then continued my stroll.

It was a beautiful day, in the mid-sixties. Just how I liked it. The fresh air helped, but my mind was all over the place.

Nathan was right. Not only was I busy, but I was filling my days so that I didn't have to spend time thinking about being outed as a clone. Part of me hoped my friends were right, that the world simply wouldn't give a shit, outside the scientific community. Well, and the religious zealots. I sure couldn't expect everyone to be as thoughtful and open to changing their minds as Cara had been. And even she wasn't fully on board.

But that wasn't the only thing bouncing around in my head. Dana was coming home. I'd asked him what had happened with Bronwyn, whether they'd worked things out. The fact that he didn't reply told me they did not. I hated the fact that I felt bad for him, but happier for myself.

There were so many things I needed to do that I'd been deliberately putting off or just hadn't found time to do. I'd promised Sinta a trip. I needed to see Macy. There was the whole situation with Weatherford and the Overseer, whatever it truly was. I needed to talk to Dynasonic and her brother. I hadn't seen Daniel in a while, either. Hell, I hadn't seen half my own team in too long.

Before I knew it, Post Street came to an end at Presidio Avenue. I stood there on the corner, surprised. Had I really been walking that long? My stomach rumbled with hunger, so I turned north and made my way to Ella's, an eatery popular with many of the Gatekeepers.

I got there just before the end of their breakfast hours and headed to the counter, where I saw a familiar figure. I made my way over and sat next to the enormous African-American man. "Hey, Derek."

The man turned and smiled. "Dyna, hey! I haven't seen you in ages!"

Derek Fisher had been one of my teammates in the Gatekeepers. But today he was dressed in civilian clothes, not his Blockbuster outfit. "I know," I said. "How have you been?"

"Wonderful," he said in his surprisingly soft voice. He pulled out his wallet and opened it toward me. "Shauna and I have a kid, now," he said as I looked at the photo of the infant. "That's James," he said. "Five months old."

"He's adorable," I said. "Congratulations!"

"Thanks," he said, then waited quietly while the waitress took my drink order and handed me a menu. Then he said, "What brings you out this way? Another chat with Invictus?"

"You know about those?"

Derek laughed. "Everyone knows about those."

"They do, huh? Well, not today. Just out for a walk." He nodded, but I could see the questions in his eyes. "Go ahead," I said. "I know what you want to ask me."

He smiled apologetically. "I'm sorry, Dyna. But is it true, that you...?"

"Yeah." I knew more questions were coming. I was used to them from the few people who knew the truth. But he surprised me.

"I'm so sorry," he said. "That must have been... I don't even have words."

I gave a half-smile. "Thank you." I'd forgotten how kind and considerate he was. I wondered why we hadn't been better friends when I was on the team. Probably because I was still a bit of a self-centered brat, then.

Derek sat with me, drinking coffee as I had second breakfast. It was, without question, the longest conversation he and I had ever had. And as I wished him well and began my walk home, I considered just how much I'd missed out on during my tenure with the Gatekeepers. Yes, I made a few excellent friends who'd even left the team to join me in the Pariah Project. And we'd had our little "Gatekeeper Girls" gatherings, which were a lot of fun.

I'd always complained that the Gatekeepers was too large of a group, with too many members to ever feel like a family. In retrospect, I was probably wrong. The team could have felt like a big, extended family, had I only given it a solid chance.

Dana arrived late that afternoon. I was waiting for him in the living room and got up when he entered. "Hey," I said, walking around the sofa to greet him. "How was the flight?"

"Long," he said, setting his bags down near the wall.

I embraced him but his response was half-hearted. "You should try Vicky's portals," I said. "If you can stand the nausea, it's definitely the way to go." I smirked, trying to elicit a smile. I failed.

"Don't think I'll be going back anytime soon." Dana grabbed his bags again and moved past me, heading for the back stairs.

"Are you hungry?" I asked. "We could–"

"No," he interrupted. He paused as he reached the doorway. "But thanks." Then he descended out of sight.

I stood there for a minute in frustration. For being a therapist, Dana was not the most open to discussing whatever was bothering him. He'd always been that way. I don't know why I expected anything different, this time.

Despite the guilt I felt over the end of his relationship, I couldn't help but be angry with him for shutting me out. But I knew better than to confront him about it. Not now, anyway.

About an hour later, my phone buzzed with a text message. It was Ali.

Dinner, grandma?

I chuckled, despite myself. *Sure,* I replied. *Where and when?*

New taqueria just opened at McAllister and Divisidero. Right across from Green Earth. I've heard good things. Say in an hour?

I knew the neighborhood. *Meet me at the NW corner of Alamo Square Park,* I said, then tucked my phone away.

I went upstairs, took a shower, and got dressed. Then I went down to Dana's room, to find his door closed.

I knocked. And waited. I knocked again. "Dana?" Still no answer. Maybe he was asleep. I quietly opened the door and peered inside. He was on the bed, but awake. He turned to look at me, clearly unhappy to be disturbed. "Sorry," I said. "I wanted to let you know I'm going out for a while." He just turned away again. I closed the door and headed out, my heart heavy.

The taqueria was about a mile from my place, as the Dyna flies. So that's what I did. I spied Ali in the park and descended to land near her. She looked up, hearing me, and laughed. "Awesome!" she said.

I chuckled as I pulled my shoes from my purse. "If you say so," I said.

She seemed giddy. "That's the first time I've seen you do your blasty thing!" she said.

I hadn't thought about it before, but I realized she was right. The most she'd ever seen me do was lift a guy to the ceiling. But before I could confirm this, she grabbed me and pulled me down for an intense kiss.

I smiled as we parted, my lips tingling. "Speaking of awesome..."

Ali laughed. "Come on. I'm hungry."

"I can tell," I said, touching my lips.

We walked the two blocks to the taqueria and arrived to find the place packed. We made small talk as we waited in line until reaching the front, where we ordered our food to go, there being nowhere to sit.

Back in the park, we found a nice patch of grass with a good view of the Painted Ladies rowhouses and the skyline beyond. The tacos were also in the awesome category.

As we chatted, my mind strayed back to Bronwyn's reaction when she realized Dana and I had our bond, again. That there was a practical reason for it didn't seem to matter. She couldn't deal with it. And that was my fault.

And what about future relationships? What if they found out? Would they, too, end things? Were Dana and I doomed to never have real relationships again?

"Are you okay?"

I looked at Ali in surprise. "Sorry," I said.

"What's up?"

"Just... a lot on my mind." I offered a slight smile.

After a moment, Ali said, "Want to talk about it?"

I finished my meal and wiped my lips, chucking the napkin into the empty bag. "Ali, what are we?"

She grinned. "We are two totally awesome bitches!"

I laughed. "True, but... you know what I mean." Ali furrowed her brow and looked sidelong at me. "What?" I said.

"Stop messing with me," she said.

"Messing?"

"With this 'what are we' shit." Before I could rebut, she said, "I know you've just been humoring me by going out with me."

My mouth fell open, I was so shocked. "*Humoring* you?"

"Come on. Why would I think you were looking for anything more than casual fun with me?"

"Why *wouldn't* you?" I questioned what I might have done to give her this impression.

"Well, let's see." She ticked off the reasons on her fingers. "One, you're a grown-ass woman, even though you look creepily younger than you are, while I'm only a few years past being a teenager. Two, you're super-smart and a legit scientist, whereas I flunked chemistry in high school and didn't go to college. Three, you're a big-time, famous hero, saving peoples' lives all the time, and I sell pizza by the slice to stoners in the Haight." She shrugged. "Should I continue?"

"I thought we determined that the age difference didn't matter."

"It doesn't, if we're just dating casually."

"But it does for something more serious?"

Ali paused. "I... don't know. But still, the other things..."

"You don't have to be a scientist to be smart. Intelligence comes in many forms. And you don't just sell pizza by the slice to stoners," I said. "You sell them salads, wings, and soft drinks, too," I teased.

"Fuck you," Ali laughed, punching me in the arm.

"Either way, it seems you've answered my question."

"Did I?"

"Well, I'm apparently not what you're looking for in a serious relationship, so..."

"Dyna, you don't even *do* serious relationships!"

I stared at her, a bit stunned. "Um... what?"

"On our second date, we were talking about our past relationships, remember? You basically told me that you only did casual, that you were into dating multiple people at the same time, like with those girls in college."

I shook my head. "Wow. I clearly didn't explain it right. Ali, I was deeply serious about both of them. Being serious does not require exclusivity. At least, not to me."

Ali absorbed this and was quiet for a bit. "I don't know." She looked up at me. "I'm not sure I could ever be serious about more than one person at a time. Not saying it's impossible, just..." She hesitated a moment. "All I know is that I like you. A lot. And I'm a little freaked that you even think we could have something serious."

"Freaked? Really?"

"Okay, bad word choice." She smiled faintly. "I guess the right word is 'flattered.' And I'm not used to that."

"That's a shame."

"Hey, this conversation is a lot heavier than I expected." She smiled wickedly. "Wanna make out?"

I laughed. "You ask stupid questions."

When I got home that night, I descended to Dana's room. The door was open, and I looked inside. The room was dark. His bags sat untouched by the bed, but he wasn't there.

I continued down to the kitchen. Dana looked up from where he was making a sandwich. "Hi," we both said at the same time.

"How was your date?" he asked.

"Mostly good," I said, walking toward the bar.

"Just mostly?" Dana said, returning sandwich ingredients to the fridge.

At the bar, I poured myself a Zaya. "It isn't my date we should be talking about," I said. Seeing what I was doing, Dana opened the freezer and telekinetically pulled out a single ice cube and lowered it gently into my drink. "Thanks."

He joined me at the corner table. "There's nothing to talk about," he said as he began eating. "You know what happened. It's not complicated."

I sipped my drink, remaining silent for a minute. Then I said, "Well, it kind of is." Dana looked at me, one eyebrow raised inquisitively. So I told him what I'd been thinking earlier, of how what had just killed his relationship could continue to do so in the future, for either of us.

"Then we just keep knowledge of our telepathic bond to ourselves," he said simply.

"But is that enough?" I said. "I mean, it's likely that someone we're intimate with will discover it eventually, right?"

Dana didn't reply. He didn't need to. "I'm going back to Sacramento tomorrow," he said.

I frowned, but had been expecting this. "Yeah," I said. "You have clients to return to." Dana let out a tiny snort. "What?" I said.

He smiled faintly. "I don't have as many clients as you might think," Dana admitted. "And most of them don't live locally." He looked up and saw my confused expression.

"Metas," I said. "You told me you had meta clients."

"Almost exclusively, now. And most of my sessions are done via video calls."

This was, in fact, news to me. But rather than express surprise, I said, "Then why haven't you moved here? Why pay rent up there when you can stay here free?"

He finished eating and carried his plate to the sink. "Ironically, to reduce the likelihood of us doing again what we did in Wales."

His reply shocked me. But rather than question him, I suddenly had a flash of memory. Something Bronwyn had said, the last time I saw her. *I knew it when I met you. I knew you were a couple.* And that had been just after Dana admitted that I hadn't been the only one with a sibling crush as a kid.

I looked at Dana, my heart pounding. "Tell me what she said," I demanded. But he didn't respond, just stood there at the sink, staring down at the plate he'd been washing for far too long. So I yelled at him mentally. *Dana!*

I saw him flinch. He finished rinsing the dish, placed it in the drying rack, and turned off the water. Then he turned to face me, leaning back against the sink while drying his hands. He didn't look at me as he said, "She accused us of being in love with each other."

Before I could express my astonishment, Dana left the kitchen and climbed the stairs to his room, closing the door behind him.

I remained in the kitchen, finishing my drink.

And a few more.

EIGHTEEN

"Have you ever had that moment when you looked back on something and said, 'Well, gosh, that seems obvious now... why didn't I see it then?' I like to call this the Face Palm Epiphany. Oh, hindsight, you magical, humbling thing."
~ Alethea Kontis

It's often said – accurately – that what we fear most is the unknown. It's human nature, really, and this fear has served us well since the paleolithic era. Without it, humans would never have made it.

But, as with most things, it's not entirely beneficial. There's a drawback, which is that this fear prevents us from exploring as much as we otherwise might. It breeds distrust of anyone different from us, leading to racism and other forms of bigotry.

Certain people, though, have always risen above their fears: the explorers who boarded ships and sailed in search of new lands, the adventurers who climbed mountains just because they were there, the researchers who studied new species in order to make the unfamiliar familiar.

I've always been in that group. Not to say that I'm fearless. Far from it. But my fears have generally leaned toward what is known to me, not unknown. These are things I tend to avoid, even when I know that by not avoiding them, the fear could be abated. Sometimes, I'd just rather not think about these things, let alone face them. And I'll go to great lengths in order to do so.

I wasn't surprised to find that Dana was gone by the time I got up the next day. There was a text from him on my phone. *I'll call you later*, it said. I knew him well enough to know that could mean anything from "later tonight" to "later this month." Likely it would be "later this week." It was just as well. I had no idea what to say to him.

I had a second text waiting for me, this one from Sinta. *When are we leaving?*

Today was the day I'd promised to take Sinta to Monterey. I checked the time. It was a bit after 7:00. I'd reserved the rental car for 8:00. *I'll pick you up in an hour or so*, I replied.

Sinta was one of the first acquaintances I made in the city and, since we lived together for a year and a half, she knew me better than most. So when, within minutes of our journey, she asked what was bothering me, I knew there wasn't much point in trying to deny it.

"Dana and Bronwyn broke up," I said. "He left for Sacramento this morning."

"Oh, wow. That's sad. I thought he really liked her."

"He did. Does."

"Then why?"

I weighed the different ways to explain it. I couldn't lie to Sinta, but I didn't want to just brush it off, either. "She was uncomfortable with me."

"Like... as a person?"

"Well, no. More like... um..."

"Oh. You mean uncomfortable with your relationship with Dana."

I felt my heart thump in my chest. "What do you mean?" I asked, glancing at her.

Sinta looked away. "Just... you know... how close you guys are." She looked out at the scenery. "Doesn't matter."

I was happy to let it go, so I quickly changed the subject. "It's weird to be driving a car again," I said. "Since moving here, I haven't needed one." I'd rented a Mustang convertible, since I'd always wanted to drive a Mustang. And I figured Sinta would enjoy having the roof down.

"I've never learned. Like you said, there's not much need."

"Well, where I grew up, we didn't have any sort of public transportation. We didn't have bus routes or anything. Driving was essential." I smiled. "I'd forgotten how much I enjoy it." Sinta just nodded and returned to watching the landscape go by.

My thoughts returned to my college days, when I'd drive from home to school every day in "Baby," my gold Renault with the horn that sounded like the Road Runner. It was a money pit, but I still thought of it fondly.

"How are things with Ali?" Sinta said, breaking my thoughts.

"I think they're good," I said, which surprised me more than Sinta, I think.

Sinta grinned at me. "Ali thinks so, too."

I shook my head and chuckled. "You really do talk to her a lot, huh?"

"Well, I might stop in for a slice every now and then."

"Right."

"And she might text me every time you guys go out."

"You're kidding."

Sinta giggled. "She said you guys made out in Alamo Square Park."

Despite myself, I blushed. "Geez. What *doesn't* she tell you?"

"You guys must have had an important talk. She seems a lot more positive about your relationship, now."

"Yeah, well... seems she thought I was just going out with her to be polite, not because I wanted to."

"I told her you weren't like that," Sinta said.

I smiled faintly, but all I could think about was how Ali would freak out, too, if she learned about Dana and me.

Our first stop was not Monterey, but Gilroy. The annual Gilroy Garlic Festival was this particular weekend, and since the town was right on the way, I figured it would be a fun side trip.

We arrived not long after the festival opened for the day and spent a couple hours roaming around, eating amazing food like garlic fries, garlic tri-tip sandwiches, grilled garlic sausages, and garlic-barbecued oysters. At the vendors, I purchased pickled garlic, garlic-infused olive oil, and a number of other items. I love garlic. Roasted garlic, garlic bread, garlic popcorn... but not garlic ice cream, it turns out.

After stuffing ourselves, we hit the road again, reaching Monterey in mid-afternoon. Our first stop was the Monterey Bay Aquarium. There, we spent hours viewing the incredible exhibits. Sinta was overwhelmed. "This is amazing," she said, probably twenty times. Her favorite, it seemed, was the sea otters. "They're so cute!"

A young docent stepped forward. Kurt, according to his name tag. "That's Kit," he said, pointing to a particular otter. "She was found stranded back in January. Only five weeks old, then. She's the youngest otter we've ever had on exhibit, here."

He said this very professionally, but he couldn't take his eyes off Sinta. She smiled politely at him. "I'm sorry," he said. "I don't mean to stare."

"It's okay," Sinta said. "I'm used to it."

"Still," he said. "It's not polite."

Sinta tilted her head as she looked at him. "You're staring out of curiosity. Most stare with disgust. I'll take curiosity any day."

The docent smiled shyly. "Thank you."

When he didn't stop staring, Sinta said, "Go ahead."

"Pardon?"

"I can tell you want to pet me," she said, causing him to stammer awkwardly. "You can. It's okay."

I smiled to myself. Sinta must have found the guy cute, which I suppose he was. She didn't offer her fur for petting to just anyone. I watched as he hesitated, then reached out and stroked the fur on Sinta's exposed shoulder. To his credit, he only did this for a few seconds. He grinned. "Wow. That's so cool," he said. "Thank you."

"No problem," she said. "Bye, now." And with that, we moved on deeper into the aquarium.

I regarded my friend. "A couple years ago, I don't think you'd have done that."

Sinta looked up at me. "Yeah, you're probably right."

I knew from our experience at the pizza shop that she still had a lot of people who stared at her in non-curious ways, which I'd told her was terrible. She assured me that she was used to it.

I told her that was just as terrible.

We spent the rest of the day shopping on Cannery Row, followed by dinner at The Sardine Factory. Then we hit the road again, but I wanted to show Sinta the scenic route. Specifically, the gorgeous 17-Mile Drive, possibly the most scenic route ever.

We drove along the coast, famous golf courses on our left, and the sun lowering along the stunning coastline to our right. Sinta didn't say a word the entire time, just sat there staring from Point Joe to Pescadero Point.

Returning north, we connected with Route 1 and began the journey home. "Dyna, have you taken that drive before?"

"Yeah. Dana took me one weekend a couple years ago."

"Cool. Well, thanks for bringing me."

"You're welcome, kitten. I'm glad you had a good time."

"I always have a good time with you."

"That's a lie, but thank you, anyway. We'll do more things like this in the future, I promise." After a time, I brought our conversation back to where it had begun, since I hadn't been able to stop thinking all day about what Sinta had said. "Kitten, what did you mean before, about Bronwyn and my relationship with Dana?"

I could feel her looking at me for several seconds before she answered. "Like I said, because of how close you guys are." I frowned, but said nothing. "Why?" Sinta said. "Did she say something different?"

Now it was my turn to hesitate before replying. I cleared my throat. "She said we were in love with each other." I forced a laugh and waited for Sinta to echo it.

"Well, yeah," she said. "That's what I meant."

I nearly ran off the road. "What the hell? Why would you think that?"

Now Sinta laughed. "Come on, Dyna. I may have never experienced it, myself, but I can tell when two people are in love. The way you act around each other. The way you look at each other, especially when the other isn't looking."

I felt my face drain of blood, despite my heart pounding fiercely. I wanted to dismiss her words, just as I'd wanted to when Dana told me that Bronwyn had said it. "What... I mean..."

Sinta smirked, as though enjoying how uncomfortable she was making me. "Dana looks at you the same way you look at him when he's not looking. Like you're the most amazing sight in the world."

I absorbed that, with some disbelief. "Is this what everyone thinks?" I asked.

"I doubt it," Sinta said, to my relief. "Most people haven't seen you and Dana together as much as I have." She paused, then said, "Wait." She looked at me with her big, catlike eyes. "Are you saying you honestly didn't realize this?" When I didn't reply, her eyes got even bigger. "Oh, wow."

My own sentiments were a bit more strongly worded.

When I have no choice but to face something I don't want to, I tend to hide. I withdraw, become reclusive, or take road trips by myself, for example. I justify this behavior by saying it's just my way of working through things, that I need time to think, etc. But, while there's some truth to that, it's primarily just running away. And right now, I absolutely needed to distance myself.

This is how I ended up sitting at a café with Dynasonic the following day. "I have so much to tell you," she said. "First, we finished recording our tracks with the orchestra. What an incredible experience!"

"I bet!" I said. "When will the album be released?"

"We still have some tracks to finish without the orchestra. Then all the mixing and post-production stuff. I don't think we can get it out in time for the Christmas season. Probably early next year."

"Are you happy with it so far?"

She smiled. "I honestly think this is the best work we've produced."

"Really? I thought *Whine* was fantastic. I can't wait to hear this one, if you say it's better," I said.

"Okay, so there's that. Also," she continued, looking around furtively, "my brother's group has made some progress. Big progress."

"How so?"

"Let's just say that the governor of California is no longer being unduly influenced by Michaels."

"Whoa," I said. "That *is* big!"

"Dana's been working on him for a long time. He was able to establish a contact in the governor's office who kept him informed of the governor's schedule. Dana would go to wherever the governor was and discretely work on unraveling Michaels' mental web."

"That's fantastic. Does the governor know about your brother's actions?"

"No. As far as he's concerned, he just gradually changed his views on things. Which would be how he believed he got to those views in the first place. He seems to know nothing of Michaels."

We were quiet for a moment, sipping our coffees. I couldn't help but remember my first visit to this world and how amazed I was by it. Not for the first time, I struggled with what I saw and what I knew. What I saw was a peaceful society with low crime and a fantastic economy. What I knew was that at least some of it was the result of mind control, making it essentially a dictatorship, without the populace realizing it. It might look benevolent, but it had dark aspects to it, not the least of which was the forced conscription of telepaths into the Overseer's network.

"Speaking of Michaels," I said, "I had a run-in with him in my world."

Dynasonic frowned. "You mean your world's version of Michaels?"

"Afraid not." I related to her the whole story of the encounter, including his ability to take physical control of seven of my friends at once, as well as his discovery of my clonehood.

"Oh, man," Dynasonic said. "That can't be good."

"Not even a little bit," I agreed.

"What are you going to do about it?"

I frowned. It was a good question. "I'm still debating."

"So why was he in your world?"

I finished my latte. "That's just one question I've been struggling with. I'm not used to this sort of thing," I admitted. "In the past, whenever there's been a bad guy, it was clear what they were doing and what I could do about it. But this whole thing with him and Weatherford..." I shook my head. "It's frustrating as hell."

"Remember the first time we met?"

"Yeah, my ears are still ringing."

"Cute," she laughed. "Well, as you recall, I mistook you for someone else."

"Your stalker."

"Whatever she is, I've seen her around a couple times, recently."

I frowned. "Doing what?"

"That's the odd bit. Nothing."

"Okay, tell me your history with this person. I gather it's not too extensive."

"It's not," she agreed. "Not counting the recent sightings, we've met three times. The first was maybe three years ago. She was in a crowd of fans after one of our shows. She was the only one not cheering, so she sort of stuck out. We stayed to sign autographs, and she hung out until the end, at which point she confronted me."

"Confronted how?"

"It was weird," Dynasonic said, toying with her empty cup. "She was aggressive, called me a 'pretender' and other unpleasant things. I thought she was high, honestly. She had that 'stoned' look to her."

"Okay."

"The second time was a few months before I met you. I don't think this encounter was planned on her part, since she seemed surprised to see me."

"Where was this?"

"I was over in the Haight, and we bumped into each other on the street. Like I said, she seemed surprised, once she realized who I was."

"So what happened?"

"The bitch hit me! Just hauled off and punched me in the face."

"Wow."

"By the time I'd recovered, she was running away."

"So she can't fly?"

"Not that I know of, no."

"And the third time?"

"That was the worst. It was just a few weeks later. I had been out and was returning home. She was waiting for me out by the gate."

"So she knows where you live?"

"Seems so. Anyway, this time, she just attacked without warning. She has electrical abilities," she said. "And they hurt."

"What happened after she zapped you?"

"Well, I screamed at her."

"And I know from experience that *that* hurts," I said.

"She seemed surprised by that, too. Like she didn't know I was a meta. So she ran off, again."

"You just let her go?"

"I thought about going after her, but to be honest, there's no way I could have caught her. She runs really fast."

"I see," I said. That made sense, as well. I can run quite fast, too. I'm not in Speed Freak's league, but I've got the energy to put into running that most people, meta or not, don't have. It stood to reason that Mistress Dyna would, too.

"So now you can understand why I reacted like I did at the Fillmore when we met."

"So the recent sightings... did she see you?"

"Yes."

"But she didn't attack?"

"Nope. Now, that could be because both situations had lots of other people around, but..." She hesitated before saying, "When she saw me, it was like she didn't know who I was, though she looked at my face with curiosity." She shrugged. "Weird, but I'll take that over being electrocuted, any day."

I smiled faintly. "Yeah."

Dynasonic frowned as she looked at me. "Okay, something's bothering you. What's up?"

I waved it off. "I came here to get away from that."

"I think it followed you."

I smiled at that. "Yeah, well..."

"Look, I know we're not like best friends or anything, but you can talk to me."

I gazed at her face, appreciating the earnest expression. I nodded. "Okay. You and your brother," I said. "How close are you?"

Dynasonic considered the question. "Well... I guess we're as close as siblings typically are. If there is a 'typical' way siblings are."

"Has that always been the case?"

"Well, no," she admitted. "When I was little, we weren't all that close. I mean, there's an age difference that means little, today, but when I was six, he was thirteen. We lived in very different worlds. And of course, he was dealing with this enormous secret of being... you know... and having to hide that fact."

"Yeah, how was he able to do that?"

"Well, it helped that we lived in a rural area. Metas weren't at all common. So he had plenty of time to get used to what he was and learn how to hide it."

"Was it commonly known that... what he is... is so rare?"

"Oh, yeah. In fact, common knowledge isn't that it's rare, but unknown completely."

"I can see how this would create a rift between you guys."

"Oh, I wouldn't call it a rift. As I said, we just lived in different worlds. We didn't start getting close until I moved to San Francisco. He'd moved here after college."

"So... you'd say you're close, now?"

"Well, the age difference doesn't come between us, anymore. On the other hand, because of his activities, we don't communicate a lot, let alone see much of each other. It's just safer that way." Dynasonic tilted her head, assessing me. "What's this about, hon?"

I looked across the table at her and saw the sincere concern in her eyes. But I had no idea how to answer her, or even if I should. So I forced a small smile. "Just... you know... seeing how much you and I have in common."

She frowned at me. "You know you can talk to me about anything, right?"

"I do," I said. "But I'm not really ready to talk about it." She nodded, then I said, "In truth, though, I'm having some difficulty adjusting to this new life."

"Is that how you regard it? As a new life?"

"I mean... in some ways, yeah." And I told her about how I wasn't sure what role Dynamistress would play, from here on out. "The Pariah Project is a different kind of team," I said. "We're not in the public eye. At least, not in the role of being a team of metas. We're becoming busier as an organization that assists in other ways, though."

"And how do you feel about that?"

"I feel good about it," I said. "After all, that's what I envisioned for the team in the first place."

"So... what's the issue?"

"I think," I said slowly, drawing out my own thoughts, "I think I feel a little guilty. Like we're not doing all we could be doing."

"In what way?"

"Well, in the sense of taking on criminals, I guess." I frowned. "It doesn't help that other metas have made such assertions about us."

Dynasonic was silent a moment. Then she said, "You told me that you used to feel that way about your brother. That you thought him being a psychologist was a waste of his meta abilities."

"That's right."

"Do you still feel that way?"

"To a degree, I guess. But not as much as I used to."

"Because it seems to me that, if anything, the Project is sort of inspired by his behavior. He doesn't hesitate to use his abilities when necessary, you've said. But his real strength is in his education."

"That's... interesting. I never considered that I may have been subconsciously inspired by him. But I can't deny the possibility."

I thanked her for that insight, then we spent another hour at the café, talking mostly about the new album and world tour that would go with it. Then I thanked her, gave her a hug, and left for home.

What I'd told her earlier wasn't entirely a lie. I really was curious to know if her relationship with her brother was similar to mine. I already knew that my late other-self's sibling relation was like mine only up to the estrangement. Her brother was killed before they could reconcile. So, I supposed this was another form of "balance." After all, Dynasonic's relationship with her brother was fairly neutral, while mine...

Mine was anything but.

Sinta's words still haunted me. "*I can tell when two people are in love.*"

The next day, I spent my morning struggling with anxiety. So much had happened recently that I'd almost forgotten that I had guests arriving. Comic-Con had ended the day before, so Sharon, Jackie, Michael, and Dinah were coming to visit.

I was anxious for a few reasons. First was just seeing them again in general. The brief time we'd had together at the airport the year before was emotionally overwhelming, so this reunion would probably be even more so. I sat in the office on the computer, staring at the photo that Michael had taken of us at the airport, which was my computer wallpaper. I was seated between Sharon and Jackie, with Dinah on my lap. Of course, I looked a bit different, now, from what the photo showed. That was a second level of anxiety.

The third issue was due to the lodging arrangements. I'd suggested they stay at my place rather than pay for a hotel. I'd done this automatically, without thinking through the sleeping arrangements. Michael was the one to solve the problem, though. He suggested that Sharon and I share a bed one night, Jackie and I the other night. Dinah would sleep with the others in the guest room. I'd agreed to this, but now I was strangely nervous about it.

Just before noon, they arrived. I answered the door, and a small blue and white streak tackled me. I looked down at Dinah, my eyes growing wide. "What the heck?"

Dinah was dressed as me. The costume was almost a perfect replica, down to the white wig. "The girls worked on that thing for over a month," Michael said.

"I was you at Comic-Con!" Dinah beamed. "I won the kids' costume contest!"

"That's amazing," I said as she disengaged from me and did a twirl, showing off the cape. I pulled out my phone and took several photos, knowing I'd have a new desktop background shortly.

I picked her up and welcomed the others inside. After hugs all around, I led them down to the kitchen, where I served them donuts I'd picked up that morning, with coffee for the adults and chocolate milk for Dinah.

"How was the Con?" I asked.

"So much fun!" Dinah said. "So many people took pictures of me!"

"I bet they did. And they asked who you were."

Dinah shook her head. "Well, some of them, but most of them knew."

"Seriously?" I said.

"Why weren't you there?" Jackie asked.

"Yeah," Sharon said. "There were a bunch of metas."

I shrugged. "Didn't get invited. Who did you see?"

They rattled off several unfamiliar names, a few familiar ones, but only two that I personally knew: Golden Bear and Miss Fire.

About the last, I said, "She's hot."

Dinah picked up on the joke immediately and laughed. The others rolled their eyes, but chuckled, nonetheless.

Throughout our chat, I occasionally caught Sharon or Jackie studying my face, but neither of them mentioned my appearance. The women told me more about their jobs and Dinah told me about her hobbies and school.

Eventually, Sharon asked for a tour of the building, so I led them around the various floors and rooms after dropping their luggage in the guest room. I avoided my lab. Explaining Hank wasn't something I wanted to do. Besides, he might scare Dinah.

We finished the tour up on the roof balcony. It was a nice day, with temperatures in the mid-sixties. "I love this weather," Sharon said, and I agreed.

"See, in my head," Jackie said, "you lived in a place with a fantastic view of the bay."

I laughed. "I wish."

"Can we see the Golden Gate Bridge?" Dinah asked.

"Of course, sweetie," I said. "In fact, if you like, we can do a tour of the city. Have any of you been here, before?"

The women shook their heads, but Michael said, "I was here about five years ago, but didn't have much time for sightseeing. By the way," he continued, "when would you like to do the photo shoot? And where?"

Before I could answer, Jackie said, "Why don't you do shots at different San Francisco landmarks?"

Michael smiled. "We could do that, if it's okay with you."

"Sure," I said. "On one condition." I looked at Dinah. "You have to be in the pictures, too!"

She jumped in excitement. "Yes!"

After a light lunch, I stood in front of my wardrobe, staring at the blue and white costume hanging there. It was what Michael wanted me to wear. Dinah, too. I understood why. It was the look most associated with me, by far. Most people didn't know anything about my outfits before or after that one. It felt odd to put it on, again. But I'd promised.

I met the others in the living room, then we walked out to Post Street, where we caught a cab. All afternoon, we went from location to location, the girls admiring the sights, and Michael shooting Dinah and me against all the landmarks: Coit Tower, the Golden Gate and Bay Bridges, the Palace of Fine Arts Theater, and more. He took photos of us separately, as well.

Nearly all of the taxi drivers seemed excited to have a real, live meta in their cabs. I made sure to sit in the front with them, Dinah in my lap, and allowed selfies for the ones who asked. Dinah got a lot of attention, too.

Many of the shots featured me in the air, which made Dinah clap and jump around. I tossed her skyward while she made "superhero flying poses" for Michael to capture. Inevitably, she asked if I could take her up in the air. After getting the clearance from the adults, I agreed. When our last cab arrived, I told the others that Dinah and I would meet them back at my place. Then I carried Mini Dynamistress into the sky.

Her reaction was just as I expected. She was absolutely giddy, and I had to remind her to hold on tightly. Eventually, her excitement calmed down, and I realized she was probably cold. Soon after, we landed on the upper deck of my home.

Naturally, we arrived well before her parents did, so after changing into normal clothes, we sat in the living room in front of the fireplace. As Dyna warmed herself after our flight, we chatted about things. She surprised me when she said, "My moms didn't think you'd really invite us out here."

"Really?"

"They said you were too busy and stuff. And that maybe you didn't want to see us again."

"Of course I did!" I said. "I'm just sorry it took so long before it happened."

"That's what I told them. And so did Michael."

"Well, you were right." I smiled at her. "No way would I miss the chance to see you again."

The front door opened, and we looked over, expecting to see the others. But it was Sinta arriving for a stint on monitor duty.

"Wow!" Dinah said. A surprised Sinta came over and I introduced them.

"So you're Dinah," Sinta said. "I've heard a lot about you."

"You have?" she replied, eyes wide.

"I sure have." Sinta nodded at me. "She talked about you a lot after you met."

Dinah smiled bashfully. Then, "Can I pet you?" she asked.

Sinta laughed. "Sure."

I watched the two, Sinta delighting in playing with the girl. The others arrived during their wrestling match, so I made more introductions. As they rested for a bit, we discussed dinner, as Sinta headed up to the office.

After a nice meal out, we returned home. We sat around our conference table, playing Go Fish. Dinah won. After we tucked her in bed, Michael retired to the living room to go over the photos. Jackie, Sharon and I headed down to the bar.

We drank and reminisced for hours. When it came time for bed, Jackie called dibs on sleeping with me. And sleep is what we did. Mostly. There was cuddling, and some kissing. Maybe a little more than that.

It was wonderful. At one point, I wept, shocked at just how many feelings I'd kept locked inside all these years. We fell asleep with me as the big spoon.

We were awakened by Dinah jumping on the bed and wiggling her way under the covers with us. I was a little concerned, since Jackie and I were both naked. But Jackie turned to face us and hugged her daughter. "Morning, Tink."

"Morning, Mommy One and Mommy Three."

I laughed. "Is that what you call us?"

"Sometimes," she admitted.

"Did you sleep well, honey?" Jackie asked.

"Mm hm," Dinah said as she snuggled up next to me. Minutes later, she was asleep. Jackie and I lay there, talking softly.

"Her hand is on my boob," I said with a chuckle.

Jackie smiled. "Yeah, she does that, sometimes."

"She's wonderful," I said.

"Mm, well, you're seeing her at her best. She can be a demon."

"What six-year-old can't be?"

"Six and a *half*," Dinah mumbled.

Jackie laughed. "You little faker!" She tickled her and Dinah scream-giggled and thrashed around, begging her mother to stop. Jackie did. So I took over.

I made pancakes for breakfast. Dinah assisted, while the others sat at the table with coffee. I glanced over and caught Michael gazing in my direction with a curious expression on his face.

As he helped me clean up, later, I asked him what caused the curious face. He said, "I was just noting how great you are with Dinah."

"Oh," I said, surprised. "Well, she's easy to get along with."

"Most of the time, yeah." Then he said, "In case they haven't told you so, I know the girls are beyond happy to be here with you."

"I'm glad to hear that."

"You have no idea how often I've heard your name over the years."

I was sincerely surprised by this. "Really?"

"I can't help but wonder if you've ever thought about doing more than just visiting."

I glanced over at the others, still at the table, chatting. "What are you saying?"

"That there maybe should be a permanent reunion."

I stopped loading the dishwasher and stared at him. I opened my mouth, but nothing came out for a moment. Then, I said, "Seriously?"

"I know all of us would love that."

I raised a skeptical eyebrow and teased him. "You're just looking for a third partner, aren't you?"

Michael smiled softly and shook his head. "Jackie is the only one I need," he said. "Sharon and I aren't sexually involved. She joins us for cuddles, but that's all."

"Oh. Well... even so, this is kind of a sudden suggestion. I mean, it's been a lot of years since we were together. We're all different people. Plus, my work here keeps me busy."

"Yeah, sorry. It was just something I've often wondered, since the girls talk about you so frequently."

I didn't even know what to say to that. I looked over at the three of them, to find Sharon looking at me. She smiled. I smiled back, but felt my face flush.

"Just something to think about for the future," Michael said.

I nodded. It was, yes.

We spent the day mostly hanging out at home. We talked a lot, mostly about little Dinah. We played Go Fish again. Dinah won again. I think she cheats.

Although I still had some anxiety, by afternoon, we were talking as we used to, as though the years had never passed for us. Dinah fell asleep in my arms in the late afternoon, and we sat there on the sofa together. Michael suggested going out to a coffee shop to pick up drinks, and the girls went with him, leaving Dinah sleeping on me.

I was totally fine with this. I held her warm body to mine, surprised at the maternal feelings that hit me. This visit felt like a dream. One that I didn't want to end. For these two days, I wasn't thinking about work. I didn't care about Weatherford or Michaels. I didn't pay attention to other Project matters. And it felt fantastic.

I woke to the sound of voices. I opened my eyes to see Sharon, Jackie, and Michael sitting around us. Dinah was still asleep on my chest. "That's adorable," Jackie said.

I smiled awkwardly as I tried to sit up without waking Dinah. I failed.

"Hey, Tink," Michael said as Dinah rubbed her eyes. "We got you a hot chocolate."

"Yay!" she said, sliding off me to get her drink.

"Caramel latte for you," Sharon said, pointing to the other cup on the coffee table.

"Thanks," I said, surprised that she'd remembered my preference.

Conversation now focused on me. Since they'd only read the media accounts, I ended up telling them all about my genetic work, how my abilities manifested, and the truth about how the lab had caught fire that night so long ago. They asked all kinds of questions about my teammates, both in the Bay Scouts and the Gatekeepers, which surprised me a little. "You guys never seemed too interested in metas when we were in school," I said.

"Well," Jackie said, "that's probably because we never expected to know one."

"Keep going," Sharon insisted.

I chuckled and told them about how I departed the Gatekeepers and started the Pariah Project. I was surprised they hadn't brought it up by now, but they finally asked about my "death."

I admit that I was nervous to tell them about the cloning. But I did. In great detail. They all listened intently, not even stopping me to ask questions. When I was finished, they were silent for a time, exchanging glances.

It was Michael who broke the silence. "Holy shit," he said.

"Language!" Dinah said. "There's a child present!"

Despite myself, I cracked up. Michael chuckled and acknowledged his gaffe. Then he said, "Sure wasn't expecting to hear anything like that."

Jackie agreed. "I mean, we were surprised at how little you seemed to have aged since college, but we assumed it was just some byproduct of your original experiment."

"Well," I said, "in a way, you're right. The genetic alterations I did included a few different ways that my body fights the aging process. Even before I went nova, I looked younger than my age. And now... who knows how the process will go?"

"I kinda hate you, now," Sharon said, laughing.

"Oh, stop," I said. "You still look fantastic."

"If I do, it's because of heavy use of expensive products."

Jackie still looked shocked. "I... I don't even know how to respond to this."

"You don't really need to."

"I mean," she continued, "we always knew you were smart, but you're like... a super-genius or something."

"No," I said. "I'm really not." Before she could contradict me, I said, "There's a distinct possibility that my aptitude with genetics is another meta ability. It seems to have been the only one that expressed itself when I was young, but it allowed me to bring out the others."

Michael looked puzzled. "So, you gave yourself abilities many years ago. But after you cloned yourself, those same abilities manifested?"

"I was surprised by that, too, to be honest. But it supports the theory that my genetic aptitude is meta in nature. I just thought I was focusing on the most obvious areas in pulling out meta abilities. But maybe I was being guided to those, subconsciously."

"Guess it's a good thing that you and your brother made up, huh? Otherwise, we wouldn't be having this conversation."

"Yeah, that was..." I shook my head. "Yeah."

"I'm hungry," Dinah said.

I glanced at the clock and was surprised at how late it was. I hadn't realized we'd been talking for so long. "Yeah, so am I," I said.

Dinah wanted spaghetti, so we went out for dinner at Colombini, only a couple blocks from my home. We had wonderful pasta and great conversation before heading home. Not long after returning, Dinah started to nod off, so Michael took her to bed, leaving the girls with me to talk.

We chatted for hours, basically just seeing how much, or little, we'd all changed since college. Finally, I brought up what Michael said about a permanent reunion. I asked if he was right about them wanting such a thing.

Sharon and Jackie exchanged glances, apparently judging which of them would reply. Sharon drew the short straw. "When we were in grad school, Jackie and I talked about that. We both wanted that, at the time. But then, as you know, life got in the way, and you became a meta and moved here. In the years since then, we often spoke of you. Obviously, since we named Dinah after you."

Jackie chimed in. "And being with you, talking with you, feels much like it did back in college. I mean, we're all different people than we were, then, but our dynamic still seems pretty much the same."

"It's probably too early to do more than talk about it," Sharon said, "but I'd be lying if I said we haven't been thinking about it."

I just nodded, not really knowing what to say. So we switched topics and chatted until the yawning started. Jackie was the first to surrender. She got up, kissed us both, and headed to the guest room.

Sharon and I stayed up a bit longer, but eventually headed to my room. We didn't do a lot of talking after this. Mainly because our mouths were otherwise occupied.

The following day was just as bittersweet as I figured it would be. We had time for breakfast before they needed to leave for the airport. I spent most of the morning paying attention to Dinah, who was sad about having to leave. I told her she wasn't the only one sad about that.

Too soon, their cab arrived. The goodbyes were filled with tight hugs and some tears. As the taxi drove away, I felt a pit of emptiness grow.

I had a lot to think about.

Several days later, Jack turned thirty-two. We had a small gathering for him at my place. It gave me the opportunity to get to know Aimee a little better. She's a lovely woman. I was genuinely happy for Jack.

At one point, Sinta came up to me as I was watching Jack and Aimee interact with each other. "See what I mean?" Sinta said.

I frowned down at her. "Oh, come on," I said. "It's obvious how they feel about each other. I mean, look... they're holding hands whenever they're next to each other."

"It's not just that," she said. "It's how they look at each other and stuff, just how they interact in general."

"Are you insinuating that Dana and I make lovey-dovey eyes at each other?"

"No, but..."

"But nothing," I said. "You're making too much of it. Bronwyn was wrong."

Sinta chuckled. "Whatever you say." Then she grinned. "I'm going for more cake!"

I'd been successfully not thinking about "the Dana issue" until Sinta brought it up again. But now that he was on my mind, I remembered a question I needed to ask him. I pulled out my phone and texted, *Are you coming to town on Thursday for that concert you had me buy tickets for?*

His reply came almost immediately. *No. You go ahead and use them.*

I wasn't surprised. Seeing a band whose lead singer was friends with your ex wouldn't be my idea of a good time, either.

The concert itself, though, *was* a good time. The Joy Formidable played a set of eight songs, and Ali and I both enjoyed their sound quite a bit. They were described as "alternative," as are so many bands, though no one has ever successfully explained to me what it's an alternative to.

After the show, Ali commented on how cute the singer was. Though I agreed, I said, "You just like her because her hair is almost white."

"Was that a backward way of complimenting yourself?" Ali replied.

I laughed. "Why? Is that why you like me?"

"Well, no, but it is rather striking."

"Says the girl with green hair."

"Admit it," she said. "The hair is why you like me."

"No, I like you because you give me free pizza when I take care of rude customers."

"That's fair," she said, clasping my hand. "Let's go eat."

"Ah, the three little words I was hoping to hear," I said.

"That's good, 'cuz I'm not ready to say those other three little words." Sensing me tense up, she looked up at me with an apologetic smile. "I just made it awkward, didn't I?"

"Maybe a little," I admitted.

"Sorry."

"It's fine," I said. It wasn't her fault, after all, that her words made me think of Dana.

August held another birthday. Lily turned twenty on the twenty-first. As with Jack, we had a party at our HQ. It was a smaller crowd than for Jack's birthday, but rowdier, given the lower average age of those in attendance.

When Lily and I had some time to talk privately, I asked how things were going at home. "Nena still feels like she's intruding," she told me, "but every day gets better. She finds it hard to believe that Kit is okay with her living there, but he really is."

"That's good."

"She still spends most of her time alone in her room, though. She'll join us for dinner and on movie nights in the living room, but that's about it. And she insists on doing most of the cleaning."

"She may need to do that in order to feel like she's contributing, rather than just living there for nothing."

"Yeah, Kit and I have talked about that. Of course, we both tend to clean up after ourselves, so that makes it easier on Nena without her realizing it."

"Well," I said, "I'm glad you were able to talk her into it. She needs that kind of stability at home."

I wished her a happy birthday again and hung out in the kitchen for a little while longer, mingling with my friends, before heading upstairs. I passed through my bedroom and into the lab. "Hi, Hank," I said out of habit.

I assessed the big guy, again amazed at the changes in him over the past two weeks. All my estimates had been wrong, since I figured progress would remain fairly steady, when it had instead accelerated. I'd allowed this business with Dana to distract me from Hank, and how exciting the whole thing was.

Hank's arms had lowered more. His mouth was almost completely closed, now, and his facial features were much more defined, including what were becoming eyeballs where only a flat surface had been. His entire progression was both fascinating and creepy.

I picked up a stethoscope and applied it to his chest, listening. So far, I hadn't heard anything, and I wasn't sure what I was hoping for. This time, though, there was something. A faint crackling noise, like someone playing with cellophane.

My heart raced at this. I'd done a fair bit of research on aluminum oxynitride and knew that it could be formed into thin films. Could this possibly be some sort of rudimentary lung being formed? The implications of that were tantalizing.

"Oh, my big, glass man," I mused. "What surprises have you got in store for us?"

NINETEEN

"It's ironic that when you go through a tragedy, you appreciate more. You realize how fragile life is and that there are so many things to still be thankful for."

~ Adam Grant

After a certain age, my parents never really celebrated my birthday with anything beyond a cake and a single gift, so I grew up thinking birthday parties were just for little kids. I held to this belief, even though I would be invited to the birthday parties of friends all throughout my school years. In college, other students made big deals of their birthdays, using them as convenient excuses to get wasted. Since I never needed an excuse to drink, I didn't need to justify it with that sort of celebration.

In fact, it's only been in the past decade or so that I've really understood the level of significance many people give to birthdays. Some seem to find it interesting or entertaining when they share a birthday with someone famous. For example, my brother shares a birthday with legendary entertainer George Burns, DeForest Kelley of Star Trek fame, surreal director Federico Fellini, and others. For the record, I share mine not only with Sinta, but with Abraham Lincoln, Charles Darwin, Anna Pavlova, and some famous folks who aren't dead, yet. At any rate, I really enjoy birthday parties, now.

Not terribly long after Lily's, another one was upon us. Marcus was turning forty. Interestingly, he shares his birthday with the state of California, itself, which would turn one hundred and sixty on the same date. I didn't know what bash the Golden State had planned, but the Golden Bear would be having a party at his favorite bar in San Francisco, where Dana and I had met him, years before. We were looking forward to it.

Around six o'clock that evening, I was upstairs debating what to wear to the party when I heard Jack yell from down below. "Dyna! Emergency!"

Actual emergencies were rare, so it took a second to process. Then I dashed down to the main floor. Jack stood near our computer monitor, listening on a headset. He looked up at me. "Explosion. Big one."

"Where?" I said, snagging an ear comm from a drawer in the wall.

"San Bruno," he said. Then, catching my eye, he said, "Crestmoor."

My stomach dropped as we exchanged looks. Crestmoor was the development where Kit, Lily, and Nena lived. From a cabinet, I grabbed two of our emergency trauma response backpacks. After sending out an emergency notice to the full team, Jack helped me swap out components, putting heavy focus on burn dressings, disposable filter masks, and portable oxygen with resuscitators. The second pack, I filled with bottles of water and strapped it around my front. I fixed my own filtration mask in place, then sprinted for the door. Outside, I tapped the power button on my earpiece and took to the sky, listening to the emergency chatter that Jack had patched into our channel.

There was so much confusion. No one seemed to know the cause. Since this was only a couple miles from the airport, the immediate assumption was that an aircraft had crashed in the residential neighborhood. Some of what I heard was quite alarming. Flames a thousand feet high, one voice said. Surely an exaggeration, I thought, but with every word, my heart pounded.

"I'm getting no response from Kit or the girls," Jack said in my ear. "I'll keep trying."

It would be several minutes before I would get there. But I saw the smoke right away. Huge, billowing, dark clouds reached for the sky, being carried eastward by the wind. Then, to my astonishment, I saw the fire. It was like something out of Hollywood: enormous, raging gouts of flame.

By the time I arrived, it was probably close to twenty minutes after the initial explosion, but these flames showed no sign of slowing. The news chatter in my ear kept insisting this was a plane crash. Nearby residents said the same, although most of them judged this from sound, not visual confirmation. Granted, I had never seen a plane crash up close, but I just couldn't imagine that's what this was. Unless a plane did a straight nose-dive, wouldn't there be debris scattered over a long path? No such path existed. And I could see nothing that resembled aircraft sections.

I was so overwhelmed by the magnitude of this horror that I didn't even have time to appreciate that the fire was not near my friends' home. There are two Crestmoor developments. Kit and the girls lived in the one on the other side of Crestmoor Canyon from the fire. Once I realized this, I let Jack know. No sooner had Jack acknowledged than Kit's voice came over the comm. "I'm here, guys. Sorry for not responding before. I was on the emergency channels. The girls are at the movies, by the way."

I was glad to have the relief of not needing to worry about them. I didn't need that distraction. "Thanks, Kit. Anything I need to know?"

"Center appears to be near the intersection of Glenview and Earl."

"It's not a plane crash," I said.

"I agree," Kit replied. "My bet is on a gas main."

"OK. I'll check in later."

The heat was incredible, even from my distance. The smoke was thick, and the wind just made everything worse. The roar of the fire was loud, much louder than I'd expected. From upwind, I was able to count a dozen homes in flames. I don't know how long I hovered there, but eventually I flew low and landed near some fire trucks. The firemen were frustrated. Evidently, the blast had broken a water main. Hoses had to be dragged for blocks to working hydrants until water could be trucked in. Local citizens helped with the hoses and, because there weren't enough ambulances, also drove burn victims to the hospitals, proving again that, in times of tragedy, regular folks are just as heroic as those who routinely bear the label.

I dove into the thick of things, occasionally finding a victim. Fortunately, all those I found were alive. After applying burn dressings and masks from my kit, I'd fly them out to a waiting ambulance or civilian vehicle. Fortunately, I ran out of victims before I ran out of supplies.

After I'd been there for close to an hour, the radio confirmed that this was not a plane crash, but a gas main rupture, which explained why the fireball was showing no sign of stopping, since the gas was still flowing.

Other reports filtered in. Pacific Gas & Electric had turned off the power to the area. I did the only thing I could, which was to help to drag hoses and evacuate residents. I saw several other metas doing the same, Kit being one of them, decked out in his full armor. I think I caught a flash of Speed Freak. Other Gatekeepers were there, unsurprisingly. Even more would arrive, but aside from assisting the same way I'd been doing, there was virtually nothing any of us could do. It was the most helpless feeling I have ever had.

I rested a bit, sucking down a tube of PowerPaste. Overhead, air tankers dropped water on the blaze and news helicopters hovered, cameras never wavering. As I watched them, I thought I saw a figure in the sky through the heavy smoke.

Weak or not, I flew up toward the unidentified meta, figuring I might as well say hello. As I neared, I realized what I'd thought was more smoke was actually an accumulation of tiny storm clouds around the young woman hovering nearby. She held her hands out toward the ground, a spray of water issuing forth from the cloudlets, raining down toward the flames. But the heat was so intense that the water evaporated before it could even reach the ground. She must have realized this was happening, so why continue?

As I neared, I heard her hysterical sobs, punctuated by coughs from the smoke. She was so focused, so distraught, that she didn't see me until I was right upon her.

Startled, she looked at me, her liquid spray fading. Her face was as soot-covered as my own must have been, the trails of her tears plain on her cheeks. I hovered next to her and shook my head. "This is no use," I yelled, my voice still mostly drowned by the roar of the fire and the sirens.

Her face again screwed up in anguish. Then, to my shock, she embraced me tightly and sobbed into my shoulder, her entire body heaving. The girl was no longer using her abilities to stay aloft, so I increased my own output. As she cried, I slowly lowered us, moving away from the fireball.

I found a patch of grass off to the west of the fire and landed there. The girl collapsed to the ground, and I sat beside her. I gave her a towel to wipe her face, then opened the valve on an oxygen tank. She held the mask to her mouth, her eyes showing her gratitude. She was exhausted, and her crying softened. After a time, she removed the mask, drew her legs up, and rested her forehead on her knees. As I put the tank away, I wondered who she knew who lived there, but certainly wasn't about to ask. Not now. Not there. So I just sat with her, trying to comfort her as best I could.

I gave her a bottle of water and a tube of PowerPaste. She accepted the water and began drinking, but eyed the PowerPaste dubiously. "Go ahead," I said. "It's chocolate mint."

She tore it open, squeezing a bit into her mouth. Her expression told me it tasted better than she expected. "Thanks," she said.

I looked at her face, certain now that I knew who she was. There were a number of weather manipulators, but only one who fit her description. Young, strikingly pretty, with intense eyes. Her profile had told me she was of Ukrainian descent, and her features definitely reflected this. I put a hand on her shoulder. She tensed up and looked at me with red-rimmed eyes. "Did you want to talk?" I asked.

Her voice cracked as she said, "I think my parents were there."

My stomach sank. "You're not sure?"

"They come here every Thursday to visit friends. Their friends' house is one of the ones destroyed." Tears welled again, but she continued. "It's possible they were out to dinner. I know they often do that together."

I squeezed her shoulder in what I hoped was a comforting way. "Don't despair before you know for sure, River."

She gave a half-smile. "I figured you knew who I was. You're Dynamistress, right?"

"I'm impressed," I said.

"It's the hair," she said.

"It's always the hair," I said, causing her to smile briefly.

After a moment, she said, "So... if you know who I am, you know there's a warrant out for me."

"I think I read that somewhere."

She hung her head again. "Will you at least let me find out about my parents before you take me in?"

I snorted. "You're not serious, are you?"

Her face fell and she looked away. "Oh."

"No, silly, I mean about taking you in!"

She looked at me again. "Really?" Tears flowed again down her face.

If I remembered right from my visits to Kit and the girls, most of the restaurants in the area were toward the east, past the interstate. "If they went out to dinner, they probably went down to San Bruno Avenue from here, right?"

"Maybe?"

"So that's likely the way they'd return. If we go down to the intersection, we might see them. There are a lot of people gathered there."

"You think?"

"It's worth a try," I said. "If you're up for the flight."

She sucked down the rest of the paste and shoved the empty wrapper into her pocket. She might help thieves, but she was environmentally conscious.

We flew low, both of us watching the houses and vehicles burn as we passed by. A few minutes later, we were hovering over the parking lot of a shopping center on the other side of San Bruno Avenue, packed with cars and people. River scanned the crowd of people, almost all of whom stared down the road at the fire, not up in the sky at us. I stayed by her side as she searched and, to my great relief, it wasn't long before she said, "There they are!"

She squeezed me in a mid-air hug. "Thank you so much," she said, crying again. "I mean it." Then she joined them on the ground. I stayed long enough to see her embrace them both before I flew off.

Even when there was nothing left to do, I stuck around. I was drained, physically and emotionally. The sun had set quite some time before. I sat, watching the fire. Kit joined me on the ground. He removed his helmet, and I could see the weariness on his sweaty face. I tossed him some water and we sat wordlessly for a while.

"When we heard Crestwood," I said, "we feared the worst."

"Yeah," he said, then drained the bottle. "Again, sorry I didn't check in."

I continued staring at the flames. The gas had finally been turned off at some point, so the situation was better, but the blaze was far from contained. It would be many more hours, I knew, before it was extinguished.

"The magnitude of this," I said, shaking my head. "Do you know how many alarms?"

"Eight," Kit said. "According to what I've been hearing on the comms, there are about two hundred firefighters here."

"I've seen one helicopter and some planes," I added.

"I helped Google and Cisco set up emergency communications."

We sat and watched the blaze for several more minutes. Finally, I said, "I don't think we can be of any more use, here."

Kit nodded weakly. "Afraid not," Kit said, then stood and picked up his helmet. "I'll see you soon," he said.

As he walked off, I combined my mostly empty packs into one, then strapped it on. It was a long flight home.

The following morning, I woke with a start from dreams filled with smoke and fire. Even though I'd showered before bed, I still felt covered in soot, so I took another.

The water was pleasantly hot, and I remained there long after I'd finished washing. My thoughts were a jumbled mess, filled with fear of being outed as a clone, doubts about my relationship with Ali, my unclear feelings for Vicky, and dread over having to face my parents with my new, younger-looking face. Weatherford. Michaels. Dana. My brain jumped from one of these to another without any real thought involved. I felt overwhelmed.

Eventually, I stepped out and dried off, then pulled on sweatpants and a t-shirt and stumbled down to the kitchen. I made coffee and spread cream cheese on a pumpernickel bagel, then collapsed into a corner chair. After eating, I phoned Dana. He hadn't returned to San Francisco since leaving the previous month, but I know he'd been planning to attend the party for Marcus.

"Sorry I didn't show up," he said. "I was going to, but... I dunno. So how was it?"

"You haven't seen the news recently, have you?"

"No, why?"

"There was a gas pipeline explosion in San Bruno, not far from where Kit and the girls live. Dozens of homes destroyed."

"Shit," Dana breathed.

"Four dead, last I heard," I told him, "but it wouldn't surprise me if that rises."

"Now I feel bad for not coming. I might have been able to help." I disagreed, telling him how helpless I'd felt, but he interrupted me. "You know I could have been helpful," he said. "I could have telepathically searched for survivors. I could have telekinetically moved debris from a safe distance. You're just too nice to point it out."

"Okay, you're right. If you'd been here that early, you could have been helpful. But you didn't come because of me."

"Dinah..."

"Don't deny it. I know it's true. Every time something comes between us, it's always my fault."

"Dinah..."

"I'm sorry I ruined your relationship with Bronwyn."

"Dinah, shut up!" I did so, reluctantly. "Look... I won't lie and say I'm not upset about Bronwyn. But the truth isn't as simple as blaming the breakup on you or on our... you know."

"Sure, it is."

"Okay, fine. The breakup itself, I guess. But I don't know that our relationship would have worked for long. I doubt I would have been able to be so far from you, either."

I felt a tightness in my chest. "Really?"

"You have to ask?"

I was quiet for a moment. I didn't realize how much I needed to hear him say that. "Pity she couldn't have come here," I said.

"Her father is getting up in years and she wants to be there for him. Besides," he said, "she still would have learned about us."

I apologized again. He told me to shut up again. And then we had nothing more to say. I made him promise to come visit and threatened to go to Sacramento if he didn't. I ended the call and trudged upstairs to the office, since paperwork waits for no one.

No sooner had I settled in at the computer than the Project's phone rang. I answered, and when the caller identified himself as working for the *National Enquirer*, my stomach sank.

"I'm following up on a tip," he said, "that was sent via email to multiple publications. It was quite fascinating," he said.

"Is that right?" I said, my pulse racing.

"It alleges that the way you survived your public meltdown early this year is that you had previously cloned yourself. That sounds ridiculous, of course, but the tip suggested we investigate certain purchases you made and claimed that you'd had some of your eggs harvested. These all checked out."

I waited for him to say more, but he didn't. "Okay," I said. "And?"

"These purchases, according to the tipster, were for the construction of an artificial uterus. Can you comment?"

"Would it even matter?"

"Well, probably not," he admitted. "You must admit, the evidence is compelling. But I'd much rather have confirmation and additional information from you."

"You're not exactly a reputable publication. No offense."

"None taken. However, though we do tend to sensationalize, our stories are factually accurate far more often than most people realize."

I didn't respond to that. I was too busy berating myself. Why had I done nothing to prevent this? I'd had plenty of time to take control of this story, but I just sat back and ignored it. But why? I'd made it clear to my teammates and friends that this was something they needed to keep to themselves, and they had. But once Michaels pulled the information from my head and told Weatherford, I think I just regarded this as inevitable. And maybe, just maybe, I was tired of keeping it a secret.

"Ms. Geof-Craigs? Are you still there?"

I snapped out of my reverie. "Sorry. Yes, I'm here. Just multi-tasking." I cleared my throat. "So entertain me," I said. "You confirmed some purchases I made and verified that I'd had some of my eggs harvested. Tell me how I allegedly cloned myself."

The caller hesitated. "Well, according to the experts I consulted, it's possible to construct something like an artificial uterus."

"You said that, already."

"So you cloned yourself using your eggs and tissues and used the artificial uterus to grow the clone."

"And in the highly unlikely event that such an effort had succeeded, that would end up with an infant. What did your experts say about that?"

"I admit, most of them were highly skeptical that there was any way to bring a clone to adulthood in a short amount of time. So that's the big stumbling block."

"It is? I'd think the big one would be explaining how a clone would have all the memories of the original."

"Well, it's known that your brother is a telepath..."

I laughed. "Yeah, he can communicate mentally. How on earth would that help?"

Another hesitation. "It's theorized that an extremely powerful telepath could perform what's referred to as 'brain taping.' And that these memories could be planted into another mind."

"That's quite the fantasy."

The caller seemed flustered. "I'm assured that it's feasible."

"It's sad that someone out there hates me to the point of wanting me in the spotlight in such a negative way, but I do tend to make enemies in my line of work. Thanks for the laughs, but I need to get back to it."

"Just one more question, please. The tipster also alleged that–"

"I'm sorry. I've wasted enough time on this. Have a good day."

Then I hung up. There was still a feeling of dread within me, but it was overshadowed by feelings of satisfaction and relief.

After finishing up with Project matters, I sent a message to my teammates on our private channel, advising them of the conversation and the doubtless forthcoming tabloid headline. *I'm hoping it's largely ignored, but you never know. Even though this isn't really a Project matter, I'd appreciate you following our standard protocol for press inquiries if you're contacted by a reporter. Thanks!*

✧ ✧ ✧

Over the next ten days, I busied myself with work, mainly so I didn't dwell on the coming storm of controversy. Much of this time was spent in my lab with Hank.

His body was warm to the touch, now, and the red specks inside were brighter and more numerous. His eyes were distinctly formed. Virtually all the extra mass at the base had been absorbed. No longer did he lack an abdomen. I half expected him to greet me every time I entered the lab.

I visited Dynasonic a few times, just to make sure nothing unpleasant was happening there, with either Weatherford or Michaels. But it was all quiet on that front.

One day in late September, the doorbell rang, and I was surprised to find on my doorstep a young woman with dark blonde hair and large, intense eyes. "You clean up nicely," I said as I welcomed Silver Storm inside.

River smiled and said, "Ash isn't really my best look." She stepped past me and I closed the door behind her. "Wow. This place is beautiful," she said, looking around.

"Thanks," I said as we made ourselves comfortable in the living room. "So what brings you?"

"I wanted to thank you again," she said, "for helping me find my parents."

"I'm happy they and their friends are safe," I said. "But you don't need to thank me for that."

"Well, then for not arresting me," she said.

"Only an asshole would have arrested you in those circumstances."

She chuckled. "Then thank you for not being an asshole."

"You're welcome," I said, laughing with her.

After our laughter faded, she said, "I have a favor to ask."

"Sure. What is it?"

She hesitated, lowering her eyes. "Arrest me now."

"Pardon?"

River stared at her hands for a moment. "I don't know how my life got so out of control," she said. "It's not that I ever wanted to help criminals, y'know?"

"So why did you?"

With a sigh, she said, "I got involved with a questionable crowd in school, I guess. I was getting into trouble, fighting with my parents. My grades dropped so much that I barely graduated. I stayed living at home, but about a year later, we got into a big fight, and I moved out. I couch-surfed for a while, staying with friends from that crowd. But it didn't take long for me to see what losers they really were. I needed to find my own place, but I'm not qualified to do anything that would provide much of an income. I mean, I can't survive on what retail pays."

"I don't think anyone can," I said.

"So it was just for the money," she continued. "But I never felt good about it."

There was so much I wanted to know. Did her parents know about her abilities? Is that what they fought about? Did her friends know? But those were questions for another time. "Still friends with that crowd?" I asked.

River shook her head. "Not even a little."

"Glad to hear it," I said. "But as for turning yourself in, you realize that, since you have a prior record, probation is unlikely."

River's expression turned somber. "Yeah, I know. But I'm okay with it. Even with the max, I'll still be young when I get out. I'll have plenty of time to turn my life around. Maybe learn some skills while in there."

We talked a while longer. Then we walked together to the Tenderloin police station, six blocks away. I remained there while she was placed under arrest and taken away.

The following day, I made an appointment with the district attorney. One of the perks of being a somewhat respected meta is the ability to see such people sooner than others might. I intended to milk that perk for all it was worth.

It was late in the day when I entered the DA's office. She greeted me politely as she offered me a seat. "It's a pleasure to meet you, Dynamistress," she said. "I admit to being a fan, both of you and the work the Pariah Project does."

"That's kind of you. I'm impressed with your work, too," I said, "especially your program giving first-time drug offenders the chance to obtain their diplomas and find jobs."

"Thank you," she said as she sat at her desk. Brushing a lock of her dark hair away from her face, she said, "What can I do for you?"

"I want to talk to you about River Smolts. I believe she's up for arraignment tomorrow."

"Okay."

"I'd like you to take into account that River not only doesn't deny her actions, but willingly turned herself in. I'm convinced that her criminal days are behind her."

The D.A. frowned. "How can you guarantee that?"

"Obviously, I can't," I agreed, "but I do have a history of being a good judge of people. Consider that her acts were done only out of desperation. She's turning her life around in several areas, including having already severed ties with those who'd negatively influenced her, and mending fences with her family. And she'll have my assistance."

"How so?"

"If you know my organization, you'll know that we can make sure she has access to just about anything she needs. And if the rest of my team is willing, she'll become a member. The kid has a good heart. I would consider her a great asset."

She frowned. "She has priors, doesn't she?"

"I did some investigating on that," I said. "In each case, the criminals she aided were caught within three days. No one was hurt during the actual crimes, and River's actions after the fact didn't cause any injuries or property damage."

The D.A. was quiet for a time, then said, "All right. I'll take all this into consideration and look deeper into both Ms. Smolts and your organization. Will you be attending the arraignment?"

"If I may."

"I have no objection, and I'll inform the judge."

"Thank you," I said.

"By the way," she said as we shook hands, "aren't you supposed to be dead?"

I chuckled. "I'm sure I have no idea what you mean." I opened the door. "See you tomorrow."

At the arraignment, the room was packed with many other defendants waiting to be called forward, one after another. I sat quietly at the back of the room, waiting for River's turn.

Finally, she was up. The D.A. nodded to River and turned to the judge. "Your honor, in the case of River Smolts, we will not be pressing charges."

The judge looked at her in surprise. "Good. Docket's full, today." And then the case was dismissed. River's face showed her shock when she turned to look back at me. I smiled and went outside to wait for her.

A week or so later, I was in the kitchen making coffee when Jasmine yelled my name. "Down here!" I shouted back.

I heard her rapid footsteps down the stairs. She stepped into the kitchen, looking at me with a worried expression. She carried a tabloid paper in her hand and began unfolding it to show me. It was Monday, the publication day for the *Enquirer*.

I sighed, but expected it. "Ran the clone story, did they?"

"Dyna, no," she said, and the painful tone in her voice made me look again, to see her holding up the paper. It wasn't the *Enquirer*, but the *Sun*. I stared, open-mouthed, at the huge photo of me with the headline:

THE SECRET INCEST OF DYNAMISTRESS

TWENTY

"Fake friends believe in rumors. Real friends believe in you."
~ Yolanda Hadid

As I've previously described, my hometown is not exactly the most progressive of places today, let alone in the eighties, during my teenage years. Many of the adults seemed to be stuck thirty years in the past. As in most small towns, gossip was common and rumors ran wild. And once a rumor (true or false) "stuck," a person (young or old) was left with a reputation that would likely never fade.

Peer pressure is always difficult for kids to resist, and it often leads to betrayals of trust, sometimes ruining friendships. When I was fourteen, I confessed to my best friend that I thought I might be more interested in girls than boys. She was surprised, but it didn't seem to affect our friendship. At least, not until she shared that confession with others.

Pennsylvania had decriminalized homosexual activities a mere five years before. It would still be two years before the American Psychiatric Association would completely remove same-sex attraction from the *Diagnostic and Statistical Manual of Mental Disorders* (after several years of simply changing the name of the "disease") and seven years before the World Health Organization would drop it from its *International Classification of Diseases*. All this is to say that, in general, America was still pretty homophobic, and that was especially true in rural areas like where I grew up.

It started one day with odd looks from other kids, then whispering and pointing. Eventually, the name-calling made it clear what the pointing, whispering, and odd looks were all about. And of course, there was only one possible source for it all.

When I stopped speaking to Rhonda, she knew why. She wasn't stupid. Decades later, we resumed our friendship after a chance meeting. By this point, of course, I'd long since stopped caring what others thought of me. Nor was I in a school environment where the effects of rumors were amplified by the constraints of the social setting.

But still, rumors abound. Since becoming known as a meta, there have been many about me. Most of them were funny. Some were cringeworthy. But all such falsehoods were always easy for me to ignore or deflect. But now, just as when I was in school, I was faced with a "rumor" that just happened to be true.

The article itself, unsurprisingly, was quite brief, with nothing to substantiate the headline. It had references to male teammates I'd spent time with, photos of me with Jack, a paparazzi pic of the "date" I went on with Transcendant, and references to the old rumor that I was involved with Invictus, which I'm sure made his husband chuckle. This was all obviously in an attempt to convince the public that I was into guys, when just about everyone who knew me assumed I was a lesbian.

Still, such flimsy evidence had never stopped the news rags before. It did, of course, call out my brother by name, referring to him as "a prominent psychologist in Sacramento." But he could almost certainly brush it off and his clients would believe him. Few people ever took tabloids seriously.

"The emotions radiating from you make it pretty clear that it's true," Jasmine said.

My stomach knotted and I pulled my gaze from the paper. I knew there was no way she wouldn't sense the truth. "So... are you gonna freak out?"

She didn't meet my eyes when she spoke. "In all honesty, Dyna, I'd always suspected it might be true."

"You... what now?"

With a sigh, she said, "When the two of you are together, your feelings are so strong that I don't even need to try to detect them."

"I see," I said.

"Someday, I'm sure I'll ask about it, but not right now."

I knew Jasmine well enough to know that she'd get over it. It was the rest of the team I was worried about.

"It's a distraction," I said.

"Pardon?"

"These tidbits that Weatherford is dropping. He's just trying to keep my attention away from his actions."

"Why do you assume it's Weatherford and not Michaels?"

"Because I'm nothing to Michaels. I don't think he gives a damn about me. But Weatherford? I've been a pain in his ass for a while, now, however slight."

Jasmine nodded thoughtfully. "You know, this could be fortuitous."

I blinked stupidly. "In what possible way?"

"Well, think about it. One paper is working on an exposé about you being a clone. Then another paper comes out with this. You think the other paper will want to ride on their coattails by releasing your story?"

"Hmm," I muttered. It was an interesting point.

"Anyway, as far as this story goes, I don't think anyone in the team will believe it."

"I dunno," I said. "Sinta figured it out before now."

"You're closer to Sinta than anyone else on our team, though."

"True, but they already know to expect a story about the cloning. The timing of this revelation would almost certainly make them assume he lifted that secret from my mind, too."

"Then just tell them it's not true."

I heaved a sigh. "I should, but I can't lie to my friends, Jaz."

Jasmine frowned and was silent for a moment. I knew she disagreed with this attitude. But then she smiled faintly as she folded the paper and prepared to head upstairs. "What, then?"

I laughed. "Guess I'll just ignore it until someone brings it up." Then I frowned. "I should call Dana, though, before he finds out from one of his clients." Jasmine headed back upstairs as I dialed my brother's number.

Dana took the news in stride, considering it easy to dismiss if any of his clients brought it up. My hope, of course, was that most people in my life wouldn't even know about it. My parents were never ones to buy the tabloids, but even so, they were sure to see them on display at the supermarket checkouts. And even if they didn't, one of the neighbors would, so it would definitely get back to them. I knew it was just wishful thinking that I wouldn't be questioned about it.

I did have one thing going for me that would make this easier. As I said, most who knew me assumed I was strictly lesbian. Only a few knew this wasn't completely true. One of those was Jack. He had evidence to the contrary in the form of a rather serious kiss we'd shared once.

Ali, though, had no idea of my history with men, or lack thereof. And I didn't need there to be any speculation from her.

I met her at work, near the end of her shift. When she was done, we took a walk, crossing Stanyan Street into Golden Gate Park. It was cloudy, but otherwise a pleasant day. We chatted a bit about her job and other little things.

"I'm guessing this surprise visit has something to do with today's *Sun*," Ali said casually.

"Can't I just visit my girlfriend if I feel like it?"

Ali stopped walking and stared at me, eyes wide. "Visit... your what?"

I realized that was the first time I'd used the "g" word. "I mean... you are, aren't you?" Her face reddened. "You're blushing!" I teased.

"Am not!" she said, burying her head into my chest. "Shut up."

"You're too cute," I said, and just hugged her until she decided to face me again. She looked up at me.

"Soooo...?" she said as we began walking again.

"Soooo... what?"

"So is it true? The paper?"

I laughed nervously. "Seriously? Anyone who knows me knows that I only date girls. Jack and I were never an item. Invictus is gay. Transcendant... well... I didn't even know he considered that a date."

"Really?"

I smiled softly and nodded. "One day, he asked me to meet him. Naturally, I assumed it was about Gatekeepers stuff." I paused, remembering my late friend. "It was so weird, Ali. Chip was handsome, well known, and popular. He had every reason to be confident. And when it came to meta stuff, he was. But he was awful, just awful, when it came to dating. He was nervous, awkward, even shy."

"And apparently clueless."

I chuckled. "Yeah. It was... well, it was kinda cute, honestly. I let him down gently, of course. Told him I was already seeing someone, which was true."

Again, we fell silent. I tried to enjoy the park, but was too anxious. Ali wasn't usually this quiet. "You still haven't addressed the incest thing," she said.

"I didn't think I needed to!"

Ali smirked. "You've been dancing around it. And, while that's been entertaining, the truth is I don't care."

"I wasn't..." I stopped in my tracks. "What?"

She turned to face me. "So is it just for sex or what?" I was so shocked, all I could do was stare at her. "Stop looking at me like I'm wearing pink," she said. "Are you in love with him?"

"Ali... where is this coming from? How are you saying this so casually?"

She shrugged. "Well... I read a lot of manga and watch a lot of anime. Sexual and romantic love between siblings aren't exactly uncommon themes."

"Seriously?"

"Yeah. And usually, at least in my experience, it's older brother with younger sister. So when it comes right down to it, Dyna," she said with a twinkle in her eye, "you're actually being cliché."

She waited for me to say something, but all I could manage was, "I... have no response to that."

"*Joe Versus the Volcano*. Great flick." I stared at her in confusion, and she laughed. "You're adorable when you're flustered, you know that?" She pulled me to an empty bench and we sat. "Oh, no!" she said. "Did I shock you? Can your old heart take it, granny? Do I need to call an ambulance?" I swatted her arm as she laughed. "Ow," she said, then continued laughing.

"If you have a bruise there, it's your own fault."

Ali smiled. "That's fair. But Dyna," she said, sobering, "you could have just denied it. I'd have believed you."

I dropped my gaze as I said, "I could have. But I don't like lying to people who matter to me. I could never lie to you, Ali."

Now she was the one to look surprised. "Oh," she said softly, turning her face away as she blushed again.

"You're adorable when you're flustered, you know that?"

"Don't quote me back to me!" she said in mock offense. "I'm... not used to being with someone who doesn't lie."

"Which means you've never been with someone who respected you."

Ali sighed and said, "And I'm still amazed that you do."

"You haven't given me a reason not to. But seriously... you're really not freaked out?"

"Not freaked out, but surprised. I mean, I've known siblings who sure seemed like they might be fucking each other, but I never pegged you for being that type."

We sat there for about half an hour. I told her everything, from the first incident to the last, including how it was that the paper received the scoop.

"And there's something else," I said. "There's another tabloid story likely coming. And I'll tell you now that it's also true."

"That you're really seventy years old?"

"Shut up," I said, laughing. "But since you mentioned it... the story is directly related to why I don't look my age." I took a deep breath. "Technically speaking," I said, "this body is... um... less than a year old."

Ali looked up at me, her eyes narrowed. "Uh... what now?"

"I kind of... cloned myself."

The look on her face was almost comical. Then she snorted. "Bullshit."

So, for another half hour, I explained all that business to her. As most people would be, she was skeptical. But by the time I finished, she accepted it.

She looked at me with a furrowed brow. "You have a seriously fucked-up life, you know that?"

As I was wholeheartedly agreeing with her, my phone buzzed. Jack had sent a text to Vicky and me, asking us to meet at his workplace. Vicky quickly responded that she was on her way. I did the same.

"Work calls," I said to Ali.

"Okay," she said, then kissed me. "Call me later, pervert."

I glared at her before smiling, then flew to Wonderland Robotics.

Vicky was already in Jack's office when I arrived. They were looking at his computer screen.

"Hey. What's the emergency?"

"No emergency," Jack said, "but... Well, just come here."

"What is it?" I said, dropping into a chair next to Vicky.

He sat on the edge of his desk and faced us. "I've been thinking about the zero-point weapons. I know you believe Weatherford wants them for defense against metas, but I think there might be a second, even more critical reason that he's so interested in them."

Before he could continue, a woman's voice came from behind us. "Fullerton!" I looked back to see Jack's associate, Paige Stephens. She scowled and pointed at the coffee cup on his desk. "You did it again, didn't you? You took the last of the Sumatra."

Jack turned a lazy gaze to his coworker. "There are no witnesses. You can't prove anything."

"What are you doing, taking it home with you?"

"Just drink the Colombian."

"I will, but it's not the same, and you know it," she pouted. She entered the office and greeted me. "Hey, Dyna!"

"Hi, Paige. Good to see you." Then I introduced her to Vicky.

"So," she said, pushing her glasses up the bridge of her nose, "what did I interrupt?"

"I was just about to tell them about a unique application of zero-point energy," Jack said.

Paige grimaced. "Oh, *hell* no." She spun, her heavy, blonde braid barely missing Jack's face. Vicky and I chuckled as she left.

"Anyway," Jack continued, "as you both know, the zero-point weapons essentially suck energy away. Given enough exposure, this would eventually kill a person."

"But you're thinking of something else," I said.

"I am." He moved aside, revealing his computer screen, which showed a ring of maybe three dozen rectangles. Lines extended inward from each, like bicycle spokes, converging at the center. "If enough zero-point energy beams were focused on a single point, it's just possible that it could..." He paused, as though expecting us to laugh at him. "...create a portal."

Neither of us laughed. I frowned. "You're suggesting that removing all but zero-point energy in one spot can... what? Poke a hole in the universe?"

"Well... yeah. Maybe. I'm not an astrophysicist, but given what I know about the behavior of zero-point energy..."

"It'll probably do *something*," Paige said from behind us, a steaming mug of something not Sumatran now in her hands. Written on the mug was:

EVERYTHING HAPPENS FOR A REASON
AND THAT REASON IS USUALLY PHYSICS

She took a sip and moved closer, looking at the screen. "I mean, if everything you've told me about these things is accurate."

"But," I said, "what's the point? He can create..." My words trailed off as I finally got it. I looked at Vicky. "He thinks this will be the portal he's been seeking?"

"Probably," she said. "I am curious, though... what made you come up with this idea, Jack?"

Jack cleared his throat. "You once told me that it didn't seem he was out to kidnap you any longer, that he'd seemingly thought up an alternative."

"And that led you to this?" Vicky said.

"Well," he said with a smirk, "I *am* pretty smart."

Paige snorted and said, "He also told me he watched *Ghostbusters* recently."

I turned back to Jack. "So you're 'crossing the streams.'"

Jack mock glared at me. "Well, more like intersecting them, but yeah," he said. "Now, this illustration is just speculation. I don't know how many of the weapons would be required. And they'd need to be calibrated perfectly to converge. On top of that, then he'd need some method of keeping the portal open."

"And he knows from Nevada how that can be done," I said.

We fell quiet, considering the implications of Jack's theory. Eventually, Paige spoke up. "I've got a meeting to get to. See you ladies another time."

We said farewell to her, then Vicky said, "I've got to dash, too. See you later."

When both were out of earshot, Jack turned to me. "Before you go, did you, um... did you want to talk about the paper?"

"Do we have to?"

"No, not at all," Jack said. He stared at the screen for a few seconds. "Okay, yes. A little."

"How little?"

Still staring at the screen, he said, "I guess just enough to confirm or deny."

"You really need me to do that?"

He glanced up at me, then quickly averted his eyes. "Well... no. I guess I don't." I breathed a sigh of relief, then he said, "I mean, I always had my suspicions."

"You *what?*"

"So... I guess that's all the discussion we need."

I was about to protest, but my phone rang. It was Macy. Deciding the conversation with Jack could wait – possibly indefinitely – I said, "I should take this."

I waved goodbye while answering the call. "Hey, Mace," I said as I walked out of Jack's office and down the hall to the exit.

"Hey, D. You okay?"

"I'm fine. You?"

"Well, you're the buzz of social media, after this morning's paper. I'm working on a response to put on the site."

"Wait, what? Macy, I wasn't planning on making any statement."

The girl chuckled. "Well, it's a statement with minimal words. I've been working on it for a bit and it will be live in about twenty minutes. I just wanted to let you know to look at the site pretty soon. And once it's ready, I'll just reply to any emails with a link to it. Though, a lengthier reaction should go out to the fan club."

"I don't know..."

"Trust me, okay?"

"All right. I'll check it out. Let's get together soon. I have something else to talk to you about."

"Sounds good! Okay, talk later!"

Macy hung up and, unable to resist the curiosity, I flew home.

Once in the office, I went to the computer and pulled up my website. A picture carousel loaded quickly, filling most of the screen. The first image was a photo of the cover of an older edition of the *Sun* with the headline, *Invictus and Dynamistress: The Secret Relationship*. Overlaid on this, by Macy, was one word: NOPE.

The images scrolled through several such cover photos from the different papers and magazines, each with a rumor about me and NOPE on it. It ended with today's cover, overlaid with SERIOUSLY?

I had to chuckle. I shot off a text to Macy: *It's great! Thank you!*

The week following the newspaper announcement was a bit rough. Macy told me that hits to my website had tripled since the news article. Damning emails were plentiful. I didn't engage on social media, but Macy told me Facebook and Twitter continued to be rife with condemning comments. Frequently, someone would point out the track record of Dyna rumors, even linking to the pictorial history of them that Macy had made for my site. There were even a few who would post in defense of consensual adult incest, which incited some heated arguments.

A few *Sun* readers mailed the article to me, care of the Project, with their own comments scrawled on it. Usually, these were along the lines of "How could you???" or "You're sick!!!"

When out in public, I got the occasional odd look, sometimes accompanied by a disgusted noise. It was probably a good thing that Dana wasn't in town. I can't imagine what sort of responses we'd get if we were seen in public together.

Fortunately, no one else on the team confronted me about it, though there was clearly an awkwardness when I was around. All in all, it wasn't a good time.

October eleventh marked the ninth anniversary of Lee's death. Part of me was shocked that it had been so long. The other part of me was shocked that it hadn't been longer. Her death itself felt recent, but those years in general felt like ancient history. I hadn't visited her grave since moving west. Next year, I told myself, on the tenth anniversary, I'd visit.

I spent the majority of the week sequestered in my lab, continuing my study of Hank. Over the past several days, his posture had changed, and he now stood properly, rather than in the death pose he'd initially been in.

As amazing as the physical changes were, I was more interested in what was going on inside his head. There had to be something, otherwise he wouldn't be "coming back to life." Pretty much everything about Hank made zero scientific sense to me. Even though I tried my best to work out how meta abilities were possible, I could only ever get so far in the process before I had to admit that I was stumped.

At our monthly team meeting, I said, "Ever since the gas explosion in San Bruno, I've been researching ways to protect ourselves from heat. Most of us have fire-resistant outfits, but that's a different thing altogether. What I've found is that there's a silicone-based treatment that can be applied to fabric to protect against heat. There's even a version of it that can be applied to exposed skin, like makeup. I suggest everyone have this incorporated into their suits. You all know Jasen. Just get in touch with him to set up an appointment."

Jasmine cleared her throat, shuffling a few sheets of paper. "Over the past months, we've had three incidents in which the hemostatic sponges were used. Thank you all for filling out the questionnaires. And that thanks is not just from me, but from the manufacturer. They're quite pleased. As are, I'm sure, the individuals who received care from you. They're all alive thanks to your actions, and the product."

The rest of the meeting was filled with mundane matters, reports on our grant funding, and so on. I was waiting for someone to mention the incest assertion in the paper, but no one did.

Once all the standard stuff was done, I announced that I wanted to offer membership to Silver Storm. I told the group her history and my reasons for submitting her for membership, just as I'd done with the D.A. There was a fair amount of discussion, but no actual opposition. When I voiced my disbelief at this, I was surprised further at the reply. Jack said, "You've shown that you're a good judge of character with everyone you've brought into the team. We trust you."

I felt my face flush and thanked him for saying this. But I questioned whether such trust was deserved. "I already arranged for her to stop by at the end of this meeting," I said, "so if you could all hang around a bit longer, you can meet her."

There were nods around the table and, after the meeting, River arrived. I introduced her to the rest of the team, then gave her the standard tour of the building, ending on the rooftop deck. As we stood there, I said, "The team has approved you for membership, if you're interested."

River looked at me with wide eyes. "What?"

I chuckled. "Seriously, our door is open to you."

She hesitated before replying. "Dyna, I appreciate the offer, but I'm already in your debt enough."

"Whoa. No, you are not. You owe me nothing."

She looked away. "I can't keep accepting your generosity without paying you back."

"Then pay it forward. Becoming a member of our team will give you plenty of opportunities to do that."

She stared out over the neighborhood for a bit, then said, "So what's required? I heard that your team does clean-up work for other teams."

I frowned at the description. "We do follow-up, not clean-up. We pay attention to the aftermath of crimes and disasters, caring for the victims and so on, providing them with help navigating all the many resources out there to aid victims of crimes. And this is why all members are required to go through training for crisis intervention and trauma counseling."

"So you're... super social workers?"

I laughed. "It's not like we expect you to get a psych degree or anything. This is just for immediate help until the victims can get the care they need. Triage, you might say."

"I see."

"Now, speaking of paying it forward... I have a special project for you." River raised an eyebrow. "I'd like you to train a friend of mine."

"Me? Train someone?"

"She has cyclonic abilities, able to create powerful vortices. You can do that, too, right?"

"Well, yes. But not as an offensive attack."

I smiled. "Then maybe you'll be teaching each other."

River considered this for a moment, then smiled.

The following weeks were busy. River got to know the rest of the group and worked with Sydney, as she'd agreed. The two were becoming fast friends, which didn't surprise me. It helped that they were the same age. Layla continued her training with Booster and Newton. All involved kept me updated with progress reports.

I had video calls with Sharon, Jackie, and little Dinah once or twice a week. Dinah dominated the calls, but I was always able to talk privately with her moms, too. I admit, I was torn. I still had strong feelings for both of them. I just wasn't sure what those feelings were. Was there really a chance to recapture what we once had? No, of course not. We were all older, different from when we were in college. Dinah and Michael were part of the picture, too, making it more complicated. Not to mention their jobs and my activities. But we could still have something, I thought. Even if it was only a visit once or twice a year.

And I finally put in motion something I'd been planning ever since I moved into my home: I hired contractors to reinforce the roof, cover it with weatherproof laminate, and install a big-ass hot tub.

Visiting Dynasonic had become my go-to escape whenever I was feeling overwhelmed. Her city was familiar, yet different, just as she was, herself. She would take me on tours, allowing me to see what my San Francisco would look like if it were clean, with no homeless problem, and virtually no crime.

But on this visit, we stayed in her home, just talking. "How's *Wanderland* coming along?" I asked.

"Great!" she said as she poured tea for us in her living room. "Our engineer, Jeff, is kind of a genius. He's been able to produce some amazing sounds with my vocals, and the tracks with the orchestra sound even better than we'd hoped for."

"Have a release date?"

"January 27," she said with a smirk. "Lewis Carroll's birthday."

"Cute," I said.

She set down her cup. "So what brings you here?"

I pouted. "Can't I just want to see a friend?"

She sipped her tea, looking at me over the cup. "You can, but you seem preoccupied."

Her perceptiveness didn't surprise me. Nor did her directness. "Dealing with a lot of frustration," I said, and proceeded to tell her all my lingering questions and concerns about Weatherford and Michaels, and how the real threat – at least, as I was seeing it – was to her own world, not mine. "I just don't know what to do," I concluded. "I feel like I'm missing something."

Dynasonic was quiet for a moment. Then she shifted in her seat and looked at me. "If I'm off the mark on this, I apologize. But do you think you're maybe a bit *too* focused on it?"

I stared back, shocked. "With what?"

"The whole thing," she said. "Weatherford, Michaels... It's all you seem to talk about. Doesn't your team have other matters to focus on?"

"Sure, as they come up, but nothing as big as this."

With a frown, Dynasonic said, "I'm not trying to downplay any of it, but you treat them like they're the most dire threats imaginable. I admit, I was concerned when you told me about the weapons coming here. But nothing has come of that, so..."

I was shocked into silence. Was she right? Is that how I was coming across to others? "You're saying... I'm obsessed."

She gave me an apologetic look. "Maybe?"

I sighed. She wasn't the first to imply it. "Don't you think I have reason to be? I told you what Weatherford did to his daughter. And the whole kidnapping of my brother and his girlfriend just to get at me and lay down a threat." I rubbed absently at my now-healed arm, from where Sinta had slashed me.

"Admittedly, that was bizarre." After a moment, she said, "Why don't you just ask Weatherford what he's doing?"

I snorted. "Yeah, right."

"No, I mean it," she continued. "Look, he clearly doesn't want you dead, since it sounds like that could have been accomplished without much effort. He let your brother go. So he's obviously not a murderous psycho."

I looked at her. On the one hand, it was a ludicrous suggestion. On the other hand, I knew from my experiences as a suicide prevention counselor that people often just want to be heard, to know that someone understands their perspective.

"What about Michaels?" I asked, taking a gulp of tea.

"Dana tells me that expansion of the telepath network has essentially stopped. In fact, by all accounts, Michaels seems to be pulling many of them back to San Francisco."

"That doesn't alarm you?"

She shifted in her chair and gazed at the flames in the fireplace. "Dyna," she said, "you and I grew up in very different worlds. You say your world is filled with crime, with poverty and power-hungry people everywhere. My world has little of that."

"Our societies do shape us," I agreed, "but don't you think this puts your society more at risk from those who want to cause harm?"

"I suppose, but again, I'm not really seeing it."

"But your brother..."

"His goal is to end the enslavement of telepaths. That exceeds any concerns he has about Michaels himself."

"But he does have concerns."

"He does," she admitted. "But if he and his group are successful with the telepaths, that makes Michaels not much of a threat at all."

I finished my tea and reclined back into the cushions. What she'd said was certainly true. Without his network, Michaels was just one guy, albeit a seriously powerful one. But for the moment, I focused on enjoying my time with my friend and tried to push other matters from my mind.

I was only moderately successful.

Twenty-One

"Because that was the problem with society. It cared too much about who you fell in love with but never about why. The why matters."
~ L. J. Shen

My death and "rebirth" have caused me to become even more introspective than usual. This was true both before and after the events themselves. In the months before, I'd done a lot of reading on the nature of self. I'd saved a great deal of information on the computer to support my view that my cloned self with implanted memories would be no different from the original "me." In the months after, my introspection mostly focused on coming to accept what I'd done, the reality of it, now that the sense of urgency wasn't clouding my judgement. And the lingering questions, of course, of wondering whether my memories were truly accurate and complete. No one had yet disagreed with my recollection of an event, but that's not a guarantee that everything was in order. I didn't speak about this, since I didn't want anyone to know that I wasn't fully confident about how things had turned out.

I kept thinking about Lily's question. What would I have done with the clone if I'd been able to stop the runaway? The clone and I would have the same memories up to a point, after which they would be unique. I suspect that would be a lot harder to deal with than what I'd gone through. And how would she identify? How would she regard our shared memories? What would she even think of me?

I chided myself for not having given these thoughts more attention a year before. I'd been too focused on succeeding with the cloning itself. I didn't have time for such an analysis. Or so I rationalize, now.

Still, I couldn't help thinking of this every time I looked at the big, glassy figure in my lab. Was "reviving" him the right thing to do, or should I have left well enough alone? Was I again "playing God"? Was my ego out of control?

Back home, I contacted Vicky and asked her about her father's office in London. Then I called and made an appointment with him. Vicky put me through a portal into her flat. And just a few hours later, I was standing in front of Weatherford's heavy oak desk.

He barely glanced at me. I could tell he was on edge, possibly waiting for me to attack him. To be fair, I was half expecting him to make the first move. When I sat in a guest chair, he relaxed somewhat, as did I.

We stared at each other in silence for a moment. Then I said, "I'm surprised you accepted my appointment."

"Curiosity is a weakness of mine," he said. "Yours too, it seems."

"True. And one of the things I've been curious about is why you have a job at all. As old as you are, surely you've amassed enough money to live comfortably."

"I have, yes. But it's often prudent to hold positions that give me easy access to information I desire. It also prevents boredom."

"Uh, huh," I said, with more sarcasm than intended.

"Now, what might be the purpose of this unexpected visit?"

"What is your association with Ben Michaels?" I said.

Weatherford looked at me with a peculiar expression before saying, "It's called a business arrangement," he said. "Perhaps you've heard of them."

"You're providing him with energy weapons and he's providing you with telepaths."

"That's correct," he said, his fingers steepled in front of him.

"Why?"

Weatherford frowned. "Obviously, because we both find it to be a beneficial arrangement."

I sighed at his non-answer. "You know, ever since meeting you in Nevada, I've never trusted you."

"Yes, well... I've hardly given you reason to, I admit," he said. "I don't expect you to start, now."

"Even so, I want to know what you're doing. You're planning on using the weapons to open what you think is the ultimate portal, aren't you?"

A raised eyebrow was the only hint of surprise he showed. "Yes."

"What do you expect this portal to do? And why are you pursuing it?"

Weatherford chuckled. "You're a scientist and you're asking me why I'm performing an experiment?"

I stared at him, and finally, I couldn't hold it back, anymore. "I can't... how could you..." I took a breath, trying to calm myself, but I could feel the energy surging, just as my emotions were. "You raped your own daughter!"

His eyes never left mine, though I could see he was tensing up. "And you raped your brother."

"*What?*" I stared at him in shock.

"You took advantage of a drunk individual who was incapable of giving true consent. What else would you call it?" He held up a hand to stop my reaction. "But you tell yourself it was research. An experiment."

I was stunned. Just how much had Michaels lifted from my memory? Calming myself, I said, "Still not the same."

Weatherford waved his hand, dismissing my protests. "Rationalize it however you need so you can sleep at night." He paused, then seemed to deflate a little. "That being said," he continued, "it was an act of desperation, not something driven by any carnal desire or any animosity toward my daughter."

"Desperation," I spat.

"I was hoping..." He looked up at me. "Well, you know what I was hoping for."

"I do, but that doesn't make it any less reprehensible."

Another nod. "You're right. And it didn't take me long to realize that. And regret it. My associates..." He looked away again. "Let's just say that their regard for me dropped significantly."

"Good," I muttered. Then I said, "What *is* the result you're hoping for?"

Weatherford chuckled. "You're expecting me to say something inane, like 'world domination' or something? You watch too many stupid movies."

"I can honestly say that idea never entered my head. Seriously, I do want to know. What is your end game? What are you really after?"

With a placating nod, he said, "Our purpose has always been to learn as much about the universe as possible, by–"

Before he could continue, I cut him off. "I mean *your* purpose. Not your organization's."

"I assure you, they are one and the same."

I scowled, not believing him. "According to Vicky, you're trying to find God or time travel or something equally as unlikely."

Weatherford shrugged. "Part of the beauty of experimentation is discovering the unexpected. I'm not fully certain what the result of this will be. But I do know it will be *something*."

"A proper experiment," I corrected him, "is to test a hypothesis that's a bit less vague than that. One formed by observation–"

"Observation is something The Nexus has done for centuries."

"And that's another thing. This whole secret society you've got going on..."

"It's not secret," he said flatly, but he looked away as he spoke. He stared at nothing for a moment. "In any case, you wouldn't understand."

"Try me."

Returning his gaze to me, he shook his head. "I see no point to that. But I will say that you shouldn't believe your assumptions about me, this project, or The Nexus are accurate."

I let my eyeroll speak for me. Silence held the room for a minute. Getting straight answers from him was going as poorly as I'd expected. Finally, I said, "Vicky also says you've been making promises to them and they're getting a bit annoyed that you haven't delivered."

"Well, that's just politics," he said. "Inevitable in large groups." I knew he was right, but didn't want to give him the satisfaction of seeing me agree. "You're feeling a bit of it, too, aren't you? Your friends think you're spending too much time fixating on my plans and not enough on matters in San Francisco."

Though it hadn't reached a critical point, he was right. I calmed myself with a deep breath. "So tell me about Michaels."

"Oh, now he's another matter entirely," Weatherford said, leaning back in his chair. "That boy has ambition. And not the purest of motives."

"Tell me."

He shook his head. "That's really not my place to share, I'm afraid."

"Are you kidding me?"

"Nothing good comes from betraying a business partner. Besides," he said, "he's not a threat. He's borderline unhinged, but not what I'd call dangerous."

"Maybe not to this world, but he's a threat to a world with little in the way of metahuman defenders."

Weatherford smirked. "Is he? Well... not my problem. And not yours, either." When I frowned, he said, "But then, you like to poke your nose into everything, don't you?"

I glared into his steely eyes, but soon looked away. "You won't share anything on his goals or actions?"

"I will not."

I clenched my jaw in frustration. "Fine. Then tell me, what can go wrong?"

"Pardon?"

"With your little portal experiment. Worst case scenario."

"Hardly worth a thought."

"Don't be an idiot. You don't attempt something like this without acknowledging the possibility."

Weatherford shook his head. "Nor without contingency plans. You know quite well how much energy is needed to keep a portal open. Cutting the power will quickly abort the procedure."

I frowned at his use of the word 'abort.' "You still haven't answered my question."

"The possibilities are practically infinite."

"And that doesn't worry you at all?'

"Did you worry about such things when you experimented upon yourself? Or when you cloned yourself?"

"Neither of those experiments had potentially world-ending consequences."

"Yet, you're certain that mine does."

"More likely than mine."

We stared at each other for a moment until he said, "If there's nothing else..."

"There is," I said, stopping him in the act of standing. He sat again and looked at me expectantly. "How close are you to attempting to open this portal?"

"Why should I tell you that?"

"Because I'd like to be there for it."

Weatherford gave a short laugh. "So you can destroy it? I think not."

"You have my word that is not my intention. Honestly, I'm curious to see the results."

He gazed at me for several seconds. "I'll consider it," he said, then stood and moved around the desk. "Now, I have another appointment, so..."

I got to my feet. "Yeah, whatever." Weatherford opened the door for me. I glared at him in the doorway.

He had the smallest of smirks as he said, "Smug comment before you leave?"

I hesitated, never taking my eyes off him. Then I sighed. I had nothing.

"Do take care," he said as I walked out.

"Mostly a waste of time," I said to Hank, once back in my lab. "I mean, I expected that, but it was still frustrating." I leaned back in my office chair, weary from the experience. "Well, not a *complete* waste," I said, setting a bag of British pastries on my desk. "I swear I'm not torturing you intentionally, Hank." I withdrew a Bakewell tart from the bag and bit into it.

A sound caught my ear, like that made when blowing across the mouth of a bottle. I sat bolt upright and looked at Hank. To my shock, I could see his chest expanding and contracting, and with each contraction, this noise issued from his mouth.

"Are you building yourself some vocal cords, Henry?" I wondered how that would work. Vocal cords need to vibrate, which means they need to be flexible enough to do so, a property not belonging to the substance Hank was made of. But then, if lung-like structures could be made, I had to assume vocal cords could, too.

I stepped over and placed my hand on his chest. It was surreal, seeing a "statue" slowly coming to life. I laughed, unable to contain my astonishment. Then I sobered and admonished myself again. I had no reason to think that Hank would have more than the most rudimentary "brain." Higher brain functions were something I was just hoping for. I didn't know why, but I had faith that they'd be there.

I returned to my chair and watched him, thinking that now would probably be a good time to determine how he should be reintroduced to the world. Or even to my teammates. It's not that they didn't know I had a big, blue statue. I just hadn't been keeping them in the loop on his progress. For all they knew, there had been no change. I should probably break it to them sooner than later.

Thinking about my visit with Weatherford brought the tabloid leak to mind. My public image was sullied. Again. But that would bounce back when people either forgot about it or concluded it was as false as all the other rumors. Hell, maybe I'd just fade to obscurity completely.

But within my team, some knew the truth. Sinta, Jack, Jasmine. More could assume it's true, but wouldn't ask me directly. Ali knew, too. And I didn't even want to think about what was going through my parents' heads. That was going to make for some fun holiday conversation.

I swallowed the last of the tart, then stood. "Okay, Hank. I'll see you later." I took the pastries and walked down to our conference area, where Vicky was on monitor duty.

"Welcome back," she said. "Was it as fruitless as I predicted?"

"Not at all," I said, placing the bag of pastries in front of her. "Some of these are fruity."

With an exaggerated sigh, Vicky said, "Who was the first person who said you were funny, and why did no one correct them?" Vicky's smirk turned into a big smile as she peered into the bag. "But I think I can forgive your sad humor in this case," she said as she pulled out an Eccles cake.

"You were right about getting anything out of him," I said. "Still, it was a more cordial meeting than I anticipated."

"And that irritates you, doesn't it?"

"A bit," I admitted.

"Did you learn anything at all?"

I pulled up a chair and slumped into it. "Honestly, I don't know. But I did plant the idea that he should invite me to witness the attempt to open the portal."

"He didn't just laugh in your face?"

"At first," I admitted, "but I gave him my word that I wouldn't try to sabotage it."

"And he believed you?"

"Dunno," I said, snagging a slice of lardy cake from the bag. "We'll have to see."

Vicky drained the cup of tea in front of her. "None of my business, but what did you tell your teenager?"

"About what? And she's not a teenager."

"About the tabloid's overshare."

"I told her the truth," of course, I said, hoping that would end the conversation.

Vicky raised an eyebrow. "And how did she take that?"

I felt my brow knit as I looked in Vicky's eyes. "What do you mean?"

Sadness washed over her face as she turned away from me. "You know what I mean." I said nothing in awkward silence for a moment, before she continued. "Look, it may not have been for a long time, but you and I were together enough for me to hear you talk about Dana a lot. Your feelings for him are beyond those of a sibling."

"And that naturally means we were sleeping together," I said, putting as much sarcasm into it as I could.

Vicky just gave a tiny shrug. "Tell me I'm wrong and I'll believe you."

"Seems you've already reached your conclusion."

"If you say it, I'll believe you," she repeated.

And there it was. The corner I'd have to lie my way out of. I took a deep breath, attempting to calm down. And then I sighed, looking away, giving her all the answer she needed. When I looked back, she was the one avoiding eye contact. "I guess this means I shouldn't hold out hope that we might be together again," I said.

Vicky was silent for a bit, then took a deep breath. "I won't say I'm not squicked by this," she said, "but I do smell some hypocrisy."

"What? Why?" She didn't need to explain. "Vick, no," I said. "What your dad did is not the same at all."

"Isn't it?"

"No! I didn't fucking rape my brother!" *No matter what your dad says*, I finished in my head.

Now she looked at me. "The story of your first time... was it him?" I hesitated, then nodded. "And was he drunk?" I dropped my eyes and nodded again. "You've often said I should be angrier. Does that mean you think your actions were reprehensible? That Dana should hate you the way you think I should hate my father?"

"Your father is way more than old enough to understand what he was doing. I was a teenager."

Vicky didn't acknowledge the point, just stared at her feet. The pit in my stomach twisted. My eyes stung with building tears. I had no words for her, though I was putting together some pretty choice ones for myself. I stood, then, as calmly as I could, and walked up to my room.

Later, in my lab, I sat at my computer, but paid no attention to it. My thoughts were all over the place. Jack's hypothesis about the ultimate use of the weapons was apparently accurate, but I was becoming more and more of the opinion that I was wasting my time by focusing so much on Weatherford. As others had pointed out, he wasn't really doing anything that warranted such attention. Michaels was much more of a threat. Maybe not to our world, but to Dynasonic's.

Not that I had any idea what to do about it. It was certainly far out of my area of expertise. It was really Dana's. Maybe I should stop thinking about it, just let the Dana of that world deal with it. I had more than enough things going on here to keep me occupied. Like Hank, I thought, looking up at him. And when I did, my eyes practically popped out of my head.

Because Hank was looking back at me.

Some people have a lot of difficulty in admitting to being wrong about anything, even when it's completely obvious that they were. My mother is a good example of this. Even though she'd made remarkable progress in becoming a more accepting person, she never offered any apology for the horrible way she'd treated me over the years. But the truth is, I don't think I'd feel any differently if she had.

Still, sometimes an apology is warranted, even decades later. Which is why I found myself in Sacramento the next day. I needed to talk with Dana. And it needed to be in person.

I arrived at the train station in the late morning, finding the weather so different from my last visit. It was in the high forties, probably. Slightly breezy. I almost felt like I hadn't left San Francisco.

I'd spent the entire trip trying, and failing, to choose the best way to broach the subject. I continued the attempt while walking the mile to Dana's place, careful to keep my thoughts tamped down. Before I knew it, I'd reached his door. I took a breath and knocked.

As expected, he was surprised to see me. He invited me in and offered me a drink. I declined as we moved to the living room. "I really need to talk to you about something, but I'm having trouble figuring out how to begin."

Dana said, "Well... it's me. Just dive right in."

I looked up at him. "It *is* you," I agreed. "Which is why you're the one who needs to dive right in." I closed my eyes and waited.

After a moment, he accepted my invitation, entering my mind and letting my thoughts wash into his. Everything was there for him, from my memory of our first time to recent conversations. Most importantly, there was the new guilt brought on by Weatherford's accusation.

I'm not sure at what point I started crying, nor how much time passed as we sat there. It seemed like hours. And then I heard him in my head. I don't remember his words, just the soothing tone of them. When I stopped crying and opened my eyes, I found that I was in his lap, his arms around me, my head on his shoulder. I must have really been out of it not to notice him levitating me out of my chair and across the room.

I leaned back and looked into his eyes. To my surprise, they held no trace of accusation or resentment, but concern. And love. "Don't you have anything to say?" I said.

"Plenty. Where would you like me to start?"

"Oh," I said. "I guess... the beginning?" My heart throbbed as I spoke.

Dana hesitated, then said, "Remember how I told you I was terrified that you were going to tell someone and I'd end up in prison? I'm glad you never experienced that feeling. Sure, you took advantage of my inebriated state. But you didn't force me. I was drunk, but I knew exactly what was going on. I allowed it."

"Why?"

He laughed. "Seriously?"

"Okay, you're a guy and it was sex, so yeah. But why did you allow it with *me*? Especially considering the fear and guilt you felt afterward."

"I wasn't thinking at all of repercussions at the time." He paused and I waited for him to find his words. "Okay, look... You know how, when I needed respite from the world, I'd take a little vacation in your mind?"

"Yeah," I said. "Creepy, but yeah."

"Well, that included listening in on your thoughts. They were always so innocent and positive. At least when you were little. As you became a teenager, they became more complex, but even with that, they never failed to lift my spirits." I smiled with him, at that. "But there were thoughts about me in there. Unexpected thoughts. You had such deep love for me. It was almost overwhelming."

"You've told me this before."

"Yeah, but what I never told you is that one of those thoughts I picked up from you was how you wanted to marry me."

I felt my face flush and I buried my head in his shoulder again. "Oh, geez... Come on. I was like nine."

We laughed together. "Oh, I know. At first, I found it kind of cute. But as the years went by, I began to realize that my feelings for you weren't the same as when you were a kid. I mean, you were still a kid, but now a teenager."

My heart felt weird in my chest. "What are you saying?"

"I'm saying that all those years of mingling with your mind made us closer than I ever expected. That my feelings for you were different. And that being drunk that night wasn't much of a factor. If I'd been sober when you suggested it, I doubt I could have refused." I looked at him, a bit shocked. "I know," he continued. "It was so wrong, and I felt..." Dana struggled to find the words. So I helped him out.

Words don't matter when you're kissing.

✧ ✧ ✧

I woke the next morning to the incessant buzzing of my phone. I ignored it, but after the call went to voicemail, it just started ringing again. Irritated, I grabbed the phone and looked at the screen to see that it was Kit. I accepted the call.

"Where *are* you?" Kit yelled.

"Sacramento," I said. "Why?"

"Check your text messages! And get here!"

Kit ended the call, and I did as he asked. There was a photo in my texts. The moment I saw it, I bolted from bed, calling for Dana in my mind while throwing on my clothes.

In the shower, he replied.

I dashed into the bathroom. "I have to go!" I said. "Now."

Sliding the shower door open slightly, he poked his face out. "Why?" In response, I held up the phone to show him the photo I still had on the screen. "What the *fuck?*"

I kissed him quickly. "I'll brief you later."

Catching a train wasn't an option. With all the stops, it would simply take too long. A taxi wasn't a good option, either, as it was bound to get caught in the morning rush hour traffic. I consumed the single tube of PowerPaste I'd brought with me, but it would certainly not be fuel enough for an eighty-five mile flight. Stepping over to Dana's small bar, I snagged the first full bottle I saw, opened it, and choked down the contents.

I owe you a bottle of Appleton, I mentally told Dana, then ran out the door, leaving my shoes inside. I texted Kit and told him to summon the entire team, then I shot into the sky.

At full blast, I estimated it would take me about seventy-five minutes to complete the flight. I only hoped the quickly metabolized rum would get me there.

My mind raced as I flew. I kept Interstate 80 to my right as a guide. By the time I reached Vallejo, my energy was beginning to fade. But I kept pushing until I could see the Bay, after which I didn't need the highway for navigation.

I was near to passing out by the time I landed on the street in front of my building. I staggered inside to find Kit and several others gathered in the living room, staring toward the stairs to the second floor.

Sinta came running over with a tube of PowerPaste. "You made it the whole way?" she said, eyes wide.

"And on only one bottle of rum," I said, tearing open the packet and squeezing it into my desperate mouth. "Thanks, kitten."

Then I turned to face the staircase, a smile touching my lips, to the confusion of my teammates. I took a deep breath, my pulse racing. "About time you get up."

The big figure looked at me from the bottom of the stairs, and a grin slowly spread on his face. His mouth opened and a sound came out, again sounding like breath across a bottle top. To my astonishment, the sound was discernable. "Diiiinaaaah," Henry said in a voice that sounded like a bass flute.

"What the actual fuck?" River blurted.

I pushed down my surprise and turned to my friends. "Yeah, so..." I began. Then Jack walked in.

"Okay, what's the emer–" He stopped and stared. "Holy shit."

"Gather 'round," I said. "Story time begins when everyone is here."

While I waited, I looked closer at Henry as he slowly lumbered to the entry of the living room. Locomotion would require some sort of equivalent to musculature. Even though he was mostly translucent, I could see nothing of the sort. But then, I couldn't see his "lungs," either. And given the number of young ladies present, it would have been a lot more uncomfortable had Henry grown genitals. But having no need for them, he was as smooth as a Ken doll.

When the remainder of the team had entered and voiced their astonishment, I started in. For the next hour, I told the team the whole story, from seeing the news article in the paper, to seeing *something* in him at the Academy, to acquiring him, the tests I ran, the dip into the furnace, and the continuous monitoring since then, along with the progress I witnessed.

The team stared at Henry the whole time, who had taken a few minutes to trudge into our meeting area, where he stood at a respectful distance. He seemed as interested in his story as the others.

There were a ton of questions, which I answered as best I could. Nena stepped over to Hank. "Can I touch you?" she asked. In response, Hank slowly reached out to shake her hand. "Oh, wow," she breathed, her face beaming, as she ran her hands over his. "It feels like glass!" She looked up into Hank's face and said, "I'm Nena. Or Neon, if you like."

"Neeeeeeonnn," Hank replied.

And the floodgates opened. Everyone wanted to touch him, to hear their names spoken in Hank's haunting voice. Once their curiosity had been temporarily sated, we gathered around our conference table.

I'd been pretty sure that he would have some level of awareness and perhaps a modicum of intelligence. But Hank surprised me, answering my questions slowly but completely.

"Do you know who you are?" was my first question.

He looked at me, and I was surprised to see that his face showed expression. In this case, consternation. Then he said, "Yoou caaall mee Haaaank."

"Yes. Do you have any memory of Henry Glass?"

Again, he paused. "Yesss," he eventually whistled.

I followed with, "Do you remember what happened to Henry Glass?"

A shorter hesitation, then, "Paaain."

I immediately felt a bond with him. We were both members of an exclusive club comprised of those who had died... and remembered it.

I stepped back and allowed the others to continue, while I listened. And learned. I learned that he didn't have the physical limitations we all knew. He didn't get tired, didn't get hungry. He had some amount of physical sensation, but said he had not yet experienced pain in this form.

And to everyone's surprise, he then asked questions of each of us, showing genuine curiosity. Jack left the group and walked me up to the office, where he closed the door.

He looked at me with the most serious expression. "Look, this is..." He paused, frustrated. "Well, it's astounding and a bunch of other adjectives. But what were you thinking? And what are you going to do with him?" Before I could reply, he continued, "More accurately, what are you going to tell his family?"

I explained that the Academy had researched this before purchasing the "statue" to put on display. "Not married, no kids, no siblings, parents deceased..." I shrugged. "If some distant cousin learns of this, we'll deal with it, then."

After a moment, Jack continued. "You have a very... cavalier attitude toward life, Dyna. The cloning. Now this." He shook his head. "I don't even know what to say."

"What would you have done, Jack? I sensed something in him... a flicker of life. Should I have ignored it?"

"I mean... no, but..."

"But what? What was another option? It was either ignore it or bring it out. That's all I could see to do."

Jack stared at me for a while, frowning. Then he said, "The things you do are mind-blowing, you know that?"

"Yeah, so I've been told."

He shook his head. "I don't even know what to say. Just... I dunno."

"I know," I said. We shared a quick hug before he left.

Back in the meeting room, Cara sat in a corner wearing an expression that seemed familiar to me. I stepped over to her and we sat under the stairs, beyond the glass wall.

"I do not know what to say," she began, before I said a word.

"You're not alone in that," I said. "Do you think I've done something wrong?"

Cara frowned and brushed a strand of her long hair away from her face. "Dyna, I don't think I can make such judgments, anymore. I'm sorry, again, for before."

"Please don't give it another thought, okay? Never apologize for voicing your opinion on anything."

Cara smiled softly. I gave her a quick hug, then returned to the main attraction until the crowd eventually dispersed.

The following Monday, the *Enquirer* published the clone story. The headline read:

**DYNAMISTRESS IS DEAD
BUT HER CLONE LIVES**

My hope was that, without confirmation, the public would accept it as just another tabloid fabrication. However, the author of the article had done a fairly convincing job of piecing together what I'd done.

Because of this, the calls from the scientific community over the next several days became a virtual deluge. The Project began screening all calls, answering those that were obviously for the Project and ignoring those from the media. Some, however, slipped through, posing as legitimate inquiries, then revealing themselves as media once a live person was on the line.

And there were letters, many of which were from various "pro-life" organizations. They threatened me with lawsuits, since California had enacted a ban against human cloning back in 2001. But I paid them little attention. As convincing as the article was, there was no way anyone could actually prove what I'd done.

And then there were the paparazzi, who gathered outside my home by the dozens. The entrance to our street required a key to open the gate, but most of them climbed right over. The security company made half-hearted attempts to shoo them away, but gave up quickly.

Those of us in the Project who could fly had no trouble avoiding them, of course. The upstairs deck served as the back-up entrance. But the earthbound members had little option other than wading through the throngs. To spare them this, I suggested that only the fliers need show up for monitor duty until the situation cleared up. I was thankful that there didn't seem to be any flying paparazzi.

Dana returned to the city a few days before Thanksgiving. The first thing he asked was to meet Henry, who was engrossed in exploring the kitchen. After a brief introduction, we let him get back to it.

"He looks like a walking glacier," Dana said. I had to agree. The blue color was much like that of thick ice. "Where does he sleep?"

"He doesn't, really. Nor does he eat or drink. His energy comes purely from sunlight or other sources of light or heat. He stores it up, like a battery."

"So... what? He just wanders around the house at night?"

"Generally, he spends it up on the deck. I'll find him standing there in the morning in the exact spot he was in when I went to bed. At first, I figured he was lost in his memories, or trying to be. But one day, I asked him. Evidently, he can form his eyes into powerful lenses. He's been studying the moon and planets."

"Damn. That's very cool."

"And he's improving every day, becoming more active. His voice, as you heard, still sounds like blowing across a bottle top, but it's clearer and less drawn out than it was."

We moved from the kitchen to the guest room, where Dana began unpacking. "I saw that Rachel's movie comes out on Friday," he said, changing the subject.

"Did you want to see it?"

"Don't you?"

"I mean... yeah, I guess."

Dana chuckled. "You know you do."

Now it was my turn to change the subject. "I hope being here won't be too uncomfortable for you, given that some of my friends know about us."

Sitting on the edge of the bed, he said, "I've been thinking about it, ever since the paper came out. Most people don't believe it any more than they believe stories about the Bat Boy. Why didn't you just deny it?"

"That seems to be everyone's question. I guess because these people accepted me, most of them without reservation, after I... 'came back.' I don't want to lie to them. They deserve better than that." I hesitated. "I know it puts you in an awkward position..."

"It's fine," he said. "I'm not in the public eye like you are." He smiled, then changed the subject again. "What are the plans for Thanksgiving? You cooking?"

I burst out laughing. "Yeah, no one wants that."

"Wait... you want *me* to cook, don't you?"

I shook my head. "It's being catered. We'll have everything set up down here. I expect the others will arrive sporadically. I also invited Macy. And Ali."

"The pizza girl?"

"Yeah."

"How serious are you guys?" he asked as he finished unpacking.

I chuckled. "I don't think we've figured that out, yet. We don't see each other all that often, between her work schedule and my activities with the Project."

"I see."

"Why? Jealous?"

"I'm not even gonna go there," he said.

As we headed upstairs, I said, "I think Vicky is."

"Things any better between you two?"

"Well, she doesn't actively avoid me, anymore." We headed up to the living room to sit near the fire. "But she's still not receptive to picking up where we left off. I don't honestly think she ever will be."

"But you think she's jealous?"

"She denies it, but it seems obvious. She's always referring to Ali as 'the teenager' and such. She's never met her."

"And you invited both to Thanksgiving."

I tucked one leg up under myself, enjoying the heat of the flames. "I figure the chances of them both being here at the same time are pretty slim." Dana just stared at me, an incredulous look on his face. "What?" I said.

"You are the absolute last person in the world who should use 'pretty slim chances' as an excuse. For anything."

I had to admit, he had a point.

On Thanksgiving, the kitchen was filled with plates, bowls and chafing dishes holding all the standard Thanksgiving fare, from turkey to pumpkin pie and everything in between. Wine, beer, soft drinks, and buckets of ice sat atop the bar.

As expected, people arrived depending on their own Thanksgiving schedules. Some didn't have family near (or at all), so they spent most of the day. Cara didn't celebrate Thanksgiving, but stopped by around noon for about an hour. Daniel and Invictus both declined.

Macy arrived around two in the afternoon. I'd invited her parents, as well, but they also declined. The same went for the Shepherd family. The girls came over, but their mother wanted to just relax, and their dad's excuse was football. Jack brought Aimee, though they didn't stay long, since they were expected at the Wonderland home.

Naturally, a lot of focus was on Henry. Though he did not eat, he hung out in the kitchen and interacted with those who flocked around him. And someone was always flocking. Dana, for example, sat near Henry most of the day.

Most of the team was friendly toward Dana. Sinta spent a lot of time talking with him, as she always did. Jasmine, not so much. Jack, nothing beyond a polite greeting.

And as Dana had predicted, Bridget and Vicky arrived minutes before Ali, defying the odds I'd stated. I introduced Ali to everyone, except for Sinta, of course. When it came to introducing her to Vicky, I was surprised.

Vicky was polite, but reserved. Ali, on the other hand, gushed. "It's so great to finally meet you! Dyna talks about you so much, I feel like I already know you. And you're just as gorgeous as she said!" This caused Vicky to reluctantly loosen up around her. They talked for a few minutes, with Vicky actually smiling once or twice, and they parted cordially.

I gave Ali a questioning look when she returned to me. "What the hell was that?"

"Thought I'd do what I could to make it painless." She grinned. "Now where's your brother?"

I nodded over to the corner. "Over there with Henry and Sinta."

Ali hesitated, her eyes widening as she stared. "And Henry is...?"

"A long story," I said. "So what are you planning to say to Dana?"

With a wicked look in her eye, she said. "What else? Threesome!"

Before I found my voice again, Ali was already beside them. I just shook my head. The girl had a twisted sense of humor. I had to keep telling myself that she was joking.

Kit, Lily, and Nena made a short appearance before going to spend time with Kit's family. Jennifer and Kim spent about an hour with us. Vicky and Bridget left (via portal) to spend Thanksgiving with Bridget's parents.

One person did bring family: River's parents wanted to meet me. They thanked me for all I'd done for their daughter. Her mother embraced me in a hug and said, "Thank you for giving us our daughter back." Then she handed me a plastic bag filled with what she said were "horishky." They were a Ukrainian shortbread cookie in the shape of a walnut with a creamy caramel filling.

"Thank you," I said, accepting the bag. "And we're all happy to have her with us," I said. We spoke for a few more minutes before they excused themselves and departed.

By late afternoon, the event was down to Sinta, Ali, Dana, Henry, and me. We'd moved up to the living room. Henry stood near the front door, looking outside, observing. Sinta had fallen asleep curled up against Dana on the sofa.

"Well, that's just too damn adorable," I said quietly, as I joined them.

Dana looked down at Sinta. "Have to agree," he said.

I sat next to Ali. "So how are you doing?" I asked.

"Great," Ali said. Then, with an excited smile, she said, "Dana said yes."

I felt my jaw drop, and I looked at Dana, who seemed undisturbed, then back to Ali. She broke out laughing. "Oh, the look on your face, D."

"I honestly didn't know if you were serious."

"That's what makes it so great! You still don't!"

Did she ask you about... something? I thought to Dana.

You mean the threesome? he responded. *Can't wait!*

"Wait, *what?*"

"Yes!" Ali said, holding up her hand for Dana to high-five. I stared between the two of them.

Dana finally broke. "I like this one," he said, laughing.

"I hate you both," I said.

"Oh, come on, D," Ali said. "It's all in good fun. Though, to be honest, your brother is kinda hot, for someone literally twice my age. I wouldn't be opposed."

I rolled my eyes. "Okay, joke's old, now."

"Yeah... not joking, now," Ali said, then rose and headed for another drink at the bar.

"Was she kidding that time?" I asked Dana.

"How would I know?"

"Probably not," Sinta said with a yawn.

I stared between Sinta and Dana, unable to form a coherent thought. Dana grinned. "You're adorable when you're flustered, you know that?"

On her way back from the bar, Ali laughed out loud at his remark. "Your brother is awesome, D." She returned to the sofa and sat again between Sinta and me. She hugged Sinta. "You sleepyhead, Sin."

"Shush," Sinta said. "Dana's comfy."

"So are you," Dana said to her, scratching her head.

"How was today for you?" I asked him. "Too uncomfortable?"

"Eh, I've had worse experiences."

"Why would it be bad?" Sinta asked.

"Some people don't understand or approve of the kind of relationship Dana and Dyna have," Ali said.

Sinta rolled her eyes. "Yeah. Because they have no idea what it feels like to have *no one* who loves you." The rest of us were silent after her statement. "Being loved is precious, and you should never turn it away, no matter where it comes from or what form it takes, so long as it's real."

"That's sadly beautiful, Sin," Ali said. "But it's not the love that people have the issue with." She leaned in, conspiratorially, and stage whispered, "It's the *sex*."

Dana turned his face away, suddenly captivated by the fire as it crackled nearby. I felt my entire head flush.

"Well, they should mind their own business," Sinta said. "Besides, that's a form of showing love, right?"

"Yeah. And it's hot as hell."

Sinta looked at her. "Really? Why?"

"Because even though I don't agree that it's morally wrong, society does. So it's kind of a 'fuck you' to conventional opinion. It's being 'bad.' Eating the forbidden fruit. That's exciting."

"Call me a prude," I said, "but I'm not sure how I feel about people discussing my... personal life... so casually."

"Prude," Ali teased.

Sinta sat up and stretched. "Okay, Ali. It's getting late."

Ali smirked. "I do love the subtlety of your hints."

Sinta got up and pulled Ali to her feet. "Thanks for Thanksgiving," Sinta said, then hugged me before planting a fuzzy kiss on the top of Dana's bald head.

When we'd said all our goodbyes, the girls stepped out into the cool evening air. I closed the door and turned to look at Dana. "Sorry about that," I said. "Ali is... um..."

"She's cool," Dana said. "I like her."

"I'm glad to hear–" I hesitated. "Wait. You're just saying that because you're thinking about the threesome, aren't you?"

Dana just laughed and gathered up the empty drinkware.

It was disconcerting to see Rachel on the big screen. She looked great. Confident. Nothing like the traumatized woman I'd known so long ago. Whether she was hiding it while acting or it was truly behind her, I had no idea. But everything I'd read about her seemed to indicate that she was doing well. It made me happy.

I missed her friendship and the fun we had while working together at the Red Devil. But that seemed so long ago, now. It was easy to push it out of my head while I sat in the theater.

The movie itself was a twist on her original show. This time, rather than being the precocious "Li'l Devilgirl," she was the adult mother of the family, dealing with mundane matters while living as a semi-demonic being. It was reminiscent of *Bewitched*, in that respect. But while the original TV show's humor was with cute and endearing situational comedy, the movie "upgrade" went with over-the-top humor, as befitting modern times. The audience seemed to enjoy it. Not saying that I didn't, but I guess I was hoping for something more like the original.

Even so, it was great to see that Rachel's life was where she wanted it to be. The hype for the movie had, predictably, raised significant interest in her show, which found a new generation of fans as the reruns were broadcast on television and the full series released on DVD. I admit I bought a set.

Rachel herself was a celebrity again. She was being linked to one Hollywood hunk after another. Rumor had it that she and her movie husband were currently an item. The tabloid articles about her were certainly kinder than the ones about me.

After our discussion about the film wound down, Dana said, "So what's on your mind? You're too quiet."

"Honestly," I said, "I've been thinking about Dynasonic."

"What about her?"

"My main concern is the situation with Michaels there in her world. I feel strongly that we need to step in and end his threat."

"Okay?"

"The problem is," I said, "that some members of the team are not on board with our intervention."

"You could put it to a vote," he suggested.

But I shook my head. "There's no point. We operate by consensus, and there's no way we'd come close to that if we voted."

"So what will you do?"

"Well, at the very least, I want to go check in with her."

"Want some company?"

I looked up at him. "Really?"

"I've been pretty curious about her ever since you first told me."

"Okay, then! We'll go tomorrow!"

Just then, my phone buzzed. I'd received a text message from none other than Dane Weatherford:

After consideration, I have come to see the logic of your proposition. One can never have too many contingency plans. I will contact you again with the time and place.

Twenty-Two

"You want to believe that there's one relationship in life that's beyond betrayal. A relationship that's beyond that kind of hurt. And there isn't."
~ Caleb Carr

When Dana was in his teens, he would often "camp out" with one of his friends by pitching a tent in our back yard. I would often join them, which his friends found annoying, but had to accept.

I'd watch them play cards or board games by lantern light and share their chips and dip. But once I'd fall asleep, Dana would carry me inside and put me to bed before returning to his friends. So I missed out on their jaunts to what then passed for a convenience store in our tiny town, where they'd buy little fruit pies, pretzels, and pop, then walk around long after the sidewalks had been rolled up for the night.

But sometimes, it would just be Dana and me. Well, and our dog, Scooter. I'll never forget those nights. We'd talk for hours, about whatever I felt like, while walking Scooter through town.

On one such midnight walk, we were awed by the sight of the Northern Lights, which we had no idea could be seen at our latitude. I remember standing transfixed, seeing the shimmering waves of light, going from orange to red to pink to white. And when it faded, it was like Dana and I had a secret that no one else shared.

On these nights, when I fell asleep, Dana didn't take me inside. I'd be there all night. And sometimes, I'd be awake when he wasn't. I'd lie there on my stomach, propping my head on my hands, enjoying the crisp night air. And, if I'm honest, I liked being awake when he was asleep, because it made me feel like I was standing guard. Like I was his protector. It was nice to reverse roles, at least for a while.

The following morning, Dana and I headed to the portal over the Bay. Dana wasn't sure his telekinetic levitation would be sufficient to carry him that high, but it was.

Man, it's cold up here, he mentally said as we neared the portal.

Wimp, I replied.

Eventually, we reached the portal and eased ourselves through.

Okay, that was a bizarrely abnormal feeling. Or is it because I'm a wimp?

No, it really is super weird.

As we slowly descended, Dana grilled me with questions about this world. I'd told him all this previously, but he appreciated the reminders. As we neared the ground, I watched him as he looked all around. *Wow*, he thought to me. *You weren't kidding about how clean this city is.*

We traveled from the Bay to Dynasonic's place just above building height, Dana frequently expressing his astonishment at the lack of homeless people, trash, and abandoned storefronts.

Finally, we reached her home, landing in front of the building that looked exactly like my own, but cleaner. I made a mental note to have the exterior of my place power-washed. Dynasonic was surprised to see that Dana had accompanied me. Inside, I was equally surprised to see her brother sitting in an armchair, sipping coffee.

I made introductions all around, chuckling at Dana's obvious envy of his counterpart's full head of hair, and said counterpart's shock at my brother's baldness. Dynasonic brought us tea as we all got comfortable.

I turned to her brother. "I'm not used to seeing you here. What's the occasion?"

"Ah, well... Michaels nearly found me," he said. "Being here is the safest place away from him."

When I looked confused, Dynasonic reminded me. "The tungsten shielding."

"That," her brother said, "and them." He hooked a thumb over his shoulder to where two young women were standing near the kitchen. He summoned them over and introduced them. They were two telepaths that he'd freed from the network. They stayed near him, acting as a mobile shield, preventing Michaels from sensing him.

The girls smiled and were polite in greeting us. But something seemed odd about them. Dana picked up on it, too. *Why are they so... timid, I guess?*

I didn't have to answer. Their rescuer saw our confusion. "These girls were taken at a young age," he said. "Their actual knowledge of the world and life is far more limited than it would have been, otherwise. They're also not terribly comfortable around others, yet." He thanked the girls, who returned to their places near the kitchen, then continued. "For the past several months, Michaels has been increasing his efforts to find me and has come close to doing so a few times."

I let that sink in, then tentatively asked, "Has this been since July, by chance?"

He looked at me in surprise. "How did you know?"

I related to them how my brother had been abducted in my world. "It's possible that he could have detected my brother's weaknesses and used that knowledge to help in his pursuit of you." As they absorbed that, I said, "I take it you've become quite the pain to him."

"Over the past year, we've successfully freed dozens of telepaths from his network and some of them, in turn, are freeing others. His surveillance efforts outside of California are severely crippled. And he's been so focused on me that he hasn't appeared to make any effort to rebuild that network."

"So you've got him on the ropes," I said.

"It seems so. Ever since I freed the governor from his control, Michaels has become angry, sloppy, and erratic. He now seems more focused on getting rid of me and my group than he is on growing, or even maintaining, his existing network. But I don't want to get overconfident."

We were silent for a bit, before my brother spoke up. "I can't help but feel partially responsible for how things are currently going for you. Had I not been captured, this wouldn't be happening."

But his other-self just shook his head. "The only one to blame is Michaels himself."

"And Weatherford," I added. "Without him, Michaels wouldn't really have known anything about Dana." I finished my tea and set the cup on the coffee table. "At any rate, we're going to help you. I'll speak to my team and see who is willing to come."

"To do what?" he replied. "Sit around and wait?"

"Well..." I began, but really didn't have an answer.

Just then, a loud crackling noise grabbed our attention, and the front door rattled. We all jumped from our seats. Other-Dana rushed his two telepaths up into the kitchen, joining them out of sight. A moment later, the frosted glass of the front door exploded inward, revealing the silhouette of Mistress Dyna.

I prepared to attack, but before I could, I was frozen in place, unable to move a muscle. I couldn't speak. I couldn't even redirect my eyes. Thankfully, I could still breathe and blink.

And think.

Can you hear me?

Yes, Dana replied.

Mistress Dyna stepped through the door frame, with Michaels right behind her. He looked at the three of us. "Hello, again," he said, looking at me. "Thank you both for guiding me here. It's quite uncommon to see airborne metas in this world." He ignored Dana and turned his attention to Dynasonic. My eyes were locked on Mistress Dyna, but my peripheral vision showed him stepping closer. "I figured it was too much to hope that your damned brother would be here," he said to Dynasonic with a shrug. "But I'm sure you can tell me where he is."

This is bad, I said to Dana. *Can you do anything? Telekinesis?*

No, he's preventing that, somehow. I'm trying to break free of his control, but can't seem to make any headway.

Headway? Really? This isn't the time for puns.

It's always the time for puns.

Michaels was now face-to-face with Dynasonic. He stood several inches taller, looking down into her eyes. A moment passed, and Michaels frowned.

"I see," he said. "Your brother has taught you some impressive resistance. But it's just a matter of time before I break through."

Dynasonic was struggling to open her mouth. Michaels chuckled. "I'm not stupid, you siren. You remain silent."

What do we do? I asked. *Can you speak with the other Dana?*

I could, but he's a bit busy with shielding himself and his friends. And possibly his sister.

I refocused on Mistress Dyna, who stood idly near the wall, seeming to be bored. No... not bored. In fact, she looked inert. Like a mannequin that breathed and blinked.

Dana! Mistress Dyna, I thought to him. *I think Michaels is controlling her, too.*

A moment passed, then he replied. *You're right. I'll try to override that.*

I saw Mistress Dyna flinch, confusion on her face. My hopes rose. And then fell, when Michaels whirled to face Dana. "Leave her alone!" he yelled, and then Dana fell to the floor. When he didn't reply to my thought-speak, I knew he was unconscious.

Michaels pushed Dynasonic aside and glared down at my brother. He opened his mouth to yell at him again, but then stopped. He was so close to me, but there was nothing I could do. Every bit of my strength was going into trying vainly to move.

Mistress Dyna, though, hadn't returned to her previous state. She continued to stare at the floor, but I could see confusion on her face. Her breathing was heavy. This grabbed Michaels' attention, and he turned to look at her.

"How?" he whispered. Then his eyes widened. "Where are you?" he yelled. "You son of a bitch!" He spun back around to Dynasonic. "Where is he?

Take me to him!" And to my shock, she began to move, shuffling zombie-like toward the kitchen.

Mistress Dyna still looked bewildered. Then, suddenly, her eyes widened and she stood quite still. Her gaze settled on me. Her brows were knit, and she seemed to be struggling against something in her head. But Dana was out, which meant it was likely that the other Dana was trying to free her from her mind control.

I hoped he could succeed before his sister unwittingly led Michaels to the kitchen. But then, Mistress Dyna reverted to her inert state and the kitchen erupted with the sounds of fighting. There was unintelligible yelling, the sound of chairs falling over and so on. I heard one of the telepaths scream.

Wake up! I mentally yelled to Dana. When he didn't stir, I kept "yelling," all while trying to ignore the noise from the kitchen. And still, I couldn't move. Just how powerful was Michaels? *Come on, Dana! Wake up!*

And then I felt him stir in my mind. *Oof.*

Can you move?

No, he replied. *It's insane, the amount of power he has.*

I briefed him on what was happening, just as I heard someone come tumbling down the steps from the kitchen. Dana had fallen with his head facing in that direction, and he confirmed that it was Dynasonic.

Focus on Mistress Dyna, I told him. *I think she's close to breaking free.*

The sounds of physical fighting were fading. I couldn't help but think the worst was happening. I focused every bit of my energy into breaking the psychic restraints on me, but it was no use. I was stuck in the same position, staring at Mistress Dyna.

Another scream from the kitchen, followed by the sound of a body hitting the floor. Both telepaths and Dynasonic were down. The noise was now reduced to grunting sounds as the two men fought.

I closed my eyes and redoubled my efforts to break my mind free. But no matter how much I struggled, there was no progress. I sighed and opened my eyes again, only to see Mistress Dyna looking more confused than ever. Her eyes were wide. She looked around the room, seeing me, seeing Dana on the floor, seeing Dynasonic at the foot of the steps to the kitchen. She shook her head, as though clearing away a bad dream. Then she stumbled, catching herself at the wall and sliding down to the floor.

Oh, shit, Dana said in my head.

I watched as Mistress Dyna sat there, staring into nothing, tears welling and spilling down her cheeks. Her breathing became short and labored, and she began to tremble.

For several seconds, she shook her head, arms crossed over her stomach, as she rocked back and forth. "No," she whispered. "No, no, no, no, no!" Then she got to her feet, her fists clenched, electricity arcing up and down her arms. "DAAANAAAAA!"

And then she bolted to the kitchen, where the sound of fighting suddenly stopped. There was a thud, and then Michaels came sailing into my field of vision, landing hard on the floor and sliding toward the front door.

"Fucking hell," he muttered, one hand rubbing his sternum, his face contorted in pain. Then he looked up toward the kitchen. He raised his arm, palm forward. "Don't!"

I heard the crackle of electricity and flinched as the bolt struck him. As he writhed on the floor, I saw Mistress Dyna approach in my peripheral vision. Soon, she stood over him, and my breath caught in my throat. Electricity crackled around her. Filaments leaked from her eyes, reminding me of another Dyna. "You BASTARD!" she screamed. "How *could* you?" And she attacked him again. The sound was deafening.

"Stop!" he yelled, struggling to stand. But she stepped over and punched him in the head. "*Stop!*" he pleaded, and the woman hesitated for a moment. She recovered quickly, however, and jolted him again. Michaels screamed in pain and anger, finally yelling, "I said STOP!"

I heard Mistress Dyna gasp, ending with a choking sound. Then I heard her hit the floor. A moment later, shockingly, I could move again. I took a moment to collect myself, then I turned, ready to blast Michaels, only to find him crouching, looking at Mistress Dyna, who lay twitching on the hardwood floor.

I watched his anger fade, to be replaced by confusion. "No," he whispered. "Get up," he said, his voice shaky, as he crawled over to her. "I didn't mean..." I stared at her, too, at her vacant eyes. "Wake up!" Michaels pleaded.

Switching to my energy vision, my heart felt heavy as I saw her life force quickly fading.... until it flickered and was gone. Michaels must have sensed this, too. He wailed and clutched her to his chest, rocking back and forth, as he wept over Mistress Dyna. Or rather, I watched another Dana weeping over his sister.

It was heartbreaking, honestly. His wails of "no, no, no" deteriorated into guttural sobs, vocalizations without words. His face showed unimaginable grief, tinged with fear and a bit of panic.

By this point, everyone was up and around, including the two telepaths. I'm not sure how long we all stood there, but eventually, the scene was disrupted by the arrival of two police officers. I assumed a neighbor had called them because of the commotion.

One of the officers knelt next to a still weeping "Michaels" and tried to talk to him, but he had mentally checked out, too overcome with grief to pay any attention to them, let alone respond. The other officer approached us. Dynasonic stepped in to handle his questions.

I spoke mentally to Dana. *Did you have any idea that Michaels was another version of you?*

I had a suspicion, he replied, *but I really didn't want to believe it. It was too unnerving to see "myself" as a villain.*

At this point, said villainous Dana looked up, as if noticing the police for the first time. In turn, he looked at all of us, ending with his nemesis, this world's Dana. There was anger in his eyes, at first, but it faded, to be replaced by a blank stare and more tears. He looked then at Dynasonic, then at my brother and me. After a while, he returned his attention to his sister. I heard him whisper, "I'm sorry" to her. "So sorry." Then he gently laid her head down before shakily getting to his feet.

He continued gazing down at her as the officers tried to question him. But he remained silent, eventually turning away from his sister and staring vacantly at nothing. I was struck by the look on his face. He seemed to realize that he'd lost. Not just lost his sister, but lost his will. It was the face of a man who'd lost everything.

The officers continued trying to get him to speak. One of them reached for him, but Michaels tore himself from the officer's grasp, causing them to pull their sidearms.

Seeing this, Michaels froze. Then, to my astonishment, he gave a faint, sad smile. With a sigh, he closed his eyes and nodded. Before any of us could react, the suddenly mind-controlled officers shot him to death.

Twenty-Three

"Hiding, secrets, and not being able to be yourself is one of the worst things ever for a person. It gives you low self-esteem. You never get to reach that peak in your life. You should always be able to be yourself and be proud of yourself.
~ Grace Jones

I once asked my brother just how difficult it was for him to keep his abilities secret for so long. He told me it was ridiculously hard, not because he feared an accidental reveal, but because he so badly *wanted* to tell someone. Had our parents not been the kind of people they were, he would have told the world.

"I see it a lot when counseling metas who maintain private identities," he told me. "They're constantly afraid. When it comes to having your enemies find out who you are, that fear is totally justified. But it still eats at you. It's not difficult to keep something secret. That's the easy part. The hard part is trying not to think about it all the time, to keep telling yourself that you must protect this secret at all costs. Look at our mutual secret," he said. "It's easy enough to keep hidden. But tell me you don't think about it. A lot."

I couldn't tell him that, because it was true. I did think about it a lot. What he (probably) didn't know, though, was that I felt like he did as a teen. I didn't want to hide this secret. I'd become quite good at not giving a damn what others thought or said about me. And hell, it seems like half my friends already thought I was in love with Dana. Or maybe it's that they just saw it, while I was in denial of it.

Over the next couple days, I spent most of my time with Henry, seeing how much of his human life he could remember. Very little, as it turned out. Some things from childhood, but not much recent besides the accident itself.

His speech improved daily. His movements became more fluid, allowing him to move perhaps half as fast as a human. For someone who was built like a linebacker and weighed in excess of four-hundred pounds, he was surprisingly light-footed. Eventually, of course, his curiosity kicked in.

"I have... a question," he said in his bass flute voice.

"Of course," I said. "What is it?"

"Why?" he said. "Why am I... here?"

I took a deep breath. I'd been expecting the question, but still wasn't entirely sure how to respond. "The truth is," I said slowly, "you're here because I'm too curious for my own good. And a bit selfish." I hesitated, then laid it all out. "When I realized there was a spark of energy inside what everyone assured me was a piece of inert polymer, I had to see if that meant that you were, in some way, alive. I just needed to know, if that makes any sense."

"I... see," Hank said.

"But if you're wondering if I'd thought ahead as to what would happen if you... well, if you became what you have become... no, I didn't. Even when I saw your body gradually changing over the past six months. And I'm sorry."

"Why...sorry?"

"Because now you're here. The only one of your kind. I've brought you into a world where you have no natural place. And you have every right to feel upset, to be angry with me."

I watched in fascination as his facial features slowly flowed into a frown. "Angry," he said. "No. I am not."

I smiled in relief. "I'm glad to hear that."

We were both quiet for a time, then he said, "May I... stay?"

"Stay? You mean here in my home?"

"Yes."

"Well, I have nothing against that idea, but won't that be boring for you?"

"No," he said. "And I can... protect." When I asked what he meant, he said, "I heard... intruders. But... could not move."

"Intruders?"

"I heard men... talking. I heard... you... but you were not here."

"Wait," I said. "Hellion. That was months ago! You were aware, that long ago?"

"Time... is still not clear to me."

I let this fact sink in. "So... whenever I was here, talking to myself, talking to you... you heard me?"

"Yes," he said. "Some... made little sense. But I heard."

I reviewed my memory for things I may have said. I felt my face flush. "Could you see things, or just hear them?"

"Sight... no. Only recent."

His answer saved me from some embarrassment. Most of the time, after showering, I just like to air dry. "Well," I said, "you're welcome to stay, of course." To my surprise, a smile formed on the blue man's face.

And that's how Henry's Home Security began.

At the next team meeting, I invited Dana to participate, and the two of us explained everything that had happened in Dynasonic's world. Dana talked about freeing Mistress Dyna from her brother's control and described what he'd picked up in her head, of how her brother had used and abused her in any number of ways. It made the man's behavior at the end seem strange to me. I'll never understand how love can become twisted that way.

At the end of the reckoning, I said, "I know some of you... well, most of you... were against the idea of interfering with that world's issues. I respect that. And as it happened, it was just coincidence that Dana and I were there when everything went down." I paused for a moment. "Well, no. In fact, it was our presence there that allowed them to follow us to Dinah's home. So it was kind of our fault."

Jasmine cleared her throat. "It's likely that they would have found her eventually. You may have accelerated that event, but without you, it could have ended far worse."

"Whatever the case," I said, not wanting to dwell on it, "the point is that only Dana and I were there."

"What are you getting at, Dyna?" Jack asked, forcing me to put my vague feelings into words.

"I guess what it comes down to is that I feel like I've been letting all of you down by focusing on situations that don't involve the whole group. We don't feel like a team at all," I said, "and that's my fault."

My friends looked at me with quizzical expressions, but it was Silver Storm who spoke up. "I know I'm the new kid on the block, so maybe I'm just confused, but when you explained the Project to me, you said that actual team endeavors weren't all that common. You said the members often had solo activities. I mean, that's how I viewed the things you're talking about. Your solo stuff."

There were nods around the table, then Sinta said, "Dyna, you keep saying that you're not the leader of the team, but you constantly act as though all the responsibilities are on your shoulders alone. And that's not what the Project is about, right?"

I had to admit, they had me, there. "Thank you both. You're right. But, if I may ask you all... Are you happy in the Project?"

Jasmine chuckled. "You'd know it if anyone wasn't." Again, nods around the table. "But as you said, you've been focused on your own stuff. I think maybe you need to know what the rest of us have been up to." She looked to my right. "River? How about you start? Then we'll just go around the table."

"Well," she said, brushing a lock of hair from her eyes, "I've mostly been learning. Jasmine has been explaining monitoring and communications. And as for the volunteering requirement, I've been looking into working at one of the camps for troubled youths. Oh, and training with Sydney."

"How's that going?" I asked.

"Very well! I'm about out of things to teach her. And I've learned a bit from her, too."

"Good! Glad to hear it. Bridget?"

"Yeah, so I'm still volunteering at the dog rescue," Bridget said. "I don't really have any solo activities, as you know."

Nena said, "No real solo stuff for me, either. But I'm working with one of the homeless organizations."

"Still a volunteer docent at the bat exhibit," Jennifer said. "An' I'm involved with NorCal Bats, up in Sacramento. Occasionally, I still do night patrols."

"And I've not noticed any mosquitoes around here, so thanks for that."

Jennifer just sighed. "Ah'm glad you can amuse yourself at my expense."

"So am I!" I said, and we both chuckled.

"Orphans," Lily said. "That's where I'm focusing my volunteer time. Outside of that, I'm still learning how to use my abilities offensively so I can be a better team player."

"As you know," Kit said, "I work with the deaf. And in the past few months, I've assisted the SFPD in two hostage situations, rescued a pair of injured hikers over in Marin, and brought in a tug with engine trouble."

Vicky was next. "I've been teaching Crisis Intervention to the police at precincts around the city. Also assisted in dousing a couple structure fires."

"I do work with my church," Cara said. "We have a soup kitchen, I believe you call it. Sinta has been helping me improve my close quarters combat. And I also do daytime patrols."

Kim cleared her throat. "I have been visiting schools as part of an anti-bullying campaign. And as you know, I do a lot of our monitoring."

"Still working with amputees," Jack said, "in addition to the day job. Most of my other activities are when I'm called in for things where I can lend an arm."

"I volunteer at the Child Abuse Prevention Center," Sinta said. "Plus regular nightly patrols."

Jasmine was last. "I still work with the Red Cross on preparedness matters. I frequently do monitor duty, in addition to maintaining our security system and our field kits." She smiled. "Now, let me tell you what the Project, as an organization, has accomplished here." She glanced at her notes. "In the past six months, we have had three hundred and twenty-nine walk-ins for help with various assistance programs. We have also been called upon to aid other teams eight times. And individual members of the team have been dispatched to help other teams or the police on a weekly basis."

I sat back in my seat, absorbing everything. "Thank you," I said. "All of you. I feel quite relieved, so I'll shut up, now," I said with a smirk. "Okay. My last item is regarding Vortex and Jammer. Any objections to making them full members?"

There were smiles and head shakes around the room. So now we were fifteen strong.

"Any other business before we adjourn?" I asked. When no one suggested anything, I said, "All right... I know some of you were wondering if we'd have a holiday bash like we did last year, and the answer is yes. A week from Saturday, we'll have it up on the roof. Holiday party and the grand opening of our hot tub! Guests are welcome, of course."

The next week flew by, filled with preparations for the party. Catering had been arranged, decorating had been done, and the weather looked like it would be decent for December. The day itself turned out to be cloudy and in the low-to-mid 50s.

The hot tub got a fair amount of use. The tub itself was beautiful, with lots of jets. It was black, with a tile mosaic of our drum logo inlaid on the bottom. The contractors had cut the balcony wall and installed a door gate. I'd set up deck furniture all around, as well as several standing patio heaters.

Over the course of the afternoon, every member of the Project showed up, many of them bringing guests. Jack brought Aimee, of course. Daniel and Ping Song dropped by. The Shepherd family accepted my invitation, so Layla and Sydney spent a lot of time talking with the people who were now their teammates. Macy was there, as was Ali. It was heartwarming, seeing them all interacting.

We'd opened the party to others, too, so several people showed up who'd been helped by the Project, including Jeremy and Nathan. Casual friends, too, including Jack's co-worker, Paige, and even Fabian dropped by. Paige praised me for having the caterers provide Sumatran coffee. Fabian brought his partner, Trent, who seemed in awe of all the metas around him.

Captain Shepherd was having a beer with Jack while his wife chatted with Aimee. Macy and Bridget were laughing together near the hot tub. Hank stood in a corner, where the younger folks gathered around him. Everywhere I looked, I saw smiling faces. And I couldn't help but smile, myself.

Vicky approached, holding two plates of food, and handed one to me. "Thanks," I said, accepting the offering.

"Nice get-together," she said.

I snagged a cube of Jarlsberg. "I'm glad everyone is having a good time."

"Does that include you?"

"What? Of course!"

"You've been keeping to yourself," she said. "You sure you're okay?"

"Well, I admit I'm still processing what happened in Dynasonic's world. But beyond that, I've been thinking of something Dana said earlier." I noticed Vicky looked away at the mention of Dana's name. "What's wrong?" I asked.

She shrugged. "I'm sorry. It's just whenever you mention him, all I can think about is... you know."

I sighed deeply. "Vick... you do realize just how minor that aspect of our relationship is, right?"

"I know! You've explained it. I'm sorry. It's just an automatic reaction I can't seem to help." She shook her head. "Anyway, what was it he said?"

"He referred to the Project as a family, rather than a team."

Vicky was quiet a moment, then said, "He's right. You've gone out of your way to make the Project feel like anything other than a business. Everyone loves you and you love them back."

"But it *is* a business," I reminded her. "And anytime you have a business that says they're 'like a family,' it's a bad sign."

"It's not like that," Vicky insisted. "Trust me, the group is solid."

I decided to take her word for it and changed the subject. "I saw you talking to Ali, earlier."

"Yeah. She's determined to make sure I'm okay with you two. It's kind of cute."

"Is it working?"

With a smirk, Vicky said, "If she keeps flattering me the way she's been, it might." She was quiet a moment before saying, "Think she's talking to Dana about a threesome?"

I looked over at the pair and sighed. "Probably. She's incorrigible."

"So I've noticed."

"Has she floated that idea to you?"

Vicky blinked. "You mean... the three of us?"

"Don't be surprised if she does. She thinks you're hot."

"Well, that goes without saying."

I chuckled, then turned to face her. "Are we okay, Vick?"

"Aren't we?" she said, looking back at me.

"No, I mean *really* okay."

Vicky was quiet for a moment, then said, "Honestly, Dyna, I don't know how to think of you, anymore. I mean, it was hell accepting that you were dead. Then more hell getting used to you being 'alive' again, but with no memories. But I did accept it," she said, looking into my eyes. "Then pizza girl entered the picture."

"I *knew* you were jealous!" I said with more than a little smugness.

But the satisfaction of the moment vanished as Vicky said, "And now the... thing... with your brother."

Choosing not to go down that rabbit hole, I said, "Are you implying that, if Ali hadn't come along, you might have wanted to get back together?"

"Didn't say that," she said quickly.

"So, are you denying it?"

Vicky hesitated, then sighed in frustration. "I don't *know*, okay? I liked what we had. But I don't know if returning to that is possible."

"It's not," I said. "But going back to what we had isn't the goal. Going forward is, and creating something new as we do."

After some silence, Vicky spoke without looking at me. "I can't do that. Not until I understand this... whatever it is... with Dana."

"Ask Sinta. She seems to understand it more than I do, myself."

"Bollocks. You just don't want to talk about it."

"Can you blame me?"

Vicky sighed heavily. "You should have just denied it. No one would have questioned that."

"I've explained why I didn't."

"You have the most peculiar morality."

"Do I?" I thought about the accusation and decided maybe she was right. "Is it too peculiar?"

"Too peculiar for what?"

"For you," I said. "Come on, you know what I mean."

Vicky ignored the question, finally saying, "Why the pizza girl? Seriously."

I rolled my eyes, exasperated. "I dunno. I mean... she's fun. She makes me laugh." I looked across at her, watching her chatting with Dana and Sinta.

"That's all?"

I frowned. "If you're thinking that Ali and I have a super-serious relationship, you're mistaken. We both realize it's casual." That seemed to relax her, but only a bit. "What's the real issue, Vick?"

"What the bloody hell do you *think*?" she snapped. "You and Dana, for fuck's sake!"

"Then why do you keep bringing up Ali?"

"Because at least I can understand that!" she said.

"Okay. Let's talk about my brother. But first, let's talk about your father, and how you seem unperturbed about him *raping* you!"

"We've already talked about that."

"Not to my satisfaction," I countered. "But the thing is... that's okay, because it's not any of my business, when it comes right down to it. I don't have to be satisfied with your explanations."

"And you're saying that it's not my business what you and your brother do."

"Well, it isn't, but no, that's not what I'm saying." I took a calming breath, trying to figure out what I really *was* trying to say. "Look, I get that there's an 'ick factor' with this."

"Doesn't seem like you do."

"That's because... for me, there isn't."

"And that's the bit I have trouble with," Vicky said. "Why is there *not* an ick factor for you?"

I hesitated, then said, "I don't think anyone can really understand that except Dana and me. But why does it matter that we don't have that reaction?"

"Any other relatives you wanna sleep with?"

"No, of course not," I said.

Vicky raised an eyebrow. "Why not?"

"Because I don't have that kind of bond with anyone else."

She looked at me thoughtfully. "You mean the telepathic link thing."

"Well, to be accurate, the link is the result of the deeper connection we have, not the other way around, though it does add to it."

"Yeah, you've said as much, before," she said. "But I still don't get it."

"Look," I said. "I've told you how Dana would find refuge in my mind when he was adjusting to his abilities. This unintentionally, but unavoidably, created a kind of mutual familiarity unlike anything either of us ever could experience with anyone else."

"So he groomed you!"

"*What?* Of course not! Vick, he was a kid! He had no idea how this would affect both of us over the years. He was just seeking shelter from the chaos of thoughts that he couldn't always block out." I hesitated, then returned to my point. "What I'm getting at is... in some ways, we really do feel like two halves of the same person. We feel incomplete without the other."

Vicky was quiet for a bit. "You love him, don't you?"

"He's my brother. Of course I do."

"You know what I mean."

I was silent for a minute, not really wanting to answer, but knowing I had to. "Ever since Sinta accused me of being in love with him," I said, "I've been trying to deny it. But... I really can't. I mean... it's not like this mad, passionate, new relationship energy kind of love. It's just a comfortable, secure sort of love. But obviously not just as siblings."

"Obviously," Vicky said, and we both were quiet for a moment. Then I took her hand. She looked at me, but didn't protest. So I leaned in closer, one hand tracing a path down her side. "This conversation was too heavy for a party setting," I said.

"Dyna..." she began, reaching to stop my hand, "don't..." Then I thrust both hands to her abdomen and began tickling, eliciting a squeal. "Oh, you *bitch!*"

I grinned as she squirmed and tried without success to escape. I didn't stop tickling until her laughter was laced with tears. When she finally started breathing normally again, she said, "Swear to God, Dyna, I'm going to tickle the shit out of you one day."

"You're waiting until I'm old and incontinent?"

"Eww!" Vicky punched me in the shoulder. "You're disgusting."

"At any rate, only one person knows where I'm ticklish, and I've sworn him to secrecy."

Vicky grinned. "Bet he'd tell me if I shagged him."

"You may be right," I said. "I could arrange that, if you like."

Vicky laughed, then looked at me, staring with her eyes wide. "Bloody hell, I think you're serious."

"I'm always serious," I said with a smirk.

"But now that you mention it, aren't you jealous, too? You weren't happy about Dana and Bronwyn."

"I wasn't, but only because of the idea of him moving to another country. Truth is, I really liked Bronwyn. And I was happy that he'd found someone like her."

"But didn't it bother you that he felt he needed someone other than you?"

I frowned. Time to reveal the hypocrisy. "I mean, a bit. But I have no doubt that I'd have gotten over it. I mean, I've always found it odd that people seem to think you can ever find someone 'perfect' for you. The chances that any one person being able to satisfy all your needs... emotional, intellectual, social, sexual, and so on... is just crazy unlikely. Besides, you remember my first relationship was a triad. There was no jealousy there."

"But with Bronwyn, you and Dana would effectively have been cheating, if she didn't know about it."

I sighed heavily. "Yeah. That's true. Kind of a non-issue, now, though."

During the silence that followed, Vicky took the opportunity to change the topic. "So... Hank." She frowned, looking over at "GlassMan," as we'd come to call him. "He's not the most... nimble... of metas."

"He's not quick or agile, but I'm sure he'll improve. One thing that'll help is that he never seems to get tired. He doesn't even sleep."

"That's not at all creepy." We were quiet for a moment, until Vicky said, "You should maybe socialize with the rest of the guests, not just me."

She was right, so I did.

While making my rounds, I found Cara and River chatting at the far end of the roof, both smiling and laughing. It was the first I'd seen Cara in such an upbeat mood. I joined them for a moment, a little surprised that they were talking about movies. Specifically, their mutual love for *How to Train Your Dragon* and other recent animated films.

Nena was entertaining others with juggling multi-colored balls of fire, the flames changing color from one hand to the other.

I found Jennifer staring absently into the currently vacant hot tub. "What's up?"

"Just guesstimatin' on how much chocolate we'd need to fill up that thing." She glanced sidelong at me, smiling at my burst of laughter.

"It would clog the jets, I'm afraid."

We were interrupted by Layla forcing her way between us. "Guys! I wanted to show you my costume!" She thrust her phone toward us, displaying a photo of her all decked out. For the most part, it looked like standard roller derby attire: skates, shorts, tank top, protective knee and elbow gear, and helmet. All done in black and gold. Her helmet had the Project logo where a jammer's star would be.

"Very cool," Jennifer said, and I agreed. Layla grinned before rushing off to show others.

And then my cellphone buzzed. It was Weatherford. The big event would be taking place on Monday.

I made the journey through Vicky's portal to her London flat, took a train to Newport, then another north to Abergavenny. The entire trip, my mind was on Weatherford. Now, there was a guy who had secrets. He was also a guy I was quite torn over.

It's true that I never trusted him. But I had to admit that I'd most likely blown that distrust out of proportion. As Vicky said, his activities in "magical" portal research weren't evil at all. I'd allowed my meta bias to shape my suspicions, failing to view it as actual research. Which it was, of course. I'd be stupid to pretend otherwise. I still couldn't comprehend the twisted sort of relationship Vicky had with him. But dwelling on that accomplished nothing.

In Abergavenny, I flew to The Little Skirrid, locating the hidden entrance to the connecting tunnel and flew its length to the secret home of The Nexus. When I reached the end of the tunnel, I saw that the portal trap to the river was gone. And the damage we'd done to the wall to get around the portal was repaired as though it had never happened. Taking a deep breath, I knocked on the door at the end of the passage.

It soon swung open, and one of the acolytes (or whatever they were called) welcomed me with a nod and motioned for me to enter. Looking around, I saw Weatherford standing next to a large, circular construct that stood on edge in the middle of the large, open room. It was similar to the machine used to keep the portal open back at Groom Lake. It stood maybe eight feet tall, nearly brushing the ceiling of the cave. Around the inside of the circle were twenty energy weapons, wired together and stripped down to just the functional bits. All were aimed at the center of the circle.

Weatherford turned from the machine and greeted me. "Ms. Geof-Craigs," he said. "Welcome."

I looked at his smiling face. "It's creepy when you act nice. Stop it."

Instead of stopping, Weatherford laughed. "I can't help it," he said. "I'm excited."

"Excited or desperate?" I asked.

With a small sigh, he said, "I can't deny there's some of that, yes."

"So tell me what you've got here."

"Gladly!" he said. "As you've certainly surmised, the de-energizers are wired to be activated remotely. Each is tuned to the frequency of one of the known planes. They are all aligned to intersect in the exact center of the circle."

"I'm curious. Where did you obtain all the 'de-energizers'?"

Weatherford chuckled and spoke softly. "Believe it or not, they come from the same world as Mr. Michaels! He has no idea."

"Had."

"Pardon?"

"Michaels is dead," I said.

Weatherford appeared genuinely surprised. "Your doing?"

"No," I said, shaking my head. "His own."

Seeing the incredulous look on his face, I gave him an abbreviated version of the events. "I see," he finally said, shaking his head. "Such a waste."

"Sorry to have lost someone else you could use for your own ends?"

"It saddens me that you have such a low opinion of me. The waste is that he was so obsessed with power that he limited what he could truly accomplish."

"You're not one to point out the obsessions of others."

"Perhaps not. But my own goals have never been as limited as his."

I studied the machine as I changed the subject back to matters at hand. "And what of the precautions you told me you had?"

"Right," he said. "We cut the power, of course."

I stared at him. "You think that will help in the case of a late-stage issue?"

"Certainly."

I rolled my eyes and stopped asking. So why was I here? To destroy the machine if it turned out he was attempting something nefarious? Or was I genuinely interested in seeing the results?

"Speaking of power," I said, "how did you manage to get it way down here?"

"Generators," he said simply.

I looked at him skeptically, remembering just how much energy the portal in Groom Lake used. In the corner, I saw a technician at what was obviously the control for the main machine. "No way you can get enough juice to power this thing just from battery generators."

"Oh, we have an exceptionally powerful generator that doesn't run on batteries."

I glanced around, not seeing any such thing. "And what *does* it run on?"

Weatherford gave me a small smile. "From what I understand, mostly alcohol. And, occasionally, something called PowerPaste."

Before I even processed what he'd said, a sharp pain exploded behind my eyes. And everything went black.

The first thing I noticed when I returned to consciousness was that there was something in my mouth. No, not just my mouth. I had a tube down my throat. I glanced up at it, seeing a funnel at the end.

I was strapped into a chair, held in place with what felt like cable ties around my wrists and ankles. I was stripped to my underwear, my body covered with more electrodes than I could count, front and back, running from me over to the control unit in the corner. My shirt was draped over my breasts, allowing some sense of modesty.

Weatherford appeared at my side, looking down at me with an expression I couldn't quite read. "My apologies," he said, indicating the shirt, which he adjusted to better cover me. "I didn't realize you eschewed a brassiere." Just as I thought this was surprisingly considerate of him, he said, "But then I saw that you don't especially need one." He changed tracks. "You may not realize this, but you are fairly predictable. Had you not volunteered to come, I was going to bring you here, one way or another. The plan has always been to use you as the primary power source."

I stared at him, pieces coming together. From his position as Director of Metahuman Affairs, he learned details on how my abilities worked. The telepaths were for rendering me unconscious and keeping me under control. Normally, I would blast myself out of this by "exploding," or at least break the cable ties with a simple flex. But my mind was as restrained as my body. I couldn't make myself blast or break the ties. It was as though I'd forgotten how to move my limbs.

I tried to give a snappy retort, but the tube prevented this. Still, the effort caught Weatherford's attention.

"I also apologize about the tube," he said. Then he turned away from me, only to produce a bottle of Everclear. "I read that rum was your favorite," he said. "I'm more a fan of a nice Japanese whisky, myself. But as we're going for efficiency, this is what you get. You won't taste it, anyway." He handed the bottle to an associate.

The room began filling with dozens of other members of The Nexus, gathering in a semi-circle near the device. I studied their faces, as best I could, looking for evidence to support Vicky's claim of Weatherford being desperate to produce results, lest he be faced with rebellion.

And I saw it. One stood with his arms crossed, a frown on his face. A few seemed disinterested and kept shuffling their feet. Others whispered between themselves, with pointed glances at Weatherford, and more than a few at me. Most of them looked disturbed by my predicament, but none said anything. As for the man himself, Weatherford's face showed nothing but confidence, and it didn't look forced.

One of his people was fussing around with the control unit. Shortly, he looked up and nodded to Weatherford. I tensed up. But Weatherford delayed activation of the machine so that he could address the others.

"My friends," he began, as one or two of them rolled their eyes, "we are here today to witness the end result of two centuries of work, the culmination of our grand experiment." He grew more somber. "Before we begin, I want to thank you all for your patience. This has been too long in coming, I agree. But I have no doubt that you'll find it worth the wait."

With that, he stepped away from the machine, chatting with the technician at the controls, who in turn glanced over at me before turning a dial on the panel.

Immediately, my entire body began to tingle. Then it grew into a strange sensation that was uncomfortable, but not painful. I felt my energy leaving me, though, and grew lethargic. Light caught my eye and I looked at the portal, where beams erupted from all the weapon nozzles, converging in the exact center.

The machine continued to draw energy from me as the technician worked the console. At this point, I was near to passing out. But then someone poured the Everclear into the funnel. It wasn't long before I felt my energy levels rising, only to be immediately sucked from me.

They took no chances with me as a generator. One bottle followed another. Eventually, I felt my bladder beginning to strain. I also worried that, despite how quickly I could metabolize alcohol, this could overtax my system. If so, winding up drunk was the least of my worries.

Finally, in the center of the circle, flashes of light emanated, seemingly changing hues randomly. Expressions of Weatherford's comrades ranged from boredom to excitement, with everything in between. Weatherford himself moved to the portal, looking closely at the center. Colored light played on his face as he nodded to two others, who came and stood at the sides of the construct.

Weatherford then plunged his hand into the flashing light, as I'd once done in Groom Lake, so long ago. The converging beams now stopped, and the others pushed/pulled the mechanism so that one edge "caught" the opening around Weatherford's forearm. And, again as I'd done, he moved his arm around the circumference, the "hole" stretching as it was held by the machinery, the light output growing brighter with every inch.

Turning his head to catch my gaze, he said, "Thank you for this. We had you on camera in Groom Lake when you reactivated that portal in this way."

I glared at him, or tried to. There was little else I could do.

Eventually, the entire circle was completed, as the edges of the opening were held open by the machine. Weatherford took a step back, squinting, then put on a pair of sunglasses he pulled from a pocket. Others did the same. I was glad I was off at an angle from the face of the portal.

Weatherford tore his gaze away from the light and spoke to the technician. "Are you getting everything?"

Without looking up from his readouts, the man said, "All looks good."

Weatherford turned back to the machine, trying his best to peer into the light. But just then, one of the telepaths yelled, "Sir!" before being hurled into the wall by a blast of wind, falling unconscious to the ground. The other two telepaths were dispatched in a similar fashion. Immediately, my mind felt unburdened.

I felt a presence behind me. Able to move, now, I managed to snap the cable ties around my wrists, then reached up and pulled out the feeding tube, while trying not to puke.

My savior stepped into view, her back to me, but her identity no mystery. Auburn hair. Metallic blue tights. Iridescent, asymmetrically-cut tunic. "Hey, Vick," I croaked.

Seeing that I was no longer restrained, the technician transferred power to the battery generator. I wanted nothing more than to erupt in a blast that would rid me of all the electrodes at once. But my brain was still reeling from the effects of the telepathic prison. And the booze. So I began tearing off the wires in handfuls, leaving the electrodes stuck to my skin.

I turned my attention to the center of the room, where Vicky faced her father, both of her fists glowing, ready to summon forth... something. To my surprise, the other members of The Nexus had stepped back, not interfering in the coming showdown. Weatherford himself looked to the technician, who said, "We're good."

After a quick glance at the fallen telepaths, he acknowledged her presence. "Victoria." When she didn't reply, he said, "Why are you here?"

"To get this gormless twit back, obviously."

"Rude," I muttered.

"And?" Weatherford prompted.

Vicky turned her head toward the portal. "And to see what your obsession ended up producing." She looked into the light. "Which... appears to be not much of anything."

Some of the others muttered under their breaths, but Weatherford just smiled. "Oh, far from it. Very far from it."

"You think you know what that light show is?" I rasped through a throat sore from the tube.

"Indeed, I do. The data collected will confirm it and, after proper analysis, allow me to recreate this portal at will."

"So what is it?" said one of the gathered crowd.

"Isn't it obvious?" he said, seeming truly surprised that we didn't know. "Vicky knows, don't you?"

She was silent for a moment, frowning. "No," she finally said.

"Oh, come now," he replied. "Combining all four prime planes and adding either positive or negative energy allows us to go wherever we want. Adding both positive *and* negative will allow us to go *when*ever we want."

"But this isn't a combination of anything," Vicky said. "This just a hole you've created."

"Not so," Weatherford said. "We've known for a long time how to artificially replicate any of the planes by using the proper combination of frequencies. It's much less efficient and more time consuming than doing it 'naturally,' but it does work. This machine is also feeding those frequencies into the portal. All that's left is to add the positive and negative energies."

"So you were expecting me to show up?" Vicky said.

"You were the obvious one to rescue your friend," he said. "Come. I know you're dying of curiosity." With that, he reached out a hand to the portal, his palm touching flatly against the "surface" of the interface. In a moment, there was a color shift toward deeper and darker tones. Then he turned to Vicky. "Will you?" he asked.

After a moment of hesitation, during which I freed my ankles and stood, ripping the leads off the last of the electrodes. Vicky stepped forward. I didn't blame her. My curiosity was certainly piqued. I struggled into my shirt as Vicky mimicked her father and placed her palm against the portal's surface. Soon, the interface lightened, returning to its former luster. At the same time, the swirling slowed and took on a different pattern, like a rainbow.

"Pretty!" came a child's voice from within the gathering.

After both of them pulled their hands back, Weatherford looked expectantly at his technician, who was busy typing something into a keyboard. Soon, he stopped, turning his attention to something I couldn't see. Then there was a beep, after which he removed a small object from a slot in the machine. It looked like a tiny TV remote. He walked it over to Weatherford, who accepted it with a smile. Though I didn't hear Vicky's words, I knew she was asking him what the object was. She nodded at his reply.

Slipping the object into a suit pocket, Weatherford turned to face the hushed crowd, his other hand turning Vicky to stand with him. "My friends," he said, "I present to you... the door of time."

"Enough of this fantasy, Dane," said a doubter in the crowd. Others muttered what sounded like agreement.

I looked back at Weatherford, seeing his jaw clenched, his eyes piercing the crowd. "This is what we've all been striving for!"

"It's what *you* have been striving for," his skeptic said. "You've been wasting our resources on this foolish quest–"

"*Foolish?*" Weatherford yelled, his face growing red. "This is without question the single most important accomplishment in the history of mankind!"

The other man scoffed. I studied the faces in the crowd. Many were nodding at the skeptic's words. Weatherford apparently noticed this, and held up a hand to silence the murmuring. "It's fair that you have doubts. But I will now dispel them. I will enter the time stream and return at this exact instant."

The crowd's murmuring returned, but Weatherford ignored it, turning again to face the portal. He looked down at Vicky and said, "Ready?"

She looked up at him in surprise. "What?"

He clasped Vicky's wrist firmly and, with possibly the haughtiest look I've ever seen, stepped through the portal, dragging Vicky behind him.

"No!" Vicky and I screamed simultaneously. I rushed forward, seeing Vicky begin to disappear into the void. One arm remained, which she was able to hook around the frame of the machine. But the frame was thick, and her grip couldn't hold. I leapt forward, reaching for her arm, just as it slipped free.

Without thinking, I continued my lunge, shoving my hand into the interface. I braced myself against the body of the machine, my left arm wrapped around the arc of the portal, as I flailed about, my heart nearly bursting as I felt it latch onto what had to be Vicky's ankle.

I pulled with all the might that my body could muster. But it was no use. She wouldn't budge, likely still in Weatherford's grip. Despite this, I kept pulling, feeling desperate tears rolling down my cheeks.

I was so weak from being used as a human battery. I knew I didn't have the strength to pull her back unless she could break free. And I remembered well just how strong he was. And a moment later, that strength was exhibited. I felt a strong pull, and I slid forward, my upper body entering the portal.

Describing what I experienced is difficult. No matter how many times I write it out, it falls short of reality, if "reality" is even the right word. The sensation of being drawn through was much more disconcerting than going through any other portal. My body felt as though an electric current was passing through it, like my very being was buzzing. Visually, it was like a kaleidoscope of images hurtling past my vision at all angles and speeds. It gave me a headache almost instantly, and I felt on the verge of vomiting. And it was loud, like being in a windstorm. I could see Vicky and Weatherford. I tried yelling to her, but I could barely hear my own words.

To my surprise, the two of them seemed to be floating in mid-air. They had no footing, so I wondered how Weatherford had managed to pull me inside without something to brace himself against. But then I felt a gust of "wind" and realized that maybe it hadn't been him, after all.

I kept my eyes on them, trying to ignore the barrage of other images. I could feel my grip on the machine weakening. I admit I was terrified of what would happen when it failed completely. But just then, Vicky's foot was wrenched from me. A wash of fear ran through me as I watched her reach toward Weatherford. I fully expected her to blast him in some way, but instead, her hand went toward the pocket where he'd slipped the "remote."

When he realized her intention, he grabbed her forearm and they began to struggle. As I watched, my arm suddenly weakened and I crossed the threshold. I was now entirely within what seemed to be the "time stream."

I panicked, flailing about. Behind me, the portal was visible, still being held open by Weatherford's machine. I looked back to Vicky and was shocked to see that Weatherford was gone. Vicky floated freely in the tumult of the time vortex.

I had to get her, to bring her back. Summoning as much energy as I could, I let loose a gentle stream of energy from my feet, propelling me slowly toward her. Vicky's eyes were closed, doubtless trying to keep the flood of sights at bay.

A moment later, I bumped into her and wrapped my arms around her. Her eyes popped open, and I could see in her eyes that she was shocked to see me.

"Blast us back!" she said.

I shook my head. "No energy! Teleport us!"

"Can't! I tried!"

We just gazed at each other, terror growing. It seemed this lasted for a long time, but was likely no more than a few seconds before Vicky's face lit up. She slid a hand inside the back of her tunic and pulled, showing me the emergency kit that was held in place there by Velcro. Opening it up, she pulled out a tube of PowerPaste.

I grabbed the tube, tore it open, and sucked it down. Then we waited for it to metabolize. We held each other close, our cheeks touching, knowing we were drifting farther from the portal with each passing moment.

"Thanks for coming for me," I said.

"Same to you," she said. Then she said, "Oh, fuck."

I turned my head to see what she was seeing. The portal was flickering. The battery generator was failing.

I had no time to wait for the PowerPaste to fully metabolize. I turned us to face the distant portal back to our proper time and place... and blasted as much as I could.

We coasted toward the portal, which continued to flicker. After an eternity, we reached it, and I pushed Vicky through. She kept hold of one of my hands and pulled me behind her. We made it through and landed roughly on the floor. It was such a relief. The noise was gone, as were the nausea and disorientation. Vicky and I laid there on the floor, out of breath. Vicky held me tightly until we both calmed down.

We were surrounded by amazed members of The Nexus. The skeptic rushed over and knelt near us, asking if we were okay. We assured him we were, and he apologized for the situation we'd found ourselves in. Then he stepped away to talk with the technician.

The room was silent as we rose, with little attention being paid to us. The only sound was the hum of the portal. Everyone waited, some staring at the portal, others at various entrances to the room, obviously waiting for Weatherford to reappear.

Minutes passed as Vicky and I recovered, occasionally glancing at the failing portal. The young voice from before said what we were all thinking. "Where did Uncle Dane go, Daddy?"

The crowd began to stir, with everyone exchanging looks, some with concern, some with resignation. And gradually, they dispersed, taking the telepaths with them. Soon, only a handful of members remained, including the skeptic and the technician, who continued to speak quietly with each other.

I turned to Vicky, confused. "Vick... what happened in there? One moment, you were struggling with him, then he was gone."

She just shook her head, occasionally glancing at the portal, but mostly staring blankly at nothing. I had no idea what she was experiencing. Her relationship with her father was too complicated for me to comprehend.

The others stood near the control panel, occasionally glancing at the battery-powered generator. For a moment, I regretted not being its power source. "Vick," I said. "Do you want me to...you know..." She shook her head, not looking at me.

My jeans were in a pile behind the chair I'd been strapped to. I put them on while we waited, which we did for perhaps five long, silent minutes, until the interface began to fade in color. The machine's draw was too great for the battery. Finally, all of us watched as it flickered and went dark.

For a minute, no one moved, including me. But then I could hold it no longer. I dashed out to relieve myself.

There was no way this was the end, I told myself while my bladder emptied. After all this time, he couldn't just be *gone*. This was a guy who could open portals to almost anywhere, after all. But then, Vicky said she couldn't create a portal while inside there. Was that because of all the noise and whatnot made it too difficult to focus? Or was it legitimately impossible to do so? This portal was different, too. He'd needed Vicky's help to create it. That explained why he tried to take her with him, but surely that wasn't what he was banking on. Then I remembered the little device that he pocketed. I had a suspicion about it, but would need to ask Vicky.

By the time I returned, Vicky and the skeptic were speaking with the technician, who soon stepped away from the device. Vicky looked over the controls, extending her hands above the panel. Then, lightning seemed to erupt from in front of her palms, frying the console and all the recorded data it held.

I stood uncomfortably off to the side as Vicky spoke with the few remaining members of The Nexus. I didn't eavesdrop. I was too busy processing what had just happened. I'd been anticipating a huge confrontation, a serious battle. But I knew now that such a thing would never happen. Sometimes, I reminded myself, endings come with a whimper, not a bang.

It wasn't long before Vicky appeared at my side again. Then she wordlessly opened a portal to her home in London and we stepped through. In her flat, I collapsed into an armchair in the living room, while she put a kettle on. I removed my shirt and began peeling electrodes from myself.

A few minutes later, she brought two cups of tea into the living room, handing one to me, before sitting beside me. "I am absolutely knackered."

"Same," I said, then fell silent. I didn't know what to say. She gave no indication of how she was feeling. Did she want sympathy? Was I capable of sincerely offering it? "Vick," I finally said, "I'm sorry." When she didn't reply, I said, "I have so many questions."

"Me, too," she said, then urged me to turn away from her so she could remove the electrodes from my back.

Figuring this was my permission to ask, I said, "First, what was that little device the tech gave him?"

Vicky frowned as she confirmed my suspicion. "The machine transferred the data, including the specific frequency combinations, into the device. It has enough power to open a portal for a moment. Theoretically, long enough for him to go through. It's his failsafe device for returning."

"But using you was his first choice, apparently."

"What?"

"Well, I mean... he dragged you through..."

"Yeah, so he could abandon me in the time stream." Before I could voice my astonishment, she continued. "If I hadn't been holding onto him..."

"*You* were holding onto *him*?" I shook my head. "Jesus, what an asshole," I muttered. Vicky didn't reply, so I said, "What's your take on what happened? Why did he vanish? And where or when did he go?"

"No way to be sure," she said, pulling off the last electrode. "It seems like he did really create a time portal, but didn't know how to control it."

I put my shirt back on. "Why would that be?"

Vicky dropped the stack of electrodes on the coffee table and sipped her tea before replying. "When we open a portal, we're breaching another plane and bringing some of it here. Or we open a portal to a specific place and travel through. This is basically done by directing our thoughts in certain ways, which I'm not about to try to explain." She shook her head. "He most likely assumed that controlling time travel would work the same way."

"You don't think it does?"

"I just can't imagine it being that easy. Each added plane makes it harder to not only open the portals, but to control the results. This being the most planes ever combined, it would have to be far more difficult."

"But surely he would have known that controlling a time portal would be much different than the other planes, right?"

"You would think," Vicky said. "But when you combine his arrogance, his desperation, and his desires..." She trailed off with a shrug. "Momentary lapses of reason are behind the fall of many powerful people."

"That would explain another flaw in his thinking."

"Which is?"

"Time and space are linked," I said. "If you move in time, you're moving in space. The world rotates at over a thousand miles an hour, at the equator. So a 'jump' of a single second would put you more than a quarter mile away. And that's not even taking into account the rate at which the earth moves around the sun. Combined, it would be approaching twenty miles in that single second. And then there's the speed of the solar system itself, which is something like a hundred twenty-five miles per second. So moving a single second in time would put you a hundred and some miles away. And it could be into empty space, or into the ocean, or into the planet's mantle." I paused, shaking my head. I saw Vicky absorbing this, realization on her face. I felt a twinge of guilt at having so cavalierly spoken of her father's almost certain demise. "I suppose it's possible that his little remote activator also contained all the specifics of where in space he'd be returning to, and a way to 'anchor' to those coordinates," I said, "but I doubt it."

Finally, Vicky spoke. "So he's dead," she said flatly.

I said nothing for a moment, then said, "Maybe, maybe not. The very existence of the 'time stream,' as he called it, adds a layer of complexity that could, I suppose, change the rules altogether. Perhaps jumps in time are automatically anchored in space, rendering everything I just said irrelevant."

Vicky wasn't the only one struggling to accept this. I wasn't even sure how I felt. I'd wanted Weatherford gone from my life, but not from life completely.

"I feel like an idiot," I said. "I don't know why I ever thought he really wanted me there as a failsafe, or as a fellow scientist. I should have had sense enough to see it was all a ruse."

"Well, sometimes you're stupid," she offered, then carried the empty cup and dead electrodes to the kitchen.

"Dana has accused me of being too trusting of others," I said as I finished my tea and followed her.

"He's not wrong."

Vicky washed the cups, then we headed to the permanent portal to her home in San Francisco.

Twenty-Four

"I think the best endings bring you back in rather than close things off with absolute finality. I'm not saying they necessarily have to be ambiguous, but we don't always need to know what happens when everyone wakes up tomorrow morning."

~ T. C. Boyle

Music has always been important to me. Like most people, I've always been drawn to certain types. I love uplifting music, for example, and I dislike angry music. But there's one type of song for which I have a particular weakness: nostalgic tunes about childhood.

These songs really hit me hard. For some reason, they can pull tears out of me like nothing else. This is odd, because my "happy" childhood ended when I was still quite young, once my mother learned of Dana's abilities and began to withhold affection out of fear. Maybe that's why such songs hit me so hard. I feel robbed of such happiness. I'm missing something I never had.

Three days later, Dana and I landed in Pittsburgh around 5:30 p.m. After collecting our luggage, we picked up a rental car. Dana whined about how cold it was. Living in Sacramento for so many years, he was definitely not accustomed to the sub-freezing temperatures. He cranked the heat as we drove Route 28 the whole way home.

We reached town and rolled down Main Street, which was festooned with its annual holiday lights and decorations on every lamp post. I asked

Dana to go through town to stop at Sheetz. He waited in the car as I went inside the busy convenience store. Not for the first time, I wished this place had existed when I'd lived here.

There was a line at the food and beverage order station. I stood at the end, casually looking around at other customers out of habit, to see if I recognized anyone. I didn't, of course. Most of them would have been children when I left town. Others currently *were* children. In fact, of all the patrons, the only one who was clearly older than I was the man in line directly in front of me.

There was something familiar about his profile. I tried to imagine him without the white hair and age lines. And then I recognized him. "Chief?" I said.

The man turned to face me, his eyes immediately going to my own white hair and noticeable lack of age lines. "Well, my goodness," he said. "Hello, Dinah. And I'm retired, now, so I'm just Bob."

I smiled at the town's former Police Chief. "It's good to see you. You look well."

"Retirement suits me." Then he frowned. "Heard you'd died. A couple of times, in fact."

I just chuckled and shook my head. "Don't believe everything you hear."

"So the celebrity comes home for the holidays?"

I rolled my eyes. "I'm hardly a celebrity."

"Around here, you are."

My heart skipped a beat. "I am?" I glanced around, noticing now how many people were looking at me, many with expressions of surprise on their faces. A few smiled at me. I timidly smiled back. I had to appreciate the irony. When I left home, I'd wanted nothing more than to become a celebrity. Now, the thought made me uncomfortable.

The line moved forward and we both ordered. Then he said, "Your mother brags about you every chance she gets."

"She what?" I said, eyes wide. He just nodded. That was certainly unexpected. And honestly, a bit uncomfortable.

As he stepped forward to accept his order, I said, "Listen, I don't think I ever thanked you for your kindness, all those years ago when I tried to run away."

"And you never needed to. It was my job. And my pleasure," he said with a kind smile.

"Still," I said, "I just wanted you to know how much I appreciated it, and I've never forgotten."

He smiled and laid a hand on my shoulder. "You have a Merry Christmas. And give my regards to your family."

"Same to you and yours," I said as he left.

A few minutes later, I returned to the car with two caramel lattes. I handed one to Dana. "All set?" he asked.

I frowned. "Even less than before. But I guess we can't put it off any longer."

My previous visit home, a year and a half earlier, had been surreal, with my mother behaving utterly differently from what I'd been used to for the past decades. But it was nothing compared to how this visit began. As soon as we entered the house, Mother embraced me firmly, laying her head against my chest, all while saying how happy she was that we were home and other hard-to-swallow statements.

"I'm sure you two are hungry," she said as she disengaged. "Let me go heat something up for you." Without waiting for a reply, she scooted into the kitchen.

Dad's hug was less intense, but warm. He urged us into the living room to sit, asking all the required questions about how our trip was. I let Dana field those, while I soaked in the memory of living in this house.

Nothing had changed, as far as the décor went. It was as though it was decorated once they bought it and had never changed anything. It had the same thrift store paintings on the wall, and the same paint job. The same furniture. The TV had been upgraded since I was a kid, but that was about it.

"Come on," our mother said, putting two plates down on the same old dining table. We did so, and feasted on reheated meatloaf, mashed potatoes, and canned green beans. I was surprised how nostalgic the food made me feel.

Afterward, we returned to the living room, where I sat in the rocking chair that was older than I was and Dana joined our mother on the love seat. The first thing out of her mouth was, "Did you bring it?"

I sighed. "I did."

"Let's see it!" she said, beaming with excitement.

"Can't it wait 'til tomorrow?"

"Come on!" she pleaded. I knew she wouldn't stop pestering me, so I grabbed my suitcase and went up to my room. There, I put the case on the bed and opened it, staring down at my blue and white costume. Why did she ask me to do this? And why did I agree?

I undressed and pulled on the body suit. It was a familiar feeling, but also a bit odd. I associated this outfit with my years in the Bay Scouts and the Gatekeepers. Did it really have a place in my current life?

I stepped over to the full-length mirror on the closet door as I fit the mask and circlet into place. Those years before the Pariah Project were bittersweet. The blue and whites felt the same way, both good and bad. But I had to admit, it felt good on my body.

A few minutes later, I descended to the living room, my boots clomping on the old wooden stairs, my cape trailing behind me. And I stood there in front of my family, feeling like a child ready for trick-or-treating.

"Oh, my gosh!" Mother said, leaving her seat and coming to closely inspect the costume. "It's got the DNA thingies!" she said, tracing a finger down my leg.

I saw Dad looking at the circlet on my head. "When you were little, you always said you were going to grow up to be a princess," he said.

"I most certainly did *not*."

"Oh, you most certainly *did*," Dana said with a chuckle.

I glared at him. "Quiet, peasant." Then I reached up and pressed the circlet's blue gemstone, which lit the LEDs like a small but powerful flashlight. When Dad seemed satisfied, I turned it off.

"Oh! The cape has pockets!" Mom reached in and pulled out my standard emergency kit and unzipped it. She and my father looked over the array of first aid supplies, the mylar blanket, the bullet wound syringe that we were field testing, and the packets of PowerPaste. The latter, she pulled out and examined.

"What's this?" she said, turning the packet over in her hands. So I explained all that went into that, including a rough estimate of how much I made from the sales, since Dad had asked.

"So that's your actual income?" he said. "Not the hero thing?"

"Yeah. Funny how that turned out. We're not one of the government teams, so most of the Project's income is from a variety of grants," I explained. "They cover our operating expenses and a small stipend for those members who need it. But DynaPaste brings in the bucks." Seeing some confusion on his face, I blurted, "POWERPaste! Not... whatever I said." Dana snorted, but I shot him a look before he could mock me.

And this is how the evening went. I answered a ton of questions about my suit, my abilities, and more. Honestly, I could not have been more surprised by their curiosity. Dana found the whole thing quite entertaining.

Finally, after promising them a demonstration of my abilities the following day, we all went to bed.

"It was unbelievable, Rhon," I said. "I had to blast stuff, fly for them... They were more curious than your kids were when they met me." I shook my head. "And we couldn't exactly do this in private, so the neighbors were all gawking. And taking pictures."

We sat in her comfy kitchen, drinking coffee and eating from the enormous Tupperware container of fruit cocktail cookies that I'd brought with me. Mother made them, knowing I'd be visiting Rhonda and her family.

"You'll be the talk of the town for months," Rhonda said with a smile. "You know, your mom has become quite active in the community."

I poured myself another coffee. "How so?"

"She joined the Historical Society. The Kaimanns Club. And she's on the Fourth of July Committee."

"Who is this woman and what did she do with my mother?"

"No idea," Rhonda said, laughing. "How long will you be in town?"

"Just until the end of the month." I looked around at the strawberry-themed country décor. "Where's the family?"

"Believe it or not," she said with a shake of her head, "shopping."

"Ugh. On Christmas Eve?"

"It's Steven's fault," she said. "Came home from college and said he hadn't done any shopping, yet."

I smirked. "Well, much as I'd love to see them all, it's nice to have time just the two of us." As Rhonda agreed, I pulled several small envelopes from my purse. "Before I forget, these are for you and the rest."

"Oh, gosh, Dinah. You didn't need to do that."

"And yet, I did," I said with a smile, while snagging another cookie.

"Gift cards, I assume."

"Puppies."

Rhonda rolled her eyes. "Well, thank you very much." Rhonda set the envelopes aside. She was quiet for a moment, looking at me, and I knew what she was thinking.

"Go ahead and ask," I said. She looked surprised, so I tried to put her at ease. "Yes, I look and sound different."

Rhonda's eyes widened. "You mean... that story in the *Enquirer*..."

"Yeah."

"I figured you just had work done."

"Did I *need* work done?" I teased.

"No! No, of course not, but..." After a moment of shocked silence, she made me spill the whole story. It took two more cups of coffee and quite a few of the cookies.

"Holy hell," she said. "That's... I mean..."

"Believe me, I know."

"Have your parents asked about it?"

"Sort of. Dad brought up the physical and vocal difference, but Dana suggested that Dad was due for an eye exam and hearing aid adjustment."

Rhonda laughed. "Dana to the rescue." Then her smile faded and I knew what was coming next. She was about to ask about the other news item. I was ready to deny it, but Rhonda was a friend. I needed to treat her like one. And yet, could I trust her? She'd outed me once. Would she do it again?

But to my surprise and relief, she changed the subject completely, asking about my team's activities. I answered her questions about the Project and such. We spent the rest of the afternoon reminiscing and playing catch-up. She filled me in on the kids' activities. And more of my mother's.

I left before her family returned, but promised I'd be back to see them sometime during the week. We exchanged warm hugs before I headed home.

Christmas Day itself was mellow. Dana and I received gifts of clothing. In my case, it was a blue leather motorcycle jacket. It was quite lovely, though I was surprised by the color, which matched the blue of my costume. Dana received three flat caps, which he was eager to show off on his bald head. In return, we'd gotten them generous gift cards. For Dad, a local golf shop. For Mom, a gardening center.

We had our traditional Christmas meal, the centerpiece of which was baked ham slathered in mustard, packed with brown sugar, and studded with cloves. I was surprised to see spiced apple rings on the table. I'd loved them as a child, but hadn't had them since I was probably ten. I looked at my mother as I held the bowl. She smiled faintly at me, and in her eyes, I saw the unmistakable expression of apology. She quickly turned away and headed back into the kitchen. I caught her wiping her eyes.

Turns out, I still love spiced apple rings.

The next several days passed quickly. Dana and I, as previously agreed, spent little time together. We both visited friends, but not at the same time, so at any given moment, one of us was typically home with the folks. We did this to minimize any chance of our parents alluding to the *Sun* article, or seeing "something" between us, real or imagined.

During one of our rare moments together, Dana and I walked up to Josephine's for pizza. The temperature hadn't gone above freezing since before Christmas, but the front door of the shop was ajar. The aroma of pizza wafted out as we approached, making my stomach growl. Inside, the heat from the ovens kept us warm. As we sat at a table waiting for our pie, we chatted idly about our get-togethers with friends.

I had my hair pulled up and was wearing one of Dana's new hats. Despite this, the spill of white hanging down was enough to draw the attention of other patrons. I nodded politely when I caught them staring. I was reminded of a previous visit, several years earlier. Then, the boys hanging out ogled me. This time, they cast jealous, resentful glances at Dana. I couldn't help but smile.

"Listen," I said to him. "There's something I need to talk to you about." I took a sip of my Dr Pepper and said, "You know about the whole book thing. Well, I'm told it's going to be split into three volumes. The final one will be about the events of this year."

"You're going to include everything about the cloning?"

"I am," I said.

"Do you think that's wise? I mean, you were able to sidestep the inquiries recently, but if you actually publish a confirmation, they'll return with a vengeance."

"Yeah, but the press won't care, since they wanted a scoop... which they won't have."

"What about the scientific community?"

"Well, I'll deal with it when it happens."

Dana nodded, but then frowned. "What about legal issues?"

I shrugged. "What are they gonna do? Fine me? Technically, I'm the result of the procedure, not the one who performed it."

"That would certainly be an interesting argument to hear."

I smiled at that, but quickly turned serious. "There's... something else." Dana looked at me curiously. I lowered my eyes and said, "I, um... I want to talk about *us*."

Dana stared at me for a long moment. "In the book," he finally said.

I nodded. "Yeah."

Squirming in his seat, he said, "Why, exactly?" When I hesitated, he said, "I mean, I understand your desire to be transparent about things. But is it necessary?"

"I mean... no. Not *necessary*. Hell, telling my story at all isn't *necessary*. And maybe it's a terrible idea. But I'm told they want these books to be about me, as a person, more than about me being Dynamistress. So I should include the things that really matter to me. Things that make me who I am."

"Don't you think you're giving it a little too much significance?"

"I really don't," I said. "I mean, the sex part isn't what I'll stress, but our love."

Dana practically cringed at that. "Save some of that cheesiness for the pizza."

I couldn't help but laugh. "Okay, fair. But still, it's true. So much of who I am is because of you."

"Okay, just let it go," he said, his face flushing. "Do what you feel you need to do."

"I know you're worried about how it'll affect you," I began, but he cut me off.

"Me? Dinah, I'm not a public figure. You're the one who'll be negatively affected by this."

"I don't really care about that," I said. "I'm more concerned about Mom and Dad."

"Well, yeah. That alone should be enough to keep it out of the book."

Our pizza arrived and we dug in. After a few bites, I said, "As I mentioned, this will be in the third book. It won't be out anytime soon. And our folks aren't getting any younger."

Dana frowned. "You're thinking they'll pass before that book comes out?"

"They're in their seventies now, so... there's a fair chance of that."

"Well, it's your call," Dana said. "Don't worry about me, though. Just make sure you're not hurting anyone else."

The last couple days with Mom and Dad were good. We spent most of the time just talking. To my surprise, they asked a lot of questions about how I'd become Dynamistress and the early years of my activities. They also asked about my teammates, past and present.

On the one hand, it was nice that they were showing such interest in something they'd once regarded as borderline evil. On the other, though, it was like they were more interested in Dynamistress than in their daughter. But after years of being treated as I was, I'd take what I could get.

One of the personal things I shared was about Sharon and Jackie, including the recent reunion and Little Dinah. Mom insisted on seeing pictures, so we swiped through my phone. "I just don't understand it. How can you have *real* relationships with two people like that? Do they *really* love you?" she asked.

"They named their daughter after me, so..."

I showed her the photos Michael had taken on their last visit, with me in costume around San Francisco landmarks. She ate it up. We paused on a candid shot of me and Dinah laughing together. A wistful smile touched my mother's face, but quickly vanished. "I'm sorry," she whispered. I looked at her in surprise. "This should have been us," she said, still staring at the photo.

The simple statement hit me like a brick. It was obvious that she regretted her behavior toward me. "Mom..." I began.

But she didn't let me speak. "I don't expect forgiveness, Dinah. I was terrible to you. And to Dana. I was just so... so *afraid.* And honestly, today I can't even say of what. Whenever I think about it now, it just sounds so ridiculous. I'm ashamed of myself." She fell silent and handed my phone back to me. "And I really am sorry."

I took her hands in my own and gave them a comforting squeeze. I still didn't know what had happened to cause such a change of heart in this woman I once regarded as a monster, but I was grateful for it.

We talked until late, and before I even knew what was coming out of my mouth, I suggested that she and my father let me fly them out to San Francisco to visit. I promised to show them around as much as they wanted. There were tears in her eyes when she agreed.

On New Year's Eve, Dana dropped me off at Sharon and Jackie's place. I introduced him to everyone. Little Dinah said he seemed like a bald teddy bear. Since the girls would give me a lift to the airport in a couple days, Dana took the rental back to the airport and flew back to Sacramento.

I had a wonderful visit. There was no nervousness, this time, no awkwardness. It almost felt like it had back in college, except that we were now much older, with all the changes that came with it. Still, it was amazing how much love I felt. I hated for it to end, but the holidays were now over.

"Listen," I said on my last day there, "there's something I want to talk to you all about. You don't need to give a response. It's just something for you to think about." I took a deep breath before just spilling it. "I'd love for you guys to move to San Francisco. I'll help you get settled, so you don't have to worry about that." As they sat in surprise, I said, "Michael, the photography opportunities out there have got to be better than in Pittsburgh. Dinah, I know you'd make lots of new friends..."

Sharon held up a hand to stop me. "We've already talked about it," she said. "Once the school year is over, we're in."

"Well," I said, genuinely surprised. "That was easy."

Upon returning to San Francisco, I dealt with the pile of mail that had come in. One fancy envelope stood out. I eagerly opened it and smiled when I saw the card.

Aimee Kaye Wonderland

and

Jack Connor Fullerton

Invite You to Their Wedding

Saturday, June 11, 2011, at 2:00 P.M.

at the

Conservatory of Flowers, Golden Gate Park

After seeing this, even paying a stack of bills didn't ruin my mood.

Speaking of weddings, I learned through one of the popular magazines that Rachel had married her movie husband. They were expecting a child in the summer. K.T.'s wedding was also coming up. I made a note to send a gift.

I spent Dana's birthday with him in Sacramento. Over dinner, I told him about the plans for Dinah's family to relocate to the Bay Area. "That's great," he said. "I know how much you want them around."

"I do," I agreed. "But not just them." I looked into Dana's eyes. "I want you to move in with me. And I want you to join the Pariah Project."

"Dinah..."

Before he could argue, I said, "Look, you're already spending half your time in the city with me. And you would be a tremendous help for the Project! If you don't mind doing *pro bono* counseling for people, anyway. And I know you'd be happy to do that."

"Dinah..."

"But beyond that," I said, "I need you. I know that makes me sound like a little kid again, but you mean so much to me. Being apart from you is just—"

"Dinah!"

I nearly jumped at his tone. "What?"

"Okay."

I stared at him, mouth open, for a moment. "Wait... really?"

Dana smirked. "Yeah."

I couldn't contain my excitement. I wore a grin the rest of the day.

Toward the end of the month, Captain Shepherd called me to discuss portals. He explained that he'd worked with the Navy to pinpoint the location of the one on San Nicolas Island. The plan was to collapse the cave in which it was found and fill it in with concrete.

That brought us to the portal to Dynasonic's world. Unlike the portals in Nevada and on the island, this one had no obvious way to close it. It had no solid surroundings, no mechanical gates holding it open. Though there was no threat from Dynasonic's world, and the portal didn't fall within any of the established airline flight paths, there was always the danger that a smaller plane might intersect with it. To that end, the plan was to make that area restricted airspace, until a way to close it was determined. I knew this was necessary, but the thought of losing contact with Dynasonic bothered me immensely.

Further, he shared, the government was assembling a team of sorts to discuss the portals in a general sense, given the differences between them all and the implications for our world. "Don't be surprised if you're invited to be on that team," he said. "No one has more direct experience with them than you do."

On our birthday, a group of us gathered for a late lunch at Pier 23 for my fortieth and Sinta's twentieth. We'd reserved an outdoor space and mingled around the patio heaters, despite it being nearly sixty degrees. Most of the team showed up, as did Ali and Macy. And there was a special guest, who arrived with Vicky. I stared in shock as Dynasonic approached and gave me a birthday hug.

I was speechless as they stood before me. "How...?"

Vicky said, "My birthday gift for you. I've set up a permanent portal between your homes."

I stared at her. "So that's why you've not been around, lately."

"So now I can come visit you, too!" Dynasonic said. "I do hope that nausea goes away, in time, though."

I looked at Vicky, I'm sure, with utter disbelief on my face. Then I embraced her. "You sneaky bitch," I whispered in her ear. "Thank you."

"Oh, and here's your gift," Dynasonic said, handing me a copy of *Wanderland*.

"Yes!" I blurted. "I can't wait to hear it. Are you happy with it?"

"Very," she said. "It'll be really hard to top this one."

"When does the tour begin?"

"Next week!"

"I'll have to come catch a show." Then I frowned. "Wait. Today's your birthday, too! Happy Birthday!"

"Thanks!"

After taking some time to introduce her to the guests, I stood and addressed everyone. "Okay," I said. "Let's try this again, with no explosions, this time!" Some strained laughter sprinkled the cheers of "Happy Birthday" from the group. Then we pigged out on fish and chips and other delicious items.

Ali elbowed me and said, "I'm gonna get a reputation for dating a forty-year-old."

"A good reputation," I said, "considering which forty-year-old you're dating."

"Oh, is *that* how you think it is?" she said with a chuckle.

"How else *could* it be?" I joked.

In reply, she just glanced over at Dana, who sat opposite me at the table. He looked between us. "I refuse to be roped into this conversation," he said flatly, stuffing chowder-soaked bread into his mouth.

"Aww," Ali whined. "You're supposed to be on my side."

"I am?" he asked.

"Well, yeah... if you want that threesome."

Dana nearly choked. Sinta laughed. I pretended not to hear it.

Dynasonic was seated between Sinta and me, and Sinta seemed delighted to have yet another Dyna in her life. Sinta had listened to the Dynasonic CDs I had, so they talked about music while eating.

After everyone had finished, we mingled more and chatted. There were birthday wishes aplenty, but Dynasonic got more attention than we did. I'd talk with her later, as I was curious about how things were going with the dismantling of the telepath network in her world. I expected her brother to be quite busy.

Eventually, Dynasonic and Vicky stepped over. "Afraid I need to get going," Dynasonic said. We hugged goodbye and Vicky escorted her back to the new portal between our worlds, wherever that happened to be.

Others showed signs of packing up, so Sinta and I stood near the door like the end of a receiving line, where everyone gave us final birthday wishes and hugs before leaving. And then, it was just the two of us, plus Dana and Ali.

On the street, Dana flagged down a taxi and we piled in, Dana in the front and the girls with me in the back.

"That was fun," I said.

"It was!" Sinta agreed.

"It was really cool to meet your teammates," Ali said. "I can't believe I got to meet them all. And 'you' from another world!"

"Yeah, Vicky sure surprised me with that one," I said. "Sinta, what do you think about Dana joining the Project?"

Sinta snorted and rubbed the back of Dana's head. "About time."

"Yeah, yeah," he mumbled.

We rode in silence for a while, until Sinta's phone buzzed. She pulled it out and looked at it, smiling. She typed out a reply and sent it. "So... I guess I have a date, tonight."

I stared at her. "Seriously?"

"Yes. Don't act so shocked."

"I'm sorry," I said. "Who's the lucky guy?"

"Kurt," she replied softly.

As I tried to place the name, Ali said, "The dude from the aquarium?"

"Mm hm. He's driving up after his shift."

"Wait," I said. "Ali knows about him, but I don't?"

"You were there when I met him!"

"Yeah, but you haven't mentioned him since!"

Sinta shrugged and leaned into me. "We've been texting and stuff."

"How'd he get your number?"

"Um... he figured out who we were, then called the Project and left a message for me."

"Gutsy," I said. "I'm impressed."

We reached our destination. Since Ali was set to work later, I had the taxi take her to the Haight after the rest of us stepped out.

Once inside, Dana headed down to "his" room, while Sinta and I collapsed in front of the fireplace. I stared into the flames, enjoying the heat, letting my mind wander.

"What's on your mind?" Sinta asked.

"Oh... just thinking about things that are important to me. Like our team," I said. "We really are like a family. And we've no political drama like so many other teams do. We're doing good work that directly affects those in need."

"You should be proud of that."

"We all should," I said.

Sinta shifted in her seat and studied my face. "You look different."

"Yeah, we've been over that," I reminded her.

"No, I mean..." With a frown, she said, "You've always had an expression that held... sort of... pain. Sadness. Anger. Not all the time, but it would come out every now and then. But I haven't seen it in a while."

I considered her words, feeling the truth in them. "I didn't realize all that. But now that I think about it, it's true that I've always had those feelings. Lately, though... not so much."

"No?"

I shook my head. "It's been... nice."

Sinta smiled. "You're happy," she said.

Again, I had to think about it. It was a word, an emotion, that people used freely. For me, it had always been a conditional term. It's easy to be happy about situations as they come, but I couldn't remember ever feeling happiness as a base state of existence.

But now? A great team. Wonderful friends. A rekindled romance, including a "daughter." Improved relations with my parents, and much more. These weren't momentary things, but as permanent as life allows.

I felt a smile on my face. "You're right," I said to Sinta. "I am. Maybe for the first time in my life."

Sinta hooked an arm in mine and squeezed, laying her head against my shoulder as we stared at the fire.

"About time."

EPILOGUE

Golden Gate Park is where the kids hang out. I don't mean children, though some of them seem pretty damn young. I mean the ones celebrating their new status as registered metas in the city. They strut around, appropriately, in Peacock Meadow, where they pose in their costumes like jocks trying to impress cheerleaders. Recruiters for government teams swoop in on them like pimps on runaways at a bus station.

As it happens, I'm there as a pimp, myself, because I go there to look for potential recruits, too. But I'm much more selective than the government scouts. I look for those who aren't so puffed up with pride. I look for the humble, not the haughty. I watch for the ones who look lost or confused, or are there just to meet other metas, rather than boast and show off. In other words, the ones the government folks tend to ignore.

But I see them all, the timid and the bold, with mixed emotions. I look at them with fond nostalgia, for I remember being one of those neophytes, not so long ago. I look at them with hope, for that's what they are – the hope for the city's future. But mostly, I look at them with pity, because "The Disappeared" is a group that just continues to grow in size.

Occasionally, one of them will almost bashfully approach and ask me if I'm Dynamistress. It probably shouldn't surprise me, but it always does. I'm not in the news much, these days, especially since the tabloid stories finally faded to nothingness. But I guess I'm still known. Interest in the "Nevada Incident" is still strong, after all, even so many years later. And sales of the first two volumes of my "memoirs" still sell moderately well. So I'll smile and offer them a seat beside me. I'll answer their questions, both about myself and metas I have known. Maybe it's because of the work I've put into these books, but I have plenty to tell them. Nostalgia takes over and I blab on and on.

I ask plenty of my own questions, too. And I never have to feign interest, since everyone is interesting. I love learning about others, hearing their stories and their ambitions. Some can't wait to show off their abilities to me. Others need to be persuaded to demonstrate. Some, in fact, never approach me and I need to summon them over.

And when I have my select audience – sometimes just one, sometimes a few – these conversations take an unexpected turn for the youngsters when I smile at them and say, "Let me tell you about the Pariah Project."

DGC, 2025

About the Author

Vincent M. Wales was raised in the small town of Brockway, Pennsylvania, where he frequently complained about the weather. Since then, he has lived near Philadelphia; in Utah; and in Sacramento, California, complaining about the weather in each location.

He has worn many hats, including writing instructor, suicide prevention crisis counselor, Big Brother, freethought activist and essayist, mental health podcast host, and award-winning novelist.

He currently lives on the northern coast of Humboldt County, California, where he finally has no complaints about the weather.

Just earthquakes.

www.vincentmwales.com

www.ingramcontent.com/pod-product-compliance
Lightning Source LLC
LaVergne TN
LVHW091643100826
845152LV00006B/145/J

* 9 7 8 0 9 7 4 1 3 3 7 7 5 *